NYALA

BOOK 1 OF THE UPSTAIRS GIRLS

MICHAEL HARVEY FRIEDMAN

Butternut Press
Santa Barbara, CA

www.theupstairsgirls.com

Printed in the United States of America

Cover Illustration: George Patsouras
Book Design: Carla Green, Clarity Designworks

Library of Congress Control Number: 2020912899

ISBN paperback: 978-1-7353924-0-0
ISBN ebook: 978-1-7353924-1-7

For my loving wife, Karen Leah Krulevitch,
without whose patience and encouragement this book
would never have seen the light of day.

Also, for my mother, Regina, who understood my heart,
and for my dear father, Marion, who loved me
"up to the sky and down again."

"You shall go to the city of enchantments! There you shall take root and enjoy the air and the sunshine, but your life shall be shortened. The long procession of years that awaited you here in the open country will shrink to a small number. Poor Dryad, it will be your ruin! Your longing will grow and your great desire and craving will increase until the tree itself will be a prison to you. You will leave your shelter and change your nature; you will fly forth to mingle with human beings, and then your years will shrink to half of a May fly's lifetime—to one night only! The flame of your life will be blown out. The leaves of the tree will wither and blow away, never to return."

—Hans Christian Andersen,
The Dryad, 1868

Chapter 1

~

THE CLUB

Month of November/Month of Ivy

The tall, exotic-looking woman stood beside the lectern in the large auditorium, which served as both the theater and meeting hall of Club Nyala, the elegant erotic play space shared by roughly 270 well-heeled lay members, each of whom paid $4,800 per year for the privilege of unlimited access to the lavishly appointed dungeon and other facilities.

Looking to be in her late twenties, the woman at the podium was one of the "Upstairs Girls," the five professional dominatrices who worked on the top floor of Nyala during hours when the club was closed to its regular membership. Clad in skin-tight black latex, with her creamed-coffee skin, jet-black hair piled atop her head, and with those long elegant legs and striking features, she radiated the energy of a jungle cat.

Her name was Mistress Jilaynie Ashe—though her friends and lovers called her Jill—and she was the MC for tonight's lecture. She stood, arms akimbo, surveying the audience, a faint smile playing on her rouged lips as she waited for them to settle in and quiet down.

Nyala lived in an old four-story warehouse bordering San Francisco's SoMa District. The building had once housed an Italian sausage factory, and years after it had gone out of business, the pungent aromas of cured meat and garlic were still vaguely discernable; a fact that some club members considered a turn-on.

The auditorium was on the second floor, along with a small fetish art gallery, while the dungeon occupied most of the third floor, and the theme rooms and administrative offices claimed all of the fourth. The ground floor held an elegantly appointed lobby that was reached through the parking lot. There was also a smaller, shabbier lobby off the street by the old loading dock, where the factory had once received shipments of meat and spices. This entrance was seldom used and all that was inside that dim lobby was a freight elevator, with the rest sealed off by a stout iron door, behind which a faint whining sound like a generator could be heard.

The club had a notorious reputation, and rumor held that it enjoyed the secret patronage of several of The City's most prominent political figures. In addition to the capacious dungeon, with its bondage racks, paddles and suspension devices, the theme rooms were equipped to resemble a Victorian boudoir, a cramped interrogation room, a Dean's Office, a vampire's cave, and the newest addition, a sensuously appointed drawing room with a retro look dedicated to Betty Page, the infamous 1950s pinup vamp. Each room was designed to accommodate couples or small groups with specific fantasies they wished to act out, some mostly playful, some a bit rough, and others—well, others that were hard to label. The theme rooms were also where the Upstairs Girls conducted most of their professional trade.

Nyala was not running a brothel, not in the literal sense, anyway, since what the "vanilla world" called sex wasn't on the menu the Upstairs Girls offered. But because partial nudity and certain types of physical contact were often part of the games they played with their clients, the club operated in a kind of legal gray zone; so management was very fussy about staying within legitimate bounds as far as possible, while also being careful not to spoil the fun with a lot of strict rules.

Nyala's legal counsel, Nellyn Greenleaf, was an expert in both local and state codes regarding places like this, and she always seemed to keep the club one step ahead of the law. For example, several months ago, when a now expelled club member had managed to slip a minor into the 'Dean's Office' for a bit of after school discipline, and the girl's parents had raised bloody hell, Nellyn had worked some kind of charm on both father and mother, and things were settled quietly.

Nyala was an odd name for a club like this, and some of the members who styled themselves 'Goddess Worshippers' believed it was the Ancient Egyptian term for clitoris; but only the Upstairs Girls knew the word's true meaning.

Until five years ago, this was just a kinky social club, named for its street address, 629. But when Headmistress Selene Mayweather—a professional dominatrix and sex educator—along with some of her friends, purchased 629, rescuing it from the brink of bankruptcy, everything changed. The club was remodeled, rechristened Club Nyala, and turned into a novel hybrid, offering professional domination services while retaining most of its "amateur" membership.

It was the "old-guard" members who first began calling the pro dommes "The Upstairs Girls." Initially it was a slur to show contempt for the professional interlopers who worked on the top floor, but the pros refused to be offended. In fact, they found the name delightful and happily embraced it. When that happened, it lost its negative connotations, and the social barriers between the old members and the pros began to break down.

If a regular member wanted to engage one of the professionals, they received a discount, and the pros quickly gained a reputation for going the extra mile to provide services that felt truly therapeutic. Some clients even claimed they'd received more healing in a single session with one of the Upstairs Girls than they had in years of psychotherapy.

One of the other changes Headmistress Selene had introduced was a public lecture series, her aim being to increase public awareness of the physical and emotional benefits of "consensual power exchange" and also to grow Nyala's dues-paying membership. Tonight's speaker would be Selene herself, and though the subject of her talk seemed a bit tame to some of the edgier club members, it was a big draw for non-members interested in the milder, sexier aspects of erotic bondage and discipline. It was also a topic that occupied a full chapter in Selene's book, *Twisted Honey*, which had become a best seller on Amazon.com.

As soon as the audience quieted down, Mistress Jilaynie stepped to the microphone and, to everyone's surprise, began to sing in a lovely contralto voice the first lines of a bawdy old drinking song:

If all them young ladies wuz fish in a pool,
I'd jump right in with my water-proof tool,
Roll your leg over, roll your leg over,
Roll your leg over the man in the moon.

She stopped there and got a round of lighthearted applause from the audience. At this, she did a curtsy so exaggerated it threatened to split her dress. She put a hand to her mouth in mock dismay and drew a hearty laugh.

"Wow, I love making people laugh," she said. "Making someone laugh is the next best thing to making them come as … uh, my sainted granny used to say." This brought an even bigger laugh from the audience, a few of whom wondered about the source of her slight accent, which might have been Irish or Welsh.

"Anyway," she continued, "I'm Mistress Jilaynie Ashe, and for those who've never been here, welcome to Club Nyala, where fantasy spills into reality. And the exploration of one luscious fantasy is what's in store for us tonight, because we have our very own Headmistress here to talk about a subject near and dear to our hearts—the subtle art of erotic spanking." This brought more cheers and applause from the room.

"Okay, great … I see I'm preaching to the already perverted. But, even better than just a lecture, we're going to have an actual spanking demonstration, right here on stage." Cheers and applause. "All right, folks, restrain your excitement. I know what you're hoping for, and I'm sorry to let you down ... but I will *not* be the one being spanked tonight."

There were good-natured boos and hisses.

Jilaynie laughed. "I know it's a crushing disappointment ... but cheer up, because we have the lovely Erica Birch bottoming for us tonight ... and what a delicious bottom she's got." There was an appreciative outpouring of whistles and foot-stomping.

"All right, then, I think you've heard enough gab from me. So, without further ado, let's give it up for our irresistible 'Goddess of Carnal Mayhem,' the Headmistress of Nyala ... Selene Mayweather!"

Beaming and waving to the crowd, Selene stepped into the spotlight from stage left, receiving a generous round of applause. She'd been on several TV talk shows recently and had built quite a local following. A honey blonde, with hair worn loose to elbow-length, the Headmistress stood about five-eight, but seemed closer to six feet in her open-toed, black stiletto heels. She had full breasts, graceful arms and a slim waist, widening to hips that were pleasingly round without being stocky. Her face was nothing short of angelic, with finely chiseled features and milky-white skin that was as smooth as anything you could hope to find on a woman who claimed to be thirty-six.

Still, the most striking thing about her couldn't be seen from the audience. Though Selene's left eye was a deep emerald green, her right was a vivid sapphire blue with streaks of violet, and from close up, the effect was hypnotic.

Her outfit was only a bit more conservative than what she might have worn for sessions with her clients or play partners. It consisted of a short, black leather skirt and a black leather top, with a plunging neckline that showed off her breasts to just an inch above the nipples. A tattoo of a tree with multihued blossoms poked up from between her breasts, a smaller version of the identical one that covered her entire back.

As Selene walked to the podium, the short-handled flogger she carried in her left hand swayed jauntily. It looked more sensuous than menacing, but she used it to give the podium a resounding whack as she took her place behind it, bringing more laughter from the audience.

"Well, hi, everyone," she said, flashing a dazzling smile. Her voice was both melodic and husky. "'Goddess of Carnal Mayhem,'" she mused (and some in the audience picked up the trace of an unusual accent from her too). "Now, that has a nice ring. I may just use it on the website! You've earned yourself a reward for coming up with it, Jill."

"Oh, goodie," Jilaynie said from stage right, where she now stood. "Do I finally get to top you?"

"Ah, many have tried, but none have succeeded," Selene quipped, bringing more laughter.

"Well," she continued, joining in the laughter. "Maybe we should just go upstairs and see who tops whom tonight. But I guess we have business to attend to first, and this gives me a perfect lead-in to our topic: Spanking! What the hell is the attraction, and maybe more importantly, how do you give a proper spanking to your lover? Also, what do I even mean by 'proper'? Well, a proper erotic spanking hurts … but only as much as your partner wants it to. And, in the right circumstances, it's the appetizer for a luscious, full course meal. Appetizer is the right word here, because even though a spanking can be a meal in itself, when I'm with a lover, my aim is to generate sizzling body heat to enhance both our erotic appetites.

"I know you're all here to see the spanking demonstration, not listen to me talk, but I think we need a little background first. Let's see … how many in the audience have never been spanked as adults?"

Most raised their hands.

Selene peered at the crowd and chuckled. "Okay, looks like we've got a lot of virgins here. Now, for those who've never been spanked as adults, how many have fantasized about it?"

At first, just a smattering of hands went up as audience members looked nervously around. Then, slowly, more hands rose until there were perhaps a hundred.

"Ah," Selene said, "seems like a lot of you are turned on by the idea, but just a little shy to admit it. Well, that's common enough. I mean, if you've fantasized about being spanked, you may be wondering what it says about you as a woman—or a man—that you've dreamed about lying across someone's lap, sticking your ass out, and willingly 'giving it up.' The thought is probably humiliating, isn't it? As a woman, you've naturally got issues about violence and your vulnerability. And if you're a male, maybe the idea of being spanked by a woman makes you wonder if you're some kind of wimp, especially if the thought gives you a raging boner."

That brought a few titters, and Selene grinned. "Maybe you're even thinking, 'No real man would ever want this,' or … 'Okay, that does it. I must be gay.'"

Peals of laughter greeted that, much of it from the gay and bisexual members of the audience.

"Well relax, boys, because if you're thinking about how much you'd love for a woman to spank you, you've got thousands of brothers out there."

That brought another round of cheers, mostly from the female members of the audience, who were eyeing boyfriends and husbands in a way that made the men squirm.

"And they're not wimps," Selene continued. "Most are virile as hell, and I know this for a fact because I've probably spanked at least half of them."

She had the audience eating out of her hand now, laughing, whistling, applauding, and leaning on every word. "Let's see, oh, right … I wanted to say a bit about role-playing. In our little community, we do a lot of that. You just saw me and Jill teasing each other, and that's often how we warm up … with words, sometimes flirtatious, other times more assertive, even aggressively challenging. But it's all good, clean fun; well, maybe it's not always that clean. It can get a little messy sometimes, but it's always consensual. And if it's not, you don't stay in our community long.

"Sometimes we do play a little rough, though. Bondage, paddling, flogging—these are all part of what we call 'power exchange.' Asses get reddened and sometimes backs are striped. But we understand the rules of playing this way and we know how to do it safely. For some of you, though, these things may conjure up nasty images. And the truth is that some of our 'games' aren't for everyone. But we're not here to discuss anything extreme tonight. We're here to talk about a teensy little spanking, like the one Mommy used to give you.

"See, even in what we kinksters call the 'vanilla' world, there is something about a spanking that feels familiar and nonthreatening. After all, unless your parents were really cruel, you cried a bit when you got spanked, then just went back to play with your toys.

"Sure, it hurt, but you knew your parents loved you and the spanking didn't change that. Your butt was sore, but maybe it also felt nicely warm. And if you look deep within, you may find there were times when you actually wanted that spanking, maybe because it made you feel cared for and loved, or maybe because you were hurting inside and just needed a reason to let those tears go. Of course, if you were destined to grow up a freak—like those of us in the scene—maybe it just felt *gooood*." There were a few chuckles from the crowd, and nods of recognition.

"In our community, we're totally attuned to the feeling of wanting to be spanked or wanting to spank someone. We love the whole ritual and seldom bother to ask why we love it. For me, spanking is the comfort food of power exchange—kind of like our meatloaf, mashed potatoes, and apple pie. It's healthy and nutritious ..." This brought another chuckle from the crowd. "... provided you also eat up all your spinach—which, when *I* am in charge, you will do without a word of complaint!" Selene slapped the podium with her flogger for emphasis, and laughter erupted that went on for nearly a minute before the audience quieted down.

"The thing about adult spanking is that even though it's not *sex*, it can get pretty sexy. For both men and women, the ass is very close to the genitals, which are easily stimulated during a spanking. Being spanked releases endorphins, which can actually be quite pleasurable. When I first started working as a domme, this became obvious when some of my submissives, both male and female, would become aroused in the middle of an over-the-knee spanking, even when I was whacking them hard.

"Now, as a domme, I might have to further punish you for getting turned on without permission, since this is supposed to be about punishment, not pleasure. Well, that's a sweet little fiction, because of course it's also about pleasure. I just pretend to be angry at you because it's another part of the game. In fact, if you didn't get turned on, I'd think I was losing my touch.

"In truth, it's not really surprising that someone who longs to submit to a powerful woman might become aroused while she's slapping their ass. After all, the submissive is having a cherished fantasy fulfilled: A devastatingly sexy Mistress is devoting her full attention to them, directing all her energy at their bare butt, scratching, stroking, and slapping—all of which creates an incredibly intimate connection. If the domme is doing it right, the spankee is in total submission to her. This can be so erotically charged as to be literally spiritual, more exquisite—and longer lasting—than what some might experience during vanilla sex."

The crowd was visibly moved now. Most were leaning forward, and there was no more laughter. Except for the sound of 150 people's breathing, the room was utterly silent.

"If this sounds hot, it's only because it is. And you don't have to be totally dominant or submissive to have fun with spanking. Anyone can do it, and you and your partner can take turns playing top or bottom. But ... you do need to understand what you're doing, and you absolutely need to spank safely, or you could seriously injure your partner, or even yourself."

Selene let that sink in for a moment. "Now… there are several classic ways to spank. The main elements are tools and position. I'll discuss position later on, but first a few words about tools. Spanking is mostly done with paddles, hairbrushes, or the human hand, gloved or bare. I personally prefer spanking bare-handed. There's just nothing to equal the sensation of skin meeting skin, the feel of your partner's gorgeous bottom growing warmer and warmer under your touch, the lovely slap of your hand meeting that firm yet tender flesh, and the way that ass literally begins to light up as your 'victim' wriggles and squirms. I swear you can almost see in the dark by the glow of a well-spanked ass."

There was a collective sigh from the audience and a few giggles.

"Okay, looks like I've got everyone's attention, so let's get our *spankee* out here and give her a few well-deserved whacks. Erica?"

There was a shriek of laughter from the audience, as Erica Birch, a slim, frizzy-haired brunette, about five-foot-five, appeared stage right—dressed as a Girl Scout! Even Selene joined in the merriment at Erica's ensemble.

"Oh, girl, you are just full of surprises, aren't you?" Selene said.

Erica gave the audience a little curtsey and then approached Selene, head down, wearing a very guilty look.

"For those not familiar with our terminology, I should mention that Erica's what's called a 'switch,' meaning she enjoys playing both the submissive and dominant roles at different times. So you know how to administer a spanking as well as take one, don't you, Erica?"

"Yes, I do," Erica said, throwing the audience a little moue. "At least that's what my bad girls and boys tell me." And there was that same accent again, so faint it was easy to think you were just imagining it.

"Okay," Selene said. "But today, it's you who's been naughty, and you are the one who needs to be punished. So face the audience and tell these good people exactly what you've done to deserve your spanking."

"I … umm … well," Erica stammered. "I … uh …"

"Out with it, young lady!" Selene demanded, rapping the podium several times with her flogger. "Confession is the first step to correction."

"I ... I sold all my Girl Scout cookies," Erica stammered.

"But?" Selene, said, drawing the word out and giving Erica a cross look.

"But ... but instead of turning the money over to my troop leader ..."

"What did you do with the money, you bad girl?" Selene demanded, flogging the podium again while stifling a grin.

"I ... I used it to buy a new dildo."

Of course, this brought another howl, both from Selene and the audience.

"Okay," Selene said, turning back to the room. "This Girl Scout bit was totally unscripted, but it's exactly the kind of role-play that can add real spice to a scene. Erica has been playing with me for a long time now, and as you can see, she's quite clever. If you're taking the dominant role and have a very creative sub, it can be a real in-your-face challenge, because the 'game' is everything, and you must be on your toes to keep your end up.

"Erica loves to play the bad little girl, and she's a real Method actress. Just look at her fidgeting over there and see how flushed she's getting. She's totally putting herself into it, and the thought of being spanked in front of all you people is probably driving her crazy with anticipation. It's this ability for both partners to fully immerse themselves in their roles that makes a scene really juicy. And the more you give yourself over to the role you're playing, the more permission you give yourself to be 'wicked,' the more fun you'll have."

Selene paused for a moment. "Now ... age regression fantasies, where the adult submissive willingly puts herself into the role of a child who is totally helpless before a grown-up ... that's about as primal as it gets. But it can make a novice feel extremely vulnerable, especially if there's a history of real child abuse. Acting out past trauma compassionately can be healing, even a turn-on; but you don't want to cause panic. The trick is to move slowly with your partner and really understand her fantasies and desires as well as her fears. That's how you build trust."

Selene turned to Erica. "So, young lady, for stealing money from the Girl Scouts, who would have used it to do good deeds for a lot of needy people, I am not just going to spank you; I will totally humiliate you in public. You know you deserve this, don't you?"

"Yes, Mistress," Erica said, eyes to the floor.

"All right, then …" Selene put her flogger down and walked over to stand behind a sturdy armless chair, next to which a small purple cushion rested on the floor.

"There are several classic positions for spanking," she told the audience, "and all have something to recommend them. Standing, bent over with hands on ankles or knees, is the boarding school method. The ass is stuck out and stretched very taut, which makes for the most painful spanking there is, especially if you use a paddle.

"But tonight, we're going to demonstrate the most familiar and cherished position—the bare-bottom, over-the-lap spanking. And though I'm going to spank a girl, with just a few minor changes, this technique works just as well on a male. Now … the first thing we need to do is get her undressed. So, Erica, strip down."

A murmur went through the audience, which, though it had been alerted to the fact that it would be seeing some nudity, was getting more and more caught up in this drama. Erica looked at Selene for a moment, then turned her eyes to the audience pleadingly, as if hoping someone might help her.

"Forget it, Girl Scout," Selene demanded. "No one is going to get you out of this mess, which you created for yourself."

Erica began to remove the clips she'd used to fasten the little Girl Scout cap to her hair, but Selene stopped her. "You can leave your hat on," she said, drawing still another laugh from the crowd.

Erica herself had to stifle a grin to keep from breaking her submissive mood as she removed her shoes and white socks, followed by the standard green dress, which she unbuttoned and let fall to the floor. In just a few moments, she was standing on stage in only her bra, a little thong and that Girl Scout cap.

"Let's go, young lady," Selene demanded. "The bra too."

Erica looked at her in surprise. "No, Mistress. Please. I can't!"

"Yes, you can, and you will. Take it off."

Erica obeyed, slowly unhooking her bra straps and removing the garment, which brought an appreciative sigh from the crowd. Her breasts were small and firm, the nipples peaked with arousal, or maybe she was just cold. As if embarrassed by her nudity, she quickly folded her arms across her chest, drawing another laugh from Selene.

"Oh, what a little show-off! I know what an exhibitionist you are. Get those arms down and stop pretending you don't relish letting everyone see your pretty tits."

Once more, Selene addressed the audience. "Just to maintain a bit of propriety—and in case there's any law enforcement in the audience—we'll let Erica keep her thong on tonight, though I doubt that skimpy thing is official Girl Scout issue."

There were mock hisses from the audience and cries of "Take it off!"

Selene now sat in the straight-back chair, adjusting it a bit to face the audience. "Obviously, complete nudity is more fun; but this should work for tonight. Okay, Erica, come here and kneel on the cushion until I'm ready for you."

"No!" Erica shouted. "I … I've changed my mind!" She began to back off slowly toward stage right, eliciting surprised murmurs from the audience.

"Stop her, Jilaynie," Selene said.

Mistress Jilaynie, who stood nearby, quickly seized Erica about the waist, just before she could dash behind the curtains. She lifted her easily and turned the squirming young woman toward Selene, pinning her arms behind her back and making Erica yelp.

"Keep still, or I'll really have to hurt you," Mistress Jilaynie said. Erica ceased her struggles, though the taller woman still held her firmly.

Selene looked at the audience and grinned. "Having an assistant is unusual, but handy in situations when your sub gets a little unruly. Another person watching can also add to the feeling of helplessness and humiliation, which in itself can be devastatingly sexy for some.

"All right, then," Selene continued, turning to Erica and pointing at the purple cushion beside her chair. "Come and kneel over here while I explain to these good people how this is going to work."

Jilaynie released Erica, who obediently walked over to kneel on the cushion. Selene's order to leave her hat on had been more than just a clever reference to the Randy Newman song about a man instructing his girlfriend to stand on a chair and slowly strip for him. The little Girl Scout cap, sitting on top of her nakedness, had the desired effect of making Erica look totally vulnerable and forlorn.

Selene stroked Erica's cheek and put a hand on her shoulder. "So, first off, in all forms of spanking, positioning is crucial. Comfort is of primary importance to the spanker, who should take a position that allows her arm maximum freedom of movement. Sitting or standing, the spanker must be higher than the spankee to assert full dominance.

"I prefer the submissive to be as comfortable as possible, too, so she can relax and surrender to the physical and emotional sensations. And the most comfortable position for the spankee is generally over-the-lap."

She patted her lap. "Okay, honey ... all aboard the Punishment Express."

"Yes, Mistress," Erica said. She stood and then draped herself across Selene's lap, so that her tummy was centered over the domme's right thigh, while her arms hung loosely to the floor, shoulders and head angled down. Her legs, with knees about six inches apart, were tucked under the chair as far as possible, toes barely touching the ground.

"Erica's a veteran and really has this down. See how she's placed herself? Her legs are spread apart and tucked in; this gets the more sensitive inside of her thighs out of harm's way. And note how she's arched her lower back down a bit. This is a little tricky at first, but it turns the bottom up even farther and opens her butt cheeks so they are harder to clench and more vulnerable."

Selene relaxed in her chair, resting her left hand casually on Erica's butt. "Okay, this is fine for a woman, but what if I'm spanking a male? Well, it's not that different, really. The position would be pretty much the same as Erica's, only forward just a bit to keep the testicles from sticking out too far where they can be accidentally pounded. Ouch! But you might want to expose those balls just a little so they can be brushed or tickled.

"As to the shaft, the best place for that is pressed firmly against your right thigh and aimed to the left, or the other way round if you're spanking right-handed."

Again, there were giggles and nervous laughter.

"Well, it has to go *somewhere*, doesn't it?" Selene said, and another huge laugh greeted this remark. She raised a hand to quiet the crowd. "I should tell you that the first time I ever did an over-the-knee spanking on a male, I got a little—well, let's just call it a wet surprise. I was a novice at the time, and it came as a total shock. I had no idea men could do that when you spanked them." Her look of mock horror produced more laughter.

"Well, okay, then," Selene said when the audience quieted down again. "Is everyone ready to watch me redden Erica's butt?"

The crowd responded with cheers, whistles, and applause.

"An important thing to remember is that, positioned like Erica is, the ass is both supple and soft. Those of you in back can't see this, but when I press a finger into her behind and release, it just sort of bounces. Now, we want to start like that, with a little stroking and patting, going from soft to firm. This primes the flesh."

Selene demonstrated by stroking Erica's ass with her left hand, then teasing slightly around the crack with her fingernails before administering a few light slaps. "Yum," Erica said, squirming a bit.

"As you can tell from Erica's reaction, these sensations can be maddeningly sexy. Ah, she likes that, doesn't she? You want a little more of that, sweetie?

"With an intimate partner, it's always fun to do lots of teasing. Don't be afraid to get a little rough, and talk dirty to them all the way through. Spell out exactly what delights you have in mind for them after their spanking, provided they behave and accept their punishment. You'll be amazed at how cooperative they become. A bit of nipple tweaking for men as well as women is a nice touch too … I hope you didn't think I made her take her bra off just to give you folks a cheap thrill."

She lifted Erica slightly and gave each nipple a hard tweak.

"Ouch! Ouch!" Erica said, then giggled.

Selene whispered something to Erica, who promptly tried to lick her hand, but Selene pulled it away and gave her face a little smack. "No! Not without permission." She looked out at her audience. "I'm not going to tell you folks what I just said to her, but feel free to use your imaginations."

The audience laughed again, but most of them were beginning to perspire.

"Okay," Selene said. "Make sure to aim your slaps at the underside of the ass. That's the sit-spot, or fillet, as we call it. Getting that nice and sore will give your girl or boy something to remember you by for days. Pay attention to both sides, but don't be predictable. Alternate slaps between butt cheeks for a while, then lay a couple right across the middle. Caress and tickle when the ass gets really red, wet your hand with your saliva if you want, and brush lightly in the crack with your finger before you go back to slapping. The uncertainty of what's coming next—pain or pleasure—is a huge turn-on. So … so …"

She stumbled over her words, startled by someone she'd spotted in the audience: A youngish man sitting in the second row. He was just under average height, with a medium build, a nice head of curly brown hair, and a handsome face that was looking very flushed. He'd just thrown his jacket across his lap in an attempt to hide the bulge in his trousers, and that quick movement, plus the flood of passionate emotion coming from him, was what had distracted Selene. His longing was intense, but the lust Selene sensed was not aimed at her or at the almost naked Erica, lying across her lap. It was all for Jill.

Selene turned and caught Jill's eye, using a subtle head movement to direct her attention to the male. But Jill had already spotted him and nodded, smiling to show that she understood.

"Now," Selene said, regaining her poise. "Let's get this butt blazing. Ready, young lady?"

"Yes, Mistress," Erica said, her voice husky. "I really, really deserve this."

Chapter 2

OLD FRIENDS

Month of December/Month of Reed

"Shit, you're out of your fucking mind, dude!" Willie shouted, loud enough to make half the customers in the bar turn their heads. The two of them had gone to the Buena Vista for Irish coffee after gorging on crab at The Wharf, where they'd killed a bottle of chardonnay at dinner. David was now on his second Irish, so he was feeling a bit too mellow for his own good.

"Keep your voice down," he whispered from across the table. "The whole place doesn't need to hear. Besides, it's not like you think."

Willie glowered but dropped her voice to a searing hiss. "I haven't even begun to say what I think. You tell me you're seeing some violent whore and it sounds like you're in love with her."

"She is not a whore," David insisted. "And I'm not in love with her. She's more like a therapist."

"Oh, now you're really scaring me," Willie said. "First you say you're seeing a dominatrix, and then she's your therapist? You're totally insane."

"Okay, 'therapist' is the wrong word. There's really nothing to compare it to. I've wanted to try this for a long time and now I'm getting it out of my system ... like I did with hang gliding?"

"Oh, right. And let me remind you that you broke your collarbone landing that contraption."

David sighed. "It was just a hairline fracture, and I only missed three days of work."

Willie Ludlow was his closest friend, but there were things it was probably better not to share with her, like when he'd foolishly confessed to having tried heroin. He hadn't shot up, and he'd done it only once, snorting just a small amount on a dare, but Willie had been ready to pack him off to rehab. Now the Irish coffee had loosened his tongue and he'd again blabbed something he should have kept to himself. Only the fact that he was half drunk could have made him think Willie would find the fact that he was now the steady client of a dominatrix deliciously edgy.

"You've done some nutty things before, David Sendak," she said, "but paying money to have some skank whip your ass is truly sick."

"It's not sick ... and don't call her a skank!" David knew he sounded defensive, but Mistress Jilaynie was "class personified," and Willie didn't get it. "Look, if you could just be rational and listen to me."

"No! There's not one rational thing you can say about this." He thought she might actually stuff her fingers in her ears and go "blah, blah, blah" to shut him out.

They had first met as sophomores at Cal fourteen years ago while struggling together through an insufferably dull statistics class, and though they'd never been lovers, they'd been close ever since. Willie had been a "hot item" at Berkeley, with countless lovers, mostly women, though a few men too. And even if she'd never turned heads with her looks, she'd made up for an unremarkable face by studying Tantra and the other erotic arts as meticulously as she'd once pored through Biblical passages as the stepdaughter of an evangelical minister. Her reputation as a sexual prodigy was a bit overstated, in part because she'd worked so hard to self-promote it, but the ability to feel the power of her sexuality instead of remaining its victim had been intoxicating in college.

Now, her promiscuous past embarrassed Willie, and she never spoke of it outside her women's group. David was the only other person who knew most of her "sordid" history; but of course, they'd been such close friends when all this was happening that there was no way he could not have known. And she'd felt safe telling him everything back then, partly because she'd never felt any romantic longing coming from him, which might have made talking about her sexual exploits awkward.

But then, just before Christmas break during their senior year, he'd suddenly made a pass at her. Early one morning, completely out of the blue, he'd simply spun her around as they were walking through the eucalyptus grove on campus, kissing her with a passion she never suspected he had in him. After more than two years of being like brother and sister, it was so unexpected that all she could do was stand there and gape as a mortified David fumbled an apology, saying he had no idea what had gotten into him.

It might have been the end of their friendship if she'd handled it badly. But instead of reacting as if she'd been violated, she just laughed—not unkindly, but with an amused tolerance that silently said, *"You're very sweet, David, and I love you dearly … but you're not strong enough to handle the likes of me. I'd eat you up in a week and pick my teeth with your bones if we were having sex."*

How she managed to get such a complex idea across, conveying both rejection and yet deep tenderness—and all with just that laugh—neither of them could have said. Maybe the pat on the cheek she'd given him helped, but he totally got it. He shook his head and smiled, realizing what a bad idea it would be for them to sleep together. And just like that, the incident fell off their radar, without ever needing to be spoken of.

Now, looking at David across the barroom table, Willie was frightened for him. Some of his behaviors were becoming riskier and riskier, especially since he'd had to put his father in hospice two years ago. Lester was suffering from Huntington's chorea and had been living at their Inverness house with a part-time caregiver for years, while David went there to provide what help he could most weekends. But as Lester's decline accelerated, it became obvious that he needed fulltime care, and David—who adored Lester—felt like a heel for warehousing him.

Huntington's could take many years to kill its victims. The gene that triggered it was inherited, and there was a fifty-percent chance that David would develop the disease himself, though an equal chance he'd escape it. The genetic markers were usually clear, and there was a test to determine whether he had the defective gene or not. It was a test he'd always resisted having because, if he was doomed, he didn't want to know. But when Lester went into hospice, David finally broke down and had the test, deciding to free himself of the uncertainty.

But, while waiting for the results had merely been nerve-racking, the outcome was utterly frustrating. The test was usually clear one way or the other, because you either had the defective gene or you didn't. But once in a while the genetic marker fell into a gray area, and that had been the case here. The medical jargon was confusing, but the upshot was that the test was indeterminate, and he still had a fifty-percent chance of developing Huntington's, but also an equal chance of escaping it, which meant he knew no more now than before.

Lester had begun to show symptoms in his mid-thirties—only a few years past David's current age, and that was fairly typical. If Huntington's was going to strike David, it could happen anytime during the next few years, after which the danger would begin to decrease. Ironically, where not knowing his fate had been emotionally manageable before, the test results sent David into a major funk.

Willie knew he was using the uncertainty as an excuse to be reckless with his life and also to avoid healthy relationships with women. But, as she kept reminding him, he was very much alive now, and the present was the only certain thing that anyone had. "Why deny yourself companionship because you *might* get Huntington's?" she'd said, so often that she was like a looping tape on the subject.

"I can't, Willie," was his typical reply. "I won't risk putting a woman through watching me die slowly. In ten years or so, my risk will be smaller. Then I can start thinking about marriage and shit like that."

Willie didn't buy it for a moment, because the fact was that he'd always had an odd sexual "vibe." David was obviously attracted to women, but he lacked the male assertiveness most heterosexual girls found attractive. Still, "assertiveness" didn't quite get at it, because David could be very confident in other areas, especially at his job, where he'd risen over several more-senior competitors to manage his software group.

But he could never approach women in a confident way. Instead, he seemed in awe of the ones he was attracted to, as if they were goddesses instead of potential conquests. That was so wrong Willie didn't even know how to explain it.

Men who were successful with women were sexually acquisitive. They let a woman know they wanted her, with their eyes, their posture, and with how they talked and flirted. A woman always knew when a man desired her. Her ability to read the signals was instinctive. But a man's signals had to be clear, and with David, they were either clumsy—like that time he'd tried to kiss Willie—or, more often, totally absent. It was confusing to women, so the ones who found him interesting—even attractive—came to see him as a "friend" rather than romantic material.

"You know what I thought, David?" Willie said, finishing the last of her Irish coffee. "When you said you had something 'exciting' to tell me, I thought, 'Oh, my Lord, …he's finally found someone. Thank you, Jesus.'"

David shrugged. "Well, I have found someone, haven't I? Why no 'Thank you, Jesus' for that?"

She narrowed her eyes. "Don't be a smart-ass. I'm a preacher's daughter, and not about to thank God you found some slut to whip you even sillier than you already are. Besides … Hey, ease off the juice, lover boy. You're sloshed enough already." He was holding his glass up to the waitress, signaling for another refill.

"I'm fine," David said, waving off her protest. "But you know, for a girl who once got passed around like a water pipe in an opium den, you've become awfully straight."

"Well, fuck you too," Willie said, without anger, because they were close enough to bandy insults with no intent to injure. "Look, you're the best friend I've got. I love you and it's hard for me to separate what you're telling me from my own history. I had no choice with Harry, but you're doing this voluntarily."

"Willie, this is totally different from your stepfather. Mistress doesn't do anything I don't want. Not ever! The chief rule is: 'Keep it safe, sane, and consensual.'"

"Okay, great. But that leaves me with one question: What exactly are you consenting to? And how much are you paying for this so-called 'service' anyway?"

David laughed. "That's two questions. The answer to the first is that what we do is none of your business. The answer to the second is that I see her twice a week, so I get the frequent flyer discount."

Willie laughed. "A discount dominatrix? What does she do, run ads in the *Bulletin* saying 'Buy one ass whipping and get the second at half price'?"

"Yeah, funny ... but the place she works at is dignified. They don't run ads."

"So where is this place?" Willie asked. "And what's her name?"

He looked at Willie and frowned. "What are you, the Spanish Inquisition?"

The waitress brought David's Irish coffee, and he thanked her as she set the glass down.

"All right, sorry," Willie said. "But can you at least tell me what she looks like? Does she have a lot of piercings and tattoos?"

"Why do you even care what she looks like?" David said, taking a sip of his drink and making a face, mumbling that the Irish here was never hot enough.

"Well, I hope she's not some weightlifter with biceps like tree trunks," Willie said. "She might break you like a twig by accident."

David took another sip of his drink. "I'm flattered you have my safety at heart," he said with a sardonic grin.

Willie shook her head thoughtfully. "It's just that I never figured you for a ... Shit, is there even a politically correct term for it?"

"The term we use at the club is 'submissive,'" David said. "And if you read Selene Mayweather's book, you'll understand that the classy subs aren't wimps. It takes courage to honor that part of yourself."

But it was the word "club" that caught her attention. "Oh, shit! You're talking about the place in the SoMa with the weird name, aren't you? That woman was on TV talking about it. She's the one you're seeing?" Willie let out a soft whistle. "Wow, she's hot as a blowtorch, but she kept babbling about how her club's a refuge for spiritual seekers. She sounded like a cult leader."

"Actually, she's very sensible," David said, so intent on justifying himself that he neglected to say that Selene was *not* the domme he'd been seeing. "She says D&S is about using the body as a channel ... as a bridge between souls. I'm telling you, read her book. It's amazing."

Willie covered her eyes with a hand and shook her head. "Okay, I may be ignorant about what goes on in these places, but one thing I'm sure of ... it's not spiritual."

When she got home, Willie fed the cat and turned on the shower, which needed a minute to get as hot as she liked. Walking into the bedroom, she undressed, hung her clothes, and threw the items that needed laundering into the hamper.

Naked, she stood before the full-length mirror and studied herself, pleased that she was holding up so well at thirty-three. Her face had always been freckled, but it was still free of lines, even though it had grown a bit rounder than she liked. Her recently bobbed red hair softened her rather flat features too much, she decided, resolving to let it grow out again.

As to her body, her trim, five-foot-two frame hadn't widened at all since college. That was partly the result of good genes, though three hours a week at the gym didn't hurt either. No one would ever call her beautiful, but she had well-shaped legs, a tight tummy, pert breasts, and a scrumptious ass, even if she did say so herself.

But now she tilted her head and frowned as she ran the tips of her fingers over the ten mottled scars just below her belly button, feeling the insult of those ridges like the plagues of Egypt. When he'd punished her with lit cigarettes, Harry had actually named those burns for the Ten Plagues. This one, he'd called "darkness," that one "blood," and there at the bottom, just above her bush was—appropriately enough—"the slaying of the firstborn." Those scars would be with her until the day she died—along with the even worse scar she'd inflicted on her own heart.

She made an impatient sound when she realized she was falling into exactly the kind of self-pity she hated, so she pushed the past from her mind and went to luxuriate in the steaming shower.

Chapter 3

⁓

JILL

27th day of Ivy, 5335

Dearest Full Sister,

It was lovely getting your letter when the Balacampa opened and the mail came through. Our portal is open so rarely during the winter moons, Janaynie, and I feel so disconnected from home when it's closed. A couple of nights ago, I dreamed I was walking through our orchard and picked a golden hollyath from cousin Blynnith's tree; it was so luscious when I bit into it. The fruit here on T'Erenya is nearly tasteless compared with what our Drys trees produce year-round.

You asked what we do at Club Nyala and how we use this place to find potential Changelings to bring home to Ausonia. Well, if humans with the spiritual ailment we also call nyala were mice, this club would be the perfect mousetrap. The name itself seems to draw them like goat milk draws starflies, even though they don't know what nyala really means.

We Meliai who work upstairs are known as "mistresses." That's a human word for a female in charge, and the closest term we have in Pandoric is probably thallalanatta, which doesn't translate well into any of the human languages I've learned.

Unlike the club's regular members, for whom dominance and submission are mainly a form of sex play, the Upstairs Girls are "professionals," and we work only with a select type of nyalic human—those who've been severely damaged, but not entirely broken by loss, betrayal, rape or any of the countless other miseries these short-lived beings inflict on one another. For the fortunate few, nyala has opened their hearts, making them compassionate, loving, and ready to receive us. But the great majority of nyalic humans are cruel and selfish, and too wounded to be of use, even to themselves. Finding just the right one is difficult. If a Meliai is careless about the human she chooses, the results can be disastrous, as we have too often seen, so we cannot afford emotional mistakes.

Once we identify our ideal match, we begin healing them as only a Meliai Dryad can heal a spiritually crippled human. Our methods are a bit like those a Shepherdess uses with her Changeling, though unlike Changelings, humans here have no idea what will finally become of them.

I know you've watched and participated in the ritual of chakchina, and you've seen how Changelings go into the erotic trance we call analu when they worship the feet of a Meliai; and the longer we defer their sexual release, the deeper into analu they go. After a time, they lose all sense of being a separate self, which gives them a lovely taste of what is to come at Edarta. Here at the club, we do chakchina with nyalic humans when we begin seeing them as clients, and if we feel them go into analu, we will see them again; otherwise, there is no point in further sessions.

30th day of Ivy, 5335

Oh, Kayla, we had a near disaster yesterday. One of Audrille's clients suffered something called a heart attack during a bolanta session. The poor male was nearly seventy, which for a human is simply too old to tolerate such energetic games. We sent for a medical rescue wagon (called an ambulance") and, to our dismay, a fire wagon and a law enforcement vehicle came with them. Fortunately, Nellyn was here and handled the situation with her usual poise.

Still, Selene was furious with Audrille and ordered her back to Ausonia for three months as penalty for accepting such a decrepit creature for bolanta. I'm not sure who will replace her, maybe Tannith Elderblossom from Second Mountain.

But I saved the good news for last, because I've found a very promising human for us. His name is David and, yes, he's male, which makes for even greater possibilities. Imagine not just a healthy Changeling, but two new daughters and maybe as many as four if we both bear twins. With our clan's population shrinking so frighteningly, think how wonderful four darling Nymphs would be.

David was sitting in the second row of the auditorium when Selene gave her talk on spanking three weeks ago. The two of us spotted him at the same moment, and his nyala was so strong we could smell it from clear up on stage. He was having what Selene calls an "erotic emergency," a state of urgent sexual need that humans sometimes have just from being in our presence. But his hunger wasn't for Selene; it was for me! I used my kash sense to send him an empathic message to let him know I'd be receptive to him, keeping the transmission subtle so he'd believe it was his own idea.

After the lecture, he walked up and began talking to me. What he wanted was obvious enough, but what he said was that I had a beautiful voice and should consider singing professionally. He was so transparent, and his longing for me so intense, that I could have taken him right back to my apartment and given him exactly what he craved. But I'd learned my lesson with Lynette.

You'll remember how drawn I was to that human girl, and how I started having sex with her right away, despite Clan Mother's warning. Well, just as Selene predicted, I was too impatient and didn't take the time to entice Lynette slowly, so she'd ignite like a bonfire once I'd piled enough erotic kindling under her. And instead of bursting into flame, she just smoldered like green wood, and a potential Changeling slipped through my fingers.

So when David asked me out for coffee, I said, "Sorry, I don't date men, but ..." I thumbed through my day planner, making him sweat a bit. "For $350, I can let you have a ninety-minute session ... Let's see ... Tuesday night at 9:00?"

My tone was businesslike, even though I'd sent him that empathic message saying I was attracted. The plan was to keep him uncertain, while not shutting the door entirely to becoming more than just my client.

The implication that I was sexually interested only in females came from an idea Selene once gave me. What she said was that when you tell a timid human male that you only have sex with females, it actually gives him hope, since it means that if he can win your interest, there won't be a powerful male rival waiting to challenge him. Selene understands humans so well.

Well, my strategy worked, because he obviously thought a session with me for money was better than nothing at all. "We're going to have lots of fun, little man," I said, patting his cheek, though I wriggled away like a getchi when he tried to hug me.

We've already had five sessions, and. I've never seen a submissive human go into analu trance so easily. It's as if he's been waiting all his life just for me. My next appointment with David is in just a couple of days, and I have high hopes for him. I'll keep you posted on developments.

Meanwhile, I send you all my love.

Your Full Sister,

Jilaynie

Chapter 4

⸎

A DIRTY OLD MAN

Month of December/Month of Reed

*D*avid pulled his Volvo into the parking lot behind the hospice and cut the engine. These visits to his dying father were always unsettling, and he was grateful for Willie's company.

Though she hadn't seen Lester in over a year, Willie had known him almost as long as she'd known David himself, David having invited her to dinner several times when they'd been students at Cal. Lester had already been ill then, though his condition had been far less advanced and he'd still been able to live at home with only a little help.

Willie liked Lester from the first; his charm, wit, and generosity of spirit were qualities he'd passed along to his son, but he was also less self-centered than David could be. David's mother had walked out on her family years before Willie had met them, but she'd have bet that the narcissism she sometimes saw in David came from Myra.

They got out of the car and walked toward the back entrance of the building, making their way around a few oil-slicked puddles from last night's rain. "Oh … a couple of things I should warn you about," David said. "First of all, he'll look like he's aged a lot since you last saw him, so don't be shocked. Also, he's started saying …

well, weird shit. I mean things that never used to come out of his mouth."

"Like what?"

"Well, he's in some kind of 'dirty old man' phase. Doctor Bellows says it's not unusual at this point. So, if he says something, you know … vulgar, just cut him some slack, okay?"

Willie shrugged. "I'm a big girl, David, I can handle it."

They checked in at the desk, took the elevator to the third floor, and walked down the fluorescent-lit corridor to Lester's room. But though she thought she was ready for anything, Willie was stunned by his appearance. Though David's father had never been powerfully built, he'd always kept himself in shape and been quite handsome. But the man she saw now had wasted away to almost nothing in the past year. Scrawny and frail, what was left of his once lustrous auburn hair was totally white, and he looked more like a man of eighty than one just shy of his sixtieth birthday.

"It's mostly the emphysema that's killing him," David whispered. "And he's had at least one stroke. It's the … *other* thing that's wasting his mind, though." Sometimes David had a problem even saying the word "Huntington's."

Don't name the thing that terrifies you, and it can't happen, Willie thought.

Lester was propped up in bed in the room he shared with a terminal cancer patient named Lindt. The two were separated by a thin curtain that hung from the ceiling. Lindt seemed comatose, probably heavily drugged, his breathing ominously ragged. The air smelled stale and the room was oppressive with the aura of hopelessness and approaching death. It made Willie want to flee, but she kept her composure as they approached Lester's bed.

"Hey, Dad," David said, laying a hand on his father's shoulder. "How's my buddy?"

Lester turned a blank expression to David, but after a few moments, his eyes lit up. "Hello, Davy," he said, giving David a big smile. "How's my sonny boy?"

"Sonny boy" was what Lester had called him as a child, and David breathed a sigh of relief because he could never be certain if his father would even recognize him. "Just fine, Dad. How've they been treating you?"

The light in Lester's eyes seemed to waver then return. He didn't answer but gestured to the water glass beside his bed. David picked it up and held it steady while his father took a few sips through the plastic straw. Lester stared at Willie, finally noticing her. At first, there was no recognition in his gaze, but suddenly his face lit up. "Myra!" he said, reaching for her hand. "Oh, honey … I'm so glad you're back."

David and Willie gave each other a troubled look. "Dad," David said. "This isn't Mom. It's Willie. You remember her, don't you? She used to have Thanksgiving with us. And she came to a Passover Seder at Aunt Hilda's too. Remember the time she gobbled a whole spoonful of horseradish thinking it was something sweet? That expression on her face? We laughed about it for weeks."

Lester grew more confused as he tried to place Willie.

"Dad?" David asked. "Can you say hello to Willie? She left work early to come and visit."

"Hello, Willie," Lester said, extending his hand without a trace of recognition. "Thanks for coming."

Willie gave him a smile, half repulsed by the bony hand and its tissue paper skin. "Hi, Lester, it's so nice to see you again." But it wasn't nice at all. She was no good at seeing death close up, had not been good at it since she'd watched her mother take nearly a year to die of cancer. She was beginning to feel claustrophobic and wished she'd declined David's offer to accompany him.

"Have you been eating, Dad?" David asked. "Are they feeding you okay?" He knew they were feeding his father, or at least trying to. The problem was he simply refused most food, almost as if wanting to hasten his death. "Look what we got you." David reached into his coat pocket, pulling out a ripe avocado, which was about the only thing Lester still liked to eat, but his father barely glanced at it. This place was morbidly depressing; but at least it was clean, the level of care was good; and seeing after a dying man while working a fulltime job was beyond David's ability.

A few minutes later, Doctor Bellows, a silver-haired woman with a harried expression, strode into the room. She'd been both David and Lester's physician for over fifteen years, and she'd agreed to reschedule her biweekly call on Lester to this afternoon, when David could be here. She shook hands with David and then with Willie when he introduced them.

David watched as the doctor checked Lester's vitals, then joined her when she called him aside. "As you can see," Bellows said, "he's not doing very well. The immediate problem is more his lungs and heart than the Huntington's. We could do another full workup at Saint Francis, but I don't see much point. I'm sorry, David, but your father's probably got four months at most."

"Right, and you've been saying that for over a year now."

Bellows offered a sympathetic shrug. "An extended death watch is hard, but we can't predict the course of respiratory failure with certainty. Right now, it's mostly guesswork. But if you'd like to get another opinion …" Her words carried a hint of reproach, and David said he didn't think it was necessary. Anyway, he'd already had a pulmonary specialist check Lester and his opinion was no different.

"What concerns me now," Bellows added, tapping David's chest with a forefinger, "is that you haven't had a checkup in over a year, and since you're at risk for Huntington's yourself, we should … Oh, I forgot, you've already had the screening. Those inconclusive results were unfortunate."

David laughed. "Sorry I disappointed you."

The doctor gave him a speculative look, wondering if he was being sarcastic, but she let it pass. "There are some new measures we can take to slow the progress of the disease if we know what's coming, so given that you're entering the typical onset age, you should be getting complete physicals three times a year. I suggest you call my office for an appointment as soon as possible."

David said he would do that on Monday, but he had no plans to and Bellows knew it. "Are you still on the antidepressants?" she asked.

He shook his head. "They were ruining my sex life, but I'm doing fine, really."

Willie was standing a couple of feet away, following the conversation attentively, and she felt her anger flare again. *You are not doing fine,* she thought. *You are going off the deep end, and your doctor needs to know about the idiocy you're up to with that whore of yours.*

For one precarious moment, a demon nearly possessed her, and she bit back words saying that David was debasing himself at a BDSM parlor. She came within a hairsbreadth of spilling his "dirty secret" to Bellows and committing what would have been a serious betrayal. Even as a compassionate intervention to get him professional help, it might have been the end of their friendship, and she breathed a sigh of relief that she'd kept her big mouth shut.

"Well that was uplifting," David grumbled, walking back to his father's bed after the doctor left. Lester was lying on his back, staring at the ceiling and taking no notice of them.

"It's hard to see, isn't it?" Willie said, putting a hand on David's shoulder. "I remember him being so full of life."

"Yeah, me too," David said, trying to fluff the pillow under Lester's head. "I wonder where he goes when he checks out like this?"

Suddenly, Lester reached out and seized Willie's hand. "Myra, honey," he said. "I haven't forgotten you promised me a blowjob the last time you were here."

Willie's jaw dropped and she leapt back a couple of feet.

"Steady, girl," David whispered. "This is what I tried to warn you about … Dad, this is not Mom. It's Willie, and it's very rude of you to talk to her like that."

"How the hell can he think I'm your mother?" Willie hissed. "And even if I was, he has no right to say that in public."

"Oh, for God's sake, Willie, just relax. You're not Myra, and he's not your stepfather. I need at least one of you sharing the real world with me right now."

Willie felt her face redden, knowing she'd overreacted. "Sorry," she said. "It's just that I've been having these flashbacks lately. It's not his fault. It's mine."

David sighed. "Okay, look. We'll be done in a few minutes and then we can go have a drink."

Willie nodded, turned back to the bed, and looked at Lester, who seemed to understand he'd done something wrong without knowing what it was. She touched his face gently, drawing a sweet smile from him. "Hey, David, your dad could use a shave. I'll go to the nurse's station and get some gear."

After she left, David sat down on the edge of the bed beside his father, taking his hand. "I've got such a wonderful wife, David," Lester said softly. "I'm a lucky man."

David stared at the floor, then at the doorway through which Willie had disappeared. Finally, he looked back at his father. "Dad, you know Mom's been gone for …" He hesitated and changed his mind. There was nothing to gain by dragging Lester back into this sad world. "I know," he said. "Mom's a peach." The words almost made him choke, but his father nodded and smiled again.

It took Willie a good ten minutes to find the shaving gear, but she finally came back, carrying a safety razor, a small can of shaving foam, a towel, and a large bowl, which she filled with warm water at the sink in the little bathroom.

The two of them sat Lester up in bed and, using a washcloth, Willie wet his face with water from the bowl. Then she applied some of the foam and began to shave him carefully and gently. He smiled, enjoying the sensation, but even more the attention he was getting from the woman he believed was his wife.

"Don't worry, Lester," Willie crooned. "We'll soon have you looking like a stud."

"Not bad," David said. "You've obviously had some practice at this."

"I used to shave Harry every day," she said evenly.

"Really?"

"Yup. But he always insisted I use a straight razor. It was the only way to get the shave close enough for him." There was more irony than bitterness in her voice.

"Jesus," David said. "Did you ever feel like ... you know, 'accidentally' slitting his throat?"

"Only every other day," Willie said matter-of-factly, focusing on Lester. When she was done, she rinsed his face and patted it dry with the towel. "There you go, Lester. The pretty young nurses won't be able to keep their hands off you now."

Visiting hours were soon over, and they said their goodbyes to Lester, each giving him a little kiss on the cheek.

As they turned toward the door, Lester reached out and gently grasped Willie's arm, pulling her close. "Take care of our son, Myra," he whispered. "And don't forget, you still owe me a blowjob."

Chapter 5

A Dangerous Obsession

*A*fter leaving the hospice, they drove to the E&O for drinks and snacks. It was only 4:00, so the place was still fairly empty, and, absent the background din, it was quiet enough for serious talk. But unnerved as he was by seeing Lester, David didn't have much energy for conversation. All he wanted was a vodka martini and a chance to decompress.

Willie, though, had other ideas. As soon as they were seated at a table, she said, "I'm sorry this is so hard on you, David. I know how much Lester means to you."

He sighed. "What am I gonna do without him, Willie? He's the one person I could always count on."

She reached across the table and took his hand. "Well, you can count on *me*. I'm always there for you, sweetie … even when I'm a pain in the ass."

"Yeah, just like a hemorrhoid."

Willie laughed. "All right, I guess I asked for that. Oh, I've got something for you." She reached into her bag, pulled out a paperback with a blue cover, and handed it to him.

Both David and Willie were mystery buffs and often exchanged books they liked, so he guessed this was the new Louise Penny novel she'd been raving about. But when he saw the title, his heart sank.

"*The Righteous Male, by Len Reynolds. A Guide to Living and Loving for Men Who Love Being Men.* Jesus, why give me this?"

His irritation surprised her, and she fumbled for a response. "I ... I just thought you might find it helpful. I told the clerk at City Lights I was looking for something inspiring to give a ... highly aware male friend, and this is what he recommended. I don't really know anything about it."

"Yeah, well I do," David said. "I read his first book, or as much of it as I could stomach. He's the high mucky-muck of the 'Alpha Men's Movement.'"

"The what?"

He shrugged. "It's an extreme response to the Women's Movement ... the idea being that what women, especially feminists, really want is alpha males. You know ... men who'll protect them, take charge of any situation, and make everything work—cowboys, knights in shining armor, and all that. Reynolds is totally contemptuous of guys who can't fit his alpha model. It's like gender fascism for the enlightened male."

Before Willie could digest that, he opened to the introduction and quickly found a passage. "Here, listen to this: 'Many so-called New Age males have metaphorically lost their manhood and been symbolically neutered by powerful, intelligent women who claim they want sensitive men, but are actually pushing them to surrender the very essence of their maleness and then rejecting them for being weak when they do. Yet women are not fully to blame for the tragic result; it's hormonally cowed men who are virtually begging to be feminized by their women.'"

"That's harsh," Willie said.

"And what about this?" David read another passage. "'If you're a man who's been emasculated by women who have misplaced their native femininity, a man who's lost touch with his primal maleness and doesn't even know it, you will instinctively hate what I say here. On the other hand, if you're one who loves everything about being male, wants to treat his woman with heart-opening love, ravish her in bed, and make her want more, then read on, brother.'"

"Yikes, that's patronizing," Willie said.

"Yeah, well ... return it and get a refund," David said, sliding the paperback across the table to her. "His first book made me feel like a gelded sheep."

Willie silently cursed her stupidity. What she'd actually told the clerk at City Lights was a bit different than what she'd just let on—*"I need something for a nice hetero guy who needs to man up a little"*—and she'd accepted the recommendation without even glancing at the book.

"Admit it, Willie. You bought that for me because of the dominatrix thing, right? Because you think I'm not man enough?"

She felt embarrassed by how close to the mark that came, though of course she'd never put it that bluntly. But rather than deny that she thought he was too soft, she tried to dance around it. "David, your problem isn't what this writer, or anyone else thinks, it's just ..."

She stopped mid-sentence, relieved when their waitress, a young blonde with a ponytail and the proverbial legs to heaven walked up and gave them a big smile.

"Hi, I'm Bliss, and I'll be your server. Have you folks decided what you'd like?"

Willie knew what she'd like the moment she looked at the waitress. "Hi, Bliss," she beamed. "I haven't seen you here before. Are you new?"

The waitress smiled again. "I just moved here from Florida. I'll be starting my PhD at Cal this spring."

David had to hand it to Willie, who could be so fearless when flirting with attractive women. "Cool!" she said. "I'm from Orlando and got my PhD at Cal ... in business."

Bliss uttered a squeal. "Business? Wow, me too. I'll be at Haas."

"Oh, it's a great school," Willie said, a bit too passionately, David thought. "And I still have contacts there. Hey, look ..." She reached into her purse for a business card, handing it to Bliss. "This is my company. Feel free to call any time if you have questions about professors, classes … or anything else."

Bliss looked at Willie's card. "Green Girl Consultants? What do you do?"

David cleared his throat, feeling like he was fading into the walls. "Um, I'm David. I was at Cal too. My PhD's in Engineering, though." His weak attempt to slide into the conversation was ignored by both women.

"We work with California businesses," Willie said, "teaching them how to comply with environmental laws while actually increasing profit. Check out our website. We're totally woman-owned and operated."

"Hey, that's great!" Bliss said, slipping the card into her pocket. "I mean, when you can make money by helping the environment. And Green Girl is such a great name for a woman-run company."

David sighed and settled in to wait it out. The flirtation went on for over five minutes before Bliss finally took their order: a Blushing Geisha for Willie, a dry martini for David, and a few appetizers, which they'd share. Willie's eyes followed Bliss till she was out of sight, at which point she turned to David and gave a low whistle. "Wow, talk about adorable."

"I noticed," David said. "And thanks for rendering me totally invisible."

"Don't feel bad, dude. You'd never get anywhere. She's strictly a girl's girl."

"And you know this how?" he asked.

"C'mon," Willie said, tapping her nose. "I can smell another dyke from across the room."

David grinned. "Hey, here's a question for you: If a straight woman who's into gay guys is called a 'fag hag,' what do you call a straight guy who loves lesbians?"

"A friend wasting his time," she said, wagging a finger at him. "David, you need to start looking at something besides dykes and dommes. There's lots of regular women out there who'd kill for a man like you."

"And what if I don't want a 'regular' woman?"

Willie shook her head in resignation. "You need a nice girlfriend, dude, one who treats you like you deserve to be treated. Not like that bitch Liz you were dating last year. She treated you like a doormat."

David looked down, embarrassed by the memory. "Liz wasn't that bad," he said defensively.

"Oh, really? First she cheats on you, and then she tops that off by giving you herpes."

"It wasn't herpes," he insisted. "It was just crabs."

"Whatever. You take her to Hawaii for two weeks, and while you're at dinner in some fancy restaurant, she stabs you in the neck with a fork when you draw the line at renting a yacht for her."

"She didn't *stab* me. It was just a little scratch."

"Right, dude. And you've still got the scar. I've been doing some reading, okay? And I've learned what can lead some men to do … you know … what you're doing now."

"Ah, you've done ze clinical research, have you?" he said, with a mock German accent. "Zo … please to enlighten us, *Frau* Doctor. Tell ze class vhat makes David cuckoo."

His tone annoyed her, but she ignored it. "Most of the literature says that men who've been badly wounded by women in the past, especially by their mothers, will go to a dominatrix because they need to keep reenacting their pain. Your mother abandoned you, right?"

This time, his voice was gentler. "Willie, this is *me*, okay? I'm not some case study. And besides, you never even knew my mother. My girlfriends have been nothing like her."

"But you've told me how critical she always was of you and Lester."

"It's not all cause and effect, girl," he said. "Not everything in the human soul has a logical reason. Some things are just there, and if a person's not hurting anyone, why try to force a 'cure' on them because you don't understand what they feel?"

"And what if it's someone you love and you think they're hurting themselves?"

David shrugged again. "Then you stand by ready to help them pick up the pieces when they crash and burn ... without saying 'I told you so.' That's what real friends do."

She sighed and leaned back in her chair. He had a point there. So what if he liked "edgy" women? After all, didn't she have a right to her own sexual preferences? No! That was completely different. Her relationships were about love, or at least mutual pleasure. His were about seeking pain and abuse, something she'd had her fill of growing up.

A busboy brought their drinks and they fell silent while Willie brooded. She knew she had to stop lecturing David or risk alienating him completely. Maybe she should work on finding him a decent woman? She'd never tried that with David because she had a firm policy against fixing friends up with each other. But if he had a real girlfriend, he'd forget about his dangerous obsession in a minute, wouldn't he? She tried to think of a heterosexual or bisexual woman friend who could be a good match, but any girl who might be healthy for him would run screaming into the night at even a hint of what he was into now.

And then she remembered Penny Thompson. The woman wasn't exactly a friend, but hadn't she been part of a threesome with a man and another woman for a couple of years? Penny was pretty sophisticated and a little off-kilter herself. Even more to the point, she was bossy as hell but also a Quaker, so she wouldn't do any serious physical damage to him. For a moment, Willie imagined David, naked but for a prim little apron, on his hands and knees, waxing the kitchen floor till it shone like a mirror as Penny stood by supervising him, sternly yet kindly. It was hard to keep from laughing at the image.

"You know, there's a woman in my group you might just hit it off with," she said. And then she recalled that Penny was well over fifty. That might work for Penny, but probably not for David, who was twenty years younger. "No, forget it. She's too mature for you."

He gave her the finger.

"Oh, relax. I meant too old. She's past menopause."

But he wasn't angry. In fact, he was smiling. "Okay, I'll stop torturing you and spill it. I happen to have a date with a very classy lady Saturday night."

It was the last thing Willie expected to hear, but she was delighted. "David, that's wonderful!" She reached to take his hand again. "Where did you meet her?"

He gave her a smug grin. "Guess."

"C'mon, dude, don't play games. Just tell me."

He took a sip of his martini. "Nope, you're gonna have to work this one out for yourself. But it's the last thing you'd expect."

She looked at him in exasperation, and then suddenly her eyes went wide as she understood. "Oh, no, you're not telling me … you asked your whore for a date and she actually accepted?"

"Wrong. She asked *me* for a date. And stop calling her a whore. She's a sex worker."

"Okay, whatever. But sex workers don't ask their clients on dates."

And there was that smug grin plastered on his face again. "You'd think that, wouldn't you? But when I went for our session last night, she said she couldn't see me professionally anymore because she was developing 'feelings' for me. She wants something more personal."

Willie saw he was telling the truth, and felt her heart sink. This was the worst possible news. As long as he was seeing that woman professionally, it was a business relationship and she would keep him at a distance, like she must do with all her johns. But this was a total game changer, and who knew what emotional quicksand he might sink into?

"David, no," she said, "don't you dare! That Selene will chew you up and spit your heart out like a cherry pit if you fall for her. For Christ sake, what the fuck do you even see in her besides looks?"

David looked at her blankly. Selene? What was she talking about? And then he remembered. At the Buena Vista, Willie had jumped to the conclusion that he was seeing Nyala's Headmistress, and he'd never set her straight. He knew he should do that now, but some impulse stopped him. Let her believe what she wanted, at least until things with Jill became solid. Once that happened—all right, *if* that happened—he'd introduce the two of them, and Willie would see how completely wrong she was.

Chapter 6

WILLIE

$\mathcal{I}$ had some errands to run after happy hour and got home exhausted but still too wired to sleep. I knew I'd come off sounding like a prig lecturing David again; but now he actually had a date with that woman? There was no way a professional dominatrix would want a relationship with someone like him, not without having an ulterior motive. So what the fuck was she really after?

As soon as I plopped onto the couch, Butter, my orange tabby, was in my lap, purring like a motor as I began scratching her head and chin. *Yes, Mommy loves her sweet Butter biscuit.* Orange females are rare, and Butter—with those limpid golden eyes—was a miraculous find when I got her from the shelter as a precious kitten. Tonight, she really wanted attention, so I thought I'd try a movie to help me unwind while I ministered to her.

But just as I was scanning the cable guide, Butter started to bristle and hiss. She'll do that just before an earthquake or during a thunderstorm, but the only thing that happened was that my phone rang. A telemarketer? No, not this late. It could only be David, because he always called to make sure I got home okay if it was after dark, and he would fret if I didn't pick up. So I leapt for the phone, spilling my protesting cat onto the floor.

"Hi, David," I said, not even bothering to check caller ID. "I got home fine."

"Hello, Wilhelmina?" I felt a moment of confusion, because that was definitely not David. And then my blood ran cold. It wasn't quite the voice that still haunted my dreams; it was older and more gravelly, but it was *him*.

I can't remember much about my real father who died when I was four, so I don't know what he called me, but even my mother never called me anything but Willie. There was just one person who called me Wilhelmina, the name that made me gnash my teeth, and that was the Reverend Harry Barton, my stepfather.

My mother and me had moved from Nashville to Orlando just after I turned eight, and a couple of months later, she brought Harry home and, just like that, said they were getting married. At first, I was crazy about him. He was very handsome, with perfect teeth and this incredible smile. He even looked a little like Paul Newman, so I knew what she saw in him.

All my friends had fathers, and not having one left a big void in my life. Harry filled that void immediately, and even though I sometimes heard him and my mother arguing at night, he treated me like a princess. He'd take me to school and pick me up when my mother had to work, and in the summer, he'd meet me after swim class, and we'd stop for whole cherry ice cream in sugar cones on the way home.

Saturday mornings, our tradition was breakfast at IHOP, where my mother would have pancakes, I'd have waffles, and Harry would complain about how awful the coffee was. It became an ongoing joke because he'd drink an entire pitcher and make a "yuck face" after every cup.

The only problem in the beginning was that first day my mother introduced us, and he bent down to look me in the eye. He let out a laugh that was a little too jovial and said, "What kind of a name is Willie for a girl? That's what you call a man's 'unit' … the thing that makes him a man … his willy."

46

My mother giggled and said, "Oh, darling, she's too young to know about such things." She explained that her father's name had been William, and mine was actually Wilhelmina (I having been named for him). And Harry said, "Wilhelmina. Now that's a real girl's name. I'll just call you Wilhelmina, if it's okay with you."

I said it was not okay, that my name was Willie. *Willie!* And he laughed again and said, "Sure, darling, I'll call you whatever you like. I'm sorry if I hurt your feelings." After that, he always called me Willie, at least until my mother died three years later.

My family was nominally Catholic before Harry. We weren't particularly religious, though we went to church on Christmas and Easter, and very occasionally to Sunday Mass. But all that changed when Harry came along. He was a Baptist minister with his own congregation, and after my mother married him, we were never allowed to miss a single Sunday in church unless we were sick.

My mother was now a preacher's wife, and she fell right in line. But that was where my real problems with Harry started. This kind of religion, with all that falling to your knees, waving your hands and praising the Lord, was like worshipping some Jesus from another planet.

I'd been baptized in church as a baby, but now Harry insisted I needed to be baptized again, not just sprinkled with Holy Water, but the real way. I was to be dunked in a pond on land that belonged to one of his flock. And in front of about fifty witnesses, Harry held his hand over my mouth and nose, put my whole body under, and kept me in that icy water long enough that I started kicking in panic. The cold I caught lasted nearly a week.

While my mother was alive, I'd hide behind her in church, hoping that Harry wouldn't make me go up and testify. When he did, I never knew what to say or what sins to confess. But I'd dutifully thank Jesus for having saved me, and after a while, I started believing it.

After my mother died, church became even more intimidating because I had no skirts to hide behind. And now Harry began calling me Wilhelmina. I'm not sure why he did it, but there was no stopping him. He also started spanking me for the slightest infraction—like not finishing my broccoli at dinner—something he'd never done when my mother was around. I began to resent him, but Harry was now my father, and at age eleven, I was dependent on him for everything.

Being called "Wilhelmina" was infuriating, and sometimes he actually seemed to taunt me with it, especially on Sundays, as I sat in church and listened to him go on and on about sin and the redemption the Lord longed to offer us, if only we'd open our hearts to Him. Every couple of weeks, he'd summon his "daughter" up in front of the congregation so she could give her testimony. "C'mon up here, *Will…hu… meeena*," he would shout, drawing my name out like it was a rubber band, and he wanted to prove how far it could stretch without breaking.

The real beatings started when I was twelve. They seemed random at first, but he'd always have some reason to point to, like me leaving my slippers by my bed instead of in the closet where they belonged. This was about the time the sex started, started so slowly I wasn't even sure what was happening. Harry would sit next to me on the couch when we were watching *Gilligan's Island* reruns on TV, and when we'd both laugh at something, he'd pat my knee in a good-natured way—just affectionate father and daughter stuff at first. But soon, the "patting" moved to my thigh, and after a while, he'd start keeping his hand there, like he'd just forgotten where he'd left it.

One evening, his little finger went up just under the hem of my skirt. I didn't know why he was doing that, but my heart started hammering. I was still basically an innocent, but I knew this couldn't be right. Fathers did not put their little finger under their daughter's skirt, not even out of simple affection. But when I glanced at him, his eyes were glued to the TV, not even looking at me. I thought maybe, just maybe, it was nothing and he wasn't paying attention to what his hand was doing. Should I just leave it there or gently remove it? And if I moved it, would he be angry and give me another beating? I left it there and tried to calm myself.

A few nights later, that finger started doing something between my legs that scared the crap out of me, going where no one's touch but my own belonged. He was invading me, but the real nightmare was how good it felt. I hated it, but was afraid he might stop.

I liked boys and flirted with them at school, but I flirted with girls too and liked them better because our minds and bodies just spoke the same language. By the time I was thirteen, I knew what I was and could tell which girls were like me. I had no trouble letting them know what I wanted and had more than a couple of takers.

Frances Longstreet, a skinny brunette with no tits yet to speak of, was part of my life for a while. Sometimes I'd skip church on Sunday, lying to Harry that it was "my time of the month" and that I was "unwell." Once he'd left, Frances would come to the house and we'd have great oral sex in my bedroom. She was the girl who first introduced me to dildos, which were my first true spiritual revelation.

Then, one Sunday, when I was fourteen, Harry came home early because there'd been a power failure at church, and he walked right in on me and Frances fucking up a storm. It was a classic teenage nightmare, but it was also funny, because at first, he thought that Frances—squirming on top of me with that flat chest of hers—was a boy. It would have been bad enough if she had been, but when he realized I'd been having sex with a girl, he went totally berserk, throwing Frances out of the house and promising to kill her if she ever came near me again.

Harry beat the shit out of me that night, saying there was a special place in Hell for deviants like me. Of course, I understood what a hypocrite he was. I knew his real problem wasn't that I was a lesbian, but that I was his property and someone else was "using" me without permission.

The cigarette burns started a few months later. By now, though, I was seriously addicted to the intense orgasms I was having with him, which made sex with my stepfather even more repulsive. It wasn't just Harry who was my foe; my own body had turned against me, conspiring with the enemy to enslave me.

He would watch me undress, throw me onto the bed, and climb aboard, with no foreplay at all. I didn't need any. He'd put his cock inside me and just start fucking. It was brutal but efficient, and after a couple of minutes, I would scream and come like a freight train. I was disgusted, but even his clammy smell on humid summer nights became a turn-on.

When he got me pregnant at fifteen, Harry convinced the doctor that I'd been raped by an unknown assailant while taking a shortcut home from school, a man who'd run off and vanished like a phantom. I meekly supported that fiction, and people believed it because, after all, he was a respected minister and everybody admired him. Abortion didn't even come up. The word never passed Harry's lips, and I didn't want one. Even though I'd become cynical about religion, I was still a Christian, and taking my baby's life wasn't something I'd even consider.

I was a smart girl, *very* smart, and a straight-A student. I'd even skipped a grade in secondary school. I was over a year younger than most of the other juniors in my high school class, and doing homework was my one real respite from Harry. He didn't dare interfere with that, and if I wanted to be left alone, I could always tell him I had a big test tomorrow, go into my room, and close the door.

But, as soon as I started to show—which was right at the start of my senior year—I was kicked out of my school, which was in a very conservative district. Today, they couldn't get away with it, but back then, the fact that I'd been raped didn't matter because everyone assumed the girl had brought it on herself in some way, or just didn't say "no" firmly enough. I begged Harry to use his influence to get me reinstated, but he wanted me at home now and didn't offer a single protest.

I'd dreamed of going to college out of state, and the farther away from Harry the better. My grades were so high that if I aced my

SATs, I could have my choice of colleges, but that dream would be dead if I didn't find a way out of this mess. I could see that taking care of an infant alone while in college would be impossible, but with three months to go before I delivered, I still had time to work things out without tipping my hand to Harry.

Putting my baby up for adoption was the best idea I could think of, and there was a good orphanage in town, run by the Sisters of Teresa, who also arranged adoptions. But when I went to talk to them, I ran into a major snag. I was underage, which meant the nuns were legally bound to interview my parents or guardian and get their permission for me to give the baby up. That, of course, was a non-starter because Harry wanted both me and the baby, and he'd never go along.

Of course, there was always the option of going to the authorities and telling them my stepfather had raped me and gotten me pregnant, but I was afraid and not even sure what I was afraid of. I seemed to have no choice but to stay with Harry and offer my baby whatever protection I could.

But then I got a break. I had a close friend at school, a gutsy, "trailer trash" girl named Loretta Fuller, who worked in the administration office and had a knack for stealing school supplies and selling them to keep herself in junk jewelry and makeup. Loretta wasn't a lesbian, so we weren't having sex, but I liked her very much. She was tough as nails on the outside and some of the other girls were afraid of her. But her heart was soft as a kitten once you got past her spiny hide, and her wicked sense of humor always made me laugh.

Loretta's family went to our church and she'd always thought that "Reverend Harry" was a fraud, even before I confided in her that he'd gotten me pregnant. We'd stayed in touch after I got kicked out of school and, one day, Loretta knocked on my door while Harry was out and handed me a flyer. It had a picture of a frightened-looking girl who seemed around fourteen, and above that the words:

Pregnant and Scared? Abortion not an option? Call us.

Underneath the photograph was a phone number and nothing else.

"I think it's what they call a baby mill," Loretta said. "They take kids whose mothers can't keep them, then sell them to families who can't adopt the normal way."

Black market babies I'd heard about that, and knew it was illegal. It seemed vile to give my own child away to a place like that, like an old sweater I didn't want. "Just call them and see what they say," Loretta said. "You don't have to do it if it feels wrong."

With nothing to lose, I spoke to a woman named Judy, who gave me an address in Deltona, a bedroom community about halfway between Orlando and Daytona Beach. I took the bus and walked six blocks from the station to a neat one-story house in a surprisingly nice neighborhood. A woman who looked about forty answered the door and invited me into her kitchen, where she offered me a ham sandwich, a bag of potato chips, and a Diet Coke. The chips were a little stale, but the Coke was cold and fizzy, and I scarfed down the sandwich like I hadn't eaten in days.

Judy put me at ease immediately, and there was something about her I trusted as soon as we started talking. She told me that she'd been doing this over ten years, working mostly with minority girls. "I hear so many stories like yours, Willie ... young girls who've been abused by family members and made pregnant, girls who have nowhere else to turn. Fortunately, there are many couples who want to adopt, and there's a shortage of babies that can be adopted through the usual channels.

"Most of the babies we get are the unwanted children of poverty—drug-addicted mothers and prostitutes. It's a sad state of affairs, but it is what it is. Babies like yours, though ... well, there's a very high demand for them and we don't see many. So I promise you, darling, there'll be no problem finding a wonderful home for your child."

"But you do this for money," I said. "I mean, you sell babies."

My reproach didn't seem to bother her, and she answered matter-of-factly. "Yes, I do, Willie. But there's a lot of risk and I could wind up in jail."

I nodded, uneasily. What would happen if the police, FBI, or whoever found out, I wanted to know. "Hopefully that won't happen," Judy said. "But if it does, I'll be the one who goes to prison. Given your age and situation, nothing bad will happen to you, and your baby will be looked after. Your stepfather, though, would definitely go to jail if the truth comes out."

Was there any chance I could ever meet the adopting family and see my child? No, once it was done, there could never be any contact. "That's a big thing you have to decide, Willie," Judy said. "Do you have the heart to never see your baby again?"

My daughter was born at the Regional Medical Center on March 8th, a week before I turned sixteen, and Harry and I brought her home three days later. She was healthy and gorgeous, with Harry's forehead, and eyes and coloring like mine. We hadn't even named her yet because Harry wanted to call her Clementine, which sounded awful to me. I fought tooth-and-nail for Morgana, but he thought that was a witch's name. "A name like Morgana is a one-way ticket to Hell for a girl," Harry said, and wouldn't budge an inch from that.

Finally, I gave in and agreed to call her Clementine because I realized it didn't matter. What Harry didn't know was that someone else was going to give our daughter her real name, since I'd arranged to bring her to Judy two weeks from Sunday, and was leaving him forever the same day.

Of course, I would need money to make my getaway, but I had an idea there too. Harry kept a wall safe in his bedroom, hidden behind a cheesy Norman Rockwell print. I knew he kept a stash of money in that safe and figured it had to be at least a thousand dollars, which should be enough to take me anywhere in the country.

How I got the combination to that safe is a story in itself. You know how some parents measure their kid's growth by standing them against a wall every few months and making a line at the top of their head to mark their progress? "Here's how tall Betsy was a year ago. Here's how tall Jimmy was six months ago. Blah, blah, blah?"

Well, what Harry did wasn't to measure my height. Instead the pervert would literally take my measurements. I swear to fucking God, he really did. He'd make me get undressed and take out his carpenter's tape measure. Then he'd wrap it around my chest, waist, and hips and call out the numbers. I was 31-20-29 at age thirteen, 32-22-31 at age fourteen, and 33-23-32 just before I got pregnant, which was when he stopped measuring me. Of all the things he ever did to me, nothing topped that for "crawl into a hole and die" humiliation.

Of course Harry thought no one else knew the combination to his safe, but the dimwit had no clue how subtle my mind was. One day, while he was taking the car for a tune-up, I walked into his bedroom, took down the Rockwell print he actually believed would hide his safe from burglars, and dialed 33-23-32—my "measurements"—and fuck all if that safe didn't open like a rosebud. My guess had been right; the depraved asshole had used my measurements to secure his safe! Lucky me, because I had no backup plan for getting that money.

When I saw how much was actually in there, my jaw dropped. I counted over $7,200 and laughed my ass off. I left the money where it was, shut the safe, and rehung the print, coming back for the cash the day I left for good.

Judy had advised me not to breastfeed my baby at all, since it was better not to form attachments that would soon be wrenched apart. But nursing my daughter when they put her to my breast at the hospital—the full realization that I'd just brought this new little human into the world and was nourishing her with my own body—it was a miracle that just overwhelmed me. So I ignored Judy's advice, kept on nursing her, and paid the price of breaking that bond when the time came.

Giving her up was agonizing, like having a limb amputated with no anesthetic, but I couldn't think of another way to get free of Harry and have a life of my own. Judy said it was best not to linger over the parting, and this time I did take her advice. I kissed my beautiful child on the forehead, and took myself away from her forever, without looking back.

Vanishing without a trace wasn't hard since I'd mapped out a wild, looping path that would be impossible for Harry to follow. With the help of Loretta's brother, who was an expert at forgery, I'd gotten several fake photo-IDs with different names, all showing me to be eighteen.

At the Deltona station, I was Rebecca De Mornay and took the Greyhound to Kansas City, where I caught a train to Houston as Louise Lasser. Then it was up to St. Paul as Jennifer Gray, where I became Patsy Cline and took a bus to Seattle, where Stella Kowalski bought a ticket to Jackson Hole, from which Billie Holiday took another Greyhound to Los Angeles, where Norma Jeane Mortenson hopped a commuter flight to San Francisco, where Wilhelmina Ludlow dumped the fake IDs and became Willie again.

It didn't take long to fall in love with The City. After Orlando, it felt like I'd arrived in Utopia. The sheer number of gay people was amazing, and instead of being part of a minority, I almost felt like part of the majority. And even if that wasn't quite true, there was no more need to hide what I was.

Inside a month, I got a waitressing job and found an apartment to share with two girls who worked at the same restaurant. I wanted to go to Cal, but needed one more year of high school with great grades and top marks in the SATs to have any chance of getting into a prestigious university like that on a merit scholarship.

But to finish my last year of high school here, I'd have to have my records sent from Florida, and I was sixteen, so still a minor. I had fake IDs with my real name that showed I was eighteen, but my school back in Orlando knew my true age and probably that I was a runaway. If I wrote asking for my grades, they'd definitely get in touch with Harry and tell him where I was.

But Loretta and I had planned for this too. Since she worked in the administration office at our school, it was easy for her to make copies of my records, with my date of birth altered, and send them directly to the high school I'd be attending in San Francisco. She even thought to include a supportive forged letter from the school's director on official stationery, saying what an outstanding young woman I was. Loretta was a great friend and I'll never forget her.

And so my escape was complete. I was in a new world now, with a new life. Still, I couldn't stop thinking about my daughter and grieving for abandoning her to who knew what. She was a ghost that never stopped haunting me.

"Wilhelmina?" the voice on the phone said again. "It's me, Harry."

Oh screw me straight to hell, I thought. *This can't be happening.*

"Harry who?" I said, fucking with his head just for the hell of it.

"Don't be a child. You know perfectly well who this is."

I wished I didn't. "How did you find me and what the hell do you want?" Probably the seven plus grand I'd taken from him, along with compound interest, I guessed.

"Believe me, finding you was hard and expensive. But I don't want anything except to make amends."

"Amends?" I said, sarcastically. "You want to make amends? What did you do, join a Christian Twelve Step group for perpetrators?"

"I lead one now, Wilhelmina," he replied. "I'm a completely changed man."

"Well if you want to make amends, you can start by calling me Willie!"

"Fine, Willie ... whatever you want. The reason I've been trying to find you is that I may not have much time left in this world and I want to make sure I'm right with my daughter before I leave it. And I want us both to be right with the Lord."

Was he trying to tell me he was dying? I wasn't falling for it. "Screw you, Harry," I screamed. "You're out of my life now, so fucking stay out."

"Still have that potty mouth, eh?" he said. "Well, that's okay. Jesus loves you anyhow."

"Look, worry about your own soul, Harry, and leave mine alone, okay? Your God is cruel and crazy. He's Hitler looking down from his fucking cloud to see who he wants to torture next. Well, time to throw that bastard out! Time for a female deity with some actual compassion."

Shit, I was totally losing it. All those years in therapy and here I was playing the victim again. He was yanking my chain like I was an overhead toilet tank, and I had to stop letting him flush me. I calmed my voice. "What do you want, Harry? If you want to say you're sorry, I accept your apology. What else you got?"

"I ... I have something of yours that I'd like to bring to San Francisco," he said.

What the hell was he talking about? It had been over sixteen years. I'd left some clothes and cheap jewelry behind, all crap I didn't give a shit about. The only thing I might want was the gold wedding band from my mother's marriage to my biological father. She'd left it to me when she died, but Harry had taken it. I always figured he'd sold it, but maybe not. It would be nice to have that ring as a remembrance of my mother. "Just mail it to me, Harry. That's all the amends I want."

"No ... this can't be mailed. Listen, here's what I'd like to do ..."

What he wanted was to fly out here and see me in person so he could finally make things right between us. But instead of saying "no way" flat out, I hesitated just a moment. Could he really be serious? Maybe he wanted to leave me the house in Orlando? That had to be worth something, and it obviously couldn't be mailed. By rights, it should be mine when he died, and I could sell it or rent it out for some extra income.

He took my silence for compliance, and then he dropped the other shoe. He wanted *me* to pay for his trip, because he was barely scraping by on Social Security plus a small pension from his church. He'd learned I had a business that was doing well and figured I could afford it. Plus, this would cancel out the debt I still owed him for the money I stole. "If you can send me just thirty-five hundred, it will pay for my trip and I'll forgive the rest of what you took. That's a savings of over fifty percent to you."

He sounded like a TV pitchman, and I'd heard enough. "Goodbye, Harry." I hung up, wishing I had one of those old-style phones you could slam down hard enough to make the other person's ears ring.

I was so unnerved I was shaking, so I thought I'd work on last month's spreadsheets to get my mind off Harry, but I couldn't concentrate on business now. What I needed was something more creative. Wait! I'd been meaning to find Selene Mayweather's website, just to get a better idea of what kind of trouble David was really in, and this was the perfect opportunity.

I had to admit her site was stunning, the design sensational, the photographs blazingly erotic. The home page showed her in slinky evening attire, impossibly high heels, hair done up in a tight bun, and makeup straight out of *Vogue*. And genuflecting at her feet was a muscular bald man, with what looked like a big eagle tattooed on his back. He was wearing almost nothing, his wrists bound behind him in a position that looked extremely uncomfortable. The accompanying text was laid over the photograph and read:

Hello, submissives and slaves. I am Selene Mayweather, Headmistress of Nyala. As you can see by this photograph and by the others in my gallery, I am both a power to be feared and a Goddess to be worshipped and adored.

It went on like that for most of the page and was followed by a list of the services she offered. These included spanking, flogging, whipping, caning, tease and denial, bondage, exotic role-play, orgasm control, full body worship, smothering, plus golden showers. That one was where a dominant pissed all over her submissive— and I mean literally—and the sub was supposed to consider this an honor. Not even Harry had ever demeaned me that way.

The last "service" on her list was something called 'financial domination' and when I read that, the answer to what Selene saw in David was clear. Financial domination was where the mistress received monthly payments from her submissive—in return for nothing, just as a tribute to her "glory."

It was obvious: What Selene wanted from David was his money. How much had he cleared selling his stock options from work—a bit over a million and a half? It wasn't a huge fortune by today's standards, but it was more than enough to make a creature like Selene drool. She was playing the classic 'long con' by making him fall in love with her. Then, once she had him, she would bleed him like a vampire.

To be fair, I could understand David's obsession: Selene was a knockout. I browsed dozens of photos of her in various outfits; lots of fetish gear, mostly latex and leather, stiletto shoes and boots, spiked collars, close-ups of her bare feet (which were quite slim and pretty), plus lots of semi-nude stuff that actually got me a bit worked up.

A couple of photographs showed off her two identical tattoos of a flowering tree with weird multicolored blossoms. One tattoo poked up between her bare breasts (and, oh, were they luscious) while the other—quite a bit larger—covered her entire back.

But it was when I came to a close-up of her eyes that my breath totally caught. They were more than gorgeous—they were unearthly. It wasn't just their size or almond shape. It wasn't just the intelligence and humor I could see in them either. It was their color that stunned me, because although Selene's left eye was green as an emerald, the right was the deep blue of a late afternoon sky, flecked with bits of lavender. Those had to be tinted contacts.

Still, I had no doubt that beneath that stunning exterior was a totally wicked soul, and now David was going to date her. I couldn't just sit here and do nothing, so I decided to take action, like loving friends did for alcoholics and drug addicts. One way or another, I would pry him loose from Selene. And since he wouldn't let go of her willingly, I had to come up with a way to make her release him and go find herself another sucker.

To do that, I would have to get right up in her face and tell her I knew what she was up to. But I couldn't just accost her on the street like some psycho. I needed to get her full attention, and the best way to do that was to be her client, to pretend I was a girl who wanted to be her slave. Once we were alone in that dungeon or whatever, I'd let her know I was on to her game and that if she didn't break it off with David, I was going to the police. I mean, what she was doing had to be illegal.

Her website asked prospective clients to contact her by email and say a bit about themselves first. So the next evening, I wrote her, fussing over the email for almost an hour to get the tone right. I said nothing even remotely true, except the part about being a lesbian, which I suspected would work in my favor:

Dear Mistress Selene,

I am a shy 33 year-old lesbian with no experience in this kind of thing, but I have ached to give myself to a powerful woman like you for as long as I can remember. I never thought I'd really have the courage to do this, but yesterday when I found your website, read your words, and saw your beauty in those photographs, my heart told me I had to act.

I am writing to request an interview as soon as possible to see if we are compatible, as you said you require this before an actual session. I know you are very busy in your work, but pray you can make time for me.

Humbly Thanking You,

Dorothy Gale

I read it over a couple of times, wondering if it sounded too servile, but it seemed like a dominatrix would expect that, so I left it alone and addressed it to HMSelene@Nyala.com and then clicked the Send button. I thought signing it Dorothy Gale was a clever touch, and I used my Green Girl corporate email account which didn't include my actual name.

It took Selene a couple of days to respond, and her tone wasn't at all what I'd expected:

Dear Dorothy,

Thank you for contacting me and, yes, I'd be glad to meet with you. In fact, I'd adore it since I seldom get to play with single women in my practice. There is a sensuousness and responsiveness in women that is often missing in males, and this is very precious to me.

As to your being a novice, that is not a problem. My clients range from total beginners all the way up to highly experienced submissives who have been in the scene for decades. All have much to teach me about human nature, and I also hope to teach them something about themselves. What I sense from you is a deep feminine sensitivity, an openness and vulnerability that would be delicious to play with. If we decide we are a match, I will explain how I like to work with new clients and we can determine your comfort level.

My calendar for this month is attached. Please contact me for an appointment.

Sincerely,

Selene Mayweather, Headmistress

I read her email three times before going to bed.

Chapter 7

_~_

THE MAGIC BOX

Month of January/Month of Birch

ill picked him up in her Prius, a surprisingly common car for such an uncommon girl. He'd pictured her behind the wheel of an Aston Martin, but the ordinariness of the Toyota was comforting, as was Willie Nelson singing _Stardust_ on the CD player.

"I had no idea you were a romantic," David said.

"_Stardust_ is so sad," Jill sighed. "Remembering someone you loved and lost? That kind of sorrow is very human, isn't it?"

"It's about the saddest thing there is," David agreed. "Especially if the person you love dies and they're gone forever."

Jill thought a moment. "Do you believe in reincarnation?"

"Not really. Do you?"

"Everything is alive, David. A tree is alive, but even stones and tables are alive, because 'life' is everything there is. And since life is everything, nothing can really die. It just changes form, like the same water flowing into different vessels, one after another: woman, goat, tree … One life, many forms."

David laughed. "If this is your 'first date conversation,' I'm in way over my head."

And now Jill laughed with him. "Sorry, I don't date a lot, so I don't get much practice."

"Really? I figured you'd have lots of suitors."

"Oh, I have lovers. But the whole 'dating' thing seems weird to me. You know: 'Be interesting, be funny and charming, ask the right questions, do this and not that.' It's so hard to be yourself."

David smiled. "Is it strange for you dating a client? I mean, can't you get into trouble with … I don't know … *someone*?"

Her laughter was musical. "Well, there's no such thing as a Dominatrix Review Board, so it's not like I have a license I can lose. But do you feel strange dating me?"

"Not strange," David said. "More like unsure how I'm supposed to act. Are you always, you know … in 'Mistress' mode?"

"Well, every domme is different. For some, it's a lifestyle. With me, it's more situational. When I'm working at Nyala, I'm 'Mistress Jilaynie.' Outside, it depends on where I am and what I'm doing. Having sex, I still prefer to run the show. But unless my 'inner mistress' pops out unexpectedly, I'm usually just plain Jill."

"Plain is something you could never be, even if you tried," David said. They were stopped in traffic and he was rewarded for the compliment when Jill put a hand on his knee, leaving it there until she needed both hands to drive again.

She took him to the New Delhi, David's favorite Indian restaurant. He came here sometimes with friends, but he'd never walked in with anyone as spectacular as this girl. None of the other patrons would have guessed what "just plain Jill" did for a living based on what she was wearing tonight: a gray peasant skirt, a black sweater, a beret made of gray felt, and a pair of leather sandals. She looked nothing like the dangerous vamp she played at Nyala. Instead, with her raven hair trailing down her back, she had a casual bohemian look that really appealed to David. It obviously appealed to the guy at the next table too, because he kept sneaking glances at Jill, much to the annoyance of his date. David's grin was a mile wide.

"What a gorgeous smile you have," Jill said. "It's nice to see you so happy."

After the waiter took their drink orders, David began to probe a bit. There was so much he wanted to know about her, especially how she'd wound up in this line of work. But since that might be a delicate subject, he skirted it and instead asked where she'd grown up. Despite her light-coffee skin tone, with that accent, he thought she'd say Ireland or Wales, so her answer surprised him:

"I'm an ethnic mix, partly Roma—you know … Gypsy blood, ancestors from Northern India. But I was born in a small town in Latvia." She named a village that might as well have been on Mars. "My mother, me, and my sister … we moved around a lot, all over the world actually, until I was ten. Then we came to San Francisco."

"You have a sister?" David asked. "Here?"

"No. She lives in Munich. We're identical twins."

That surprised him. "Hard to imagine there's another girl on Earth as gorgeous as you," he said, wondering what it would be like to be with both of them.

She gave him a wicked grin. "Oh, right, don't you wish."

He felt himself blushing. "I'm *that* transparent?"

Jill laughed, covering her mouth with a slim-fingered hand. "Clear as glass, but maybe you'll get to meet Janaynie someday."

"Her name's Janaynie?"

"Yes. Mother named us Jilaynie and Janaynie, after her own mother and aunt, who were also twins. Twin girls run in our family."

"And your father?"

She shook her head. "Never knew him." Her tone discouraged further probing on that topic.

"So … what does your sister do in Munich?" he asked instead.

"Oh, she's an escort."

"Excuse me?" David wasn't sure he'd heard her right.

"A high-class hooker." She said it so casually that David's jaw dropped, and again she laughed. "Now I've shocked you. I guess sex work runs in our family too. My mother was a nude artist's model who sold sex on the side to support us. We never found anything shameful in it, David. It was just a way for pretty girls from poverty to make real money. We were clean and honest, and gave good value to our clients."

"So before you became a domme, you ...?"

"Worked as an escort? Yes, for a while. Then, a few years ago, I met Selene and learned I could make just as much flogging as I could fucking. It gave me more control and I always liked passive men anyway, so I switched careers and never looked back. Does my history change your mind about wanting to date me?"

He shook his head and smiled. "Does your sister know what you do?"

Jill thought that was funny too. "Of course. We tell each other everything. She keeps asking me to teach her how to be a domme so she can top her girlfriend."

"Ah, she's gay."

"She's bi ... like me." And when David smiled again, she said, "You hetero males are so weird. You go into cardiac arrest thinking about two guys having sex. But picture two women doing it, and you want to slide between us like a slice of ham inside a sandwich ... Oh, don't pout. I know you can't help it. You're just wired that way."

They started out with a couple of Taj Expresses made with fruit juice, plus vodka and rum. But when the waiter came to take their food order, Jill surprised David again. "Do you mind if I order for us?" she asked.

"Go ahead. The lamb *korma* here is great."

Jill turned to the waiter, and David's eyes went wide as she began speaking fluent Hindi! The waiter stared, as dumbfounded as David; then he gave her a delighted smile and the two of them began chattering a blue streak. Jill said something that made the waiter laugh, and he said something that made her smile. This time, she spoke in English. "This is my friend David. David, meet Mahesh."

The waiter chuckled. "You have a fine lady here. Not only is she as lovely as the moon, but she tells funny jokes in real Hindi. Treat her well or I will surely steal her."

"You're just one surprise after another," David said when the waiter had gone. "Have you always spoken Hindi? Because of your ancestry, I mean?"

She shook her head. "I was traveling through Asia a while ago and spent six months in India. I just sort of picked it up, I guess."

"You learned Hindi in six months? Well enough to tell jokes to an Indian waiter and make him laugh? No, wait; don't tell me … the 'gift of tongues' runs in your family."

Jill smiled. "The 'gift of tongues' … I've never heard that. What a sweet way to put it." She looked at him earnestly. "But you don't mind me flirting with the waiter a little, do you? I was just playing."

David shook his head. "I enjoyed him envying me."

She reached across the table to touch his hand. "I don't want us to get off on the wrong foot, so I should confess that I'm a chronic flirt, with both men and women. It doesn't mean anything, but if it bothers you, just tell me, okay?"

"It's a deal," David said. "But do I get to flirt too?"

"Sure, as long as it's only with me." He raised an eyebrow, but she was grinning like the Cheshire Cat. "Mistress has special privileges."

Their food came quickly: *Mattar paneer* for Jill and the lamb for David. They scooped up the delicious concoctions with chunks of *naan* bread as they talked and sipped hot chai.

She asked David a lot of questions about himself, wanting to know about his own childhood and family. But he was having trouble thinking straight because she was looking at him with those big gray eyes, and he was sinking into them like quicksand. That was when he spotted it—a subtle difference between her right and left eyes. The right eye, and only the right, had a few golden flecks inside the gray iris. They were hardly noticeable unless you looked closely, but they sparkled like tiny gems.

She saw his stare and tilted her head. "What?"

"I just noticed your right eye has these little golden jewels. They're beautiful."

Jill gave him another smile. "Janaynie has the same spots, but they're in her left eye. Mother used to say we were born with stars in our eyes."

They took their time with dinner, and after their dishes were cleared, the waiter set two *firni* puddings in front of them. "Compliments to the lovely lady and her fortunate fellow," he said, then rushed off to serve another table.

"A girl who gets free dessert," David said. "I'd better stick with you a while."

She leaned toward him and spoke in a whisper. "Just save room for the 'special' dessert I'm serving at my place."

The evening was going beautifully, the chemistry felt great, and David should have been in heaven. But as they drove to her building, he was a bundle of nerves because Jill's implicit invitation to a night of passion terrified him. Of course he wanted her. He'd been thinking of almost nothing else since he'd first seen her at Selene's lecture. Yet in his wildest fantasy, he'd never thought this might happen on their first date. What if he disappointed her? A woman like Jill would expect a lover as skilled as she was.

He was tempted to beg off, to invent some excuse, maybe about having to work tomorrow. *Jesus, you're thinking like a wimp,* he thought. *Man up. She made it plain what she wanted. Just thank the "Powers That Be" she's making this so easy for you.*

Jill parked behind her building, opened the driver's door, and started to get out. But David just sat there, totally immobile. Here he was, on the brink of a great moment and paralyzed by performance anxiety.

"What's wrong?" Jill asked, and then she saw it in his face. "Don't worry, honey. Mistress won't bite … unless, of course, you want her to."

But her sexy banter didn't help much. David turned to her and smiled weakly. "Listen, I have to be honest. The first time I saw you at that lecture, I thought you were the most incredible woman I'd ever seen. I mean, I knew I wasn't in your league, so I don't know how I got the courage to even talk to you."

She cut him off. "Sweetie, you don't have to do this."

But now that he'd started, it all came rushing out. "You seemed so approachable, though … the way you were joking with the audience and all. And I thought maybe if I could just get you to have a cup of coffee with me …"

"David, shut up and listen. I'm crazy about you, and I'll die if I can't have you in my bed tonight. You think you know the kind of girl I am, but you don't have a clue. I'm the one who's not in *your* league. That's why I want to jump your bones right now, before you come to your senses and run from me as fast as you can." She leaned toward him for a kiss that was tentative but promising, like testing the water's temperature with your toes and finding it very swimmable. Her breath was warm and sweet in his mouth, and David took more initiative, deepening the kiss and savoring her pleased response.

When they got out of her car, she took his arm and they walked around to the front of her building, stopping beneath a flickering streetlamp near the stone steps that led up to the entrance. The night was cool but not cold and they kissed again, this time with fierce urgency. Her three-inch height advantage made him raise his mouth to hers as he fought the impulse to stand on his toes, which would have felt silly. But his erection was pressing against her thigh and he made no attempt to disguise it.

"Now that's what I'm talking about," she said, giving his cock a squeeze through the cloth of his jeans.

The building was a three-story walk-up, and as they climbed the stairs and reached the second landing, an elderly woman opened her apartment door and stuck her head out to see who "that tramp upstairs" was bringing home. "Good evening, Mrs. Ray," Jill said as they passed by. "This is David. And yes, we're going to have sex, if that's okay with you."

Mrs. Ray gasped and quickly withdrew into her apartment.

"Jesus, girl," David said. "You are wicked."

"Totally incorrigible," she agreed, pausing at the top landing in front of a brown door painted with a tracery of ivy. "Well, here we are. Be brave, lover."

Inside, she gave him a tour of her snug, neat apartment. The living room held a sofa, a couple of easy chairs and lots of art, mostly paintings and pottery. There were several hanging plants, flowering vines with purple blossoms he didn't recognize; but there was one plant sitting by the window that David did know. "You have a Venus fly trap?" he asked.

"Yes, that's Miranda. Closest thing to a pet they'll let me have in this building."

David walked over and gingerly touched one of the sticky red leaves, which snapped shut instantly. "Jesus," he said, pulling his finger out. "Miranda just tried to eat me."

Jill laughed. "She can be a bit of a slut."

She showed him the kitchen and bathroom, which were efficient and spotless, but the centerpiece was her bedroom. Its drapes and wall hangings were decorated with pastoral scenes, as were the linens and quilts on the big four-poster bed, whose canopy bore a fantastical night sky, with dozens of multicolored stars and—for some reason—two moons, one larger than the other. A fountain in the shape of a little waterfall gurgled atop her dresser, and the room smelled faintly of lilacs.

Jill told him to sit on the bed while she lit a few candles and turned down the lights. "This room is incredible," David said, looking up at the bed's canopy. "That sky is like something from another world."

She sat beside him and put a hand on his. "A girlfriend made it for me. I love lying on the bed and looking up at it."

There was a pitcher of water and two glasses on the night table and she filled them, handing one to David. Leaning close, she sniffed him and sighed. "I love your scent."

"My scent?"

"Yes. You smell like sex."

"I smell sweaty?"

"No … well, yes … but it's *sex* sweat. It makes me want to lick you."

David smiled. "Feel free."

She gave his neck a long, wet slurp, from collarbone to ear. "Mm …you taste as good as you smell."

"That was nice. May I …?"

"Taste me? Sure."

Jill tilted her head, baring her neck to him, and he licked her just as she had him. She tasted musky, sweet, and just a bit salty.

She sighed. "Well, that made my toes curl."

Oh, fuck, did I ever luck out, David thought.

Jill asked if he felt like getting high. "I've got something wonderful. It's kind of spacy, but it's perfect for lovemaking."

When he said that sounded good, she walked to her dresser, opened the bottom drawer, and removed a beige linen bag. She brought it back to the bed, opened the drawstring, and removed an ornate box about twice the size of a thick paperback novel. It seemed to be made of ivory, its lid covered with little carved figures. She handed him the box, and he saw it wasn't ivory at all but some kind of cream-colored hardwood. The tiny clasps looked like silver and gold, one of each.

The figures on the box were of nude and semi-nude young women in what looked like an orchard. A couple of them were wrapped sensuously around the branches of trees, while little groups were singing, playing pipes, or doing some ritual dance.

"What are they?" David asked, running his fingers lightly over the carvings.

"They're fey girls, wood nymphs. Wait a minute ..." She opened the drawer of her night table and pulled out a magnifying glass. "Try this. It's all hand-carved."

David peered at the box through the powerful lens, and the incredible detail leapt out. Each leaf on every tree was individually rendered, as was the texture of the bark. Every feature on every girl's face—noses, lips, ears, right down to eyelashes, stood out clearly. The entire box seemed alive and had to be priceless.

But as David studied it more closely, he noticed something odd on the far right. One of the girls was kneeling by a tree and seemed to be crying, her face buried in her hands. "What's this?" he asked, pointing. "The others are all happy, and she looks out of place."

"But she's not out of place at all," Jill said, leaning closer. "See how everything draws your eye to her? She's the focus of the whole scene." David saw that she was right. Once you noticed the weeping girl, your eye could go nowhere else.

"It's mysterious, isn't it?" Jill said. "I call it my Magic Box."

"I can't believe someone actually carved all this by hand," he said, fumbling to undo one of the clasps. "Where did you find it?"

"Careful," she said, gently taking the box from his hand. "Those are very delicate. I spotted it in a little antique shop in Galway. It cost a mint, but I couldn't resist it." She carefully undid the little clasps with a fingernail, opened the box, and showed him what was inside. David stared at the contents, totally baffled. She'd invited him to get high, and he'd been expecting pot, but inside the box were several ... well, they looked like jellybeans, sparkling with every color of the rainbow, like tiny Faberge eggs.

"What're these?" he said, removing one of the jellybeans. "Hash-laced candy?"

"No, don't eat it," she said when he started to put it in his mouth. "Just watch."

She took the jellybean from his fingers and reached into the linen bag again, removing what seemed to be an un-inflated transparent balloon. "Just watch," she said again, placing a finger over his lips to silence another question.

Jill pushed the jellybean through the nipple of the balloon and began to inflate it. The inside should have clouded with the moisture of her breath, but it didn't. As it expanded, David could clearly see the speckled jellybean rolling around inside, as Jill continued to blow.

When the balloon was about the size of a volleyball, she pinched off the nipple with her fingers and began to shake it vigorously, like she was mixing a cocktail. To David's astonishment, the jellybean began to vaporize, filling the balloon with clouds of mist, dotted with sparkling pinpricks of light—green, red, yellow, violet, winking on and off like a constellation of stars.

David laughed delightedly. "Wow, that's amazing! You could go on stage with a trick like that. How does it work?"

He started to reach for the balloon, but Jill pulled it away and gave him a mischievous wink. "A lady never reveals the tricks of her trade. But here comes the best part." She released the balloon's nipple, letting out a hiss of mist, which surrounded their heads in a cloud of swirling colors. David drew back apprehensively.

"Trust me," she said, inhaling the mist. "It's harmless. Just take one breath."

"But what is ..." Too late, it was already entering his mouth and nose. He sniffed experimentally, then smiled and breathed deeply. The aroma was delicious, like a blend of cinnamon, honey, cloves, chocolate, and something earthy he couldn't identify. It was strong, but he didn't cough.

David blinked, and quickly two things happened. He heard a musical tinkling, like little wind chimes, and then he was smacked head-on by an oceanic rush. He closed his eyes and heard a voice say, "Holy shit!" It took a moment to realize the words had come from him, and when he opened his eyes again, he was lying on his back, looking up at Jill's face, which was enormous as it hovered just above his nose.

"How are you doing?" she asked with a grin.

David was doing just fine. It was like floating in a warm bath made of gauze, so buoyant he couldn't sink if he tried. He was totally relaxed and happy, loose as a goose and incredibly horny. When he looked at Jill again, her skin seemed made of rose petals, lit from within by a soft iridescence. He held his own hand in front of his eyes, and it was glowing with the same ethereal light, like a Japanese lantern.

"Magic," she whispered.

And then he was somehow looking down at himself from above. He saw his body lying on the bed, arms spread wide as if embracing eternity. He felt warm and glowing with pleasure. David had heard stories of out-of-body experiences and always thought they were hallucinations. But this felt absolutely real. His consciousness was on the ceiling, yet that was his body down there, with a gorgeous woman sitting next to him, holding his hand.

Jill looked up, directly at the spot where he was floating, and gave him a lupine smile. She could actually see him up here, so this had to be real. "Better come back down, sweetmeat," she said. "You'll have more fun if you're all in one place." And with that, his awareness drifted back into his body as delicately as a falling leaf.

Then he was flat on his back, looking up at the spot where he'd just been floating. Jill giggled and leaned down to kiss him, nibbling softly at his lower lip and running her tongue across it. He wanted to tell her what a great kisser she was, but he was having trouble talking, so he stopped trying and reached up to pull her down on top of him. His arms stopped dead about four inches above the mattress. That was when he realized he was naked and shackled to her bed by his wrists and ankles, with no idea how he'd gotten that way.

He blinked a couple of times. "Shit, how did *this* happen?"

Again, Jill put a finger to his lips to silence him. "Your body asked me to do it when your spirit was up on the ceiling. Don't worry. You're safe. Just focus on me." She stood and slipped out of her clothes, first the sweater, then the sandals and skirt. It was the first time he'd seen her completely naked and she took his breath away.

"Like what you see?" she asked, running her hands over her breasts and belly, then doing a little spin so he could see the rest of her. All David could do was grin stupidly. "I'll take that as a yes," she said, pointing to his erection. "Now, just breathe and let me do the rest."

Jill sat beside him on the bed, her sea-gray eyes fastening on his. She touched his lips with her fingertips, caressed his neck, his belly, his inner thighs, circling his cock but not touching it yet. She didn't have to. Her fingers were silken fire, setting every nerve in him alight. And when she rested the flat of her hand on his stomach, it seemed to sink right through him, down into the core of his flesh. Where on earth had she learned to do that? It was inhuman, maddeningly erotic, almost enough to make him come if she hadn't paused to let him recover.

"You like that?" she asked. And when he moaned in response, said, "I'll take that as another yes."

Now she climbed on top of him, flattening his hard cock against her belly, and again began kissing him. With his body tied to the bed, he couldn't even wrap his arms around her. Jill was running this show and all he could do was let her have her way. She'd let him see her breasts during their last session at Nyala, but hadn't allowed him to kiss or touch them. Now, though, she put the left one to his lips. "C'mon, baby, they're aching for you."

They were luscious, neither large nor small, but full and firm, the areolas chocolate brown, smooth and inviting, her nipples peaked with arousal and pointing down at him. He tried to be gentle, to kiss lightly and explore with just the tip of his tongue. But that wasn't what she wanted. "No … not like that. Devour them. Get them wet and don't be afraid to slobber. You're starving for me, and my tits are your banquet."

He filled his mouth first with one breast, then the other, suckling and running his tongue around her nipples, pressing his face between her breasts and inhaling her. She giggled again. "You want me to smother you, don't you? Don't worry, I will, but you'll have to wait till I decide how to do it—with my tits, ass, or pussy. Maybe I'll even use my pretty feet, or do them all, one after another. You'd love that, wouldn't you?"

She rubbed her belly against his cock, making him buck beneath her and sigh with pleasure. "Careful," he said, "I'm getting too close."

Jill reached down with her hand to give his cock another squeeze. "Hold just another minute and I'll let you come."

"No," he said, "it's ladies first."

"Where I come from, it's lady's choice," she whispered, breathing into his ear. "We're playing on my turf now, so remember which of us is the domme and which the sub. You'll come when and how I tell you. And you'll make me come when I say."

David wasn't about to argue and didn't care if "real men" had sex like this or not. His cock was throbbing against her, and just a few moments more of what she was doing would send him plunging into erotic oblivion.

But instead of taking him the rest of the way, she got on her knees, putting her sex just inches above his face and using her hands to spread herself wide for him. "No. No licking yet," she said as he tried in vain to reach her with his tongue. "This is my flower, David. My source. Isn't it beautiful? Just look at it and breathe it in."

She was open to him like a moist water lily and David used all his willpower not to explode, just from the bliss of having that pink heart of her so close to his mouth. "Jill, please … I'll die if I can't …"

"The longer you wait, the sweeter the treat," she said, moving herself away. "You have a gorgeous cock, David. It's like a big juicy lamb chop, and I'm going to suck every drop of marrow out of that bone. I'm going to use my lips and tongue and teeth, and I'm going to lick and slurp until I drain you dry."

She pushed her hair back over her left shoulder to get it out of the way, then leaned over to flick her tongue across the tip of his cock and catch the drop of pre-cum that was glistening there. "I didn't have the lamb for dinner, and I need protein," she said, grinning wickedly. "I want at least a pint of cum from you."

Despite his urgency, David had to laugh. "I think you're too optimistic about what I can deliver."

"We'll see," she said coyly, beginning to tease his shaft with her tongue and the fingers of her left hand.

He groaned with animal pleasure. "Honey … oh, God, that's so good."

She circled his cock with her tongue, making little sounds of contentment. "You are so delicious, Lamb Chop. Don't hold anything back. Just come in my mouth."

Now she began to engulf him, her mouth blissfully warm and wet, drawing him in deeper, down into her throat, slurping and sucking, using her hand to stroke him when she drew back, cupping his balls so that some part of her covered every inch of him.

"Jill, I … God, I can't hold on."

"Give it to me," she mumbled, reaching to slip two fingers into his ass.

That was the trigger, and he exploded into her mouth with a cry like a man being gut-knifed. It went on and on, jet after jet. It felt like every cell in his body, from his toes to his hair follicles was deep in orgasm. "God, I'm dying," he croaked hoarsely, as she continued to slurp and suck, drawing every drop of marrow out of him and swallowing it down.

"Mm … protein," she mumbled.

It was just before nine Sunday morning when he woke alone beneath the down comforter on Jill's bed, her female scent in the linens and all over him. They'd been awake most of the night, making love twice after that incredible blowjob. And then she'd finally let him go down on her, giving him what he'd kept begging for, coming again and again, pulling his head into her, screaming like a hurricane and drenching his face with her torrent.

Now David sat up abruptly, looking around, listening for her in the next room; but the apartment was dead silent. For a moment, he doubted her existence, feared the exquisite night had been a figment of his fevered imagination. But he was in her apartment, and her bed and walls were real enough.

He had to pee, so he slipped from beneath the covers and spotted the robe she'd left for him at the foot of the bed. He put it on and was about to head for the bathroom when he saw the folded note on the night table. On the outside, she'd drawn a rough pencil sketch of an erect penis, with the words *Lamb Chop* written beneath it.

Unfolding the note, he read:

Went for a run. Not a smidge of food in the fridge, so I'll pick up eggs, brie, strawberries, and croissants. Coffee's on the kitchen counter, so if you're up before I'm back, get it started. You can fix us a couple of brie omelets later.

Hope you're all recovered from last night, because running makes me horny, and I'm going to want you again while I'm nice and sweaty. Sex first, then breakfast. ☺

XOX

Mistress J

Chapter 8

༄

THE UPSTAIRS GIRLS

Month of January/Month of Birch

"Wow, check it out, Tyler," the boy with the red hair said. "I told you they'd get naked." The two fifteen-year-olds were crouching behind a driftwood blind they'd made on the clothing-optional stretch of Baker Beach, passing a pair of binoculars back and forth to gawk at two women who had just spread their blanket and removed their shirts to take in the sun, oblivious to the fact they were being watched.

"C'mon, Scott," Tyler said, grabbing at the binoculars. "You're hogging them."

"Fuck off, asshole," Scott said, clutching the glasses tighter. "Oh, man, I can't believe it … They're feeling each other's tits." The two women were oiling each other's chests with lotion.

"Check out the blonde," Scott said, finally handing the binoculars to his friend. "Man, she could poke your eyes out with a set of cannons like that."

"The other one's mine," Tyler said, focusing on the tall brunette. "Damn, I'd love to crawl between those legs."

Scott sneered. "You wouldn't know what to do if she grabbed your cock and tried to shove it in herself."

"And I suppose *you* would?"

"I'd screw her blind and have her begging for more," Scott said proudly. "You've never even been with a girl, limp dick."

"Fuck you. I hooked up with Nancy Bell at Felton's party and everyone knows it."

Scott laughed derisively. "Yeah, right ... in your dreams."

In January, even on a sunny day, most would have found it far too chilly for nudity, but Selene and Jill were used to being sky clad in weather like this and they liked having the beach to themselves.

"So it sounds like things with David are going well," Selene said, accepting one of the sandwiches Jill had brought.

Jill nodded. "Even better than I'd expected. Last night, he confessed his deepest fantasy about me."

Selene raised an eyebrow. "Tell me."

Jill sighed. "His fantasy is that we're making love so blissfully on the beach that he literally melts all over me when he comes, and the only thing left of him is a coat of oil that I rub into my warm, bare skin—my feet, my legs, my tits and ass, my neck and face. He sinks right down through my pores, flowing into me until he disappears forever. That's what he said."

Selene's voice was a hoarse whisper. "Kayla! You broke him open, Jill. I've never seen it happen that fast. He might actually be ready for transformation right now."

Jill's smile was wistful. "As he was leaving my apartment, he almost said he loved me."

"What stopped him?"

"He was probably afraid of scaring me off. But he'll say it when I see him again Thursday. I'm sure of it."

"And what will you tell him when he does?" They'd been over this material before, but Selene wanted to make sure Jill understood the best technique for thoroughly ensnaring a *nyalic* male.

"I'll be 'deeply touched,'" Jill said, "tell him that I like him very much and want to keep on seeing him ... but that I'm not ready to rush into anything."

"Say it like this," Selene said. "'I really like you, David. I like you a lot. And the sex is incredible. But I've been hurt too many times, and I'm afraid of giving my heart away before I'm sure of you ... so can we take it a little slow for now?'"

Jill nodded. "Okay. I guess that sounds better."

"Much better. Saying you've been wounded in love will make him want to prove himself ... to show you he's not like all those other men who've hurt you. Remember, though, humans always confuse love with need. And it's important to make him *need* you so badly he can't let you die, no matter the cost to him."

Jill sighed again. "But ... don't you ever feel that what we're doing to these humans is just ...well, wrong?"

Selene took her hand. "*Pleesha*, you're such a compassionate soul, and I love you for it. But the Meliai have been taking humans from *T'Erenya* for thousands of years because we have no choice. Compassion for them is fine and well, but we can't let it cripple the project. Besides, doesn't Kayla say *nyalic* humans were made to become Changelings, and that we're saving them as much as they are us?"

"I know, but I'm starting to like David."

"Well, of course you like him. He wouldn't be your match if you didn't. Just don't let your heart overrule your common sense again."

Jill finished her sandwich and brushed a few crumbs off her lap. "No worries, Selly. I learned my lesson with Lynette. He'll be totally addicted to me soon enough."

"That's my girl," Selene said, patting Jill's knee. Suddenly something down the beach caught her eye, and she laughed. "Hey, look ... we've got a couple of admirers."

Jill followed Selene's gaze and spotted the boys, who'd poked their heads above the blind they'd made. "What a couple of bandits.

Why can't they just walk up and appreciate us openly, like a civilized Meliai, or even an Oread, would?"

"Because young human males aren't civilized," Selene said. "Hey, let's have some fun with them." She began running her fingers sensuously over and between her breasts, moving down across her tummy to stroke the inside of her thighs. Jill caught on immediately, laughed, and began doing the same.

From the blind, Scott stared through the binoculars. "Oh, man, they see us," he said. "And they *want* us. We're gettin' laid, dude!"

He handed Tyler the binoculars and his friend stared in amazement. Sure enough, both women were beckoning to them. "Holy shit!"

"C'mon, let's go," Scott said. "Blondie's mine."

Scott started to get up, but Tyler held back. "I don't know, man. They're kind of old."

"So what? They're cougars hunting for young man meat, and we're lunch."

Tyler looked through the binoculars again. "Yeah, but mine's got kind of a big nose."

Scott stared at him incredulously. "You won't be fucking her nose, asshole."

"Yeah, but what if it's a trick? They could be a couple of psychos who'll lure us into the mountains, kill us for Satan, and drink our blood."

Scott sneered again. "Shit, you watch too many dumb movies. They're just a couple of horny babes."

"Why don't you go first?" Tyler said. "Signal me if it's safe."

Scott shook his head disgustedly. "Jesus, what a lame-ass. Watch me and learn how it's done, dude."

"Well, here comes one of them, anyway," Selene said, watching the red-haired boy strolling toward them. "And he's even *nyalic*. Can you feel him?"

Jill extended her *kash* and felt the boy's spirit. "Yes, but he's vile. What would we even do with him?"

"I'll show you," Selene said as Scott walked up, stopping in front of them.

"Hey, pretty ladies."

"Hey yourself, handsome," Selene said. "Where's your friend?"

"Aw, he's chicken shit. I'm Scott."

"Well, aren't you the cutest thing? I'm Selene and this is Jill. Think you can handle both of us?"

"One at a time or both together … your choice. Hey, you sound like you're from another country, right?"

"We're from Ausonia," Selene said.

"Oh, yeah, I heard of that place. It's near Germany, right?"

Selene grinned. "What a clever young man. You really know your geography."

Jill bit her lip to suppress a giggle.

Scott's courage grew and he gave Selene an appraising look. "That's not *all* I know."

"Well, good," Selene said. "We love men who know what they're doing. You really seem to like my breasts, Scott."

"Yeah, they're okay, I guess."

Selene glanced at Jill, whose face was turning red as she tried to contain her laughter. "Wow, that's … that's quite a compliment. I'll bet you'd like to touch them, wouldn't you?" She gave him a seductive smile. "You can if you want."

The invitation stunned the boy, who couldn't believe his luck. He looked down the beach toward Tyler, who was watching intently through the binoculars, and Scott knew this would make his reputation when word got out.

"So?" Selene said. "Don't keep a girl waiting. Do you want to touch my tits or not?"

"Yeah, sure," Scott said.

"Then what are you waiting for? Come closer."

Scott took a step then hesitated uncertainly.

"What's the matter?" Selene said. "You aren't afraid of me, are you?" He shook his head and took another step forward, so that he stood just a foot in front of her.

"Okay, I'm sitting here on this blanket and you're standing way up there. You don't expect a lady to get up just so you can touch her, do you? Get down on your knees." She cupped her breasts, offering them to Scott.

Scott felt a wave of misgiving. Something suddenly felt wrong here, but there was no way to pass up an opportunity like this. He kneeled in front of Selene so that he was level with her. "Be gentle with me," she said. "Dryads don't like to be mauled."

Scott had no idea what a Dryad was, but he tentatively reached for Selene's left breast, trying to keep his hand from trembling. Before he could touch her, though, Selene struck like a cobra, grabbing his cock and balls through his shorts and squeezing hard.

"Ah-owww!" Scott screamed, turning pale. "What ...?" He tried to pull her hand away, but her grip was like a vise. He screamed again, doubling over so that his forehead was on the sand.

"See, now *that's* the correct position for you, Scottie," Selene said, "bowing before your mistress."

Jill couldn't control herself any longer and convulsed with laughter.

"Let go," Scott moaned, sweat breaking out on his face. "You're killing me."

"Oh, no. If I wanted to kill you, I'd do this." Selene tightened her grip.

"Arggh. Stop!"

"Oh? You don't think this is sexy? Well, all right. But if you want me to let go, you must say these words exactly as I tell you: "'Please, Mistress Selene. I apologize for my inexcusable rudeness in spying on you and Mistress Jilaynie like the piggy I am. I humbly beg you to forgive and release me.'"

"No!" Scott shouted, trying to hang on to a shred of dignity. "I'm not sayin' that."

Selene squeezed even harder.

"*Oh, shit!* Okay! Okay!" It took Scott three tries to get the words exactly right before Selene loosened her grip, though she didn't completely release him yet.

"Now," she said calmly. "Listen carefully. If I ever catch you spying on us or any other girls on this beach again, I will rip your balls off and stuff them in a sandwich bag along with a pickle to take home to Mommy. Are we clear on that?"

"Ye-yes," Scott stammered.

"Yes, *Mistress*," Selene corrected.

"Yes … Mistress," he repeated. Selene finally let him go, and he fell onto his side, moaning and clutching his groin.

"Good. Now get lost. And if you ever want a real BDSM session, start saving your allowance and come back in ten years when you're old enough and can afford me."

"Fuck you," Scott said miserably. Then he stood and staggered off as Selene and Jill convulsed with laughter.

Chapter 9

NYALA

Two weeks later ...

*W*illie found the buff-colored building by its street address, 629, which appeared in faded letters over the entrance. But only when she walked into the tiny lobby and saw the placard to the left of the freight elevator was she sure this was the place:

Club Nyala
All Deliveries 3rd Floor
No Solicitors

Willie shivered. *Jesus, what a creepy place!* She'd been expecting something high-tone, but the tiny lobby was unadorned, shabby and drafty, and as she pressed the elevator button, Willie remembered that this was once a sausage factory—a bit of weird history she'd gotten from the club's website.

Aside from the elevator, there was nothing to see, but Willie heard a quiet humming from behind a metal door covered with peeling green paint. Intrigued, she walked over, and when she pressed an ear to the door, it sounded like they had a generator running back there. Her curiosity was cut short by the large elevator's rattling arrival, and she hurried to get into the cage before its doors jerked shut.

Willie spotted the control panel and pressed the button marked 4, hoping the ride would be brief because her claustrophobia was especially bad in elevators, even capacious ones like this. She waited, but the car didn't move, so she pressed the button again, then pressed it a couple of times more. The damned thing wouldn't budge, and there seemed no way to get the door open. What if she was trapped in here? Willie pressed the red alarm button, expecting the clamor of an emergency bell, but there was only silence. She was just about to shout for help and beat on the door when the elevator lurched and began to climb, creaking and swaying ominously.

Her original idea had been simple. As soon as she confronted the Headmistress, she'd drop her pretense of being a prospective client. Then she would come right out and say she knew Selene was trying to get David's money and that if Selene didn't cease and desist, she would go to the police.

But as she thought more deeply, Willie saw it would never work. Dating a man for his money was crass, but hardly illegal, and if David wanted to lavish his girlfriend with cash and gifts because he was smitten, that was his privilege. No, she needed a way to put some genuine fear into Selene Mayweather. So what if, instead of going after the woman directly, she went after her precious club—threatened to get it closed down?

The problem there was that, although the place was a viper's nest, there was nothing illegal about a private club whose members practiced consensual bondage and discipline, provided no minors were involved. But the minimum age for members and guests was twenty-two, and that was rigidly enforced, so she was unlikely to gain leverage there.

It was only when Willie began to research clubs like this that she spotted Nyala's potential Achilles' heel. Unlike similar places, this club lived a dual life: It was first a social club where members could meet and practice their twisted hobby, but it was also host to several professional dominatrices who plied their trade on the top floor. That was unusual, because establishments where professional mistresses worked had more in common with kinky massage parlors than social clubs, and massage parlors were sometimes closed down on prostitution charges, weren't they?

Club Nyala had a separate website for its pro dommes, and the home page insisted that none of the mistresses offered sex of any kind as part of their services. But was that really true? Willie suspected that some form of sex was being offered on the sly, and if she could discover the "what and how" of it, she might have a weapon.

So Willie studied the local laws on prostitution, and what she found was encouraging. San Francisco had a broad view of what constituted sex for sale. Anything that involved "touching the genitals or buttocks for the purposes of gratification" was considered prostitution if money was exchanged. All the pro dommes at Nyala, including Selene, advertised spanking among their services, and spanking obviously involved touching the buttocks.

The phrase "for the purposes of gratification" was the key. Absurd as it seemed, charging money for a spanking that hurt was apparently permissible, while one that produced sexual pleasure was not. She knew all too well that the line between pain and pleasure could be a thin one, so if a client was sexually aroused during a spanking—even accidentally—Nyala could be at risk.

Suppose I go there as a client and let her spank me—and I mean hard enough to bruise so I've got proof? That gives me a bargaining chip. "If you don't leave David alone," I'll say, "I'll go to the authorities and tell them you did something sexual to me during a spanking that I paid for. Your whole club will be closed down as a brothel. So, here's the deal: Keep seeing David and I get you busted. Drop him now and I fade away like a bad dream."

The elevator lurched to a halt, its doors opened and Willie stepped out into a dim, empty storeroom. The walls were shabby bare brick, the cement floor was dusty, and the air smelled vaguely of garlic. This couldn't be right. Selene had told her to come up to her office on the fourth floor, but there was nothing here except this big drafty room, lit by a few bare overhead bulbs.

"Hello?" Willie said, first tentatively then louder. "Is anyone here?" But there was only the echo of her voice. Was Selene on to her already? Was this a trap of some kind?

Then she spotted a fire door to her right, hurried over and threw her weight against it, just managing to force it open. What Willie saw now was another world entirely. On the other side of the door was an elegantly appointed hallway, the walls and thick carpeting done in velvety earth tones. The lighting came from sconces that cast a soft illumination whose source must have been electric, though it had the feel of gaslight.

Willie eased the heavy door closed so it wouldn't slam and walked forward, the soft carpet muffling her footsteps. She passed a closed door marked *Interrogation*, another labeled *Vampire's Cave*, and then one marked *Betty Page*. Finally, she spotted a door that read *Headmistress, by appointment only*. But before she could knock, it opened and a woman stepped out.

It took Willie a moment to recognize her. Instead of the sensuous slut she'd been expecting, she saw a conservatively dressed blonde, perhaps her own age, hair done up in a tight bun. Even in flats, Selene was a good four inches taller than Willie, making her around five-seven or eight.

She was wearing a modest blue dress that reached to mid-calf and retro nylons with black seams up the back. A plain gold necklace with a single pearl, plus a thin gold bracelet on her left wrist were her only adornments; no latex or leather, no spiked collar, no stiletto heels, no blood-red lipstick or fingernails.

Jesus, Willie thought, *she looks like the dean of a girls' boarding school.*

Selene scanned Willie in one quick motion, then allowed herself a tiny smile. "I wasn't expecting you for another ten minutes," she said. "Why did you take the freight elevator?"

"Uh, I didn't see any other way."

"The members' elevator is in the main lobby, off the parking lot. There's a sign out front, but I guess you missed it." Selene finally introduced herself.

Willie had put her glasses in her bag, so it wasn't until she stepped forward to accept the proffered handshake that she got close enough to appreciate how beautiful the Headmistress actually was. Yes, she'd noted that on the website, but seeing her like this, without all that dominatrix kitsch, took it to another level. There was something almost patrician about Selene Mayweather; a face at once sensuous and angelic, with high cheekbones, a finely etched mouth, perfect teeth and skin like porcelain. Willie couldn't help thinking how graceless her own small hand—a "pudgy" hand, she'd always thought—felt in Selene's elegant one.

And then there were those uncanny eyes: the left one emerald green, the right an electric blue. Their effect was even more stunning in person than on the website. The colors were so pure they could only be tinted contacts. Willie was mesmerized and it took a moment to realize Selene was speaking to her.

"It's good to meet you, Dorothy," she said. "Please come in."

Willie was baffled. What had Selene just called her? *Who the fuck is Dorothy?* Had she gotten her mixed up with another client? Then she remembered … *yikes, of course! Dorothy Gale*—the name of the person she was pretending to be. She'd almost blown her cover.

Willie managed a weak smile as she walked into the conservative business office. It was a smile Selene apparently took for shyness because she put a reassuring hand on her arm and led her to a comfortable chair on the far side of a large oak desk. "Relax," she said, sitting down opposite her. "It's normal to be nervous the first time you visit someone like me."

Willie removed the knit cap she was wearing and shoved it into her bag. "Oh!" she said, producing a plain white envelope and handing it to Selene. "This is for you."

She'd read this was the correct etiquette for clients with any type of sex worker (even one who didn't offer actual sex). The "tribute" or "offering," as it was called, was presented in an envelope at the start of a session to get the business part out of the way. Selene accepted the envelope, thanked her, and dropped it casually into the top drawer of her desk.

"It's $300 for the first hour," Willie said, gesturing vaguely toward the drawer where Selene had deposited the envelope. "Is that right?"

"Yes, thank you."

"You … you're not going to count it?"

"No need," Selene said.

Well, there was another surprise. If Willie were running a business where deceit must be common, she'd definitely have counted it. There were four fifties and five twenties in there, but for all Selene knew, that envelope was full of cut-up newspaper and she wouldn't suspect a thing until she was preparing her next bank deposit. As a businesswoman, Willie had to wonder about such a nonchalant attitude toward money. So far, nothing was going as she'd expected.

"You understand," Selene began, "that all we're doing today is getting acquainted? I never do actual work with a client until we're feeling comfortable together."

Willie fidgeted in her seat. "I feel comfortable already."

"Really? You seem very tense."

"No, no … I'm fine. I can't wait to get started."

"Good. Then tell me about yourself. I'd like to know a little about your history and expectations. Then I'll give you a tour of our facilities."

"Well … I don't really have much of a … umm … history," Willie stammered. It had taken months to open up enough to confess her sordid past in group, and she was not about to tell someone like Selene.

"Everyone has a history, Dorothy, and histories are often difficult. You said you were a lesbian?"

"Um, mostly," Willie replied. "But right now, I'm not with anyone."

Selene nodded. "I see. No interest in men?"

Willie shook her head. "Does it matter?"

"Not at all," Selene said. "It's just for my information. The more I know about you, the easier it will be for me to give you what you need."

"I'm afraid I'm not sure what you're asking for. I'm pretty ordinary."

"No one is 'ordinary,'" Selene said. "Everyone has a unique story. Is there a history of abuse in your family? I've helped lots of people heal from that. What's your hottest fantasy? Any special fetishes I should know about?"

Willie blushed and fell silent.

"Come on, Dorothy," Selene insisted. "You wouldn't be here if you didn't need something special. Nothing you tell me leaves this room."

She hadn't expected this, and Selene's questions were making Willie nervous. But she was afraid the woman might end the interview if she refused to cooperate. "Well ... let's see ... I, uh ... have a leather corset I sometimes like to wear." It was a total fabrication, but it seemed like something a dominatrix might relate to. *Why can't I just get to the point and tell her I know what she's up to with David? Because for this to work, I have to let her spank me. Christ, if only she wasn't so gorgeous.*

"You have a leather fetish?" Selene asked, leaning forward. "Lovely! Leather can be so primal during a session."

"Yes," Willie said, relieved to have found something that registered on Selene's perversion meter, so she embellished the lie. "I love the feel and smell of leather. I have a pair of those long leather gloves too and ... a matching collar with, um ... metal studs?"

"Well, I can certainly wear leather in our sessions if you want. We both can. I've got lots of gear like that. I've also got a couple of lovely leather floggers and a suede blindfold that's very soft. And all the toys we use are disinfected after each session. So, you could be completely naked when I tied you to the bondage horse and not have to worry about who was on there before you. The horse is specially made so the saddle horn rubs against your clit and labia when you're tied up. It's lovely."

Willie forced a smile, hoping Selene wouldn't see her revulsion. "Uh ... I think I'm ready for the tour now."

"Just a few more questions. Then we can go downstairs and see the main playroom."

"What's on this floor?" Willie asked. "I saw those doors in the hallway."

"Those are the theme rooms. They're used by club members, mostly couples and small groups, but we pro dommes also use them with clients. You can see those too if you like."

"Does all the umm ... punishment stuff happen in the dungeon?" Willie asked.

"Depends on what you mean by 'punishment.' If you're talking about impact play like flogging, that can happen anywhere. As far as the dungeon goes, we usually call that the 'playroom.' See, to us, Nyala is just a big playhouse, only instead of dolls and fire trucks, we have grown-up toys like whipping posts, suspension devices and bondage crosses. We've even got a Fucking Machine."

"A what?" Willie asked, not believing she'd heard right.

Selene laughed. "A Fucking Machine. That's actually the product's name, and it's even trademarked. It's so popular we're getting a second one, but the company is back-ordered six months."

Willie shuddered. "It sounds like a mechanical rapist."

Selene smiled reassuringly. "It's harmless, just a piston-driven dildo, really. You can adjust the speed and pressure, and it doesn't have an ounce of malice. Iron John—that's what we call it—is well trained and can make you come like no male ever will because it never loses its erection or stamina. It's a real eye-opener for kink virgins."

"I'm not a prude," Willie said defensively, wondering if she was being patronized. "I do have a vibrator."

Selene shrugged. "No offense intended. Everyone here is very supportive and compassionate. Whatever your needs and limits, they're respected and honored."

"And you're sort of like the House Mother, aren't you?" Willie said. "Making sure all the kids play nice together?"

Selene laughed and clapped her hands. "What a great image. That's exactly right. One of my jobs is to be the 'mommy.' I make sure my children play nice and clean up their toys when they're done. You have good insights, Dorothy."

Willie wondered why Selene's approval pleased her so much. This woman was the enemy, and she needed to watch herself. "So, do I get the tour now?" she said, impatient to get it over with.

Selene raised an index finger. "Just one more thing. Did you ever play that trust game as a child? You know, where somebody stands behind you and you fall back into their arms, trusting they'll be there to catch you?"

Willie nodded.

"Well, what we do here will be a lot like that. Your main job is just to let yourself fall and trust I'll be there to catch you. Can you do that, Dorothy?"

"Yes … I think so," Willie said.

"You *think*?"

"No … I mean, yes. I'm feeling really at ease with you now."

Selene gave Willie a dubious look, but nodded. "Okay, then give me some idea of what you're looking for in a session."

Willie sighed. *At last, we're getting down to it.* "Well … what I've been craving for years is an old-fashioned spanking. My last partner wasn't into it at all, and since I'm single now …"

"There's no one else to turn to," Selene said, finishing Willie's thought.

Willie nodded again. "And I want it really hard. Hard enough to turn my ass purple."

Selene raised an eyebrow. "That's quite severe for a first session. You won't be able to sit for two weeks. I'd suggest starting out with something a bit less … 'colorful.'"

"No!" Willie was surprised at how emphatic she sounded. "I want the real thing."

Selene narrowed her gaze. "Well, it's my job to give you what you need. But if you really want deep bruises, I'll have to use a paddle or hairbrush."

Willie fought back a wave of terror because Harry had sometimes beaten her with a hairbrush. "Whatever … you need to do."

Selene nodded slowly. "So why will I be spanking you?"

"Uh … I'm not sure what you mean."

"I mean, if I'm going to punish you, I need a reason, don't I? What have you done to deserve a spanking that severe?"

Willie was stuck. She'd read these people liked role-playing games. Why hadn't she prepared a story? "Does there have to be a reason? I just want to be spanked, that's all."

The dominatrix frowned, steepling her fingers in front of her chin, and Willie suddenly felt apprehensive. *Why is she staring at me like that?*

"You know," Selene said, "some people are what we call 'pain sluts.' They're pure masochists who just love the rush they get from being hurt, and there's really nothing they want to act out or heal. There are lazy dommes who love subs they can just wale on like that, without having to interact or be involved with them. Is that what you are, Dorothy? A pain slut?" Her tone sounded mocking.

"I … I don't understand," Willie said. "Did I say something wrong?"

Selene ignored the question. "See, for me, pain sluts are boring. I mean, physical pain that doesn't lead to emotional catharsis—what's the point?"

Willie was caught off balance. "Why would you say that? I'm not a 'pain slut.'"

"No," Selene said. "I don't think you are. What you are, though, is full of shit. You're not here to be my client, are you?"

"Yes, truly … I am," Willie said. "I gave you $300, didn't I?"

Selene opened her drawer, retrieved the envelope, and sailed it across the desk to Willie. "I don't want your money. What are you really doing here?"

"I … don't know what you're talking about," Willie protested, her heart hammering.

"I've been doing this far too long," Selene said sharply, "and I'm not a fool. That email about wanting to submit to a woman like me was a load of crap. What's your game?"

"I don't have any game. I'm just inexperienced and didn't know how to talk to … a professional like you."

"Don't patronize me!" Selene said, pounding the desk with her hand. "Either get real or get out!"

Willie felt like a mouse cornered by an alley cat. Selene's eyes were burning right through her and there was no place left to hide. "Well, if you thought my email was full of crap, why did you offer me an appointment?" she demanded. Why not just ignore it?

"Curiosity mostly. I suspected you were a fraud but wondered what you were up to. And once you actually got here … oh, girl, that nonsense about wanting me to spank your ass purple." Selene's laugh was mirthless. "A mousey little thing like you, and brand new to this; you'd want to get your feet wet slowly to see if it was actually for you. Now tell me what you're up to."

Willie fumed inwardly at being called a "mousey little thing" but let it pass. Instead, she took a deep breath and told it quickly: "Okay, my real name is Willie Ludlow. David Sendak is a friend, and I know you're using him. I came here to stop you."

Selene's eyes widened. "David? What are you talking about? I've got nothing to do with him. He's Jill's boyfriend."

"What? Who's Jill?"

"Look," Selene said testily. She tapped the keyboard of the laptop on her desk a couple of times and spun it around so that Willie could see the screen. "That's Mistress Jilaynie. She's one of our most popular girls and she's crazy about David."

Willie stared at the screen and whistled softly. "Yikes! I can see why he'd be stuck on her. But you can't expect me to believe she's got no hidden motives for dating him."

"Why? Do you think someone in this business would never want a relationship with a good man? You think we never get lonely? Or maybe you don't think enough of your friend to believe he might appeal to a beautiful, sensuous woman. Jill's got no hidden motives. If anything, she's afraid she'll lose him because she works here. You have no idea how many times that happens to us and how much it hurts. I almost feel like I should be protecting her from *him*."

Willie groaned and put a hand to her forehead, the depth of her folly now clear. "Shit. I'm such an ass." Her voice was almost a whisper.

"Yes, you are. But what I don't get is how pretending to be my client was supposed to 'save' David."

Willie blushed and shifted uncomfortably in her chair. She'd believed her plan was brilliant, and now she was exposed as a complete fool. "I thought you were after his money, and I wanted to scare you away. I was going to have you spank me hard enough to make bruises. Then I'd threaten to go to the authorities and say you'd tried to arouse me sexually, so I could …"

"Have my club closed as a brothel if I didn't stop seeing David," Selene guessed.

Willie nodded. "I wasn't really going to report you. I just wanted to warn you off. It was a dumb idea."

"No, it wasn't dumb," Selene said. "It was vicious." She stood, walked around the desk, and smacked Willie's face hard. "Get out."

Willie was stunned. She'd made a well-intentioned mistake, and Selene should understand that she was only trying to help a friend. She put a hand to her smarting cheek, searching desperately for something to say, some scathing remark to put the woman in her place. But she could think of nothing clever enough, so she stood and walked from the room with as much dignity as she could muster.

Selene watched her go and smiled. *You didn't really come here to help David, did you, Willie? That may be the story you told yourself, but you came because you were dying to meet me. How sweet.*

AN OFFER HE CAN'T REFUSE

Month of March/Month of Ash

*W*illie was half an hour late for work this morning, but knew her partner Glenda Roth would already be there and have the coffee brewed. Green Girl Consultants, the company they'd owned together for five years, was still a two-woman operation, but their client base was growing, and they'd begun looking for someone to help with the routine office work.

As Willie walked in the door, she saw Glenda on the phone in the back office. A tall, thin woman just shy of fifty, with closely cropped graying hair, Glenda's cool energy and unflappable temperament made the perfect counterpoint to Willie's emotional heat and tenacity. When Glenda spotted Willie, she held up an index finger to say she'd be just a minute. Then, making a wacky face, she traced a few circles by her head to let Willie know she had a "loopy" client on the line.

Willie grinned, walked into the tiny kitchen and poured a cup of coffee, which she carried into her office. Glenda had left a Krispy Kreme by Willie's keyboard, and she groaned, wishing her partner would stop tempting her with junk food. But she picked up the donut and took a large bite, rolling her eyes and sighing with pleasure at the sinful confection. Her email contained the usual crap, including three appeals for contributions to pro-environment political candidates, and an ad for penis enhancement pills guaranteed to "make her yours forever," which had managed to slip through the junk mail filter.

The rest consisted of two meeting requests from clients, a response to her query about ad space in a trade magazine, the weekly newsletter from her women's group, a message from David confirming their lunch date, and one from ... Oh, double fuck, Harry! The message was a follow-up to his latest phone call in which he'd told her he'd be willing to pay his own fare to San Francisco if she'd agree to see him. She'd refused point-blank, but he was obviously undeterred because this message gave her his arrival date and flight number.

Willie sighed and answered David's note, giving him a brief update on Harry and signing off with, "See ya at 12:30, dude." She was just starting a response to the first client when Glenda came in. "Looks like we've got a teensy-weensy problem, hon," she said. Willie cringed, because in Glenda-speak, "teensy-weensy problem" always meant disaster was brewing.

Without waiting for a response, Glenda walked over to Willie's computer and took hold of the mouse. "Check out today's *True-Post*." She clicked the shortcut for the popular news site and it popped up quickly.

"What am I looking for?" Willie said, taking back control of her mouse.

"Scroll down," said Glenda, absently grabbing Willie's half-eaten donut and taking a bite. "Keep going ... keep going ...there!" She tapped the screen with an impeccably manicured fingernail, pointing at an article by Chuck Learner, a *True-Post* agitator who always had a hair up his butt about one thing or another.

Willie didn't have to read very far. "Yikes! He's crucifying Masterson!"

Jack Masterson was the CEO of Welgro, an agri-business that developed pest-resistant crop varieties using only natural methods, and they were Green Girl's second biggest client. Willie continued reading: "'Violating the public trust' ...yadda, yadda, yadda ...

'Unreported genetic modifications on W32' … 'Dangerous zombie food.' Fuck, this is bullshit!"

"Relax," Glenda said, laying a hand on Willie's shoulder. "Look, we know Learner's full of crap, right? W32 isn't gene-spliced. It's a natural hybrid, and we can prove it. Why don't you come up with a rebuttal for publication? I'll give Masterson a call. If he hasn't seen this, I'll prep him ever so gently. If he's already seen it, I'll talk him down from the roof before he jumps."

"Thanks, Glenda," Willie said, regaining her composure. "Set up a meeting for 3:30. I have a lunch date, but I can whip out a response to show him in plenty of time."

It was 12:40, and the Mexican joint on O'Farrell was packed as Willie spotted David sipping *Tecate* from a can at a patio table. He was dressed in Bermuda shorts, a funky Grateful Dead T-shirt, and ratty-looking loafers with tube socks. Not that outrageous for a software engineer in casual California, but bad enough to make Willie—who was a firm believer in traditional business attire—sigh in resignation.

She'd spent years trying to "smarten him up," steering him to elegant men's stores and even accompanying him a few times to make sure what he bought was properly coordinated. Then, a couple of months ago, just when she was finally getting somewhere, Jill had come into his life and undone whatever progress Willie had made by not giving a shit about what David wore. Though Jill herself was always exquisitely turned out, she seemed to think that clothes on David were more a hindrance than anything else. She'd even told Willie that she preferred having her "Lamb Chop" naked at home, for reasons graphic enough to make Willie blush.

David and Jill were now living together at the Inverness house, and despite Willie's initial misgivings, she'd come to like Jill. The girl was smart, funny and unabashedly sexy, and Willie couldn't remember a time when David had seemed happier. Okay, so Jill was a sex worker, but if he didn't mind her occupation, Willie felt it was time to give him a break and let David live his own life—well, at least, she was *trying* to feel that way.

"Sorry I'm late," Willie said as she dropped into a chair beside him. She was a bit breathless, having walked here rapidly from her office because she hadn't been to the gym in over a week and badly needed the exercise.

"No biggie," David said, taking a sip of his beer. "I told Bernie I was taking an extra hour for lunch so I could 'prepare.' He was so relieved to fob this shit off on me that he said to take as long as I needed … just as long as I got back in time to fire Elise by the end of the day."

"I can't believe the bastard's making you do his dirty work," Willie said. "I mean, he's Director of Engineering. Isn't this supposed to be his job?"

David shrugged. "We need to cut someone, and Bernie says she's on my team, so it's up to me. This stuff usually gets done by senior management, not a mid-level stiff like me, but it's a delicate situation and he's scared shitless of bad publicity."

Their conversation was interrupted by the waitress who came over to take their order. She was a cute brunette, with a slinky mermaid tattooed on her right forearm.

"Hi, I'm Deirdre, your server," she said to David, not even glancing at Willie.

"I love your tattoo," David said, with a broad smile. "Are *you* a mermaid?"

The waitress laughed. "Well, I was on my high school swim team."

"Hmm … I never learned to swim. Maybe you could teach me?" His tone made it clear the request had nothing to do with swimming.

Willie's eyes went wide at the smarmy pickup line, and she was sure the waitress would be mortified.

But Deirdre just laughed again. "Well, I do give lessons ... and I'm a great teacher."

"And I'm a *great* student," David said, his tone even more suggestive.

Willie sat, stunned as he flirted confidently with the waitress, who flirted right back. Was this also Jill's doing? Not only was he more self-assured than she'd ever seen him, but he seemed sexier in a way she couldn't put her finger on. Willie had never had romantic feelings for David, but was that a twinge of jealousy she felt as Deirdre walked off with their order? She quickly put the idea aside because it was too absurd to consider.

Still, she almost asked David what had gotten into him with that uncharacteristic display of lechery, but changed her mind and returned to their interrupted conversation. "Elise is the only woman in your department, right?"

"She's not just the only woman," he replied. "She's a single mom with two autistic kids."

"Yikes! So why pick on her with all those men to choose from?"

"Well, her work's great when she's actually there. But the husband split for parts unknown and she's got no one to help with the kids. One of them's too damaged even for daycare, so she's been out a lot lately."

"And the answer, of course, is to fire her," Willie groused.

"Fuck," David said. "I don't even know why I'm still working there. It's not like I need the paycheck anymore. Maybe I should shit-can the job and focus on my photography. Jill wants me to shoot a new portfolio for her web page and thinks I might get some paying work from the other Upstairs Girls. Having those babes actually pay me to take kinky shots of them would be totally awesome. I might even pose a couple of them together, doing girl-girl stuff. Maybe I'll become an erotic fine-art photographer."

David had a good eye for photography, but calling smut "fine art" was nuts. Willie gave a derisive snort. "Oh, right. I'm sure Jill would just *love* that."

"Well, she suggested it and even offered to set the shoot up with her friends."

Willie couldn't fathom that at all. What self-respecting woman would encourage her man to take pornographic pictures of her girlfriends and even arrange it? "Well, you've still got a job to do *today*," she said, "and you can't just turn your back on it. It's not like Elise gets to stay if you refuse to fire her, so she might as well hear it from a good guy. Just be sympathetic and break it to her gently."

"Problem is I really like her," David said, taking another swig of his *Tecate*. "What's she gonna do with those kids and no job?"

Willie patted his shoulder. "You're such a soft touch for women. I'll bet she's a leggy doe-eyed blonde, with tits out to here, right?"

"Well, actually, she's got the face of Winston Churchill, and must weigh one-seventy. But she's a kind-hearted soul."

The busboy brought the chips and guacamole, and they busied themselves eating for a while before the conversation turned to Willie's problem. "So Harry's really coming out here?" David asked.

Willie sighed and nodded. "May 14th."

"Well, that's still weeks away. A lot can happen in that time. Maybe he'll keel over and die."

"Yeah, fat chance."

"And you've got no idea why he's so intent on this?"

"That's what really scares me. He says he wants to make amends, but Harry always had hidden agendas for everything. I doubt he's ever forgiven me for running out on him and taking his dough like I did."

"Can't you get a restraining order to keep him away?" David asked, munching a tortilla chip.

Willie shook her head. "I can't prevent him from flying out here, and I can't serve him with papers unless he harasses or threatens me ... and I'm not about to hire a bodyguard."

In a bad Mafioso impression, David mugged, "You want me and the boys should lean on da creep? Maybe take him out to sleep wit da fishes?"

Willie laughed. "David, he's in his seventies now."

"I don't care how grown up he is. I'll make him an offer he can't refuse."

Willie smiled. "My hero. Where were you when I really needed you back then?"

"Let's see ... I'd have been thirteen, so I was probably jerking off to *Penthouse* centerfolds. It's a ritual all Jewish boys go through to get closer to God, kind of like Communion, except you don't get those tasty wafers."

Chapter 11

WILLIE

That night ...

*O*ur meeting with Masterson had been a bitch-and-a-half, and Glenda and I had a lot of "soothing" to do. Long story short, I was wiped when I finally got home, too beat to fix myself anything but "emergency rations" for dinner: a prefab frozen soufflé that tasted a little like cheddar cheese but mostly like the plastic container it came in. I gulped it down anyway because my blood sugar was low and I was famished.

Crappy as it was, the food brought me back to life a little, and I decided to read some of the book I'd bought on the way back to the office after lunch. I dug it out of my bag and looked at the cover: two black riding crops crossed like swords over that same tree illustration that was tattooed on Selene's body. In black lettering, the title read: *Twisted Honey, a Mistress's Tail, by Selene Mayweather.* The subtitle was clever, with the word "tail" substituted for "tale." Not everyone would get it of course, but Selene had found the perfect pun for what she did, since tail was both another word for ass and also for whip. Whatever else she was, this girl was no dummy.

Still, why would I pony up $34.95 for this thing? I mean, I was literally lining the pockets of a slut who'd bitch-slapped me when I'd gone to see her trying to save my friend. Okay, so I'd technically gotten it wrong and she wasn't after David's money, but she was still victimizing lots of other saps, wasn't she? Someone like Selene almost made me ashamed to be a woman.

I flopped down on the sofa and waited for Butter, who leapt into my lap with a little chirp. She did a couple of turns, starting to purr even before she settled in to be petted. I indulged her a bit then opened the book, just skimming at first, reading bits and pieces from different chapters. To my surprise, though—and almost to my disappointment—it was better than I'd expected, way better. I'd wanted to ridicule it, to hate it, but I couldn't because the book was funny, perceptive, and totally engrossing. Soon I wasn't just skimming pages; I was totally locked in. I had to hand it to Selene, she could write like a demon.

In one chapter, she talked about how every pro domme had her own way of working, ranging from girls who enjoyed playing seductively with their clients, right up to vicious vixens who got off on humiliating and hurting weak men. Selene didn't rate herself on that scale, leaving it to the reader to decide where she fit.

She also talked about the different kinds of submissives she'd known over the years and explained that they varied as much as dommes, from those who just wanted something sexy and playful to those who hungered for the really dark and painful. There were lots of anecdotes—some hysterically funny, others just plain gross, and one that was oddly touching:

> *I had a client, a very sweet man of about thirty-five. I'll call Darien. Darien had been seeing me for about two years when seemingly out of nowhere, he was diagnosed with a rare form of cancer and given six months to live—it was a terrible blow to someone still so young. He'd visited me regularly every few weeks, maybe thirty times by now.*
>
> *Sometimes, he'd ask me to wear a leather skirt and smother him with my ass after he'd sucked my toes for a while. These are very common fetishes with clients. Other times, he'd want to be spanked across my lap with his pants and shorts down around his ankles while I was wearing red leather boots. He never wanted*

his pants and shorts taken off completely. Having them down around his ankles was a crucial part of the ritual, as was the color of my boots.

Few people are as obsessive and compulsive as submissives are. Everything must be just so for them, as if the smallest detail of a fetish, like the exact shade of toenail polish the domme is wearing when they worship her feet, is as vital as air. A mistress knows many quirks about her regular clients, and she learns how to use them to make their endorphins flow, which is what keeps them coming back.

I would spank Darien fairly hard, talking to him all the while, for about fifteen to twenty minutes, until his ass was beet red. Many subs like being told how bad they've been to deserve such punishment, but Darien was different; he didn't want to be chastised in any way. He didn't hate himself or feel a need to be humiliated. Instead, he wanted to hear how nice his ass felt against my hand as his butt grew warmer and warmer from the spanking. He just loved giving his ass to me because it felt good.

I always had a nice time with Darien and there was never a question of anything overtly sexual, though he would usually have quite an erection by the time I was finished. He was far too respectful to even dream of asking me to touch him sexually, though with steady clients I've built rapport with, I'll sometimes invite them to masturbate at the end of a session to relieve the tension. As long as I don't touch them, there's nothing illegal about it. I just watch and encourage them.

Once, I invited Darien to masturbate for me because I wanted to see him come all over himself while he lay on his back on the floor and I smothered him with my bare feet. I was surprised when he declined, but the reason he gave was lovely. He said my essence was totally inside him and he wanted to keep me there instead of just ejecting me in an orgasm. That earned him a lot of points in my book.

Darien didn't seem to be in pain as his illness progressed, but he was becoming noticeably frailer each time he visited me. It was *sad to see, but he lived alone and had no family, so it felt good to know I was providing him at least some kind of intimate contact and comfort as his end grew near.*

One day, he showed up for an appointment and calmly told me it would be his last visit because he was about to enter a hospice where he expected to die, and he would soon be too weak for any kind of session anyway. He looked very gaunt and his skin was quite sallow.

I probably felt more affection for Darien than someone in my line of work should allow herself for a client, but there it was. I wouldn't grieve when he was gone, but he had the kindest eyes and I would miss him.

I asked what he wanted for his last session and he said he wanted me to decide. He just wanted to feel taken. I didn't need to think about it much; what I wanted was to make him come in some really earth-shattering way, but I couldn't do it if he was here as a client. I told him what I planned and that I wouldn't take no for an answer. I wouldn't take his money, either. This would be a gift from one friend to another.

I'd never seen him this nervous, but he wasn't frightened. It was the kind of giddy anticipation a boy about to lose his virginity might feel, and it was delicious to see. Suddenly he no longer looked sick; in fact, he was positively glowing.

I told him that I was going to spank him and that we would both be naked. I wanted him to rub his cock against my thigh until he ejaculated as I spanked him. He was not to hold anything back, not to try keeping me inside. I wanted him to cycle me right through his body like an electric current, and then to empty himself completely while I held him. You wouldn't have thought this was a man who knew he'd be dead in a month or two. He seemed totally drunk on life.

I undressed him and then had him watch me undress—I gave him a real show too. I suspected he'd imagined seeing me completely naked many times, and I loved his awestruck expression as I slowly disrobed for him.

The Goddess classically has three modes: Aphrodite, the lover and enchantress; the fecund Mother Goddess, who gives birth to and nurtures the universe; and then the Dark Goddess, the force that devours all life, taking it back into herself as the substance she will use to begin a new round of death and rebirth. Today, I would be all three for Darien.

I sat down in an armless chair and had him lie across my knee as usual. What was different this time was that we were skin on skin. I even oiled my thighs to make them slippery and increase the pleasure for him. I started out by lightly caressing his balls and anus before putting a couple of lubed fingers into him. As I expected, this drove him absolutely wild. His cock was already like a ramrod and I told him to hold on and not come too soon, to let the energy build before he released it.

I was just about to begin spanking him when I had another thought, which turned out to be an inspiration. I told Darien to imagine he was a condemned prisoner about to be hanged, with me as his executioner. There was no escape for him and all he could do was let go and surrender his life to me.

Now, you might think it was cruel, reminding a sick man of his impending death this way. But my instincts didn't fail me. He moaned, as if I'd plucked some really deep chord of his sexuality. And then I felt him drop into subspace—the euphoric, trancelike state submissives can enter when in total surrender to the will of a dominant. He was totally aroused, yet completely at peace. And he was totally mine.

The narrative stopped there, like the reader was supposed to guess the rest of it. To be honest, the story not only turned me on, but there was a tenderness there that really touched me. It sounded so different from the beatings I'd suffered at Harry's hands. And the Selene who was writing this seemed nothing like the one I'd encountered at her club. If Jill's touch with David was anything like Selene's was with Darien, I could understand why he was so obsessed with her. If he was really going to get Huntington's, I hoped Jill would be there like that for him.

But I was too tired to think about it anymore. My eyes were falling out of my head, so I marked my place, closed the book, and dropped it onto the coffee table. It was barely 9:00, but I needed sleep right now, so I took a quick shower, brushed my teeth, and crawled under the covers. I would have loved a nice orgasm, but I didn't have the energy to give myself one, so I turned out the light and shut my eyes.

The phone rang just as I was nodding off and startled me awake. Caller ID said it was a blocked number and I was going to let it go, but something prompted me to take the call. The voice on the line was female: "Willie?"

"Yes, this is Willie Ludlow," I said. "Who's this?"

"Hi, Willie. It's Selene Mayweather."

I had a sudden flash of déjà vu. I'd just been reading her book, and it was like I'd known this call was coming. "Hello," I said. "Umm … how are you?" Utterly lame, but I had nothing better to say.

"I'm fine. Am I calling too late?"

"Uh, no," I lied.

How weird was it that she'd call right after I'd been reading her book? I was so off balance that I was relieved when she skipped the small talk and got right to the point: "I'm calling to ask if you'd like to meet for a walk."

"Uh …why?" I said. My response was a little brusque, but I was totally baffled by how out of the blue this invitation was.

"Well, I was hoping we might get to know each other a little. And … I guess I also want to make sure you're not going to be a loose cannon aimed at my club."

Now there was something I'd never have expected from her. It had been more than a month since that slap, and she was actually afraid I might still hurt her club. It seemed to put us on a more even footing, and I liked that. "Where and when?" I said calmly, though I could hear my pulse hammering.

"How about we meet in front of the de Young Museum Saturday at noon? We can go for a walk in the park and then the Japanese Tea Garden? Or maybe the de Young?"

I agreed, but I said 12:30, just to assert myself a little.

After we hung up, I kept replaying the conversation in my mind. Did we just arrange peace negotiations, or had I been asked on a date?

> "Your perspective on life comes from
> the cage you were held captive in."
> —Shannon L. Adler

Chapter 12

⁓

HER LEFT FOOT

Month of April/Month of Alder

On a sunny Saturday afternoon, Willie and Selene were strolling through Golden Gate Park, moving among the crowds of joggers and mothers pushing strollers, past boys tossing Frisbees and young couples lolling and canoodling in the grass. The air was mild and Willie was dressed casually in a pink blouse, sneakers, and a calf-length gray skirt, with Selene more provocative in a short leather skirt and halter top that revealed most of the tattoos on her upper chest and back.

Willie had felt nervous about seeing Selene and she'd almost canceled their meeting, but so far, she was enjoying the day and starting to relax. "I read your book," she said as they stopped to pet a playful Jack Russell, which had decided they looked and smelled interesting enough to tug its elderly female owner in their direction.

"Oh?" Selene said, bending to scratch behind the dog's ears. "What did you think?"

"It surprised me," Willie said, kneeling to work the dog's chin as it sniffed the intriguing sent of cat on her and wagged its tail feverishly.

"Surprised how?" The attention from the two women was making the Jack Russell very happy, and its owner allowed it a few more moments before coaxing it away.

"Well, I didn't think it would be so ... so soulful."

"Ah," Selene said as they resumed walking. "You were expecting pure sleaze?"

"I was," Willie confessed. "You seem to treat your clients with more respect than I'd have thought."

"None of my girls are big on humiliation. Most of what we do is just intense role-play between dominant and submissive: lots of Goddess worship, but also some bondage, flogging, and, of course"—she gave Willie a wry look—"spankings."

Willie blushed, remembering their first meeting. "Yeah, well, some of it still shocks me. But that story about Darien ... it was so sweet it almost made me cry."

"Yes, he was lovely," Selene said. "In fact, David reminds me a little of Darien."

"Really? How so?"

"Darien had a melancholy spirit and David's is a bit lighter, but he sees the Goddess in women just the way Darien did."

Willie frowned. "I guess, but ... Well, I know Jill's your friend and all, but I still worry he's not strong enough for her."

Selene laughed. "Are you kidding? Jill adores him. And he seems a lot more confident."

Willie had certainly seen that. But as much as she liked Jill, that girl was clearly a "player" and not the type who could be a one-man woman for long. It just wasn't in her, and David was too blissfully in love to see that. Jill might "adore" him now, but how long would that last before she got bored and dumped him? Willie's instincts told her that when the other shoe dropped, as it surely would, it would fall hard.

They strolled around the park a bit more and, after a while, Selene suggested they have lunch. The two women headed back toward the café, and now Selene got around to why she'd asked Willie for this meeting. "So were you surprised when I called you?"

"Stunned, actually. I never expected you'd want to apologize for slapping me."

"Is that what you think this is about?" Selene asked.

"Well, you said you didn't want me to be a 'loose cannon aimed at your club.'"

"And I need to apologize to keep you from becoming one?"

"Well ... it wouldn't hurt. Besides, you called me 'a mousey little thing,' lest you forget."

Selene laughed. "Okay ... I apologize. You're anything but 'mousey.' But you were way out of line trying to blackmail me."

"Well, David and I have always looked out for each other," Willie said. "He's vulnerable to a certain kind of woman, and when he told me he was seeing a dominatrix, I just assumed the worst."

"He's very dear to you, isn't he?"

"Yes, very." Willie told her how, when she and David had been housemates during their junior year at Cal, he'd been invited to spend a spring break week in Puerto Vallarta by a bodacious forty-year-old divorcee who'd picked him up at an outdoor concert.

"She was sexy, rich, recently divorced, and looking for something cute, young and fuckable," Willie said. "I guess David fit the bill, so she pounced. It was great for him because he was still so inexperienced, and having a foxy older woman take him in hand for a week was just what he needed. He was totally stoked, and I was happy for him because she told him exactly what she wanted, and he had no illusions that it would be anything more than a week of sun, partying, and wild monkey sex.

"But then, four days before he was supposed to leave, I come down with meningitis and wind up in the hospital. It was a mild case and I pulled through okay, but the doctors told him I'd need home care for ten days, so ..."

"So he gives up a week of 'wild monkey sex' to stay home and nurse you?" Selene guessed.

Willie nodded. "I was floored. I mean, I wasn't his girlfriend or anything like that."

"So he took care of you and now you take care of him, right?"

"I suppose. But our relationship goes deeper than that. We're almost like siblings."

"And you decided to save your 'brother' from me because I was a 'dangerous whore' out to fleece him?"

"Okay, I overreacted," Willie said. "I guess I owe you an apology too."

"Accepted. But there was more to what you did than just trying to rescue David."

Willie gave her a curious look. "Like what?"

"C'mon, you contacted me because you saw my web page and were turned on."

"What? No!"

"Look, let's be honest, okay? One reason I called was because I was interested too. I mean, we had a little tiff, but there was also some chemistry."

Willie was surprised but flattered. "You're saying you're attracted to me?"

Selene put an arm around her shoulder. "Willie, a great part of your appeal is how unaware of it you are."

At the de Young Café, they were quickly seated at an outdoor table where both ordered salads and hot tea.

"There's something I've been meaning to ask you," Willie said. "Your eyes are so amazing, one green and one blue. I was just wondering ..."

"If they're contacts?" Selene said.

"Well, some girls wear tinted lenses to enhance their eyes. But those colors are just stunning."

"Everyone thinks they're contacts at first, but these are my real eyes." Selene leaned closer, turning her head and opening her eyes wide to let Willie see she wasn't wearing contacts. "It's a genetic condition called heterochromia that makes each eye a different color. My grandmother and her twin sister had it and so did my mother. It seems to run in our family. In their case, the right and left eyes were only slightly different. In mine, well, the difference is pretty stark."

The waiter brought their salads and tea service, and the women selected tea bags from the large assortment, pouring hot water from the two china pots and setting the bags to steep.

Willie sighed. "Sometimes I wonder just how much 'gorgeousness' one woman is fairly entitled to. You seem to have gotten your share and mine too."

Selene shook her head. "Stop diminishing yourself, Willie. You're a peach. I mean, you've got this natural beauty that radiates from you."

Once again, Willie blushed. "C'mon, I saw those looks coming your way in the park. None of them were for me."

Selene smiled. "You should come shopping with me. You've got a hot little body. A slinky dress, some shoes to add a couple of inches, then a little eye makeup and lipstick … You'll be on the receiving end of as much lust as you can handle."

Willie shook her head. "I'm not much for sexy clothes. In fact, I try to avoid them."

"But why?"

Willie hesitated a moment, then shrugged. "I had a stepfather, a preacher, who molested me for years, and sexy clothes like yours just make me … uncomfortable now."

"Oh, sorry. I had no idea."

Willie shrugged. "We get the lives we get, but … God, I know I'm prying, and don't answer if you don't want to, but I've read that most women who … you know, do any kind of sex work, are molest survivors."

"It's not uncommon," Selene said. "But nothing like that ever happened to me or any of my girls. I started thinking of being a mistress at sixteen, when I read a novel about a man who falls for a dominatrix he meets at the beach. She was so hot, and I said, 'That's what I'm going to be!'"

Willie grinned. "In church, they'd call that finding your vocation."

Selene laughed, chewed a forkful of salad, and then asked a question of her own. "So, is he still living ... your stepfather, I mean?"

Willie didn't talk about this easily, yet suddenly she began opening up to someone she hardly knew—a woman who actually flogged people professionally. "Funny you should ask. Until a few months ago, I had no idea if he was dead or alive because I hadn't seen or heard from him in seventeen years. Then he suddenly calls and wants to come here from Orlando to see me."

"That must have been a shock. But the question is do you want to see *him*?"

"Fuck no! It's just that he's found out everything about me through some detective agency. He'll be here in a few weeks, and I've got no way to stop him. The thought of confronting him ... it scares the shit out of me."

When she hesitated, Selene took her hand and, gathering her courage, Willie continued. "It started when I was twelve, though at first I didn't know what to call it. My mother was dead, I was lonely, and ...well, being touched was comforting in a way ..." Tears were running down Willie's cheeks, and Selene dabbed at them with a napkin.

That was when Willie noticed a couple of well-dressed women who'd just been seated at the next table, and they seemed to be looking this way. They were whispering together, and it was making her uneasy. Had they overheard what she was talking about, or had they recognized Selene from her TV appearances?

"Go on, honey," Selene said. "Don't mind them."

Willie took her eyes from the women and lowered her voice. "In the beginning, it was mainly oral sex, and sucking him off gave me some power, because I learned to make him come when and how I wanted. But the first time he stuck his dick in me, I hated it, because now he had all the control and I was powerless.

"So I fought him and that was when the beatings started. He would call me a whore and burn me with cigarettes, tie me to the bed face down and beat my ass with a belt buckle. And, believe me, nothing about it was consensual." Willie paused to catch her breath, tears flowing freely now.

"Stop if you want to," Selene said. "Don't torture yourself."

Willie shook her head. "No, it's okay. The thing is that, after a while, I stopped fighting him. I … began having orgasms when he fucked me. I was actually enjoying it."

Selene shook her head. "Orgasms don't mean you were enjoying it, Willie."

"No … I was. Sometimes, if he was too tired for sex, I'd make a fuss and whine till he came to bed with me. But I hated him and was totally disgusted with myself."

"At least you're free of him now," Selene said. "Even if he shows up here, he can't hurt you anymore."

Willie sighed. "There's more, Selene, much more."

Now she told her how she'd become pregnant by Harry—told her all of it. How she'd broken into his safe and stolen his money. How she'd given her baby up to a total stranger and run. "It kills me to know I have a daughter out there with no idea what became of her. She'd be seventeen now, a year older than I was when I abandoned her. Where is she? Is she even alive? I dream about her, Selene, and the dreams are all bad. Like she's calling to me from some awful place; calling for me to help her."

Willie began to weep again, and Selene moved closer, put an arm around her shoulders, and let her cry. "What an awful thing, honey. I'm so sorry. What can I do for you?"

Willie sniffled and wiped her eyes with her hand. Then she gave a small, ironic laugh. "I don't know. Can you give me a different past?"

Selene shook her head slowly. "No, but there is something I can do to make you feel better now. Will you trust me?"

With tear-swollen eyes, Willie looked at her. "Trust you how?"

"Just that I won't hurt you."

It was an odd request coming from a woman who'd slapped her the first time they'd met, but somehow Willie believed her. "Okay," she said, almost in a whisper.

Selene reached for her bag, opened it, and removed a pen and small notepad. Then she began to write.

Willie looked on, perplexed. "What are you doing?"

"Hush," Selene said, tearing off a sheet and handing it to her. It read: *Move your chair as close to the table as you can.*

Willie gave her a questioning look, but Selene just stared at her silently, so Willie shrugged and moved her chair right up to the edge of the table. It felt claustrophobic, but she went along.

Selene began to write again, taking a bit longer this time. She tore the second sheet off the notepad and handed it to Willie, who read it three times before the message sunk in: *Don't say anything! Hike your skirt up to your waist and spread your legs as wide as you can.*

Willie was shocked. "What! Are you serious?"

Selene just put a finger to her lips then silently mouthed the words: "Trust me."

Willie closed her eyes, took a deep breath, and did as Selene asked. Abruptly, a hot fist of desire ignited in her belly and spread slowly into her chest and down her legs. It was like Selene had simply willed her to become aroused.

What Selene had in mind quickly became clear, because Willie felt a shoeless left foot begin to caress her right ankle and work its way slowly up her calf, tickling gently when it reached the inside of her knee. Willie squeezed her eyes tight and shivered.

A nudge from Selene made her look to see another note: *Keep your eyes open. Stay in the moment and look at me.*

Selene moved down a bit in her chair to get a better angle, her toes inching their way up Willie's thigh until they worked their way under the hem of her panties. Willie gasped as Selene paused to tickle and tug at her pubic hair. She felt like a butterfly pinned to a specimen mount, but it was wonderful.

A fourth hastily scribbled note read: *Move lower in your chair and lift your hips.* Willie obliged, lifting higher as Selene's foot hooked the top of her panties, then tugged them down to her knees in one quick motion. Selene's toes entwined themselves in Willie's pubic hair again, gripping and tugging so hard that Willie stifled a squeal of pain. She glanced uneasily at the two women at the next table, who were now staring intently, stunned at the brazen act they were witnessing. "Selene. No! We're being watched."

"So much the better," Selene said archly, working her way to Willie's labia and starting to slide up and down it with her big toe. Finally, she found Willie's clit, pressed experimentally, kneaded gently, then paused, stroked, rubbed, and paused again.

"Oh, my God," Willie whispered, sure that every patron on the patio knew exactly what was happening and could smell her heat. And yet the wave of shame that washed over her didn't diminish her lust one iota; instead, her helplessness just inflamed it.

Again, Selene's toes worked Willie's pubic hair, tugging as if to yank it out by its roots. Willie bore the pain, wanting more to laugh than scream. And then she did laugh, laughed explosively, before quickly covering her mouth with a hand.

Selene held up another scribbled note that read: *Don't fight it. Just let yourself come.* And with that, Selene's big toe found Willie's core and thrust itself inside without warning, the penetration so sudden, so fierce it made Willie gasp. A wave of obscene delight coursed through her, and without conscious effort, her hips lifted again, her legs spreading wider to accommodate Selene fully. She felt utterly defenseless, longing only to remain that way—a toy for

Selene's amusement, totally objectified and floating off in mindless bliss.

Willie's cunt was drenched as Selene's big toe found her g-spot, rubbing, coaxing, and demanding surrender. How was she doing that? It was incredible that a single toe could fill her so completely. Moments later, a portal opened, and Willie was sucked blindly through it. A convulsive wave of orgasm shook her, melting her, driving her soul from her body.

She made a guttural sound and bit her knuckle to keep from screaming, wishing she could have some part of Selene in her mouth—breast, fingers, toes—anything at all to suckle as she kept on coming. Her juices were flowing down her legs, the ecstasy going on and on, wave after blissful wave until, with a series of slowly diminishing spasms, it finally ended, and she was back on the patio, looking into Selene's hypnotic eyes.

"Feel better?" Selene asked.

Willie nodded and grinned, trying to catch her breath and focus. She looked at the next table, now boldly meeting the eyes of the two women, who turned away red-faced and began eating their lunches.

Just then, the waiter appeared. "Can I interest you ladies in a slice of fresh cherry pie?" he asked.

Willie and Selene burst into laughter as the waiter glanced back and forth between them. "Okay," he said uneasily. "I'll … just get your check."

After leaving the café, they walked together toward California Street to find cabs. "I had a lovely time," Selene said. Then she took a business card from her bag and jotted something on the back. "This is my private number. Call anytime and we'll get together again soon."

Willie glanced at it, smiled, and pocketed the card. "That would be nice," she said, trying to sound more casual than what she was feeling.

Just before falling asleep that night, Willie remembered something odd. She had the distinct impression that Selene had written all those notes left-handed, but she was absolutely sure she'd seen her print her number on that business card with her right hand. Very few people could do that. But it was even stranger in light of a couple of things David had told her a while back. He'd said that Jill was totally ambidextrous—and that she could do amazing things with her toes.

Chapter 13

⚜

JANAYNIE

17th day of Alder, 5336

Jilaynie,

The Portal has been open for six days now, and I have had no further word from you about the David human. What progress have you made with him? Spring is turning to summer and slow blight continues to spread through the Drys orchards, taking tree after tree and many of our dear friends along with them. To make matters worse, blight has been attacking the Oros forests as well, and our Oread cousins are becoming more of a problem, stealing humans from us at the rate of more than two per week. Over a dozen have been taken in the past five weeks alone, and who knows what the Oreads are doing with them?

They constantly distract us with border skirmishes, and even though we can beat them back, we haven't enough troops to protect all our humans at the same time. We desperately need you here as soon as possible to help organize better defenses, so it is crucial you wrap this human up and bring him soon.

Of course, you haven't told him what you are and want of him, but a few hints might help you gauge how pliant he would be. Before Aneel brought that William human over, she asked if he'd sacrifice himself for her if her life were at risk, and he swore he would. If you put that question to David and he gives the same reply, I'd say he's ready right now. But even if he's not, take him by force, if necessary. The time for observing traditional Meliai niceties has long passed.

Your Full Sister,

Janaynie

Chapter 14

ｰ｡ｏ

JILAYNIE

20th day of Alder, 5336

Dearest Full Sister,

My apologies for not writing sooner, but between moving into David's house and helping Selene train two new mistresses, things are very hectic again. David and I are settling nicely into domestic life, and our bond grows deeper every day. Soon he won't be able to imagine life without me.

I did speak with Selene about your concerns over the Oread situation, and she feels you're overstating the problem. The number of humans they are stealing from us is troubling, but Tristelle seems able to contain the situation for now. Take a few deep breaths, Janaynie, and don't panic because I'm confident that, with Kayla's grace, our clan will weather this temporary shortage of humans as we have always done in the past.

David has left his oppressive work in San Francisco and seems much happier this way. He spends a lot of time doing photography and has taken some "scandalous" pictures of me and the other Meliai at Nyala. Érichea and Wynter love posing for him, and we all keep encouraging David to display his pictures at galleries that feature erotic work by local artists.

By the way, he keeps asking about my twin sister and whether you have plans to come and visit us. He hasn't said so, but I'm sure he has fantasies of photographing the two of us sky clad together. It would be lovely if you and I could be here at the same time but, of course, Full Sisters are prohibited from doing that.

About Aneel's idea of asking David if he'd give his life for me, well it's just silly—at least in my Lamb Chop's case. You've said that William is the ascetic type, so it would be just like him to see a question like Aneel's as some kind of spiritual test he couldn't let himself fail. But David would treat it as a joke and laugh it off. You really must trust me and let me handle him my way.

Though you don't usually like males, I think you'll appreciate David as much as I do when you meet him. He's intelligent, funny and very sweet. It's rare to find a human male with the deep qualities of heart and spirit that he has, so I'm sure he'll make a perfect Changeling.

I'm sorry I still can't say for sure when I'll bring him; but soon, Janaynie, soon.

Your Devoted Full Sister,

Jilaynie

Chapter 15

ARRIVALS AND DEPARTURES

Month of May/Month of Willow

Selene and Erica waited just outside Security. The overhead monitors showed that Flight 1455 had landed ten minutes ago, but there was no trace of its passengers yet. "Hold your sign up the moment they start coming out," Selene said. "We can't let him get by us."

The two were dressed in matching outfits consisting of dark trousers and lightweight jackets—conservative and totally nonthreatening. Their attire would have labeled them as generic business staff anywhere, and it spoke of the variety of costumes available in the wardrobe room at Nyala. It wasn't all leather and latex. If a submissive's fantasy called for being "captured" and interrogated by a female CIA agent, there was always something appropriate for the Upstairs Girls to wear. And with a bit of creative mixing and matching, they could accommodate pretty much any scenario.

"How do we recognize him?" Erica asked. "Did Willie give you a description?"

"No. I casually got his flight information from her, but that's all. She mustn't suspect we're doing this."

"Then how are we supposed to find him?"

Selene shrugged. "That's the whole point of the sign, right? He's going to find us."

"Oh, right." said Erica. "My brain is half asleep this morning."

Selene laughed. "You need to cut back on the late-night playtime, girl. How's that new little sub of yours coming, anyway?"

Erica shook her head. "Tie a knot a teensy bit wrong, or touch her ass in a way that doesn't suit her, and she screams bloody murder: *'No! Not like that, Mistress! Can't you even tie an angler's knot? And don't use your hand. I can hardly feel it. Use the slapper I bought you!'*"

Erica's whiny impression had Selene in stitches. "You and Wynter seem to attract a lot of those." Wynter was one of the Upstairs Girls who worked at the club, a five-foot-four, full-figured Meliai with curly, jet-black hair and skin like Snow White. She was a favorite of clients who liked a gentler, more playful type of domme.

"Something about modern human females," Erica sighed. "I mean, those dance hall girls were meek as kittens when I was here 150 years ago, but *these* … they all want to tell you how to top them. I guess you and Willie are doing okay, though … if we're doing this, I mean."

"Yes. She's not a pure sub, but she's been damaged and desperately needs what I give her. I just want to get her stepfather out of the way so she can relax and stop obsessing about his visit … Okay, here they come. Get that sign up higher so he can see it."

A stream of passengers, exhausted by the long flight from Miami and laden with carry-ons, came pouring out of the terminal, heading for the baggage claim. Erica promptly held up the large card Selene had prepared: *Welcome, Rev. Harold Barton.* "I still wish we knew what he looks like," Erica said. "If he doesn't know we're waiting for him, he may not even notice us."

"No, that's him!" Selene said quickly, pointing to a tall, tanned, handsome man with steel-gray hair, wearing a beige tropical suit, and with a small carry-on slung over his shoulder. He was slim and tidy looking, and he hadn't spotted them yet.

"How do you know it's him?"

"Trust me," Selene said. "That's Harry."

"Okay, so who's that with him?" Erica asked, indicating a freckle-faced young woman who was glancing around nervously. The timid-looking girl was about five-eight, in her late teens, with long auburn hair and completely unadorned by makeup or jewelry. She was following so closely behind the tall man, she was almost huddled into his body.

Selene gasped. "Oh, Kayla … he's got Willie's daughter!"

"Impossible. You said Willie put her up for adoption."

"Yes … but it looks like Harry found her."

"Are you sure?" Erica said dubiously. "I say it's his jail-bait girlfriend."

"Probably both," Selene replied. "I mean, look at her hair and freckles, and just feel her energy. That is absolutely Willie's daughter—the 'big surprise' he was bringing. Damn, this really complicates things."

"Okay … so now what?" Erica asked.

Selene shook her head. "There's no way to separate them without causing a scene, so follow my lead until I get this figured out. Whatever happens, we have to keep them away from Willie. If she finds out he's got her daughter, she'll go mad."

Selene waved animatedly at the couple. The man looked startled when he spotted the "Welcome" sign, hesitated a moment, and then began walking toward them with long purposeful strides, the girl firmly in tow.

"I'm Reverend Barton," he said, looking them over skeptically. "Who are you?"

Selene ignored the patronizing tone in his voice. "We work for your daughter, Reverend," she said. "Ms. Ludlow asked us to pick you up and take you to her home."

"So … she's finally changed her mind about seeing me, then?" Harry said.

"I wouldn't know anything about that, sir. She just asked us to come out and collect you … and who is this lovely young lady?"

Harry looked at his companion, who was staring at the floor, unable to make eye contact with Selene or Erica. "This is … Clementine," he said, without further explanation. "We have hotel reservations."

"We'll cancel those for you, sir," Selene said quickly. "There's plenty of room for you at the estate." She'd pulled the word out of thin air, and it immediately impressed him.

"She's got an *estate?*"

"Well … more like a small mansion, really," Selene said. "But I'm sure you'll find it comfortable."

Harry looked thoughtful, trying to sort out the unexpected turn of events. "I wasn't expecting such a grand reception."

"Ms. Ludlow wishes to supply everything for your comfort, Reverend," Selene said, letting her hand fall casually on his shoulder. "This is Paula and I'm Maxine. Our job is to make your stay here as pleasant as possible. Paula, why don't you help these good people get their luggage? I'll have the limo brought around."

"Right this way, Reverend," Erica said. She took Harry by the arm and led him off to Baggage Claim, the shy Clementine trailing behind them.

Selene took a deep breath and tried to focus. *What the hell do I do with the girl?*

She pulled out her cell phone and speed-dialed Wynter, who was waiting in Short-Term Parking with the van. "Trouble," she said when Wynter answered. "There's two of them." She listened a moment. "No … It's a girl, and I'm sure it's Willie's daughter … Right, that's exactly what we have to avoid … No, there's no way to split them up. We'll have to send them both through and sort it out later."

Selene listened again for a few moments. "Good idea. Bring the van now. I want to get them to Nyala as soon as possible, and

I'll need both you and Erica to take them through the *Balacampa*. Once you're in Ausonia, get them separated quickly. Keep Harry locked up, but take the girl straight to the Upper Village and limit her contact with others. She'll be your project, so treat her like sugar and spice and stay with her 24/7 ... Okay, I'll leave that to you. Just keep her calm until she gets used to things. We'll see you out front."

Erica stowed the luggage in the back of the blue Explorer, as Harry and Clementine watched. Then she hopped into the front seat next to Wynter, who was wearing the same generic outfit as the other two Meliai, with the addition of a rakish chauffeur's cap. Selene introduced her as Shirley.

"I thought you said there was a limo," Harry said, looking dubiously at the van.

"Sorry," Selene said. "I forgot it's in the shop." She'd initially planned on sitting beside Harry in the back seat, where she'd have little trouble surprising him with a quick injection. Everything she needed was in the gym bag on the floor, but it would be more challenging having the daughter to deal with too. Fortunately, she'd brought a spare hypo.

"Let's give Clementine a window seat," Selene said to Harry as they climbed into the van. "You take the other and I'll sit between you. That way you can both enjoy the view." Being in the middle would make it easier for her to inject both of them.

But Harry insisted on taking one window seat and putting Clementine in the middle, which made things more difficult. Once again, Selene had to improvise. "You know," she said, "let's put Paula back here and I'll ride shotgun. She's smaller than I am, and it'll make things more comfortable for three."

Harry had no objection, so they made the switch, and Selene had just enough time to shoot Erica an empathic message telling her what she wanted.

"Okay, folks," Selene said, after everyone was seated. "Buckle up. We're on our way."

Harry buckled himself in, and Erica helped Clementine do the same, stealthily leaving her own seatbelt undone so that she could move into action quickly.

Once they were on the road, Selene suggested Erica pass her the gym bag to give their passengers more leg room in back, and it was easy for Selene to pull out a hypo, then turn and jab Harry in the neck, all with one deft motion.

"Ow!" he screamed. "What the hell!" Before he could unbuckle his seat harness, Selene took cuffs from the gym bag and vaulted into the back to secure his wrists.

"What is this?" Harry shouted. "Who are you people?"

Clementine began to cringe and whimper, and Erica used the spare hypo Selene handed her to inject the girl. But she did it as gently as possible, whispering to her and stroking her face. "Relax, honey," she said. "No one's going to hurt you, I promise."

Clementine buried her face in Erica's shoulder and lost consciousness quickly, though Harry hung on to his wits like a man clinging to a cliff by his fingers.

"Where are you taking us?" he demanded.

Selene laughed. "To a better place, Reverend."

Harry was becoming groggy, but sheer stubbornness kept him from going completely under. "Let ... us ... go, you ... whores. Where's my Wilhelmina?"

"Steady, Wynter," Selene said, climbing back into the front seat. "Just get us to the club and try not to draw attention. These two aren't going anywhere for now."

"Aye, aye, Captain," Wynter said with a grin, throwing Selene a mock salute. "Steady as she goes."

Wynter stayed well within the speed limit as she drove north along Highway 101. The last thing they needed now was a police stop, what with two trussed-up passengers in the back seat. All the while, Harry continued to mumble curses, struggling weakly against his bonds, a little stream of drool rolling from the side of his mouth.

"My ... such foul language from a Man of God," Selene tsked. "Things will be much easier if you just let yourself go under."

The insolence in her tone revived him a bit. "You women are mad! I demand to see Wilhelmina! I have my rights!" Selene wished she had one more hypo for him, marveling at the strength of will that kept him from succumbing to a dose of Pentothal that should put two humans his size out cold.

"Is this Willie's daughter?" she asked Harry.

"Go to hell," he mumbled, his head starting to droop.

Of course she's the daughter, Selene thought. *Just look at her. She's a younger Willie when you subtract a few inches from her height. Sending her through is my only choice for now. But then what? Do we keep her? No, I'll worry about that later. What's that adage humans have? "Sufficient unto the day are the evils thereof?" That's so sensible, it's almost like a Meliai thought it up.*

When they reached the junction to Highway 80, Wynter followed it to Fourth, where she exited, swung left onto Bryant, and then left again, before turning onto Folsom. Traffic was heavy, and it took another twenty minutes for them to reach the club.

"Park in the lot," Selene said.

"Wouldn't it be better to park out front?" Wynter asked. "It's closer to the Portal than the members' entrance."

"No, there'll be traffic this time of day. The club isn't open yet, so no one will see us around the side. Erica, go in and get the Portal ready and call me when you're done."

Wynter pulled into the parking lot and Erica hopped out, rushed to the main entrance, and then disappeared inside the building.

Selene looked into the back of the van, where she'd covered Harry and Clementine with blankets en route. The only movement was the slow rhythm of their breathing. The Dryads waited patiently, doing a *saphala* meditation, falling into it easily, as they'd learned to do when they'd been Nymphs centuries ago.

In about five minutes, Selene's phone rang. "Ready," Erica said.

"Okay," Selene said to Wynter. "You take Clementine, and I'll bring Harry. Let's get them inside before they wake up." She pocketed the phone and got out of the van.

Wynter hopped out of the driver's seat and lifted Clementine out of the back, cradling her as easily and delicately as if she were a child. Then Selene reached in, took hold of Harry, and hoisted him out far less gently. "Let's go, Reverend Rape," she said, slinging him across her shoulders. Moments later, the two Meliai, along with their human cargo, were inside the main lobby.

Although Clementine remained unconscious, Harry was beginning to stir again.

"Let's get a move on, Wynter," Selene said. "I want to get them settled on the other side before he wakes up."

But Harry did wake up abruptly, thrashing and kicking so hard that Selene had to set him down for a moment. Immediately, he tried to run. But with his wrists cuffed and his legs rubbery from the effect of the Pentothal, he lost his balance and tumbled onto his behind within a couple of steps, yelping in pain.

Selene grinned and helped him to his feet. "Relax. You're in no shape to go anywhere."

"What is this?" he demanded. "Who are you and what do you want?"

Selene faced him and growled. "We're your worst nightmare, Harry. We're demons and we're taking you to hell."

"No!" He was more frightened than angry now and tried to aim a kick at her shin. Selene deftly avoided it, giving his face a smack that made him recoil. Then she had an idea that made her laugh. "Hey, Wynter, let's show him the 'torture equipment' before we take him through."

They got into the elevator, Selene dragging Harry along while Wynter cradled the still-unconscious Clementine. Selene pushed the button marked "3" for the dungeon floor, and after a few moments, the doors opened into the club's main play space.

"Oh, Lord," Harry said, when his eyes fell on the whips, chains and other "toys" scattered about the place. "It's … a charnel house."

Selene and Wynter both laughed. "That's right," Selene said. "We're going to flay the flesh right off you."

Harry tried to bolt again, but Selene increased the pressure on his arm until he whimpered in pain and settled down enough to let her lead him through another door at the back of the dungeon, followed closely by Wynter carrying the still-insensate Clementine. He stumbled as they walked down a passageway, then through a fire door and took the freight elevator down to the dim service lobby.

Erica stood there waiting for them beside the green metal door with the strange humming sound coming from behind it.

"We're almost home, Reverend." Selene said.

"What's in there?" Harry asked, his voice shaky as he eyed the door suspiciously. "It sounds like an electric chair. You're going to kill us, aren't you?"

"*You* probably deserve it," Selene replied. "But that would be a horrible thing to do to an innocent girl—especially if she happens to be my lover's daughter." That got his attention in exactly the way she'd meant it to.

"Well, I should have known," Harry sneered. "I brought Clementine here to reunite her with her mother in the hope that Wilhelmina may have changed during all this time. But now I've just got a mind to take her daughter back to Orlando, since Wilhelmina obviously remains an unfit mother."

"You are just totally full of yourself, aren't you?" Selene said. "I mean, first you rape Willie for what … five years? Then you father her child, and now you have the nerve to call her an unfit mother?"

Harry's face reddened in fury. "She told you that? Well, it's a complete lie. Wilhelmina is not my blood daughter, so there was never any incest, not according to the Bible or the Law. And nothing happened that she didn't freely consent to."

Selene rolled her eyes. "Okay, whatever. As far as the incest goes, we won't even mention Clementine for now. But the point is you're not going to hurt Willie again, and your 'relationship' with Clementine—whatever that may be—is finished too."

"What right do you have to do this?" Harry demanded. "Who the hell are you?"

Selene laughed. "He wants to know who we are, ladies. Maybe it's time to show him. Wynter, let him see your eyes."

Wynter smiled. "Okay … Give me a hand here."

Selene released Harry and took Clementine from Wynter's arms. His eyes darted about, seeing there was no place to run. He watched in astonishment as Wynter slipped her thumbs and index fingers into her eye sockets and … —removed her eyes. More precisely, she removed the brown-tinted contacts that were disguising her natural eye color. Harry's jaw dropped in disbelief. Beneath the contacts, Wynter's left iris was the color of burnished gold, while the right was a pool of quicksilver starlight.

"Your turn, Erica," Selene said, and Erica removed her own contacts, revealing a gray left eye and a violet right.

"Now look at my eyes, Harry," Selene said. "See? Like I said, we're demons straight from the hot place." Balancing Clementine carefully in her arms, she pointed downward with an index finger, her meaning unmistakable.

Harry moaned and began to shake violently. "Oh, Jesus, my Savior … help me."

Clementine stirred and mumbled something inaudible. She was coming to, and Selene handed her back to Wynter before seizing Harry by the arm again.

"Okay, go ahead," Selene said to Erica, who put her weight against the green door and pushed it open. Harry saw what seemed like a dark storage room, but with a purplish glow in the shape of a huge egg floating in midair. The glowing egg was semi-transparent, flickering slightly as it hummed and crackled.

"What is it?" Harry said, mesmerized by the sight.

Selene ignored him. "Okay, Wynter," she said. "Take Clementine through, but gently."

The girl opened her eyes and looked up into Wynter's face, smiling beatifically. "Are you an angel?" she asked.

Wynter laughed and kissed the girl's forehead. "No, sweetheart. I'm a Meliai. The only angel here is you." She stepped through the door carrying the girl, pausing just as she reached the glowing egg. Then she looked back at Selene and grinned. "See you soon." With that, she took a step forward and vanished along with Clementine.

Harry gasped. "Where did they go?"

"You're about to find out," Selene said. "Take him, Erica."

Erica took firm hold of Harry's arm, and he moaned again, too weak with terror to struggle against her surprising strength.

"Remember to keep them separated," Selene cautioned.

"Okay. But ... where should I stash him?"

Selene thought a moment then broke into a grin. "Let's put him with the goats."

Erica laughed and nudged Harry forward. "This won't hurt much," she said.

When she pulled him into the glowing egg, Harry felt like he was swimming through molasses, bathed in light with static electricity coursing through him. It tickled more than hurt, and he had a maddening urge—impossible to gratify—to scratch his heart and liver. For a moment, he tumbled sickeningly, down and down, before falling out onto soft, sweet-scented earth. He had a brief impression of trees and dense green light filtering down from above, just before he lost consciousness again.

*"To her Changeling, the foolish Dryad says 'thou art mine,'
But the wise one adds 'and I am thine.'"*
—*The Book of Kayla*

Chapter 16

⚹

"Goodnight, Lester"

Month of May/Month of Willow

"Myra, honey," Lester said, reaching for Jill, who took his bony hand between both of hers. It was after visiting hours, but David had made arrangements with the hospice for them to come at 6:00 this evening to accommodate Jill's early shift at the club.

"Dad," David said, "this isn't Mom. It's Jill, my girlfriend. You've met her before, when we came to visit. Remember?"

Lester nodded. "Thanks for coming, Jill. David is lucky to have such a lovely lady."

Jill smiled, lifted Lester's hand to her mouth and kissed it. "And he's lucky to have such a sweet father." She turned to David, who was near tears at seeing Lester's further deterioration. "He seems a bit better tonight," she whispered. "Don't you think?"

David knew she was trying to cheer him up and that she probably didn't believe it, but it was comforting to have her company. "When I was here Friday, he kept calling me Fred and said he forgave me."

"Who's Fred?" Jill asked.

"Search me. The guy Myra left Dad for is Frank. Maybe that's who he was forgiving."

They were speaking quietly as they sat by Lester's bedside and David was sure he couldn't hear them. "Forgiveness like that is hard to muster when you've been so wounded," Jill said. "I can see where your generous heart comes from, Lamb Chop."

"That generous I'm not. Lester was never strong enough for Mom."

"What do you call *strong*?" Jill said. "I'm never sure what people mean by that, outside of physical strength."

David shrugged. "In his case, 'strong' would have been not letting himself be pushed around by her."

Jill laughed. "Like I do with you in bed?"

"That's playtime. You're never emotionally abusive."

"Okay, but you've been carrying this bitterness against your mother around forever, and it's hurting you way more than her."

"You know, I actually used to be angrier at him for wanting her back than I was at her for walking out in the first place? That really sucks, doesn't it?"

Jill felt the knife-edge of pain in him. Physical pain was something any Meliai could understand, but the emotional agony humans inflicted on themselves was impossible to fathom. Still, if *nyalic* humans weren't so emotionally crippled, there would be no Changelings and then no more Meliai.

It was hard to deny that human misery enabled Dryads to survive. But the Meliai weren't the cause of that misery; they were simply using its by-product—*nyala*—to stave off their own extinction. Like all Meliai, Jill had been taught as a Nymph that they were healing humans by giving them the gift of perfect bliss and immortality, while asking just one trifling thing in return.

But having David as her "project" was becoming much too personal for her. Not only was he touching her heart in disturbing ways but so was Lester.

Lindt, Lester's cancer-ridden roommate, had passed away, and David's sizable cash donation to the hospice had persuaded management to let his father have the room to himself for now, despite their waiting list. David didn't care about the money or their waiting list. The important thing was for Lester to have some privacy, without having to listen to the moaning of a terminal patient in the bed behind that curtain.

David sighed. "Dad's a better man than I'll ever be ... not that it got him much."

"So are you feeling sorrier for him or yourself?" Jill asked.

"Can't get anything past you, can I?"

Jill laughed again. "Get something past your Mistress? You know better than that."

David smiled. He was the proverbial open book to her, and she always seemed to know exactly what he was feeling, as if with some sixth sense. It was uncanny and sometimes disconcerting that he could hide so little from her. But it was also delightful because she never used her insights as a weapon, and being so emotionally naked to Jill could be devastatingly sexy when she was devouring his body and soul with such erotic ferocity.

Lester seemed to be sleeping again, and David looked at his watch. It was nearly 7:00 and he was getting hungry. "This might be a good time to slip out," he said, getting up from his chair. "I'm starved. We should get some dinner and let him rest."

Jill stood to leave with him, but just as she did, Lester's eyes opened, and he managed to prop himself up on one elbow. "You're leaving already?"

"Well, um," David said, "it's a long drive and we haven't eaten yet." But the truth was that seeing his father in this place depressed him terribly and he just wanted to be home in bed with Jill.

"Come on, David," Jill said, calling him David instead of Lamb Chop, as she did when she wanted to scold or light a fire under him. "We can stay a few more minutes."

Lester was obviously following this, because he said, "Not you, son. You can wait outside, but your mother promised to sit on my face last time she was here."

David felt a rush of anger. "Dad, this is Jill, not Myra! I won't allow you to speak to her that way."

But Jill laughed and led him out into the hallway. "It's okay, Lamb Chop, really. He didn't mean to insult me. In fact, I'm actually kind of flattered."

"Flattered? For God's sake, why?"

"It's just what I feel. Does there have to be a reason?"

"He's my father, Jill. And he has no right to say things like that to you."

"But he's sick and can't help it. Have some compassion."

Abashed, David looked down at the floor. "You're right, I guess. The old man hasn't been with a woman in over twenty years."

"Yes," said Jill. "Which is why I'm going to do it."

"What do you mean, 'do it'? Do what?"

"Give him his wish, of course."

It took a moment for David to get what she was saying. "You can't be serious, Jill. That's worse than crazy … it's sick."

She stood ramrod straight, seeming to tower over him. "David, listen to me. It is not sick. Your father is dying, and I want to give him a loving gift, a gift of myself. Surely you can't be jealous. It's not like he's stealing me away from you. And it's just this once."

"No! Absolutely not! I forbid it."

Jill put her face against his, nose-to-nose. "You forbid it? *Forbid?* Don't make me go all domme on you, David, or I will flog the shit out of you when we get home … and it won't be a prelude to anything sexy."

In their four months together, she'd never torn into him like this, but now she was a veritable Fury, and David took two steps back, suddenly afraid of her.

But as quickly as the storm struck, it was over and she softened. "Oh, Lamb Chop, I'm sorry. Of course I wouldn't do it without your permission, but Lester needs this so badly." She slithered up against him, wrapped her arms around his neck, and kissed him. "Think of it as a gift, not just from me, but from both of us—a sweet way to send him into the next life. Let's be generous together. You're not going to lose me, I promise."

When she put it like that, it seemed petty to refuse. But this was his father, and when he thought about it *that* way, it was revolting. Still, David's own nature had forced him to shed a lot of conventions long ago. Was he now going to be a tight-assed pillar of social orthodoxy, instead of allowing his father a little comfort before he died?

"But why does it have to be you?" he said. "What about one of the other girls at the club?"

Jill nodded. "I'm sure Erica would be happy to oblige. And Wynter really likes you, so I'm sure she'd do it too, if you explained and asked nicely."

David breathed a sigh of relief. "Okay, then. Lester always loved big tits, so he'll be crazy about Wynter. We'll dress her up as a nurse and sneak her in the back way."

"Well, maybe," Jill pouted, taking his hand and nibbling at his finger. "But it wouldn't be as personal, would it? I mean, Wynter's never even met Lester … and she's not your beloved like I am. So it wouldn't really be a gift from both of us, would it?"

He knew he was beaten, so there was no point in drawing this out. "Jesus, Jill, I can't believe I'm agreeing. I mean, what sane boyfriend would let the girl he loves fuck his father? It's just … not normal."

"Don't worry," she said. "I'm not going to fuck him. Just let him give my pussy a couple of friendly licks." She leaned in to kiss David again. "I love my Lamb Chop, and I'm going to show him just how much when we get home. Do you want to watch? This is a gift from both of us, after all."

David shook his head. That was something he definitely didn't need to see. "Pass," he said. "I'll stay out here and make sure no one comes in."

Jill nodded. "Okay, I won't be long."

It took about fifteen minutes and was lovely, Jill thought. Lester had been fully aware and skilled enough to give her a nice orgasm once he understood what she wanted, which was just for him to lie on his back as she straddled his face on the bed. He'd even gotten a slight erection, though she hadn't touched his cock, both in deference to David and since it wasn't what Lester seemed to want anyway.

Afterwards, she stood at the side of the bed, hiked her skirt up, and gave him a long look at her ass as she bent and wriggled back into her panties, marveling that David had actually agreed to let her do this. Why had she pushed him into it? *To take the measure of his courage, of course,* she thought. *If he was willing to give me this, he'll never be more ready than now to be my Changeling. But, Kayla, I don't feel ready. Is there any way to give it just a little more time?*

She tabled the question and looked down at David's father, who had a big smile on his face. "Goodnight, Lester," she said, planting a small kiss on his thin lips. "David loves you very much, you know."

Chapter 17

JILL

Later that night ...

David was sound asleep, making that awful growling sound called "snoring." Nearly all humans I've been with have done it in their sleep, so I'm used to it by now. But the first time I heard it, I thought Lynette was choking to death on a bug that had lodged in her throat.

I acted to save her, and when she woke with a start, the poor creature found I was giving her *silach oon*, which is what humans call the Heimlich maneuver. She had no idea what was happening and screamed so loud I thought the whole building would hear, and that nosy Mrs. Ray downstairs would call the police.

I eased myself out from under the covers gingerly, so as not to wake David. I felt vile for having hurt him so badly, but I was desperate and running out of time to save my tree and, with it, my own life. I needed to see how far he'd actually go to please me, and when he'd flatly refused to let me have sex with Lester, I panicked and just dominated him with my will until he'd finally relented.

David barely said a word as we drove home, and when we got into bed, he'd sullenly refused to make love for the first time ever. I was miserable, but the unexpected opportunity Lester had given me by thinking I was his wife was something I couldn't pass up, since it might be months before I got a chance to test David like this again. What if he left me, and everything I'd been working for fell apart?

I made my way into the little kitchen of the Inverness house, with its old gas stove whose burners had to be lit with a match, its chipped enameled sink that would never stop dripping, and the tiny wooden cabinets with glass windows that let you see the dishes inside. I took the goat's milk from the refrigerator, poured out a cup, and began heating it on the stove, hoping it would help me relax. David hates the taste of goat's milk, but I can't drink cow's milk, which no Dryad can digest.

It was nearly 3:00 a.m., and I was sick with worry. After failing with Lynette, what was I going to do if I lost David, especially with Janaynie pressing me to get him back to Ausonia for transformation as soon as possible?

But who was I kidding? I wasn't just afraid of failing to secure a Changeling. I was afraid of losing *him* because I had feelings for him, and that was even more dangerous than my Full Sister's fury, or the Tribunal's wrath. Not only was I risking my own life and Janaynie's, but my love for David was jeopardizing the long-term survival of my entire clan, because time was running out for all of us. I had to stop this madness and get back on program.

Besides, it wasn't like I was going to harm David. In fact, if he was doomed to get Lester's illness, I'd be saving him. But, then again, there was no way to be sure he'd even get sick. When humans carry a serious genetic defect, a Meliai can sense it with *kash* and have an idea of how long they have to live. In David's case, though, I couldn't get a fix on his condition, no matter how hard I tried. Sometimes, when I looked inside him, there was a shadow there and it was obvious that he soon would become ill. But other times he seemed perfectly healthy.

Of course, he had no idea I was examining him, and I could hardly tell him I was using my empathic abilities to sift through his genes like a gardener looking for one blade of crab grass in an otherwise perfect lawn. But still, I could tell no more with my own probing than his human doctors could with theirs.

The safest thing for David would be to take him home and begin his transformation quickly, because no human ailment can persist after that first dose of *Fleen*. But the irony was that in giving David what Kayla called "The Luminous Gift," I would lose the part of him that had become so precious to me—the quality that made him uniquely David. Finding the human who would become her Changeling was supposed to make a Meliai celebrate, yet I'd been miserable for weeks.

I took the pan off the stove, poured the milk into a cup, stirred in a teaspoon of molasses plus a pinch of salt, and sat at the kitchen table, sipping my favorite Meliai sleep concoction as I tried to think this through. My wanting to keep David human wasn't really "love," was it? It was desire, a selfish need to keep him just as he was so I could—so I could what? Keep on fucking him? There was nothing in *Sufadel* that forbid something as natural as sex. In fact, sexual fulfillment was a requirement for living "The Harmonious Life." Without experiencing sexual ecstasy at least two or three times each day, a Meliai's soul might become as twisted as an Oread's.

If I framed it like that, saying that David was the most transcendent sexual partner I'd ever had and that my *thalla* would shrivel up without him, The Tribunal might give me a special dispensation, their permission to keep him as he was while I found another human to transform.

But, of course, that was nonsense. David was a nice play partner, but he couldn't measure up to Selene, Nellyn, or any of my Meliai lovers. The sex was good and getting better, but that wasn't why I wanted to keep him. David touched something in me that no Meliai ever had; that was the truth of it. The Tribunal would see right through my story and remind me that not only was my life at stake, but I was endangering Janaynie and the entire clan, which could hardly afford to lose two more girls. The Meliai were dying out, and every *nyalic* human we took was the raw material that could help save us. That was what we were taught as Nymphs, and it was truer now than ever.

The humans we chose had a destiny to fulfill, and trying to keep David as he was—well, it was criminally selfish. Suitable *nyalic* humans were rare; they didn't grow on trees like *peloons*. And with the speed at which the blight was spreading, we needed every appropriate human we could find. Our mages calculated that if we didn't stop the blight soon, we had two hundred years, maybe three at most, before we became extinct. Reason told me that David belonged not just to me, but to all the Meliai, and I had no right to withhold him. But reason was savagely at war with my heart.

I was so wrapped up in my thoughts I didn't hear him come padding into the kitchen in the suede slippers I'd bought him last week. "Trouble sleeping, huh?" he asked coolly, sitting in the chair beside me.

I looked at him and nodded. "You're still angry with me, aren't you?"

"It's okay. I'm over it." His denial was unconvincing.

"No, you're not."

"Okay, I'm *trying* to get over it ... and to get over hating my father too."

"Lester is very sweet," I said. "He would never do anything to hurt you ... and neither would I. You know that, Lamb Chop, don't you?"

His answer was pointed as an Oread's knife. "Do I?"

He was being childish hated, and I fought the urge to snap at him again. "Of course you do. I mean, how can you possibly doubt that?"

He shrugged. "That whole thing was just so weird. I didn't know how to say 'no' to you ... or even if I really wanted to. I mean, Lester hasn't got long, and he's given me so much. I felt like a heel for saying 'no' and a wimp for saying 'yes.'"

"Poor baby," I said, caressing his cheek. "I put you in a terrible spot, didn't I?"

He looked at me sadly and shook his head. "I'm not even sure where we go from here. I keep thinking how Willie told me it was dangerous to fall in love with you."

He seemed so forlorn. How could I fix this? *Tell me, Kayla,* I prayed. *Give me the right words to say to him.*

At first, there was only silence, and then she spoke in my mind. *Remind him of the first time he said he loved you. Remind him of what he did.*

I understood immediately. "Do you remember that poem you read to me the first time we spent a night at your apartment?"

"'The Song of Wandering Aengus' by Yeats? Yeah, I remember."

"You said that I was the magical girl in the poem."

David laughed. "You seemed that way at the time."

"Read it for me again," I said. "It's so beautiful."

"You want me to recite a poem … now?"

"Yes … please."

He thought about it a moment and smiled. "Maybe … but what's in it for me?"

"I'll give you one of those special foot rubs you love so much."

He laughed again. "Oh, right. I know how those always end up."

"That's the whole idea," I said, giving him a mischievous grin. "Do you remember how it goes or should I get the book from the study?"

"No … Yeats is my favorite poet. I know that one by heart.

"I went out in the hazel wood,
Because a fire was in my head,
And cut and peeled a hazel wand
And hooked a berry to a thread;
And when white moths were on the wing,
And moth-like stars were flickering out,
I dropped the berry in a stream
And caught a little silver trout.

When I had laid it on the floor
I went to blow the fire a-flame,
But something rustled on the floor,
And someone called me by my name:
It had become a glimmering girl
With apple blossoms in her hair
Who called me by my name and ran
And faded through the brightening air.
Though I am old with wandering
Through hollow lands and hilly lands,
I will find out where she has gone,
And kiss her lips and take her hands;
And walk among long dappled grass,
And pluck till time and times are done,
The silver apples of the moon,
The golden apples of the sun."

After that we went back to bed, and he loved me like I was the only girl he'd ever had and feared I'd vanish like a phantom if he didn't hang on tight.

Chapter 18

⸱⸱⸱

The "Fish Bowel"

Month of May/Month of Willow

"*I* don't get it," Glenda said, picking a curried shrimp out of the carton with her chopsticks. "I mean, it's been four days and he's never even called?"

Willie scooped up another forkful of spicy eggplant. "Nope … never showed up and never called to say why. The fucker's flight arrived on time Tuesday, and he was definitely on the plane, but then, *poof* … he evaporated into thin air."

Willie and Glenda were sitting in what they affectionately called the "Fish Bowel," the tiny conference room at the back of Green Girl's offices, sharing a lunch of curried shrimp and spicy eggplant from Brandy Ho's.

The room's actual name was the Fish *Bowl* because of its glass walls, but spelling was not Glenda's strength, and when she'd sent Willie an email saying "meet me in the Fish Bowel" their first week in business, Willie had teased her about the invitation to meet inside the shit tube of a fish. They'd both laughed so hard that the Fish Bowel had been their pet name for the room ever since.

They usually quit work at noon on Fridays to give themselves an early start on the weekend, and their delivered lunch before leaving the office had become a tradition. Not only did it give them a chance to go over the past work week, but it was one of the few chances they had to get caught up on their personal lives.

"You tried calling his hotel?" Glenda asked.

"A bunch of times. They had him booked with his wife: Reverend and Mrs. Harold Barton, but they never checked in or canceled." Willie speared a couple of Glenda's shrimp with her fork, then took a sip of Diet Coke.

"You never said he remarried after your mother died."

"Are you kidding?" Willie said cynically. "Why would he need a wife when he had me? It obviously happened after I left him."

Glenda reached across the little conference table with her chopsticks and nimbly plucked some eggplant from Willie's carton. "Maybe he was afraid to face the grown-up you, so he chickened out and flew back home."

"I thought of that," Willie said. "But if he did, it wasn't on the same airline. Besides, he wouldn't just turn around and go home. Not after spending all that dough to fly out here. It's like he just fell down a rabbit hole."

"Hey, maybe he was kidnapped by Barbary pirates and you'll be getting a ransom demand any day now."

Willie grinned. "I think it's a couple of centuries late for pirates. You have a fevered imagination, girl."

Glenda laughed, reaching for more eggplant. "Speaking of my fevered imagination, I'm dying to know the story with you and this new love of yours. I mean, except for the Harry thing, you've been walking on cloud nine."

Willie grinned. "You know I'm not a kiss and tell girl."

"Oh, the hell you aren't. Come on, Willie. Who the fuck is she?"

"She's just someone I met ... thanks to David, I guess."

Glenda's ears perked up. "David introduced you to a friend of his? Tell me, tell me!"

Willie immediately regretted dragging David's name into it. After all, it was a story that might embarrass him too. But Glenda was in full interrogation mode.

"No," Willie said hesitantly. "I mean, he didn't actually introduce us. It's … well, it's kind of hard to explain."

That piqued Glenda's curiosity even more. "Oh, my God … she's David's ex, right?" She leaned forward and wagged her chopsticks at Willie. "No, no, wait … she's someone he has a crush on, and you went in and gobbled her up behind his back. Wow, you are wicked."

Willie shook her head. "C'mon, I'd never do that to David. Stop inventing shit."

"Well, you're being very mysterious, Willie Ludlow," Glenda said. "I can't begin to tell you the intrigues I'm imagining right now. If there's great sex happening, I require details, uncensored, X-rated details." She used her chopsticks to bat Willie's fork away when she reached for another shrimp. "Tell me all the dirty stuff or no more shrimp for you. Oh, my Lord … you're blushing."

"I am not."

"Oh, no? You should see your ears. They're redder than my lipstick."

Willie rolled her eyes, but she was actually ready to have the story pried out of her. In fact, she was dying to share it. "Okay, but it doesn't leave this room. Swear?"

Glenda spat on a finger and crossed her heart. "Slut's Code of Honor."

Willie laughed. "There's no such code."

"Okay, okay. Then friend-to-friend … my lips are sealed."

And so she told Glenda the whole story, or at least most of it: how David had fallen for a dominatrix and how she herself, trying to protect him, had gone to Nyala and inadvertently threatened the wrong domme in an attempt to "free him from her clutches." Then, carefully omitting the part about how the Headmistress had slapped her, she told Glenda that Selene had been attracted and phoned her for an afternoon date in Golden Gate Park. "After that, I guess one thing just led to another."

Glenda's jaw dropped. "Holy shit, you're actually dating a dominatrix …and a famous one at that?"

"You're disgusted, right?" Willie said. "I knew you would be. That's why I haven't told you before."

"Disgusted? Willie, this is so deliciously kinky I'm thrilled to my toes. You rock, sister."

Relieved, Willie smiled, now feeling a bit smug. "I do sort of rock, don't I?"

"Have you told David about you and Selene?"

Willie sighed and nodded. "After that sermon I gave him about his relationship with Jill, it wasn't easy. But he's my best friend, so I bit the bullet and fessed up."

"Ouch!" Glenda said. "That can't have been easy. He must have chewed you a new asshole after you gave him such a hard time for doing the same thing."

Willie smiled ruefully. "That's just it. He didn't do anything like that, though God knows, he had a right to. He just said he was happy for me. And as it turns out, Jill is a sweetheart and hot as hell. He needs to be careful, because every guy she meets hits on her. But other than that, she's the best thing that's happened to him in years."

"Well, good for him," Glenda said. "I could never understand why he had so much trouble finding women. I'd roll over like a cat for him if I was into men." She broke open her fortune cookie, contemplated the slip silently, and then read it aloud: *There is no blessing like a forgiving friend.*

"Wow, no kidding." Willie said, breaking open her own cookie. She looked at the note, laughed delightedly, and then read it to Glenda: *Convention is oft' the enemy of passion.*

"Shit," Glenda said. "I get dorky sentiment and you get steamy sex. So, tell me, does Selene tie you up? I've always fantasized about that."

"No, no …. That's just for her clients. But she's got all these, well, tricks …"

Glenda cackled. "I'm sure she does."

"Okay. If you're going to get snarky, I'm done here."

"All right, all right! Sorry. So what exactly does she do that 'regular' girls don't?"

Willie wondered how to say it without sounding debauched. "It's a little weird, but it's just so fucking luscious. She does a lot of stuff I'd never even imagined before."

"Like what?" Glenda asked, giving Willie a lascivious grin.

"Like … well I know this may sound silly, but she does this thing with her feet."

"Her feet?" Glenda said, barking out another laugh. "She fucks with her feet?"

"Well, yes and no. It's hard to describe. I mean, that's not all we do. But I swear, Glenda, I've never in my life had orgasms like the ones I have with Selene. It's like I'm finally starting to understand how sex was meant to be."

Glenda was no longer laughing. She was silent for a few moments, then said, "So … does Selene have any single friends?"

Chapter 19

JANAYNIE

12th day of Hawthorn, 5336

Jilaynie,

The letter I received from you today was devastating. Your decision to let David remain human is madness and cruel beyond belief. It's not enough that you robbed me of my birthright, now you are endangering my very life.

But my own survival is secondary. Do you realize that you're in direct violation of Sufadel and putting our entire clan at risk? Surely you know The Tribunal will learn of this. Not from me, of course, but they'll hear about it soon enough and force The Council to take action against you. What that might be I don't know but, at the very least, you'll be banished from Ausonia. Who knows, they may even decide to eliminate both you and David as a warning to others.

The idea that The Tribunal will go easy on you because you hold a Council seat is incredibly naïve. In fact, your position might even weigh against you if they want to prove they play no favorites. That's the reality of life in Ausonia right now. "Desperate times require desperate measures." Isn't that another of those human sayings our Clan Mother is so fond of?

Please, Jilaynie, think again about what you're doing. If you care so little for your own life, at least send David through the Balacampa alone, so that I can collect him on this end and transform him myself. You have my word that I'll treat him with kindness.

Still, I beg you to abandon this deviant plan and bring him yourself, so that we can make him our Changeling together. I have no wish to see you banished from home or worse, and I don't want to see the human you've put so much effort into go to waste.

If you come to your senses now, we can still salvage this situation before The Tribunal discovers you've gone rogue. I will destroy your letter and we'll forget you ever wrote it.

Your Faithful Full Sister,

Janaynie

Chapter 20

❧

JILAYNIE

19th day of Hawthorn, 5336

Dear Janaynie,

I don't blame you for being furious with me. I have no excuse, except that I just can't bring myself to do it. There is something precious about David that won't let me transform him, even if it costs me my life. Meliai rarely fall in love with the humans they choose—and when they do, we see it as a dangerous obsession. But having deep affection for them is important, and maybe that's all I feel for him. Not love but just an overwhelming fondness for who he is—his kindness, his smile, his endless passion for me and yes, that adorable dimple in his chin. Or perhaps T'Erenya really has corrupted me beyond hope and I am "in love" with him.

The truth is that I'm just too sentimental for this task, and The Council should have sent you instead of me. I was always the dreamer, and you the practical one, and this job requires a realist whose feelings won't get in the way of doing what's necessary. I was sent here to save both of us, and I've utterly failed. Now you must save yourself, darling, so come here and do what I couldn't. If I'm banished or die, the Council must allow that. Find another human to be your Changeling. Take anyone but David, who is wrong for you in so many ways.

You never liked males anyway, so choose a female human you're compatible with. And if you want a daughter, you can always borrow a male from one of the other girls to give you a Nymph. Aneel would be happy to lend you William for a night or two in the orchard, don't you think? A human female as your Changeling and Aneel's male to give you a beautiful daughter; it sounds perfect.

It's not likely we'll see each other again, Janaynie. I'm not sure where I'll go, but I must leave soon. I can't take David, though I'm sure he would follow me anywhere if I said he'd lose me otherwise. But his father is dying, and it would be cruel to make him choose between coming with me and staying to care for Lester. Besides, if I asked him to go with me, I'd have to explain why I can't stay, and I'm done lying to him.

There is just no safe way for me to remain with David. Selene doesn't understand why I keep making excuses for not taking him through the Portal when he seems so ready, and eventually I'd have to tell her the truth. Of course she's my friend, but even if she lets me keep David as he is, The Tribunal wouldn't be as understanding. If they found the two of us living together, with me still bent on keeping him human, it would go badly for both of us, and their wrath might fall on Selene too. I'm not worried for myself, but I couldn't bear to see Selene and David hurt because of me.

I don't know, maybe I'll come back for him someday, especially if I feel him becoming ill. My kash is so in tune with him now, I can sense what he's feeling every minute and could do it from halfway around this insane world.

I want to stay with him, Janaynie, but I know I must leave quickly and without a trace. Please forgive me. And if you can still find room in your heart, say a prayer to Kayla for me.

Ever your Full Sister,

Jilaynie

Chapter 21

⚜

ASHES AND ANGELS

Month of October/Month of Vine

"*Y*ou're not planning to keep these in the house, are you?" Willie asked, gingerly touching the urn resting above the fireplace. "I mean, you're going to scatter them outside, right?"

The Inverness house was now officially his, or would be after Lester's will was read next week. But to David, it felt like his father's energy was still as much a part of the place as the ratty old furniture Lester had never been able to let go of, because Myra had decorated the house and Lester feared she'd be upset if she came back and found he'd changed the look she'd worked so hard to create decades ago.

David took the urn off the mantel and wiped at a smudge with a buffing cloth. "Well, Lester wanted to be cremated but never said what to do with the ashes. I figure I'll have some kind of memorial out by the oak tree in a couple of months and scatter him around the roots. He planted it for Mom and it's not doing that well, so maybe his ashes will revive it."

"Okay, but why wait?" Willie said. "Keeping his ashes around is morbid."

David put the urn back on the mantel and contemplated it. "I guess I'm not ready to let go of Dad yet, and scattering him seems so final."

"Yeah, well, fuck cremation," Willie said. "I want to be buried when I die. At least there'll be something left of me, even if it's just bones. The thought of having my ashes blow away in the wind is just too scary ... like turning into nothing."

David shrugged. "What's wrong with that? Some Buddhists say that when you die, you just evaporate like a snowflake dissolving in air. They think it's beautiful."

The idea made Willie shiver. "You're giving me the creeps, dude. Can we talk about something else? Like have you told your mother Lester's dead?"

He nodded. "I called her Wednesday. First time in over a year we've spoken."

"How did she react?"

"About like I figured: 'Oh, dear. So sorry to hear that. But sick as he was, I'm sure it was for the best.' I could almost hear her struggling to find just one genuine emotion. I have to keep reminding myself that it's not personal with her. She's got her current life and has no time or energy to think about the one she left behind."

Willie adjusted her glasses with a forefinger. "You've got what ... two half-brothers?"

"Don and Phil," David said. "I guess they'd be fifteen and seventeen now. I haven't seen any of them in three years and have zero desire to go to Oklahoma City again. That time I went for Christmas ... it was like walking into the home of this perfect TV family from the 1960s. I mean, they felt almost fictional: no bickering, no cursing, everyone sits down to dinner at exactly 6:00 and says grace. Then soup, salad, main course, and dessert, all served up like clockwork. And everything is 'please pass the turnips,' and 'may I leave the table now?' You've never seen a house that spotless. I swear, their live-in maid dusted and vacuumed every day.

"I felt so out of place all I could think about was stealing their silverware and kicking their yappy little dog. I was like the Grinch who stole Christmas. I mean, when it was time to leave, I just slithered off to the airport on my belly."

Willie laughed. "Your heart didn't grow three sizes like the Grinch's, huh? Jesus, I'm amazed people survive their families at all. You're lucky to have had Lester."

David was silent for a moment. "I miss him, Willie. And, God, I miss *her*."

Willie knew that "her" did not mean his mother. She put an arm around David and led him silently to the sofa, where she sat him down, then walked to the liquor cabinet to get the vodka and a couple of shot glasses. Lester had died quietly in his sleep six days ago, and coming just three months after Jill's death, it was too much for David.

Losing two people you loved in such a short time was more than anyone should have to endure, but tragedies like that happened, and people either grieved it out and went on with their lives, or else fell apart. So, when Lester died, Willie had taken time off from work to stay with David, making it her job to see he took the former route and not the latter.

Of course, Lester's death had long been expected and as Dr. Bellows predicted, it was respiratory failure, not Huntington's, that finally killed him. Jill's death, though, had been a staggering shock, coming just a few days after she'd agreed to marry David. He still hadn't come to terms with it, and now, with his father's passing, he was so fragile that Willie feared he'd crack like a china teacup.

She carried the vodka bottle and glasses back to the sofa, set them on the coffee table, and poured them each a shot, handing one to David, who downed it in a single gulp. *"Na Zdorovie,"* he said, offering the traditional Russian toast and pouring himself another.

"I think you're supposed to say the toast before chugging, not after," Willie said.

"I know, but I remembered too late, so I'm starting over."

"Cute, but drinking yourself unconscious again won't change anything." She raised her own glass and offered another toast. "To Lester's memory ... and to Jill's."

"To Lester," David said and clinked glasses, though this time he drank slowly.

"Why not to Jill?" Willie asked, taking a small sip from her glass.

"Because Lester's gone for good and Jill's just missing. I won't drink to her like she's dead."

Willie cringed inwardly. He hadn't brought this nonsense up in weeks, and she'd been hoping he'd finally let go of the pathetic delusion that Jill was still alive. "David, cut it out! You've got to face facts. Jill is dead."

The pain in his eyes made her regret her brusque tone. But it wasn't going to help him if she coddled this absurd fiction. "Look, honey, I'm so sorry about everything you're going through. But you can't keep living in a fantasy world."

David downed the rest of his vodka and set the glass down. "No. She can't be dead. They never even found a body, just her empty Prius."

"Look," Willie said, keeping her voice calm despite a growing irritation with this nonsense, "she fell asleep at the wheel and her car went off a cliff into the ocean. That is a fact. The police say she was washed out to sea and they'll probably never find her body. Selene was her closest friend and she believes Jill's dead, so why can't you?"

David started to pour himself another drink then paused. "And why can't *you* see the police report is moronic? If she was washed out to sea, how come the passenger door was closed? Did the ocean open it, suck her out of the car, and then close it again?"

"Well, that's the only logical answer, isn't it?" Willie said. "There was a strong tide that night, and there are no other theories."

"Except for mine … which says she was conscious after her car hit the water, and she managed to open the door and swim to safety. She must have closed it herself, hoping it would keep the car from filling with water and sinking. Jesus, Willie, Sherlock Holmes would spot that without breaking a sweat."

Willie regarded him silently as she finished her vodka. She'd heard some new version of this tale from David at least half a dozen times the first couple of weeks after Jill's accident, and each time he embellished it, it made even less sense. "David, even if Jill survived the fall, she'd have drowned in that surf."

"Wrong! Jill could swim like a mermaid, and she'd easily have made it to shore. I mean, it wasn't more than thirty feet."

Willie thought about it as she poured herself another vodka. David's fantasy was about as plausible as winning the Powerball lottery, but there was an even bigger flaw in his tale. "All right, then," she said. "If that's true, where is she? The accident happened in July. If she survived, why hasn't she shown up?"

"Amnesia," he said matter-of-factly, changing his mind about the vodka again and pouring himself a third shot. "She's wandering around out there with no memory of who she is."

This was a fresh-baked tale she hadn't heard yet. "Sorry, but that's nuts, honey. People don't just wander around with amnesia for three months ... except in the movies. You've got to stop torturing yourself. You had the love of your life for a while, your soul mate. Most people never find that at all. But loss is always part of the package when you love someone, and we all have to cope with it sooner or later. You can't start healing if you won't let her go."

"But, how can I let her go when it feels like she's a second heart beating inside me? Look ... I know this sounds crazy, but Jill has been talking to me the past couple of nights."

Willie's eyes narrowed. "What do you mean, she's been 'talking to you'?"

He shrugged. "It's like I've been hearing her voice ... mostly just before I fall asleep."

"So where is her voice coming from, under your bed?" The sarcasm had escaped her lips before she had a chance to catch herself, and she regretted the remark instantly.

David slammed his hand angrily on the coffee table. "Jill has powers you can't even imagine. She could always talk to me without having to be in the same place. I could hear her even miles away."

Willie stared in horror. *Oh, God, he's totally losing it. Please don't let it be an early sign of Huntington's.*

"David!" she said. "Can you hear how nutty that sounds? Jill was human … a generous but flawed woman who worked the sex trade … not some kind of angel. She was flesh and blood and very imperfect, just like the rest of us. And she's dead. If you don't wake up from this fantasy, you'll never have another relationship, because no real woman will ever measure up to her."

"I don't need another relationship, Willie. She's alive, and no one—not you or the police—can shatter my faith in that."

His high-pitched urgency sent a chill down Willie's spine. He wasn't simply in denial. He was unraveling right in front of her. Reasoning with him was doing no good, so she moved closer on the couch and just hugged him, pressing her cheek into his and whispering. "It's okay, baby. The last thing in the world I want is to take away your faith. It's wonderful that you can feel her presence."

He returned her hug and then, to Willie's relief, began to sob. "Oh fuck, who am I kidding? She's gone, Willie. There's never been a woman in my life like her … and now she's gone forever. And so is Lester."

Again, Willie sighed. He hadn't really cried for Lester before this, but now a dam had burst and his grief—both for Jill and his father—was pouring out in a torrent of bewildered anguish. "I don't want them to be dead, Willie. I don't."

"Neither do I," she said. "But just cry it out. Tears are good. They're always the start of healing." She knew it was a meaningless cliché, but it didn't matter. This was exactly what he needed. Willie took the box of Kleenex from the coffee table and handed him tissue after tissue, taking the used ones from his hand and tossing them onto the floor.

"Thanks, "Willie." he sobbed. "Thanks for being my friend. I adore you."

"Oh, shut up and stop being so maudlin," she grinned, giving his ear a tweak.

After about twenty minutes, his weeping finally stopped, not because he was done grieving but because he was completely dehydrated. "God, I'm thirsty," he whispered.

"See, that's what happens when you drink too much vodka," Willie said, kissing his forehead. "You dry up like a prune." She got up, went to the kitchen, and came back with a glass of water. "Don't gulp," she said, handing it to him. "Take small sips." He drank, then Willie let him put his head in her lap, and they stayed that way quietly as she rubbed his shoulders.

When he was ready to talk, he told her a story about Lester she hadn't heard before. "I was six, maybe seven," he said, "and I had this fall off my bike and skinned my elbow. It wasn't that bad, but the mercurochrome Dad put on it stung like hell. After he bandaged me, he put me on his knee and asked, 'Do you know how much I love you, son?' And when I said I didn't, he said, 'I love you up to the sky and down again. Up to the sky and down again.' He said it twice to make sure I really got it and, fuck, I totally did."

Willie felt a flash of envy as she compared Lester's fathering skills to what she'd grown up with—because when Harry had her on his knee, it was not to express tenderness. "Hmm, good thing Lester's ashes are sitting on your mantle," she said dryly, "or I might have to talk you down from thinking he was still alive and got locked in the broom closet."

The remark might have sounded cruel to someone who didn't understand David as she did, but Willie knew it would make him laugh and it did.

David went to bed as soon as Willie climbed the stairs to one of the spare rooms, but he lay awake fitfully as sleep eluded him. He thought about masturbating, wondering if it might help him relax, but he needed some sort of fantasy to arouse himself. He'd kept a couple of the vintage "girlie" magazines he'd found while cleaning out Lester's closet, but the prospect of a meaningless orgasm inspired by an old photograph that smelled of mildew was depressing. Jill's absence was a huge hole in his gut that would never be filled.

"But I'm here, Lamb Chop. I'm with you right now."

David moaned and put a pillow over his head, trying to shut out her imaginary voice. "Stop torturing me. Your car went off a cliff."

"I'm not that easy to kill, Lamb Chop. I swam to safety, just like you said. I'm alive. Believe in me, not Willie."

"No. Willie's sensible," David mumbled, "and you're all in my head."

"Don't listen to her. She's petty and wants to keep us apart."

It was definitely Jill's voice, but what she was saying was totally unlike her. "What? You always liked Willie."

The "voice" quickly changed its attitude. *"Yes ... yes, of course, I like her. I'm being silly. I'm just upset because I miss you so much. But it's hard for me to talk to you this way for long."* Her words were growing faint, like the beam of a flashlight with failing batteries. *"Just have faith in me. I'll be with you when the Portal opens and then you'll understand."*

"Portal? What portal?" There was no answer, and when he called Jill's name, there was only silence.

David turned on his bedside light and looked around, almost expecting to see some shade of Jill floating in midair like a helium balloon, but there was only the familiar bedroom with all its trappings and furnishings. Yet Jill's voice had seemed totally real, and he wondered if he was becoming ill. Lester had never heard voices as far as he knew, but Huntington's could do strange things to a person's mind. After all, his father had believed both Willie and Jill were Myra when they'd visited him.

He knew there was no way he'd sleep now, so he reached to the night table for his copy of *The Void Captain's Tale* by Norman Spinrad. He'd read the eerie science fiction novel once before, about twelve years ago, when Lester—then still clear-minded—had given it to him, saying, "This book will blow you away, David." It had done just that, and he and Lester spent hours talking about how haunting the cautionary story about erotic and spiritual obsession was.

The story was set thousands of years in the future, in a time when humans traveled between the stars in gigantic "void ships," using a kind of warp drive powered by a mysterious alien device and a female pilot's soul-shattering orgasms. At her moment of climax, the ship she was piloting somehow "went along for the ride," vanishing from one part of space and reappearing light years away in just an instant. (A key element of the story was that a void ship pilot could only be female, because men did not have the physiology needed to be "attached" to the strange alien device.)

A pilot experienced what was called "The Jump" as transcendent rapture, an out-of-body nirvana far more intoxicating than ordinary sex or any drug. But it was also insidious because it was highly addictive, increasingly debilitating, and eventually lethal to the pilot. These women were typically wretched, short-lived creatures, ill-kempt and caring for nothing but the ecstasy of the Jump. They were treated as pariahs by society, yet their occupation was a necessary evil, because without the Jump, interstellar commerce and culture would collapse and human civilization would wither and die.

The story was mainly about the taboo relationship that develops between the void ship *Dragon Zephyr's* male captain, Genro Kane Gupta, and its mad pilot, Dominique Alia Wu. The captain develops a fatal obsession with his pilot, longing desperately to feel what she does when she "jumps the ship." But the experience is unattainable for a man, and Gupta rages against his fate at having been born male.

Ensnared by her cunning, the captain begins a sexual liaison with the pilot, who implies that she can help him share her indescribable bliss if he does one little favor for her. The "favor" turns out to be something truly unthinkable, though after much hesitation, he finally agrees. But instead of fulfilling her promise—which anyone but Gupta can see is impossible—Alia uses him to bring about her own narcissistic goal. In the process, the *Dragon Zephyr* becomes a kind of ghost ship, and its captain and thousands of passengers are doomed to spend eternity in a terrifying inter-dimensional limbo, even as Alia gets exactly what she's always longed for.

David read until his eyes ached. When he finally put the book down and turned out the light, he was asleep almost instantly and drifted into a long and vivid dream.

A red sun is setting behind him over the ocean as he walks into an alley between pastel-colored buildings that look Aegean and very old. The sunset is giving the stucco a warm glow, and the day's heat is radiating off the walls. Soon he's lost in a maze of twisting stone passageways that become narrower and narrower, until he's finally wedged tight where two salmon-colored walls come together at a sharp angle.

He feels a wave of panic, but now a doorway appears to his left and he pushes his way through into the busy kitchen of an upscale Italian restaurant, where chefs are preparing gourmet meals, and waiters and waitresses are shouting orders or porting food out to customers in the dining room. Plates rattle and he smells braised fish, tomato sauce, and loaves of fresh bread. A huge pizza whizzes by, held aloft by a dwarf in black pants, starched white shirt, and a red bow tie.

Somehow David knows that Jill works here as a waitress, but he doesn't see her in the kitchen, so he walks through a set of swinging doors into an elegant dining room. A circus clown is playing the accordion, serenading the patrons with an impassioned version of "Sorrento," and David struggles not to laugh at him. He does a quick circuit of the room, almost knocking over the dessert cart and getting an angry shove from the black-jacketed maître d'. But there's no sign of Jill.

He dashes back into the kitchen, grabs hold of a young busboy, and demands to know if he's seen Jill. The startled kid says he doesn't know anyone named Jill, so David describes her in detail: tall, light-coffee skin, sharp nose, long black hair, and a body to die for. "Of all the waitresses here, she's the only one you'd let tie you to a chair," he says.

The kid ponders this briefly, and then his eyes light up. "Oh, you mean Botticelli. She's out there." He gestures with his thumb to a side exit from the kitchen.

Botticelli? Somehow that name sounds right, and David flies through the side door and out onto a grassy field in morning daylight. Jill is about twenty feet away, casually naked and leaning against the oak tree that should be behind the Inverness house. Her arms are crossed and she's looking right at David, giving him a dazzling smile.

He runs, praying she won't disappear, and when he reaches her, they fall together like a pair of ravenous wolves trying to swallow each other whole, kissing, licking, and stroking. Finally, they pull apart and just eye-gaze.

But something is wrong because those golden flecks glittering like stars inside her left iris should be inside the right one, shouldn't they? David looks at her, trying to concentrate, trying to remember something important. Maybe the flecks were always in her left eye and he's just forgotten.

Jill smiles and cups his face between her hands. "Look up," she whispers. "That's where we're going." When he tilts his head and peers upward, he's speechless. That oak tree, which had never been more than twenty feet tall, has become a towering sequoia whose top is lost in the clouds.

Suddenly he understands what she expects him to do: He's meant to climb this titanic thing with her. But it's an impossible task. Jill has always been able to scamper up trees like a squirrel, but he's never been any good at climbing, and the lowest branch on this behemoth is a good fifty feet above them.

"Jill, I ... I can't."

"Don't worry, it's easy," she says, giving him a wink. Jill crouches and leaps, and in an instant, she's gripping the side of the tree lightly with fingers and toes, looking down at David from six feet above. "C'mon, Lamb Chop," she says. "I won't let you fall."

David jumps, and suddenly he's clinging to the bark right beside her, like a gecko, so weightless and free he laughs with the exhilaration of it.

They scamper up the tree effortlessly, reaching the first branch in moments. There they stop to look at a nest where a spotted owl is tending two little owlets, feeding them scraps of meat from something freshly killed. "What a good mother, you are," Jill coos, reaching to stroke one of the owlets. Astonishingly, the mother coos right back at her like a cat, having no problem with Jill caressing one of her brood.

They continue climbing—almost floating up the massive trunk—until they reach a height of around a thousand feet. There they stop again, perching lightly on a branch to gaze out at the incredible vista that spreads below them like a shimmering tapestry. From this height, they should have a bird's-eye view of the entire Bay Area, and they do. But to David's shock, every structure, everything man-made is gone. There are no roads, no buildings, and no ports. All he can see is lush forest, bright rolling hills, and shadowed valleys.

"Where did everything go?" he asks. "The City should be down there, and Oakland over that way. And what the hell happened to the Bay Bridge?"

"Everything's right where it's supposed to be," Jill says. "Look!" She points to a spot directly beneath them, and he sees a small village comprised mostly of wood cabins, with a few buildings that glow like white marble, all winding from a shaded valley up to the summit of a sunny hillside, where the densest concentration of buildings is clustered. That should be Beacon Hill he's looking at, but there's not a single city street.

David stares in the direction of Fisherman's Wharf, but nothing is left there either. In place of the Art Institute, Coit Tower, and the pier, there's just more rolling forest, a simple landing at the water's edge, and a few sailboats drifting across the bay. The entire Embarcadero has vanished too!

"Let's go," Jill says, kissing him. "We're still a long way from home."

David woke before dawn, tasting her kiss and savoring it as long as he could. The fact that it was a dream didn't matter. He knew that Jill was alive, and this time he wept with joy.

Chapter 22

~

THE G-SPOT

Month of October/Month of Vine

*W*illie and Selene stepped out of the cab in front of The G-Spot, the trendy boutique near Union Square, where the moneyed glitterati and lady perverts came to browse the racks of fetish gear. For Selene, this was a professional, tax-deductible shopping spree, and the fact that she was about to have some serious fun helping Willie get her mojo on was a nice added bonus.

Miss Ginger, the store's owner, was a full-figured redhead and a longtime club member at Nyala. She let out a delighted squeal, greeting Selene with a hug the moment she and Willie stepped through the door, offering them fresh-brewed espressos from a machine near the register.

Selene's invitation to come shopping here had intrigued Willie, though it had taken awhile for her to work up the nerve to do it. She'd never set foot in a place like this and had been expecting a peep show cellar with throbbing music and flashing lights, suffused with the cloying reek of cheap incense, so she was surprised at how refined the store was. The mood was of stylish decadence, and the female customers were convivial and anything but cheap. "The Power Ladies," Selene called them.

The sound of soft jazz came over the store's audio system, and if there was an actual aroma, it was the primal scent of leather. Selene inhaled deeply as they sipped their espressos and said, "Shit, Willie. Doesn't the smell of leather just make you want to flog someone?" Then she laughed delightedly at Willie's horrified expression. "Relax, girl. How many times do I have to tell you this is all just a game? Like cowboys and Indians for grownups." Willie had heard her say similar things before and still didn't buy it.

It was when Selene spoke about how much she relished her work, that Willie had the most troubling doubts about her. Which was the real Selene? Was it the one who'd been such a tender lover, so gentle and protective from the start, or the perilous creature who made her living as an infamous dominatrix? But maybe the bigger question was what her girlfriend could possibly see in someone as tame as she was when Selene could easily have her pick of the kinkiest lovers in town?

When Willie asked about that early in their relationship, Selene had replied, "Because, my love, I get my fill of kink at work, and right now old-fashioned vanilla with you is like a smoothie from heaven." The words had touched Willie, though sex with Selene seemed anything but "vanilla," because she was easily the most creative lover she'd ever had. And if their intimacy sometimes had a bit of extra spice thrown in, it was just the right amount to turn a nourishing meal into a gourmet feast.

But sometimes, she was still uneasy about being seen with Selene in public. What if they ran into one of Willie's business clients? Selene was a scandalous public figure in the Bay Area, and many knew her face, even if not her name. Willie's Green Girl clients were mostly liberal, but going around holding hands with a professional dominatrix was pushing the envelope pretty hard. So far, though, the sky hadn't fallen.

As they wandered through the racks of clothing, it seemed to Willie that every item was made with one purpose in mind—to turn women's bodies into objects of lust. Even worse, the accessories for sale were more like instruments of torture than anything designed to enhance pleasure or intimacy. But Selene saw it all as through the eyes of a child walking into a candy store with a month's allowance, and no parents to tell her she'd rot her teeth if she didn't curb her greedy appetite for sugar.

Today they were shopping not for leather but latex, and Selene was eagerly snatching garment after garment off the shelves to bring into the fitting room. Her arms were soon so full of merchandise that she began offloading some to Willie.

The staff all knew Selene on sight and treated her like royalty, calling her "Mistress" or even "darling" if they were especially chummy with her. Selene took it all in stride. She was a legend here, and there was even a prominent display rack of her book for sale at the front of the store. One customer—a painfully thin woman in her thirties—bought a copy and asked Selene to sign it. And Selene happily obliged, asking the woman's name, chatting her up a bit, and then writing a personal inscription on the book's flyleaf.

Some of the fawning attention was also coming to Willie, who found it a bit disconcerting. Selene was introducing her as "my partner," something she'd been calling Willie for a while now. It was a term whose meaning seemed perfectly clear to everyone except Willie because Selene was still keeping everything so light between them. Willie had never gotten a single declaration of love from her, and for all she knew, the word "partner" meant little more than "temporary fuck buddy" to Selene. But she wasn't confident enough to ask her girlfriend for a definition of what "partner" actually meant to her for fear the answer would be disappointing.

In the fitting room, Selene primped in front of the mirror, wearing her stiletto heels to get the full height effect as she smoothed a few wrinkles from the skimpy black number she was trying on. To Willie, the latex looked impossibly tight, almost like a layer of paint, displaying every voluptuous curve to full advantage and revealing an abundance of Selene's luscious cleavage. Willie could imagine how helpless with lust Selene's clients would be seeing her like this, and it seemed unfair to do that to a man she had no intention of fucking.

Selene rolled the dress up over her head and stood naked in front of the mirror, casually sifting through the pile of other garments on the bench. She was heartbreakingly gorgeous, and the next thing Willie knew, she was standing in front of Selene with her head buried between her breasts, face pressed against that tree tattoo with its spray of colored blossoms, inhaling her fragrance.

Selene laughed. "What are you trying to do? Smell the flowers on my tattoo?"

"Mmm." Willie sniffed again. "I guess it must be your perfume."

"I'm not wearing scent today," Selene said, as she casually picked a red latex dress up off the bench.

Willie stepped back to take in the whole of that tattoo. She never tired of looking at it, and each time she saw something a little different. The tree's leaves were reddish green and serrated, and the flowers that dotted it were like nothing in the real world, each one having its own unique shape and color. And now, when she looked closely, Willie saw what looked almost like a human face etched into the bark. "I keep meaning to ask where you got this," she said.

Selene gazed at her reflection in the mirror and ran her fingers across the tattoo. "It's one of Wynter's. She's great with a brush too. Remind me to show you her art gallery at the club." Willie had met Wynter a couple of months ago. She was another Upstairs Girl who worked at Nyala, a voluptuous brunette, just a bit taller than Willie with deep brown eyes and a complexion like Snow White's.

"You should let her do something for you," Selene said, holding the red dress up in the mirror, though it was clearly too small for her.

"A tattoo on me," Willie asked, laughing. "No way."

"Why not? You've got gorgeous skin. It would be a turn-on seeing you decorated with something sexy."

A lot of girls were getting elaborate tattoos lately, and the younger ones nearly all seemed to have some body art. Willie had to admit that a couple of stunning pieces in just the right spots could look really hot on a girl. On the other hand, tattoos could look hideous by the time that girl was a woman in her fifties. "Jesus, Selene. I'm thirty-four. A tat might look okay on me now, but in twenty years when I'm all wrinkly ... yuck!"

"Don't be silly, you'll look just as great in twenty years as you do now."

The flattery was sweet, though Willie knew it was nonsense. But still ... "Maybe I could just get a little Aries symbol on my wrist or something."

"Forget the symbol. We'll have Wynter cover your entire stomach with a ram! I can arrange it for you."

Willie cringed. Tattooing a ram on her stomach felt decidedly brazen, which both excited and frightened her. Though a ram was a male symbol, she knew she'd always associate it with Selene, making her feel like some helpless female, owned by a sexual being far more potent than she was. Mercifully, Selene dropped the subject and handed her the red latex dress she'd been holding. "Here, this should fit you." Willie held the garment up in front of the mirror, guessing the tiny thing would scarcely cover her crotch.

"I dunno, this stuff looks great on you, but ..."

"But nothing! Why are you so afraid to let yourself look like something incredibly fuckable? Come on, Willie, you can't wear *that* to my fetish ball." She pointed at the conservative blue suit Willie still had on from her day at the office.

"Oh, right ..." She'd almost forgotten about the Halloween party at Nyala, probably because she half wanted to. "I've been meaning to talk to you about that."

"Shit! You're not bailing on me? I've already told everyone you're my date!"

"No, no ... I'll be there. But can't I just go as the Wicked Witch or something? I mean, you know outfits like this creep me out. I hate being leered at."

Selene put a hand on her shoulder. "Look, Willie. There may be lots of perverts at the club, but the real predators don't come anywhere near us because we can pick them out in a flash. Nyala is safer than most churches."

Willie began undressing, and when she was naked, Selene shook some talcum powder from a can and began applying it over Willie's skin, starting at her shoulders then working down across her back and ass, before turning her around and powdering her breasts and belly. "This makes latex slide over your skin without sticking so we don't tear the dress," she said. But Willie was gone, drifting off into a lurid fantasy …

Selene is sitting naked on the bench amid all that latex, spreading those incredible legs. And Willie is on her knees doing the dirty, with Selene holding her head, pressing it gently into the warm wet heart of her, humming like some infernal queen bee. And Willie, her happy little drone, is drunk on the taste of the royal jelly Selene's honeyed flood is feeding her.

But then, it goes horribly wrong, because in walks this big fat guy with his arms full of ladies' leatherwear that will look totally ridiculous on him. And of course, he immediately spots what Willie is doing, drops the clothes he's carrying and screams in horror, which brings Miss Ginger running quick as a ferret to see the cause of this uproar in her fitting room.

The fat guy blubbers, pointing at Willie, calling her a brazen little harlot, and Miss Ginger gets the security guard, who's already six years past retirement age, and would be in the park playing with the grandkids right now if he didn't have to keep working to help his useless son avoid losing his home on account of those gambling debts.

The guard immediately cuffs Willie's hands behind her back, waving a stun gun in her face, just because "Miss G" finally bought him one and he wants to show how badass he looks with it. And the next thing Willie knows, she's being hauled off to jail for public indecency—just Willie and not Selene, because the cops are all Selene's clients and afraid she'll rat them out to their wives.

"Willie," Selene said. "Have you heard anything I was saying?"

"What? Oh, sorry … I was just thinking about work." *Shit, why can't I even have a decent fantasy without fucking it up?*

"I said I invited David to the ball, and he said he'd be there."

That surprised Willie, who'd actually floated the idea to David, though he'd flatly turned her down. "I can't believe you got him to say 'yes.' He told me he couldn't bear to come back to the place he'd met Jill."

"Nonsense," Selene said. "He's mourned long enough."

"What the fuck did you say to him to change his mind?"

Selene mimed holding a telephone to her ear and put on her sexiest pouty voice. "'Oh, David, honey … you have to come to our party. We girls just miss you so much.' Do you really think he could resist that?"

Willie grinned. "I wouldn't be fool enough to bet against you."

"Good, then it's settled. Now, try this dress on. I'm dying to see you in it."

Willie held the tiny red dress at arm's length, like it was a serpent ready to strike. "Shit, I'll look like a total slut in this thing."

"That's the whole point," Selene said, stroking Willie's ass sensuously.

A flush went through Willie at Selene's touch. "Well, it's one thing being a sex object when I'm alone with you, but the idea of being one in public is humiliating."

"Well, feeling humiliated is a choice you can make," Selene said. "But here's another option. You can wear the label 'slut' with pride. Meet the eyes of every man and woman who wants you with a seductive smile. Let their lust fill you like the scent of fine cognac. It's a lovely exchange of energy, but you're just putting on a show; it doesn't mean you want to fuck them."

Willie shook her head sadly. "I can't display myself like you do, Selene. It's not who I am." She looked at her naked body in the mirror and, without thinking, covered the burn scars on her belly with a hand.

Selene had seen her do that before and knew the gesture was unconscious. Whenever Willie was feeling insecure, her hand just drifted there, even when her scars were hidden by clothing. Now

Selene reached for Willie's hand and moved it aside to uncover the burns. "No, baby," she said. "That's part of what makes you the powerful woman you are. You survived Harry, so wear those scars as a badge of honor and don't hide them. Not from me or anyone else."

> "A picture is a secret about a secret,
> the more it tells you the less you know."
> —*Diane Arbus*

Chapter 23

⌁

PICTURES AT AN EXHIBITION

All Hallows' Eve

Selene's Halloween ball was scheduled to begin in two hours, and The Upstairs Girls were feverishly rushing about Nyala's dungeon, putting the final touches on the decorations, setting up the open bar and unpacking the catered snacks.

The dungeon had been turned into a haunted castle, complete with ceiling-to-floor spider webs, black lights, and filaments of vapor oozing from fog machines. There were zombie mannequins that groaned and leapt out of cabinets, and later there'd be piped-in sounds of thunder and pelting rain when Swallow My Flesh—the Goth band whose drummer was a client of Mistress Tannith—was between sets.

Except for the suspension device and a St. Andrew's cross, which would be part of the scheduled entertainment, most of the dungeon's gear had been stowed away to create more space for the free bar and food tables, the bandstand, and a sizable dance floor. Three of the theme rooms had been reserved in advance for private parties, but the Betty Page room would remain open to anyone who wanted to use it for spankings and floggings that all were free to watch.

Willie was doing her best to help with setup, but everyone else seemed to have a specific assignment, and she was mostly getting in the way. Selene spotted her fumbling with a vampire backdrop and walked over to hand Willie a cup of rum punch. "No, sweetie ... that belongs by the bandstand. Why don't you just relax and let us handle this?"

"Well, I can't get into costume yet," Willie said, taking a sip of punch. "I'll swelter in that latex thing for an extra two hours, and I don't know what to do with myself till the party starts."

Selene nodded. "Okay, finish your drink and I'll take you downstairs to Wynter's gallery. This would be a great time to see her paintings."

The small gallery was on the second floor, behind the auditorium. It would be closed tonight because they were expecting nearly two hundred guests, and Wynter's pictures were too special to risk damage by drunken revelers. But Selene unlocked the room just for Willie, telling her she had lots of time to enjoy the paintings. "I'll come get you half an hour before the party starts and help you get dressed," she said, giving Willie a quick kiss and closing the door behind her.

The framed oil paintings, each measuring 48 x 36 inches, were displayed beneath banks of museum lighting, and only the pictures themselves were lit, leaving the spaces between in dramatic shadow. The sole furnishings were twelve viewing benches placed around the gallery, three in front of each wall. The black leather benches stood in stark contrast to the white walls, and the only colors in the room were the dazzling tones in Wynter's art. There was literally nowhere else for the eye to go but deep into these intense pictures.

As she gazed at the first painting on the east wall, Willie tried to view it with an open mind, which wasn't easy. The picture had a small plaque beneath it bearing the title, *Bad Girls Go to Heaven, Good Girls Stay Home*. It showed a domme seated on a throne before a black curtain, holding two short riding crops crossed in front of her chest. She was wearing a white latex body suit with gossamer wings that stuck out from each shoulder, and her smile seemed at once angelic and menacing. It bore testimony to Wynter's skill as an artist that she could portray both those impressions in the same smile.

On the floor in front of the domme was a naked woman lying on her back, face turned toward the viewer, grimacing in pain as the mistress pressed the heel of a six-inch stiletto shoe into her navel. It took a couple of moments for Willie to recognize the face of the domme. *Oh, my God. That's Jill. David would totally freak.*

Ironically, this first painting was the most "ordinary" in the exhibit. Several others were blatantly pornographic, and one of the most shocking bore the meaningless title, *The Blessed Fleen*.

The scene depicted several women wearing filmy white gowns, pushing dildos into naked women's vaginas, mouths and rectums, in some cases more than one object at a time. Off to one side, two naked men sat on a couch, drinking something from earthenware bowls as greenish liquid dribbled down their chins, and two more women in translucent gowns knelt between their legs, performing oral sex on them. In the background was a long judicial bench at which sat three robed women, wearing regal headdresses, each with palms raised, as if sanctifying this profane event.

Despite the obscene themes, Willie had to admit that the paintings were masterful in their detail, their harmony of light, shadow and color. The human bodies and faces were gorgeous and blazing with fierce erotic energy. Wynter was clearly a superb artist, even though her sensibility was utterly twisted. *What a sad way to waste such brilliant talent,* Willie thought.

But as she continued to view the pictures, something unexpected struck her. When she focused on the facial expressions of the people in these vulgar scenes, she began to see a quality that was almost romantic. She wouldn't call it love, but there was a tangible kindness in the faces of the "victimizers," as if these violations were not for the sadistic satisfaction of the dominant partners, but more a tender gift to the submissives. The orgiastic sex wasn't turning Willie on, but it didn't repulse her either. Selene's rum punch was definitely affecting her, though, because she was feeling giddy and the room seemed to be getting warmer.

As she moved to the next wall, Willie saw a series of paintings quite different from the last group. The first was actually rather sweet. It showed a nude female couple—a blonde and a dusky-skinned girl, her hair a mass of tumbling black ringlets—sitting on a bench in a forest glade, embracing and kissing fervently. There was nothing even remotely crude in it, rather there was a kind of "lost-in-each-other" passion that reminded Willie of Rodin's sculpture *The Kiss*—except, of course, that this was a female couple.

Now that's more my speed, she thought. *These girls are in love.*

But the next picture undid all the tenderness in the previous one. This was a twilight scene in which a group of gowned, flower-garlanded girls were seated at a picnic table in an orchard feasting on the flesh of another group of girls who were the main course in this gory banquet. With a shudder, Willie recognized the blonde from the "kiss" painting, now consuming the left arm of her dusky-skinned lover. The most unsettling thing was that the girls being eaten alive didn't seem to mind, laughing and talking with the girls who were in the process of devouring them.

Above the table, winged pixies flitted about, filling wine glasses or hand-feeding little dainties to the girls who were the main course of this "feast." The table was brightly lit by lanterns that resembled fruits, which hung in multicolored clusters from trees whose crowns formed a canopy above the scene. It was like the Mad Hatter's Tea Party seen through the eye of a voluptuous cannibal. Willie knew she should be disgusted but found herself giggling instead.

The first painting on the north wall offered yet another drastic change in subject, showing an orchard filled with fruit trees beneath a green sky and two crescent moons. In the foreground, one of the trees appeared to be blighted, and an old woman with white hair knelt beside it, gnarled hands covering her face as she wept bitterly. A young woman who could have been her granddaughter knelt beside her, trying to comfort the crone.

Why a dying tree should cause the old woman such grief, Willie couldn't guess, but something about it was incomparably sad, and her eyes began to fill with tears. She'd had that rum punch over half an hour ago but seemed to be getting drunker by the minute.

As odd as this collection was, the final two pictures were the strangest yet, and she stared at the first in bewilderment trying to understand what she was seeing. It was entitled *The Nursery* and showed a stand of sapling trees at the center of which stood the figure of a slim, naked man, no more than twenty, with a mass of frizzy black hair, whose lower torso was a tree trunk with roots delving deep into the earth. The change from human skin to bark was gradual and very natural-looking, and a small branch jutted from his groin like an erect penis, with a spray of tiny white blossoms shooting from its tip like semen.

Standing beside the tree-man were two young women who seemed to be twins, and they were each licking one side of his serene face. In the background was a bed of California poppies, their orange essence brilliant, almost insolent against the lush green grass and a pale green sky. The colors were intense, alive and electric, like something out of a dream or a fairy tale picture book. Willie felt a flash of déjà vu as she took in the scene, but the sensation passed quickly.

The last painting, entitled *Midwives*, was clearly related to the previous one, but it was even more astonishing. This scene was set inside what appeared to be a Greek temple, through whose rear pillars one could see a night sky—a sky filled with bright stars and two full moons, one of which was either larger or closer than the other.

There were five women inside the temple, and the four who were standing were clothed in the same translucent gowns that seemed so common in these paintings. The fifth woman—a naked redhead— was reclining on a couch, her splendid upper body raised just far enough for the viewer to see her face, which held an expression that Willie could only think of as transcendent joy. The entire scene was like some classical Greek set piece, though it was totally post-modern in its bizarre, fetishistic content.

Behind the reclining redhead, another woman stood rubbing the girl's temples, as if trying to relieve her of a headache. The standing woman—a tall brunette with a sharp nose and full lips—was singing or chanting, and again, Jill seemed to be the model.

The chest of the redhead on the couch was covered with the tattoo of a tree, something like the one Selene had, only this illustration was incomplete. The tree's crown began just below the redhead's neck and covered most of her upper chest and shoulders, before the trunk began its descent between her breasts and down toward her belly, where it came to a sudden, jagged halt just above her navel. It was obvious that the tattoo was unfinished, because at the redhead's right stood a brunette who was Wynter herself, holding a tattooing needle in her left hand, poised to complete the missing portion of the image.

But it was the bottom of the redhead's body that was most startling. The woman's legs were raised, knees up and spread wide in the classic position of childbirth. She was clearly not pregnant, but the suggestion of a woman about to give birth was unmistakable.

The physical transformation began midway down her thighs. Like the young man in the previous painting, her legs were turning into tree trunks, the smooth skin becoming gradually more mottled as it dipped toward her knees, which had taken on the shape of wooden boles, brown and gnarled as an oak.

Her calves were already fully altered, the rough-looking bark sprouting an array of slender shoots, at whose tips pale-green buds were opening. What should have been lovely ankles and delicate feet had become thick, woody clumps, and what had formerly been toes were now long roots, which were being shepherded into a large pot of soil by a small woman with a shaved head, who was helping guide this remarkable transformation.

As if all of this were not strange enough, another woman was leaning in from the left, her small breasts barely visible through her flimsy gown. She was bent over the reclining redhead, a long strand of saliva trailing down from her mouth directly onto the redhead's sex, where the pinky of the spitting woman's right hand was stimulating the "tree-woman's" clitoris. Willie stared at the astonishing scene for several minutes, trying to understand it, wondering if there was even anything there to understand.

Suddenly she felt a rush of fear. Would this tree-woman still have lungs when these "midwives" were done with her? And if her lungs also turned to wood, how would she breathe? Willie felt a tightening in her chest and recognized the start of a panic attack, the kind she would have when Harry was about to burn her with a cigarette.

The room began to spin and Willie swayed unsteadily, staggering over to one of the benches where she sat and tried to regain her composure. She felt clammy, sick to her stomach, and a loud pulse was hammering in her ears, so she lay down on the bench and closed her eyes, hoping Selene would come for her soon.

Chapter 24

✿

MAN IN A BANANA SUIT

"Sorry," the salesgirl said, "but there's three big fetish parties in town tonight and the kink gear has been, like, flying off the shelves all week. All we've got left is a chest harness, but it's extra-large and you'd look puny in it." The ash blonde had about the palest skin David had ever seen, and wore a silver ring in her nose and a smaller one in her left eyelid. Her employee nametag read LaTreece.

He'd put off the decision to attend Selene's party until the last moment. Now, at nearly 6 P.M., this was the only costume shop still open, and he was almost relieved there was no S&M gear left. It was Jill who'd made living out his fantasies safe, but dressing in submissive gear and going to this party by himself was a prospect he was just as glad not to face.

That still left a problem, though, since he couldn't very well go to a Halloween party without a costume of some kind. He thought briefly about giving up and driving home. But Selene had pleaded with him to come, and then he'd agreed to meet Willie there when she'd promised to introduce him to a new friend from the club—a dominant girl named Eva she thought he'd hit it off with. At first, he'd insisted that he wasn't interested in a new relationship, but then Willie said, "Believe me, dude, Eva isn't into relationships. All she wants is sex, and you're just her type."

He hadn't been with a woman since Jill, and now, with the prospect of getting laid within reach, he didn't want to turn around and drive all the way back to Inverness with nothing to show for it. "Do you have any costumes at all in my size?" he asked LaTreece, who seemed impatient to close up for the night.

She thought for a moment then shrugged. "Well, if it doesn't have to be kinky, there may be something. I'll go check." She disappeared into the rear of the shop and came back a minute later with something yellow and green. "Here, this should fit you."

David held the outfit up and stared in bewilderment. "What's this supposed to be, a banana with hair?"

LaTreece gave him the exasperated look she reserved for straights and idiots. "Duh. A banana would be stupid. It's an ear of corn, and the 'hair' is corn silk, see?" It was basically a speckled yellow-and-green tube made of thin oil cloth, with head and arm holes, plus a hood topped by a crown of soft fibers. It smelled like a rain poncho.

"No one will have a clue what I'm supposed to be," David said, groaning.

"Sure they will," LaTreece insisted. "Halloween is a harvest thing and corn is, like, the hugest part of that."

All the other party guests were tricked out in edgy or else very glamorous gear, and when he'd arrived in that absurd costume, he felt mortified. But then a woman dressed in practically nothing, who claimed to be a succubus, asked him to dance, and when he told her he was an ear of corn and not a banana, she gave him a smile and said, "Well, you're luscious enough to slather with butter and eat, little man."

He racked his brain for a sexy comeback, but timing was everything and he missed his chance. *Shit,* he thought, the moment she walked off, *I should have said "I've always dreamed of having my kernels popped by a succubus." Why do I only think of the snappy lines when it's too late?*

Most of these guests were club members who knew one another, and David felt awkward and out of place. He recognized a few faces but no one by name, except for Wynter and Erica, who were working the bar.

Willie had promised to meet him by the bandstand with Eva at 9:30, but it was now after 10:00 and she was nowhere in sight, nor was she answering her cell phone. The mob around the bar had kept him away since he'd arrived, but the line was shorter now, so he walked over, queued up, and waited to be served. Wynter and Erica were working feverishly, pouring wine and beer, and mixing cocktails as if they'd been tending bar for years. Both were dressed as seductive vampires and getting a lot of flirtatious attention from men and women alike.

"David, it's so great to see you," Wynter said, giving him a big smile when he reached the head of the line. "It's been ages."

Her effusive greeting pleased him, though being at Nyala without Jill was depressing him more and more by the moment. "I'm fine, but it's kind of hard being here so soon after … well, you know …"

He was fishing for words of sympathy for losing Jill, and it seemed like Wynter should be feeling her loss too. After all, the women had been friends and co-workers, hadn't they? But Wynter ignored his gloom and her lighthearted manner threw him off balance.

"Outrageous party, isn't it?" she said, practically shouting above the din. "The band is just blowing everyone away … So, what are you drinking tonight?"

David fumbled for a reply. "Yeah, uh, great party … Can you do a Stoli and tonic?"

"You got it, Banana Boy," Wynter said, reaching under the bar for a fresh bottle of Stolichnaya and opening it. She took a plastic cup and poured him what must have been three full shots of vodka. "Standard party drink," she explained, winking when his eyes went wide at the extravagance.

Swallow My Flesh wasn't half bad, though they were excessively loud and played mostly old punk covers. David danced with a woman in her forties, done up as a ghoul, with elaborate makeup that must have taken hours to apply. She was attractive in a butch sort of way, with muscle tone that suggested lots of time at the gym. But she seemed to have no interest in him.

After the band's second set, Tannith announced there would be a demonstration of suspension techniques by Master Damien and his sub Little Miss Molly, two of the regular club members. It quickly drew an audience in one corner of the dungeon, but David wanted some air, so he made his way past the leaping zombie dummy and out into the hallway, where he was greeted by a bizarre scene. A woman with a shaved head was holding a younger woman—with hair so white it could only be a dye job—by a dog leash.

The bald woman's "pet" was on all fours, wearing a harness that said "service dog," licking her owner's bare feet, while her mistress chatted nonchalantly with a third woman: "I'm telling you, Lydia, that idiot roofer has fucked this job up twice now. I mean, it's just a small leak, not Noah's flood."

"Oh, I know, Betsy, I know," Lydia said. "Finding decent contractors these days is impossible. I mean, you wouldn't believe our electrician. When I walked into the kitchen from my pottery shop last week ... instead of replacing the circuit box like he's supposed to, he's at the table swigging a *Dos Equis* and coming on to my sixteen-year-old daughter. And I'm paying the fucker eighty-five an hour for this shit."

Betsy's "dog" began whimpering at her feet, and she reached down to give the woman's head a scratch. "It's okay, Nadine. We'll go walky-walks soon."

"Thank you, Mistress," Nadine said, looking up at Betsy with limpid eyes.

David felt like a voyeur staring at the tableau which, if Nadine had been an actual dog instead of a leashed woman, would have made the scene totally mundane. As it was, the moment was surreal.

Betsy suddenly noticed David standing there and gave him a small nod. "Um … that's a beautiful dog you have," he said, hoping it was the right thing to say.

Betsy's face lit up. "Oh, thank you. She's a lab-sheltie mix and almost house-broken. Go ahead and pet her if you like. She won't bite. Say hello to the nice man in the banana suit, Nadine." Betsy unhooked Nadine's leash, and the dog-woman scuttled over to David, getting up on her "hind legs," pawing at him and whimpering for attention.

"No, Nadine!" Betsy said sternly. "Sit! We do not jump on people. You know better than that."

Nadine ignored the admonition, whined, and stayed as she was, pawing at David again. "She gets this way when she feels neglected," Betsy sighed. "You'd better pet her or she'll never stop." So David rubbed Nadine's head and let her lick his hand in return, then said goodbye to Betsy and her "dog" and walked off to find the restroom.

The men's room was brightly lit, clean and unoccupied. There were three urinals, and David chose the nearest, but when he reached down to unzip, he found to his annoyance that this stupid outfit lacked a pee slot. He had to urinate badly, so there was nothing to do but bend down, grab the hem of the costume, and raise it up far enough to work his penis free and get it pointed in the right direction. Unfortunately, a man in white evening clothes and top hat picked that moment to walk into the men's room. He took in the "peeing banana" for a moment and doubled over laughing.

Grumbling, David washed his hands and walked back into the party, scanning the room for Willie again. It was unlike her to say she'd meet him somewhere and not show up, and he was becoming concerned. He checked his iPhone to see if she'd called, but there were no messages. "Nine-thirty by the bandstand" was what she'd said, and it was already after eleven.

He went back to the bar for another drink, and Wynter greeted him warmly again. "Are we having fun?" she asked, pouring him an even more potent Stoli and tonic.

"Yeah, but listen, have you seen Selene? I was supposed to meet Willie here, and I can't find her. I figure they're probably together somewhere."

Wynter shook her head. "I haven't seen Willie, but Selene went home with a bad cold. She was here to help set things up, then left feeling terrible. Poor thing; she worked so hard on this party ... Oh, I almost forgot, a woman was here looking for you."

"For me? What did she look like?"

"Let's see," Wynter said. "Tall, blonde ... wearing some kind of princess outfit. She had one of those eye mask thingies on a stick so I couldn't really see her face. I think she's supposed to be Cinderella. She was over there talking to Tannith after the band's last set, but I don't see her now. Just mill around; I'm sure she'll find you."

David had no idea who Wynter was talking about. "Did she say what she wanted?"

Wynter laughed. "Don't be silly. She wanted *you*. Now go drink your drink and just let life come to you. It'll do that anyway, whether you like it or not."

Walking to the bandstand, he saw no one dressed like Cinderella or anything even close. But Willie had wanted to introduce him to someone named Eva, so maybe Eva had come searching for him. There was no way he was leaving without at least getting a look at her.

By 2:00 AM, the guests had thinned to a handful of stragglers, and there was still no sign of the "mystery princess." He'd been back to the bar a couple of times to check with Wynter, but she'd just shrugged, poured him a couple more drinks, and said she hadn't seen "Cinderella" again.

Now the bar was closed, David was exhausted, and all he wanted was to get home to bed. But, tired and drunk as he was, he doubted he could make it back to Inverness tonight. He tried calling Willie twice more to ask if he could come over and crash on her couch, but she still wasn't answering. That she hadn't shown up at the party could be explained by the fact that Selene went home sick, and Willie had gone to take care of her. But that she hadn't called and wasn't answering her phone was very odd.

Suddenly he felt a tap on his shoulder and, turning, he saw a burly man with a full gray beard, hair tied in a ponytail, and decked out as a Hell's Angel. "Hey, Princess Blondie down by the service entrance says to tell Banana Guy she's waitin' on him," he said gruffly.

David's ears perked up. "Is she dressed like Cinderella?"

"Yeah, I guess you could say that."

"Is her name Eva?"

"What the fuck do I look like, Facebook?" the biker growled. "Go ask her yourself."

The biker did say how to find the service entrance, though, and David made his way unsteadily through three corridors, a fire door, and then down two flights of narrow metal stairs into a dimly lit lobby that smelled like garlic. But all he saw besides a freight elevator was a green metal door with a humming sound coming from behind it.

"Hello?" David said, at first tentatively, then louder so that the empty lobby echoed his voice. There was no response, but he heard faint breathing and then a soft giggle. "Look … I'm too tired for games. If you don't show yourself, I'm leaving."

"No, please don't go, kind sir." She'd been standing just a couple of feet away, hidden in shadow, so he'd missed seeing her. But now she stepped into the light looking just as Wynter had described her: tall and slim, long blonde hair, wearing an elaborate princess gown and holding a stick mask over her eyes. "I was expecting Prince Charming," she said, her voice pouty. "But I guess I can put a banana to good use." The voice was a bit huskier than the one he remembered, but still unmistakable. His jaw dropped and he gaped.

Cinderella dropped her mask, then shed the blonde wig and stood there beaming at him. It was Jill.

Come away, O human child!
To the waters and the wild
With a faery, hand in hand,
For the world's more full of weeping than you can understand.
—"The Stolen Child,"
William Butler Yeats

Chapter 25

WILLIE

I was somewhere in a field and there was a scent of lilacs mixed with cinnamon. A gentle breeze was blowing across my skin, making me sway, languid as a dancer: whoosh … whoosh … whoosh. I could feel the grass beneath my feet, and my toes were curling into it. A delicious sensation, cool and moist, was flowing through my body, and I was tall and lithe as a willow tree.

And then, a choir began to sing; no words, just this celestial melody, coming from everywhere. It was jubilant and glorious, but it was also deep-down erotic, like some Pagan Hallelujah Chorus. But that's when I started feeling nervous, because it seemed wrong for heaven and earth to mix like that—for spirit to crave the flesh so shamelessly.

I was torn, because I really needed to sing with that choir, felt like I would shrivel up and die if I didn't. But what if the price for singing was my soul? I tried to stop myself. I mean, I really, really tried. But temptation was impossible to resist. Okay, then—let the Devil take me. I was primed for surrender. But when I tried to open my mouth and start singing, I suddenly didn't have a mouth. I couldn't see, either, because my eyes were gone. And now my skin was on fire, blistering and bubbling off my arms and legs. That's when I knew I was in Hell.

I jerked awake, fighting for breath. I have sleep apnea, and sometimes at night, especially in the middle of a nightmare, my breathing just stops. I thrashed and gasped two or three times. *Oh, God, oh, God, please!* Finally, air came into my lungs, but my heart was hammering, and I was drenched in sweat. I was alive, but where was I?

I rubbed my eyes to clear out the gunk and saw I was tucked under a green comforter, in an unfamiliar bed. The room was unfamiliar too, about twenty feet long by maybe twelve wide, sparsely furnished, with bare walls made of knotty pine. A stream of greenish light was shafting down through a triangular window high above my bed, and that "angelic" chorus I'd heard in my dream was actually coming from outside, but now it was just a mockingbird's song—sweet, though ordinary enough.

Looking up, I saw a vaulted roof and guessed I was in an A-frame cabin. A wasp was zipping up and down the length of the central rafter, buzzing angrily as it clicked off the end walls, each barrier making it turn and head back the other way in wicked frustration. I wondered how long it could keep going before it cold-conked itself and fell struggling onto my bed, at which point I would probably get stung.

I lay on my back, staring up at the ceiling, breathing deeply, trying to figure out how the fuck I'd gotten here. I had a vague impression of some bizarre paintings in a stuffy little room. Looking at them had made me dizzy, and I'd walked over to a bench to lie down, closing my eyes for just a moment. And then Selene and Erica were kneeling next to me, babbling in some language I couldn't understand. My memory ended right there.

I sat up in bed and realized I was naked. There was no one else in the room, but I pulled the covers up around my chest anyway, looking around for—for what? Spy cameras? Peep holes? I studied the room carefully. The triangular window about eight feet above my bed was matched by an identical one at the far end of the cabin. There were two large, square windows, one on each side of the room, a door behind me, and two others near the back of the cabin. Simple as the room was, the bed was luxurious—a four-poster, intricately carved with lush female figures, snaking sensuously around tall tree trunks.

There was a night table beside the bed, with a beaded lamp, a pitcher of water, and a glass with a note propped against it. I grabbed the note so fast I nearly knocked the glass over. Then, mustering some dignity, I slowed down, filled the glass and took a sip before reading the note. It was long, and the handwriting was hers:

Dearest Willie,

I know you're feeling disoriented right now, but don't be scared. I have brought you to my home, a world called Ausonia. Some of our Guests think of it as an "alternate universe Earth," which is a good way of seeing it.

But however you want to think of it, you are perfectly safe here in your own little bungalow, which has all the amenities you could ask for. The door behind your bed leads out onto the front porch, the one straight ahead is to the bathroom, and the one on the far right leads to a little kitchen that's stocked with delicious food, including some of those chocolate éclairs we both love. The armoire beside the bathroom has all the clothing you will need, plus extra blankets and pillows, and there are sandals at the foot of the bed. The pellet stove by the window on the left will keep this place as cozy as you want, and its glow is very comforting at night.

Now, for the hard part: Yes, you have been abducted, but you haven't been abandoned. I've returned to San Francisco to finish up some business, but I'll be back in about six weeks, and then we'll have lots to discuss.

Once again, there is nothing to fear. You are an honored Guest of my clan. We are called the Meliai, and everything will be done to make you happy and comfortable. When you find out who we are and why you're here, you may want to stay forever. But if not, you'll be free to return to your former life, and we will never interfere with that life again.

Outside your front door are several trails. The one to your left leads up a hill for about half a mile, and will take you to the General Store, which is available to you every morning. There, you will find more food, clean clothing, candles, books, and many other nice things. Everything in the store is free, so just help yourself to whatever you want. There's lots of excellent wine, hard liquor if you like, and something very much like hashish.

The path to the right leads to the Dining Commons, in case you want company and don't feel like cooking for yourself. Breakfast is from 7:30 to 10:00 and dinner from 5:00 to 7:00, but you're on your own for lunch. This path is also great for jogging and will give you a nice workout. (A pair of running shoes is in the armoire, along with shorts and some t-shirts.)

The trails are well lit at night, so no fear of getting lost if you venture out after dark—as long as you stick to the paths. Leaving them is one freedom you don't have, darling. When you go out walking or running, you must stay on the trails, no matter how tempted you are to explore the forest.

As you look straight ahead from your front porch, you'll see a hill with a village on it. That's the Upper Village and it cannot be reached by any of these paths. You'd have to go through the forest, and I can't warn you too strongly against trying this: Should you go into the forest alone, you will almost certainly get lost, and it will be difficult for anyone to find you. Also, there are some things in there that are unsafe. The Meliai Guides can be recognized by their white gowns and are here to help you and answer most of your questions. They will tell you anything, except why you are here; that you will learn from me in due time.

Don't worry about your cat. I promise she's being loved and well cared for. Please trust me and enjoy the many wonderful things we have to offer.

All my love,
Selene

I read the damned thing two more times before I realized I was crying. I'd been kidnapped by someone I trusted and loved. Worse, she was crazy as a loon, expecting me to believe she'd spirited me off to some alternate universe. Exactly who were these Meliai whose "Guest" I was supposed to be? Probably some cult. Selene was not only a liar, she was a lunatic.

Well, fuck my nutcase girlfriend—I'd give her a piece of my mind when the time came. Meanwhile, I had to pee, so I used the comforter to wipe the tears from my eyes, then wrapped it around my body and hopped onto the floor. I walked to the foot of the bed, found the sandals, and slipped them on. Then I went to the back of the cabin and into the bathroom. It was spotless, with a toilet, sink and vanity, a shower, a full-length mirror, a small bathtub, and even an actual bidet. All the taps and faucets, except those in the shower, were polished brass and looked brand new.

I dropped the comforter to the floor and, while I sat on the pot, glanced out the window by the sink. Now I could see why the light coming into the main room looked greenish: There were trees surrounding the cabin, big leafy ones, and the morning sun was filtering down through a dense canopy. I couldn't see a thing but trees. Not even a hint of sky from this angle.

I stood, flushed the toilet, and moved to the sink, twisting what looked like the warm tap. The water sputtered for a moment but soon came out steady and hot, hot enough that I had to add some cold. There was a bar of soap on the shelf above the sink, plus toothpaste and a new toothbrush. I washed my face, used the hand towel beside the sink, and then brushed my teeth. The vanity held dental floss, a hairbrush, tampons, plus a few other items that would come in handy if I was going to be here a while.

Walking back into the main room, I checked the view from the two big windows, trying to get a handle on where I was. Same scene both times—nothing but tall, densely packed trees and not a glimpse of sky. I was obviously in the forest somewhere, probably in Mill Valley, but I'd figure that out later. Right now, what I needed was a shower, so back into the bathroom I went.

The shower, a standalone enclosure, looked like an afterthought, something cobbled in from the Home Improvement catalog. The tub seemed inviting, but I was more a shower person and I badly needed a hot shower to wash away the sweat and feelings of betrayal. I stepped inside the stall and closed the glass door, turning the single lever that adjusted both temperature and pressure. I hate those single-lever things, but I got it figured out before freezing or scalding myself. There was a bottle labeled "Shower Gel" and another that said "Shampoo," and both smelled like honey and mint.

Hanging from hooks in the shower were a washcloth and a real sea sponge. I used them to soap and scrub every inch of my skin, then shampooed and let the hot water run over my back for a couple of minutes, feeling my knotted shoulder muscles relax.

As I stood beneath the water, I thought of David. When would he realize I'd vanished and try to find me? I began to seethe with anger again, thinking how I'd trusted that bitch Selene. I'd known from the start there was something wrong with her, but I'd let my heart get the better of the common sense that usually guided me.

Then I happened to glance down. My eyes had been closed while I was washing and for the first time since getting out of bed, I actually saw the lower part of my body. It was one of those deals where you register something half-consciously the first time you see it. I mean, you look right at it and your mind reads it as something ordinary, like a brown ball of lint on your pillow. Then you focus and suddenly see it for what it really is: a giant palmetto bug, crawling right at your face. But this was not a bug. I screamed, jumped out of the shower, and ran to the big mirror without even toweling dry.

The mirror was covered in steam from the shower, so I grabbed a towel and wiped it down till I could see myself. Right there on my lower belly, what I'd momentarily taken for a bunch of fibers from the washcloth, was a tattoo of a ram!

It was maybe six inches by five, with nasty-looking horns, standing on a grassy field, its head turned to the left, its beady eyes challenging the world. I screamed again and touched it gingerly. The design was intricate, especially those striated horns. The colors were fresh and vivid, but my skin didn't feel raw, so the tattoo couldn't possibly be from last night. When had Wynter done this to me? How long had I been kept unconscious?

I was furious, but as I stared at the tattoo and kept stroking it, I suddenly realized that my cigarette burn scars had been incorporated into the design, and though they were still there, and I could feel the ridges, I could barely see them. Then I smiled because I had this weird conviction that I'd become some kick-ass "bad girl," with this aggressive creature carved right above my pussy. *"Screw with me again, Harry, and I'll skewer your nuts with these horns and pull them right out of your scrotum!"* I didn't think rams snarled, but that's what part of me wanted to do.

But fuck that. I had not given anyone permission to do this. My body had been violated yet again! It was like Selene had somehow marked me as her property, and Willie Ludlow was no one's property! Not anymore! I dried myself with the big towel and opened the bathroom window to let the steam out. I wrapped the towel around myself, slipped the sandals back on, and walked out of the bathroom.

In the main room, I opened the armoire and peeked inside. There were three full-length items on hangers—were those supposed to be dresses? They looked more like night gowns, though they seemed meant for casual daytime wear. All were identical, made of a lightweight gauzy cloth, their green color so pale it was barely discernable.

Beside the gowns hung a thick hooded robe; the fabric was also pale green though rough to the touch. On a low shelf was something that looked like a rain poncho with matching boots, made of sturdy oil cloth, all in that same shade of green. The promised shorts and running shoes were there too; the shorts were pale green, the shoes white.

The deep drawer contained several pairs of tube socks, plus t-shirts, woolen pajamas and sweats, all again an insipid green.

Apparently, I wasn't expected to wear bras or panties, green or otherwise.

There was no trace of my personal stuff anywhere in the room— no purse, no wallet, no cell phone. I could live without the rest, but that damned phone was my lifeline to the world. I dug desperately through the armoire's drawer, cursing and tossing items onto the floor, not even sure what I expected to find. But now I finally got a break, because either Selene or one of her minions had made a careless mistake, and there, at the bottom of the drawer, was my iPhone in its silver case. I would call 911 for help! My relief was short-lived, though, because as soon as the phone booted, I got the damned "No Signal" message. *Fuck all.*

I calmed myself, thinking I'd try the phone again from the porch. But the cabin was chilly, and I was starting to shiver, so I dropped the towel, took the thick robe from the armoire, put it on, and headed for the front door. That was when I realized how hungry I was—no, not just hungry, but starving. I'd probably been drugged and unconscious in that bed for over twenty-four hours, and I was too famished to even think straight. I'd deal with the phone later but for now, food was the first order of business.

I turned and walked into the little kitchen, which was as spotless as the bathroom, though it was cheesy, like something straight out of Martha Stewart: frilly curtains covering two small windows, checkered dish cloths hanging above the sink, a little breakfast nook, including a table and two matching chairs with stick-pole backs. It was like the entire kitchen had been pre-fabricated and shipped in as a unit, to fit someone's idea of what a kitsch magazine housewife from the early 1960s might like.

There was an old-fashioned circular clock on the wall, black and white with a sweep second hand. It said 1:38—so okay, it wasn't morning after all. I didn't care. My mouth and stomach were demanding breakfast. I needed coffee and carbs right now, so I surveyed the kitchen and saw a coffee maker sitting on the sideboard, plugged into a wall socket. There was another note from Selene beside it.

Sumatra, baby. Blended with something special you've never tried. Nice and strong, just the way you like it. There's a whole pound in the freezer, plus as much as you want up at the General Store. I've stocked the fridge with all the goodies I know you love, so you won't waste away anytime soon—S.

The coffee maker was a Krupp's, primed with water and coffee and ready to go. I flipped the switch, and it began to hiss and gurgle quickly, the dark brew steaming and dripping into the glass pot, its rich, chocolaty aroma filling the air and making my mouth water. Damn! It was comforting, yet this kind of homey comfort was something I didn't want right now, much as I needed it. And what was that "something special" in the coffee Selene had mentioned? Was it spiked like her Halloween punch must have been? My need for caffeine outweighed my fear of being drugged again.

While the coffee brewed, I took one of the two mugs from above the sink and set it on the counter, then opened the refrigerator to see what I could scrounge up. But no scrounging was necessary because it was loaded and obsessively well organized. Breakfast stuff was on the top shelf: eggs, bacon, and sausage; a loaf of unsliced dark bread that looked homemade; several jars of jam and marmalade; numerous packages and containers labeled "goat butter," "goat cheese," and "goat yogurt," plus a small bottle of "goat half-and-half."(Apparently goats were all the rage here.)

On the second shelf were half a roasted chicken and some kind of barbequed meat in a plastic container. (Was that really Tupperware?) Another container was full of mashed potatoes, while the crisper bin on the left held salad makings, plus raw, cut broccoli, baby carrots, string beans, and Brussels sprouts, all in their own little packages. The other crisper held several varieties of fruit: pears, oranges, some odd-looking berries, plus a couple of things that looked like small white apples.

Two jars in the door shelves contained salad dressing: blue cheese in one, red vinaigrette in the other. The bottom shelf had a box with four fresh chocolate éclairs, along with a quart bottle of goat milk, not homogenized, because the dense, yellow cream had risen into the neck. I hadn't seen milk like that since I'd been a girl and spent a summer working on our church farm.

The freezer held a small ice maker, a bag of coffee, and two quarts of something like frozen yogurt, which I sampled with my fingers. I couldn't tell the flavors, but they were seriously luscious.

I closed the freezer and moved to the pantry, which was likewise loaded: There were dried beans, rice and barley, several kinds of pasta plus jars of sauces, a box of oatmeal, a jar of pale honey, a variety of tea bags, canned goods of every description, and lots more. Selene was right; I wouldn't starve anytime soon. Everything here appealed to the indolent side of me. But if I gave in to being taken care of, I'd be what—a bird in a gilded cage? Well, that was not going to happen! I would work out my escape plan as soon as I'd eaten.

I reached into the fridge and took out the half-and-half, plus the box of éclairs. Fuck good nutrition. I wanted sugar. The coffee was ready, so I poured myself a mug and added a splash of half-and-half. The brew was hot and strong, with a spicy kick. I sampled one of the éclairs and, much as I hated being manipulated with treats, put it on a plate, shrugged, and added a second one. Then I took the pastries and my coffee over to the breakfast nook, set them on the table, and sat down to eat.

I finished the éclairs and had two more mugs of coffee, longing for a cigarette for the first time since I'd quit smoking five years ago. The caffeine was sharpening my mind, and slowly a plan took shape. There had to be an urban center nearby. Civilization would lie through the woods Selene had cautioned me to keep out of. If that wasn't my escape route, why would she warn me off?

It was nearly 3:00 and the day was too far gone to leave now, so I'd get a good night's sleep and wait until morning. I'd wear the sweats and running shoes, and take a pair of shorts plus a t-shirt for when it got warm. I'd pack those into a pillowcase along with some lunch and, once I got into the woods, I'd follow the sun and make for the coast. At the first town I came to, I'd go straight to the cops and say I'd been kidnapped. That would put an end to Selene's little game.

First, though, I had to get the lay of the land, so I went back into the cabin's main room and walked to the front door. The porch was sure to offer a better view of the terrain than the windows, and maybe there'd be cell phone reception outside.

I stepped out into the afternoon light and waited for my eyes to adjust. Then I took a deep breath, peering into the distance at what was up on that hill. I saw cultivated fields, orchards, and vineyards; and then further up, a cluster of Doric temples made of pink-and-white marble that sparkled in the sunlight.

But the most impossible thing of all was that green sky and those two moons. Where the hell was I?

Chapter 26

❦

THE GENERAL STORE

Month of Reed/Month of December

avid had been clerking at the Lower Village General Store for a couple of weeks now and liked the easy work, which had none of the deadline pressure or office politics he'd endured as a software engineer. He did only what he wanted, knowing that if he didn't get around to finishing some task, Nareen or Nyleen would cheerfully handle it.

Restocking the shelves with freshly laundered gowns was the only thing the twins had asked of him today, and he was carrying the last stack of garments out from the storeroom, trying to scratch at his new beard without dropping them. The gowns were all the same pale green and came in several sizes, from extra-small to extra-extra-large; and, because they were the main item of clothing the Meliai provided, all the Guests routinely wore them.

David's memory of landing here was fragmentary. He'd gone to Selene's party costumed as either an ear of corn or a banana, and he'd had too much to drink. He had a vague impression of a bald woman with a dog that could talk. And then he remembered searching for Willie, who was supposed to introduce him to a girl named Eva, and a Hell's Angel saying that Cinderella was waiting for him by the service entrance. Figuring it was Eva, he'd staggered downstairs and was stunned to see Jill, miraculously returned from the dead. When he'd rushed to embrace her, he felt, what ... a cold pinprick in the side of his neck?

The next thing he knew, he was waking up in a cabin, finding a note from Jill saying he was in a place called Ausonia and that she was some kind of alien. He was only slightly annoyed at being kidnapped. Mostly, he was overjoyed, because it meant seeing her at the party wasn't a dream; she was alive and well, just as he'd always believed. As to that business about taking him to another world—it was obviously one of the little role-playing games she loved. For whatever reason, Jill had been gone for months and now wanted a dramatic way of stepping back into his life. Telling him he was the captive of some sexy creature called a Meliai was just like her, and she'd be walking through the door any minute now.

That hadn't happened. He'd waited a good two hours before finally stepping outside his cabin and realizing he truly was on another world. It was a shock, of course; but, human or not, Jill was alive. That was what counted. The big question was where was she?

In her note, she'd promised to be back in six weeks and answer all his questions. "Then we'll be together forever, Lamb Chop," was what she'd said. The days tended to blur into one another here, but David's best guess was that he'd been in Ausonia for over two months now, with still no sign of her.

The Meliai were the most stunning girls David had ever seen. His new friend Baba Bill—who'd been in Ausonia nearly a year and seemed to know a thing or two—said they were a type of Dryad, the female "tree tenders" from Greek mythology. But though the Meliai were happy to answer questions about themselves and their world in general, the biggest question—why they were abducting humans and bringing them to Ausonia—was something none of them would answer. All they would say was that the reason was "lovely" and would soon be revealed. Meanwhile, humans were meant to enjoy this paradise and know they were "in safe hands."

The Meliai called their human captives "Guests," and what nearly every Guest David spoke to could agree on was that anger at the Meliai for kidnapping them was hard to sustain in a place where everything conspired to seduce the mind and senses so completely. The colors and scents were hypnotically vivid. The weather, even now in what should have been mid-winter, was almost always balmy during the day. The food in the Dining Commons was varied and delicious, and every Guest had his or her own little cabin which, though hardly luxurious, was cozy and comfortable.

The little town where Guests were housed was called the Lower Village, and it was filled with humans David had much in common with. All—both men and women—had fallen in love with a Meliai and, after a time, been abducted and brought here, with only a note from their lover promising to return soon and "explain everything."

There were about 150 humans currently housed in the Lower Village, most from the Bay Area, but David had met others from different parts of the country, and some from as far away as Europe or Asia. He'd heard a Meliai speaking fluent Italian to one man, and others conversing with Guests in German, Spanish, and once in what might have been Turkish. A Dryad named Dalsara sometimes sang in Gaelic to entertain Guests in the Dining Commons, accompanying herself on the hammer dulcimer or a goatskin *bodhrán*. And then there was Pandoric, the Meliai's own language, which they spoke mostly among themselves.

There were no phones, computers, TV or radio; virtually no modern electronics at all, except for an MP3 player loaded with music in each cabin. But there was adequate electricity for lighting and appliances, all supplied by wind generators and solar power. There was a library of books from Earth, and board games including Monopoly, chess, and Go were available at the General Store. David and Baba Bill played Go every day, and David, who was a novice, had learned a lot from Baba, whose Zen-like focus made him a master tactician.

Life here was an odd mixture of indolent freedom and strict regimentation. The Meliai's chief aims were to keep their Guests relaxed, well-fed, and as sexually starved as possible. The latter was both frustrating and puzzling in light of the fact that, on Earth, the Meliai had wrapped themselves around their human consorts like seductive boa constrictors.

As to male and female Guests coupling with each other, the logistics were tricky. Men and women were housed in different areas of the Lower Village—"campuses," they were called—and contact between them was kept to a minimum by the Meliai Guides, who were really more like "minders" than aides.

Logically, humans should have been up in arms at their captivity. But there were no urgent meetings demanding action and no riots for the Meliai to quell, because the longer Guests remained here, the more accepting of their confinement they grew. It was as if Ausonia itself acted like an opioid, replacing anger and anxiety with a languorous sense of well-being. Guests called it "The Ausonia Effect," and it held everyone spellbound.

Day followed night. The sun and the two moons rose and set. The meals were never late and always delicious.

There were lots of interesting people to talk to, and a variety of trails to hike, ranging from easy to challenging. The main thing David missed besides Jill was Willie. If he ever got back home, he'd tell her about Ausonia, and she'd think he'd gone completely off the deep end this time.

Though Guests were never required to work, chiefly out of wanting something to do, David had asked the Meliai named Nareen if he could spell her behind the General Store's counter two afternoons per week. She'd readily agreed, though his claim of being bored puzzled her. "You're bored?" she'd said incredulously. "Honestly, David, why don't you go for a swim in the lake? That should get your juices flowing." Well, his "juices" were flowing just fine, thank you, because he was always horny as hell.

Maybe a dip in the lake would have helped, but when he'd confessed that he'd never learned to swim, Nareen had offered to toss him in the water and see if an Alanoie saved him from drowning.

She was joking, of course, though the idea intrigued him. He'd yet to meet one of the aquatic Naiads, but they were allegedly as sensuous as the Meliai, and maybe that was why most of the rivers and streams were off limits to humans. Rumor had it that the Alanoie didn't care about the Dryads' silly rules, and maybe the Meliai didn't trust them enough to keep their hot little hands off their Guests.

But if the Meliai weren't having sex with humans, what they did among themselves was another matter, and they didn't seem to care who watched. David might be out for a stroll, following one of the footpaths through the Ponderosa grove, and there were two Dryads in the act of passion, splayed out on a carpet of pine needles right in front of him. Or, he'd walk out in the early evening and find half a dozen of them on the grass, writhing in ecstasy behind his cabin.

To call these scenes orgies seemed blasphemous because they were more like erotic revival meetings, into which David longed to hurl himself. But he was like some heathen from a far country, allowed to view the holy-of-holies from a distance, but too spiritually primitive to enter the tabernacle itself.

He was in a state of almost constant sexual tension, so to hide it—and maintain some semblance of dignity—David often wore running shorts under his gown to contain his erection. Those who wore nothing beneath their gowns might just as well have gone naked, though most of the longer-term Guests seemed used to the flimsy attire—"like pet cats get used to wearing collars," he'd heard one human woman say. It was also true that some Guests were excited by the feeling of sexual vulnerability the semi-transparent gowns imparted.

The Meliai loved erotic ritual, and there was a custom that David found charming when Nareen explained it. Whenever two Meliai made love, one always dominated, while the other submitted to her. There was nothing violent or abusive in it. It was more like one or the other orchestrated the encounter and was the pleasure-giver— the ravisher—while the other took a passive role and accepted the ravishment eagerly.

The ritual went like this: When two Dryads wanted to share pleasure, both would remove their sandals. Then, one would place her right foot over the left foot of the other and stroke it lightly. Right foot over left meant something like "I want to ravish you." But if the second Meliai responded by putting her *own* right foot over the left foot of the first, it meant something like, "Actually, I would prefer to ravish you."

In such a standoff, there followed an erotic battle of wills fought solely through eye contact, in which one Meliai would finally overwhelm the other with her gaze. Nareen demonstrated this for David and melted him in seconds; but when he tried to show his eagerness to be ravished, she laughed and wriggled away.

Despite the erotic starvation diet imposed on humans in the Lower Village, tales of what went on in a place called the Upper Village were enticing. There were rumors of lavish bacchanals, with food and drink, and a dizzying array of sexual exercises involving Meliai and humans. For humans who'd been in the Lower Village for months, the prospect of going to the Upper Village—where so many exotic pleasures were believed to await them—was practically all they ever talked about.

At first, David found the dizzy prattle about going to the Upper Village—or "going above," as it was often called—cloying. These people were like children looking forward to the treats at a big birthday party that couldn't come fast enough. Now, though, after a couple of months in the Lower Village, he sometimes heard himself spouting the same nonsense.

The thing was that nobody knew when they'd be taken above. It just happened when it happened, generally a couple of months after a Guest's arrival from Earth, or *T'Erenya* as it was called in Pandoric. Occasionally, though, a new Guest would be taken above in just a few days. This caused some envy, but there were no behavioral guidelines to follow, no curriculum or exams that might help a Guest go above any sooner.

Besides being housed on separate campuses, there were different times of day during which male and female Guests were permitted to swim. Swimming was always nude, yet strangely, despite all the gender segregation, men and women could watch each other swimming naked. David had watched the women swim once and never again, since it made him feel like a pervert.

Because there was just one General Store and all the Guests needed access to it, it was open to women only from 8:00 to 12:00 in the morning and men from 1:00 to 5:00 in the afternoon—this to prevent undue fraternizing between genders. Desperate to get closer to the female Guests, David had tried to 'cheat' the rules by asking for the morning work shift at the store, saying that he played Go with Baba Bill most afternoons. But Nareen just laughed and told him to play in the morning or evening, as if the solution was absurdly obvious.

There were always refreshments on offer at the General Store. Fresh-brewed coffee was available any time of day, as were tea and cocoa. On Tuesdays, Thursdays, and Sundays, there were cucumber and goat cheese finger sandwiches, made with the rich, black bread that was a staple in Ausonia. The sandwiches were scrumptious, especially with the Meliai's *sauvignon blanc*, and the Guests gobbled them with enthusiasm. There were also plates of crisp, raw vegetables and dip every day, plus fresh fruits, some of which were unknown on Earth. David especially loved *peloons*, the little white spheres that were crunchy as perfect apples but tasted like a cross between raspberries and tangerines.

The store looked like something out of an old Western movie, and bore witness to the Meliai's fascination with human culture. There was an old wagon wheel on the porch, and a quaint sign above the entrance that said "Lower Village General Store," in large, ragged letters. The place was a bit less than a quarter mile from the men's campus and just over half a mile from the women's. This was a cause of irritation on the part of some female Guests, who didn't see why they should be made to walk farther to obtain supplies than the men were made to.

210

The store's interior was lit with colorful lanterns, like those that illuminated the paths at night. There were braziers burning sweet-scented wood, which gave the place a feel that was vaguely mystical, and there was always *haraka*—the hash-like drug the Meliai smoked—on offer.

David had introduced Nareen to George Winston's version of *Carol of the Bells*, and now she frequently played it on the store's sound system. Like all Meliai, she had a gorgeous voice and loved to sing along wordlessly: "la-la-la-la ... la-la-la-la" ... this while dancing down the aisles of the store, leaping like some enchanted woodland fairy.

Since everything in the store was free, there was no way to shoplift and no need to keep an eye on customers. The counter David manned was mainly there for providing information about where to find things and recording items taken so they could be restocked. The shelves and racks near the front of the store were devoted to clean linens and garments. Farther down were food items for those who liked to do their own cooking, and at the very back were toiletries and a variety of uncategorized items, which were virtually impossible to find without help from the clerk behind the counter.

Down the central aisle were several tables that held things like glowing glass balls, quartz crystals, and an assortment of carvings and clay figurines, some animistic, others with traditional religious themes, like the Virgin or the Buddha. But David was only interested in the glass balls, which appeared to dance with colored lights from within. He'd helped himself liberally to those, along with a brazier, in which he burned frankincense as he read or sat sleepily at night by the glow of his pellet stove.

It was just after 5:00 PM and the end of David's shift when Nareen walked in, accompanied by her Full Sister Nyleen. They wore nothing beneath their white gowns except their lovely skin, so that every luscious curve, as well as the thick red thatch between their legs, was visible through the gauze-like fabric.

The Meliai didn't go in for the pubic shaving that was increasingly popular among humans, and David found the "natural" look mysterious and enticing. Fortunately, his shorts hid at least some of his excitement. Not that the twins didn't know the effect they were having on him. The pleasure they took in their erotic power was evident in the provocative way they stood—each with a hand on her jutting hip, her rosy nipples poking at the flimsy fabric of her gown, and those big, luminescent eyes drilling right into the soul of him.

As with all Dryads, the iris in each girl's left and right eye was a different color, though in Full Sisters—which was what Meliai twins were called—the eye colors were always reversed. So, while Nareen's left eye was green and her right the color of liquid silver, Nyleen's left eye was silver and the right eye green. The small birthmark just above Nareen's right nipple was in the identical position above Nyleen's left. David had met six sets of Meliai Full Sisters so far, and each girl was the exact mirror image of her twin.

"Arthur was a bad boy today ..." Nareen said, walking over to plant a little kiss on David's cheek.

"So we had to give him a spanking," Nyleen concluded. They often finished each other's sentences that way.

"I guess being bad has advantages around here," David sighed.

Nyleen came over to take David's arm. "You don't have to misbehave to get spanked," she said archly. "You just have to ask for it. Arthur likes it when we make him feel wicked, so we do."

"But if you want a spanking," Nareen added, "you'll have to lose these silly shorts. They're supposed to be for sports, not to hide your lovely *salesh* from us." *Salesh* was the Pandoric word for penis, and Nareen grabbed the waistband of David's shorts and gave them a hard snap, right through his gown.

"Hey, stop teasing," he protested half-heartedly.

The sisters laughed, and Nyleen rubbed her hand through his new beard. "I love this," she said. "It reminds me of Spanish moss."

The light outside was beginning to deepen when Nyleen glanced at the window. "Oh, Kayla, I have to run," she said. "I'm taking a Guest to the Upper Village, and I want to get her there in time for a late dinner at the Inn." She gave her twin a quick kiss on the lips and hurried out.

David turned to Nareen. "So when do *I* get to go above?" he demanded, knowing it sounded whiney. "I've been here over two months now."

"Everything happens in its own time," Nareen said. "Why don't you go for a nice jog? You're starting to tub out a bit there." She poked his tummy lightly, though her smile took some of the sting out of the remark. He knew he was gaining weight, but didn't much like having it pointed out by Nareen.

"Well, I guess that means sex tonight is out of the question again," he said, grinning.

"You know the rules," she said, then gave his ass a playful whack and headed off to the stockroom, her own behind swaying unmercifully. David sighed and walked out of the store. It was nearly time for dinner, and at least there was always as much food as he could hope for.

He took the path that wound up toward the Dining Commons, past the *jilly* flowers with their lavish purple blossoms, then through the stand of poplars, and finally past the Lane of Fountains with its twelve Meliai statues pouring streams of water into reflecting pools from pitchers that never ran dry. The marble glinted pink and the water sparkled in the late afternoon sun. A flock of birds that were *almost* geese flew calling overhead, and the air smelled of cloves and ginger. Sex or not, it took some effort not to love this place.

Looking east, he saw the smaller moon—the one called Yemanya—just rising over the mountains. When the dime-sized orb was full, as she was tonight, and you spotted her just as she was rising, it meant some glorious opportunity was at hand—or so the legend went.

Turning his eyes back to the path, David smiled and headed up the hill toward the Commons. After a minute, he began to jog awkwardly, and soon he was huffing and puffing, his leather sandals flapping against the soles of his feet.

Chapter 27

❦

BABA BILL

12th day of Ivy/November

Sita Ram, Guru Dass,

Why this hunger for what amounts to personal annihilation? Every Changeling feels it, but it's not really a death wish. I believe it's a longing for union with the Divine Feminine, the sensual lover and birth mother of the universe. According to the Meliai, this craving is caused by a condition found in less than one in a thousand humans. The Pandoric word for it is nyala. It doesn't translate well into English, but every human the Meliai bring here suffers from it to some degree. We feel it as a continual sense of lack, a need for something so fulfilling we cannot live without it. It nags at us throughout our lives, though we don't understand exactly what we need until we're found by a Meliai. Perhaps the real tragedy is that so many of us are never found by them at all.

Nyala begins to haunt us at about age seven or eight, when a once happy boy or girl will gradually become morose and uncommunicative. Our minds become lost in daydreams. In fact, nyala may be a direct cause of what we call attention deficit disorder.

As children, we have trouble fitting in at school. Some are victimized by bullies, while others become bullies themselves, simply acting out of blind frustration. The symptoms vary from child to child, but the core indicator is always a deep sense of incompleteness or inadequacy. Once we reach puberty, nyala may manifest sexually, often in the form of odd obsessions. The idea of death may become morbidly eroticized with dreams of fatal seduction by mythical beings. Some people experiment with sadomasochistic rituals like bondage, flogging, cutting the flesh, or erotic asphyxiation.

Perhaps such "perverse" sexuality is hardwired into us at a very early age because of childhood abuse, but sometimes nothing in our history can account for it. It is simply a predilection. One female Changeling I met said she'd walked into a sex shop looking for videos of an act so heartbreakingly aberrant I won't shock you by naming it. Fortunately, the owner of the shop was a Meliai who brought her here for healing and transformation.

I know you don't like to talk about reincarnation, but I often think the karmic burden of our past lives would explain so much if we could remember them. If there was no sexual victimization in this life, maybe it happened in a past incarnation and we still carry the painful stamp of these experiences.

As adults, we humans with nyala may be gloomy and uncomfortable in our own skins. It's much like having an unreachable itch. Some of us might suffer from eating disorders, alcoholism, or drug addiction; or we may become religious fanatics and join severe monastic orders.

When you first meet a Meliai and make love with her, you finally understand what you've been searching for all your life. Is that just a juvenile fantasy? Not to a human suffering with nyala. These Dryads offer a kind of salve that is both physical and spiritual. Maybe they are Devi—celestial beings with the physical form of human women and the spirit of Rati, the Hindu goddess of sexual passion and slayer of demons.

Whatever they are, the Meliai take away the ache of nyala, and the one thing they ask in return is that we become their life-giving Drys trees and bond with them forever in bliss. We have the right to refuse and return home, but for me, trading my broken life for the ecstasy Aneel offers was the bargain of a lifetime.

Have you ever seen Bernini's painting of St. Theresa's rapture as she's pierced by the spear of an angel? It's about as close to overt sexuality as

Catholic iconography ever gets. This is what she supposedly said of her experience:

> *"The pain was so great that I screamed aloud; but at the same*
> *time I felt such an infinite sweetness that I wished the pain*
> *to last forever. It was not physical but psychic pain, although*
> *it affected the body as well to some degree. It was the sweetest*
> *caressing of the soul by God."*

When I was a boy at St. Vincent's, we used to snicker about that story behind the nuns' backs: "Yeah, sure. I'll just bet her soul was pierced by an angel ... haw, haw!" Of course we were just children with spirits that hadn't begun to ripen yet.

But whether Theresa was "pierced" by an angel or the penis of the handyman at her convent, the ecstasy sounds divine, doesn't it? Funny, but now that I've left the Church, I'm less cynical about this story. Just visualize God as a passionate lover ardently devouring your body and that image is electrifying. If you can sense Theresa's ecstatic state at that moment, who or what caused it is almost secondary. The Church might be horrified at this suggestion, but that's what it's like to be taken in passion by a Meliai: to be loved with such ferocity that you feel yourself melting into the wet, loving womb of the Mother of Creation. It is the sweetest kind of death.

I am helpless to fight the lust that surges through me when touched by a Meliai. Imagine a sixteen-year-old boy on Viagra. Show him a naked woman and you could hang a trench coat on his erection. I never seem to run short of desire or energy because the Fleen supplies me with as much as I need. Sometimes I think I'm as enthralled by the symbionts that live in the Fleen as I am by the Meliai—enslaved by a hundred billion microorganisms that require my intense sexual release in order to feed, multiply and, in the end, reshape me to their needs.

Let me describe the moment of Edarta. Everything we experience, from the instant we receive our first infusion of Fleen, guides us toward this completion. What does it feel like? It hasn't happened to me yet so I don't know, and no Changeling who's gone through Edarta can ever speak to tell the tale. But watching someone who's been your friend undergo it is both a miraculous and terrible thing.

You see them disappear and become another life form right before your eyes. Where have they gone? Are they dead or living? Should you grieve their death or rejoice at their liberation? I've watched three Edartas and the impact is always the same.

During those final minutes of transformation, the Changeling is in a deep trance and there appears to be no pain. Time seems to slow down as you watch. Your breathing becomes shallow and often a flush goes through your body, settling into your 2nd chakra—the energy center of sex. There's an almost carnal scent in the air.

The Meliai train us for spiritual surrender through sex, and it is a good thing because Edarta requires total surrender. So becoming aroused as you watch is a reflex that's impossible to control. The knowledge that this will soon happen to you, and the fact that you're helpless to prevent it may be frightening, but it also delivers a thrill that resonates through your entire body.

When all goes well, the last expression on the Changeling's face is luminous, as if they were in a state of Samadhi. The eyes look inward, but what kaleidoscopic visions are they seeing? And what are their final thoughts as their sapience evaporates like mist in the sunlight? Just before the end, there is a strange reflex that causes the Changeling's arms to rise and become rigid, like branches reaching for the sky. It happens without fail. At this point, they are only moments away from the final consummation.

If the Changeling hasn't stopped breathing, there may be a last scream of delight. Then the face explodes into a crown of leaves, and whatever is left of the human body vanishes beneath a layer of bark. Your friend is gone, and in their place stands a Drys sapling. You don't know whether to laugh or cry.

Within a few months, the sapling is mature enough to be transplanted into an orchard and bond with its Meliai. Immediately after that bonding, the Meliai's original Drys, now covered in blight, will drop its last leaves and die. The Meliai's new tree grows very quickly, bearing its first crop of fruit in less than a year.

Aging is terribly unfair to human women, and I'm hardly the first to make that observation. We men can remain virile and desirable well into our 60s, sometimes even our 70s. But as for women, well, there's no need to belabor what happens to them. It breaks my heart that a gorgeous 18-year-old girl, with not a spiritual thought in her mind, will never be lovelier than she is at this moment, yet a 70-year-old woman, with all the wisdom and experience of a full lifetime, is seen as a crone at the very time her spirit is fully ripening. In a just world, she would be as radiant and alluring as Aphrodite, but most men in their prime are not interested in a 70 year-old woman because the packaging doesn't shine like the gift within.

Yet it's different with the Meliai, which is one reason I never want to leave this place. These females remain ageless and seductive just as long as their Drys trees live, and all the while their spirits continue to ripen. By the time they've reached a thousand years, they are true Goddesses.

As you know, Hindu mythology is filled with heroes and deities who transform from one thing into another, sometimes turning from male to female, female to male, or even into some entirely new type of being. Wasn't there a Goddess named Tulasi who was turned into a tree by her husband? Such transformations occur frequently in the Vedas. Both Gods and mortals undergo radical changes as the result of blessings, curses, reincarnation, or what have you. And sexual congress between Gods or Goddesses and mortals often serves a spiritual purpose.

I almost feel that I could ...

Chapter 28

⁂

THE BUDDHA AND THE CAR THIEF

The Lower Village Dining Commons was a large, circular building made of stone and sunbaked clay, with an earthen roof that held a vegetable garden that supplied some of the kitchen's produce. The roof also provided excellent insulation, and drainage from the rain was filtered and piped below for drinking water and cooking.

The Commons was set amid a grove of eucalyptus-like trees on a cliff overlooking the ocean. From here, you could smell the sea and hear the breakers on the rocks, along with the cry of blue-winged gulls circling below. From a window seat, you could see the *almost* pelicans diving for fish all day, as they competed with sleek seal-like creatures for the choicest morsels.

Early in the morning, you might also see the colorful sails of the Alanoie fishing fleet spread out across the bay, their wakes crisscrossing in fine, white traceries. Sometimes, the Alanoie—who were amphibious and also expert sailors—would dive into the sea to catch fish with their bare hands and toss them up onto the decks of their boats, just for the fun of it.

Large windows made of strong glass circled the Commons so natural light filled the entire space from dawn to dusk, and spectacular sunrises and sunsets were viewable year-round. Guests who did not wish to cook for themselves were served breakfast and dinner here if they wanted it, and many did. Of the 150 or so humans currently residing in the Lower Village, there were usually about 40 to 50 at breakfast and perhaps 100 to 125 at dinner. Yet the Commons could accommodate over 300 diners, so if this were a restaurant on Earth, it would be in deep trouble due to a lack of customers.

Meliai chefs prepared the food in a steaming, commissary-style kitchen, passing it out through a window, where it was served at a chow line and eaten at picnic tables made of dark hardwood. But the food itself, despite the military way in which it was served, was nothing like army chow. The meals were luscious and well-balanced and always left you with a sense of languorous well-being.

Dinner was served not on tin or plastic plates, but on elegant ceramic ware—a product of the Meliai pottery studios. Different sets of dishes were used each day of the week, and this evening's design featured a fleet of tiny sailboats on a shimmering nighttime bay, presided over by two gibbous moons and a sky full of glittering stars, as pods of dolphins cavorted below with silver-haired Alanoie Naiads.

Tonight, there was a choice of venison in a white wine sauce for meat-eaters, or eggplant parmesan with rice pasta for the wheat-intolerant vegetarians. Of course, you could have both entrees if you wanted.

There were three people ahead of him in line as David stood holding his empty tray thinking about Willie. He had been gone a long time and knew she would be frantic worrying about him by now, maybe even given him up for dead. Last week, he'd asked one of the Guides whether there was a way to send messages to anxious friends and family back on Earth; his question was met with gentle laughter, which clearly meant "no."

"Next!" It was his turn to be served, and David stepped to the counter. A brunette Meliai named Aliyah was on duty tonight, ladling the food out from large chafing dishes. Her left eye was chestnut brown, while her right was a fiery gold, and David knew she was Nareen's lover. Like all the Meliai servers, Aliyah was eager to make sure Guests got enough to eat and made sensible nutritional selections.

"Would you like another piece of venison, dear?" she asked David, when his plate was already overflowing. "Another scoop of garlic mashed potatoes with gravy? You should really have some of the green casserole too. Oops … ha, ha …better let me put that on another plate for you. Here … and don't forget your *peloon* pie."

"Screw the *peloon* pie," David said. "Your slutty girlfriend thinks I'm getting fat."

Aliyah looked aghast. "Which slutty girlfriend?"

He raised his eyes in exasperation. "Nareen, of course."

Aliyah's mouth dropped open. "Nareen says you're fat? Well, that little butterball is a fine one to talk. It's just plain piffle."

David stared. "You sound like something out of *Gone with the Wind*. I mean, who says 'piffle' anymore?"

Aliyah thought for moment. "Hmm. Now, wherever did I pick that word up? Seems like I've been saying it forever. Well, no matter." She reached over and stroked his stomach. "You're not fat at all. I like a soft tummy to lay my head on."

"Yeah, right," David muttered. "Just like Nareen. All talk and no action."

The human woman in line behind him groaned in exasperation. "Would you stop that disgusting crap and get on with it? Some of us are here to eat, you know."

David turned and saw a slender human woman of about twenty-five, with thick glasses and pencil-thin eyebrows. Her name was Gloria, and she was a notorious pain in the ass who was constantly venting her irritation at men.

"C'mon, Glo," David said. "We're just flirting a little here."

Gloria gave him a look that would have curdled cream. "She's not going to suck your puny little dick, so just take your food, go stuff your face, and give the rest of us a break."

"Hey, bite me, bitch," David said. "I'm not your whipping boy."

A pained look came over Gloria's face, and abruptly she began to cry, in loud, racking sobs. Her reaction was so unexpected, it left David flustered. He set his tray down and put a hand on her shoulder "Hey, take it easy. I didn't mean to ..."

She shrugged his hand away and continued to sob. "They're sending me home when the Portal opens," she moaned. "I know I can improve, but they won't give me a chance."

Immediately, a Meliai who'd been stacking clean plates nearby hurried over, taking Gloria by the arm and leading her away while consoling her gently.

David gave Aliyah a quizzical look. "What's her problem?"

"She's not very stable," Aliyah said. "We're doing our best to help her, but I'm afraid she's kind of ... What do humans call it?" Her voice became a whisper. "Borderline?"

The diagnosis sounded harsh, but before he could say anything, Aliyah placed a piece of pie on his tray and gave him a big smile, all full lips and perfect teeth. "Come back for more if you want," she said, signaling to the next person in line.

David carried his tray over to the self-serve beverage counter. As always, there was coffee, tea (hot or iced), water (plain or mineral), goat's milk, cold beer or tepid English ale, and jugs of generic red and white wine. David poured himself a glass of red, balanced it precariously on the overflowing tray, and carried it over to the men's section.

There was only the one chow line, but male and female diners were made to sit on opposite sides of the Commons. It was as annoying as the separate "campuses" for men and women, but the gender segregation was strictly enforced. The one time David had tried to defy convention and sit with a group of women at dinner, he'd been shooed off like an errant puppy by a Guide who was nursing her child. "No, no, no," she'd said, pointing him toward the men's section and sending him off with a pat on the behind.

The ochre coastal light that marked this time of day was streaming through the windows from the west, and the clouds above the bay glowed crimson and gold. The ruddy light here had a very different quality from the ubiquitous soft green sky a bit farther inland. There, the cool forest light was a sensuous narcotic—feminine as a swoon. The warm light up here felt like the one truly male thing in Ausonia. If there'd ever been boy Dryads, they probably partied up here on this cliff, dancing like drunken satyrs and howling at the sunset.

He spotted a picnic table with room for eight, though just two men were seated there, both of whom he knew. Like all the other Guests, they were wearing pale-green gowns. The first, a stocky blond man in his mid-twenties, was Sheldon Cappellini, who usually went by "Shel." He was boisterous and not very bright, but as a dinner companion, he could be amusing.

The other man, taller and in his early forties, with shoulder-length salt-and-pepper hair, was busily writing in a notepad. His name was William Neeson, and he was both a lapsed Catholic and a former Hindu monk. He'd been in Ausonia nearly a year, making him the "senior" resident of the Lower Village. The small canvas pack he always carried was on the bench beside him.

Neeson was an eccentric, even by local standards. Sometimes he could be seen balancing on the pointed roof of his cabin, frozen in the one-legged karate "stork" position. He could stay that way for hours, totally motionless, his mind journeying in who knew what abstract realms.

He'd been poised like that the first time David had seen him, unshakable as a tree, arms spread more like branches than wings. Fascinated, David had watched him for at least fifteen minutes before Neeson so much as blinked. The guy was either a Buddha or an absolute lunatic, but, for whatever reason, David felt drawn to him and the feeling was mutual, because Neeson had taken him under his wing as if he were a younger brother. David began calling him Baba Bill, or just plain Baba, and Neeson didn't seem to mind.

"Gentlemen," David said, sitting down opposite Baba and Shel as he began to unload food and silverware from his tray. "How are we this evening?"

"Cool, man," Shel said. "Extremely cool."

"The eggplant's great tonight," Baba Bill declared, quickly setting his notepad aside and jiggling his pen at David. "And you should really avoid meat. It gives you cataracts and prostate cancer."

"So does masturbation," David replied, slicing off a chunk of venison and chewing it appreciatively. "But no real man would let that keep him from doing his duty."

"The Catholic in me would call masturbation a mortal sin," Baba said, taking a sip of goat's milk. "But my inner Hindu says that if you're feeling lonely, it's less mortal than suicide."

David grinned. "Writing to that guru of yours again?" he said, gesturing at the notepad. "I don't know why you even bother when the Meliai won't deliver it."

"I write for posterity," Baba said, setting the pen down atop the notepad. "Maybe someone here will find my letters someday and learn something about me."

"Posterity, my ass," Shel said, laughing. "What a wanker. Hey, David, Mr. Wanker here says he spent yesterday in the Upper Village."

David's eyes widened. "What, again? C'mon, man. Spill it. What do they do up there, anyway? Maypole dancing and shit like that?"

Bill just shook his head. "Sorry. I'm forbidden to say."

David leaned forward. "Jesus, Baba, don't be such a dipshit. You've gotta tell us *something*."

"There's sex up there," Shel said, pointing in the vague direction of the Upper Village. "These Meliai girls give you as much poon as you can handle, don't they, Neeson?"

Bill again shook his head, looking down at his plate. "I've experienced things you wouldn't believe, my friends. The vulgar and the sacred made one. That's as much as I can reveal." He was playing with them, David knew.

"Screw you, Baba," he said. "Just how vulgar does the 'sacredness' get?"

Bill traced a phantom zipper across his lips, indicating the subject was closed.

"See? I told you he was a wanker," Shel said. "Lots of talk, but a lot more of this." He made a pumping motion with his fist.

Baba ignored the obscene gesture, but David laughed and took a bite of the green casserole Aliyah had virtually forced on him. "So, Shel," he said. "How did you ever wind up in Ausonia? You've never shared that."

Shel, an avid talker, was happy to oblige. "Well, I'm from back East, see ..."

David nodded. "I guessed from your accent you were a New Yorker."

"New York? Fuck, no, man! Metuchen ...that's a town in Jersey! Hey, do you know what we call New York back where I come from?"

David shook his head. "No, but I guess you're about to tell us."

"'New York, the gateway to New Jersey,'" Shel said, laughing. "See, my brother Tony, he used to do standup comedy, and that's what they call a 'reverse'—you know, a joke that switches things around so it's backward from what you expect. Because, see, New Jersey is always called the gateway to—"

"Yeah, we get it," David said, wishing he hadn't gotten Shel started.

"Okay," Shel continued. "So here's how it went down ..." He proceeded to weave a convoluted tale about being arrested on a "grand theft auto" charge that wasn't really his fault, because all he'd been doing was riding shotgun to Asbury Park with his buddy Mule, who'd stolen this silver Accord from in front of a Starbucks when its woman driver had run inside—probably to take a leak—leaving the keys in the ignition and the engine running, practically begging someone to cop her ride.

"Dumb, huh?" Shel went on. "Anyway, it's about midnight when Mule and me hit this sobriety check point. 'Course the cops, they make the Accord right away, and I get nailed as an accomplice. Can you believe my dumb luck? I mean, I'm already dirty on an old coke thing, so I get sent up for eighteen fucking months. But, dig this. On appeal, I get this unbelievably hot babe as my PD, my public defender, right? Nellyn was her name, but I just call her Nelly." Shel paused for a moment to catch his breath.

"So?" David asked.

"Well, Nelly does some hocus pocus lawyer shit with the judge, and suddenly I'm sprung. Badda bing, badda boom!" Shel snapped his fingers. "And then, my first night of freedom, she shows up at my place and hops into bed with me. I swear it's true. Most incredible lay I've ever had. Man, she did everything."

Baba Bill looked at Shel and shook his head. "The real tragedy is you'll never even know how lucky you are to have a Meliai share your bed."

Shel gave a sarcastic snort. "Lucky, my ass. I'll bet I've fucked fifty times more chicks than a wanker like you, Mr. Baba. Maybe a thousand. I'll bet you can't even screw like a man. You just pay to have your face sat on and your dick sucked. Am I right or am I right?"

Instead of responding angrily, Bill just smiled and gave David a conspiratorial wink. David shook his head, admiring the man's composure. Nothing ever seemed to ruffle him "Okay, so get this," Shel said, slathering a quarter stick of goat butter onto a piece of black bread. "Me and Nelly, we're hot and heavy as weasels for two weeks, right? And then, one night, I go to sleep with her in my arms, and like I wake up here. That was over three months ago, and I haven't seen her since."

"And you don't recall anything else, right?" Bill asked.

Shel shrugged. "I dunno. All I remember is waking up in this cabin with a note from Nelly telling me she'd be back in a few weeks."

"And she told you she was a Meliai, right?" David said.

"Meliai, Shmeliai," Shel said dismissively, chewing a hunk of bread, as crumbs tumbled from the sides of his mouth. "There was a bunch of crap about that, I guess. But all these chicks are gonzo." He finally swallowed. "Still, I figure, 'Look, this girl's one great lay, and maybe she'll actually be back.' Meanwhile, I got no place else to go. So, for now, hey, I'm saddled up for the ride."

"And that's it?" Bill asked, incredulously. "I mean, you look around at this—this place we're in." He gestured at the Commons and its vast wall of window. "You think some gang of female crazies just built this world out of whole cloth? Invented food you'd never tasted, animals you never knew existed? Put a second moon in the sky, for Christ's sake? Do you think these girls are even human?"

Shel shrugged. "Fuck if I know. But, hey, the food and everything else is free. So why worry? I just go with the flow."

A couple of white-gowned Meliai, with ready smiles, walked past their table, greeting them cheerfully. The three men followed them with their eyes as the Dryads strolled through the women's part of the Commons, and David noted that the female Guests stared after them no less avidly.

"What the hell makes them so irresistible, do you think?" David asked. "I mean, I know they're beautiful, but I'm talking about how they get under our skins."

"They're empaths," Bill said, toying with what was left of his pasta, looping it around his fork, but making no attempt to eat it. "That much is obvious."

Shel gave him a skeptical look. "You mean they read our minds or something?"

"Not quite. But they can read our emotions. Well, more than that, actually. The Meliai read our souls. They see right through our bodies to the light within, and they seduce that light with their own. It works just as well on women as men."

Shel hooted derisively. "What the hell is it with you Holy Roller types? Sex always has to be about something mystical, doesn't it? Instead of old-fashioned wood, all you got is airy-fairy in your pants. Like a girl who's just a great fuck isn't enough for you? She's gotta be some kinda saint, like Snow White with big tits."

David laughed. "Sounds like he's got your number, Baba. Does Aneel have big tits, I mean?"

Bill smiled. "Well, that's not really the point."

"Point fucking zero," Shel said. "You're really just another horn dog, Mr. Baba. Why can't you cop to it?"

"Sex is always about more than you think it is," Bill said as he took a sip of milk. "Our attraction to the Meliai comes from the invisible realm."

Shel was about to reply sarcastically again, when David held up his hand. "Wait a minute. I think the Baba Man is onto something here."

"Oh, really?" Shel said. "Okay, then. Since you're such a smarty, why don't you enlighten me? What makes these Dryad babes so different from regular women?"

David took a bite of his pie, which was delicious. He smiled and pointed at his nose. "It's all in what we smell," he said, swallowing. "I figure the Meliai's pheromones are irresistible to humans. So it's almost like a spiritual attraction."

"Sure," Bill said. "Pheromones are chemical sex signals in perspiration and other bodily secretions. All animals, including humans, have them. It's Nature's way of perpetuating a species."

"Yeah, well," David said, draining his wine glass. "Dryad pheromones are everywhere here, I'll bet. Not just on Meliai's bodies, but in the air too."

Suddenly, a group of men at the next table raised their voices and began harmonizing a rendition of *On Top of Old Smokey*, inviting a camp-style sing-along.

There was general laughter in the Commons as other voices, both male and female, joined in.

"Oh, fuck," David sighed. "I hate this damned song."

Bill laughed and raised his baritone voice:

> *"The grave will decay you,*
> *And turn you to dust*
> *Not a girl in a million*
> *A poor boy can trust."*

As the song ended, to another chorus of laughter and some applause, Shel said, "Hey, here's how we used to sing this shit when I was locked up in juvie. He cleared his throat and began to croak his own off-key version:

"On top of spaghetti,
All dripping with cheese,
She bit off my pecker,
For not saying 'please.'"

He laughed uproariously, but his amusement trailed off quickly when David and Baba Bill ignored him.

"Well, if you'll excuse me," Bill said, stuffing the notebook into his backpack, shouldering it and picking up his tray. "I've got things to do."

"Yeah, and I'm beat," David added, taking his own tray and following Bill to the waste bins, where Guests disposed of food scraps and stacked their dirty dishes. "Shel's a bit of a knuckle walker, isn't he?" he said, scraping his half-eaten casserole into the compost.

Bill laughed. "He may be sharper than you think. Hey, let's you and me go back to your place and have a nightcap, okay? I'm in the mood to talk."

Chapter 29

↗ə

BABA BILL

$\mathcal{W}$e were sitting outside David's cabin under a starry sky, our rockers creaking on the porch. It was around nine, and we'd been talking for a couple of hours, David sipping bourbon, while "pure" me, who hadn't had so much as a beer in over two decades— was drinking mineral water. He'd thrown together some fruit and cheese, plus chunks of black bread, and the platter was sitting on the wicker table between us. The night was a bit nippy, so we were wearing our *loobas*—the thick, hooded Dryad robes—along with wool socks inside our sandals to keep our feet warm.

I'd gone down to my cabin after dinner to change and bring up a couple of bottles of mineral water—a fifteen-minute hike each way, but I liked walking the trails at night. The lanterns hanging in the trees were shaped like globes of glowing fruit: *peloons* and *hollyaths*, or clusters of green grapes and lavender cuddleberries. Their light made the trees look ethereal. Still, you'd come back to earth fast if you stepped on one of the getchi, the six-legged lizards that lay on the paths after dark, soaking up the last of the gravel's daytime warmth.

On my way back up the hill, I'd encountered a pair of Shari, or "tinkerbelles," as they're sometimes called. These are the little winged humanoids that live in and pollinate the Drys orchards of the Upper Village. The exquisite creatures are a bit larger than hummingbirds and dart about just as quickly. Since they glow after dark—the females with an intense violet light, the males a brilliant blue—they are easy to mistake for lanterns when they perch in the trees.

As the tiny couple dropped down from the branches, the male settled on my left shoulder, the female on my right. "Take care," the male squeaked. "Oreads are about," the female added, just before the two of them buzzed away. The Shari liked the Meliai and Alanoie, who often used them as messengers or to perform simple tasks, but it wasn't without reason they feared the Oreads, who viewed them as pests to be exterminated.

From the porch, we could see Ausonia's two moons, both full in the sky tonight. Pale-yellow Salome—close and looking huge this time of month—had risen a couple of hours ago and was hanging over the mountains like a pregnant Dryad's belly, its single lava "sea" forming a dark navel just off center. Meanwhile, little Yemanya was high in the sky, featureless and icy white. The two moons together shed more light than a full moon on Earth, and their ghostly illumination was enough to see the forest's edge clearly. All the shadows were doubled, with the light from the two moons falling across the landscape from different angles, so the *leeothie* tree in front of David's cabin had a V-shaped shadow trailing behind it. The landscape was eerie in this light.

I told David that, next month, the two moons would line up exactly, so the little one was eclipsed by the big one. "Salome is closer," I said, pointing up at her. "So she circles the planet faster." I traced an imaginary orbit with my finger. "And when they're perfectly aligned and the smaller moon is covered by the larger, Salome slowly moves aside to reveal Yemanya, so you can imagine she's giving birth to her." I demonstrated by putting one fist in front of the other and moving it aside.

David laughed. "Wow, you're just a walking planetarium, aren't you, Baba?"

I ignored the gentle sarcasm and mentioned the myth that told how Salome, a Dryad goddess, had given birth to Yemanya, a

Goddess worshipped by the Naiads, or 'Alanoie' as they were called in Pandoric. "The Alanoie are probably a genetic offshoot of the Dryads," I said. "So maybe that's the meaning behind the fable of Salome being Yemanya's mother."

David nibbled a piece of cheese, washing it down with more bourbon. "Shit, I feel like I'm living in a fable. This whole place seems like a fever dream."

His words triggered an old memory. I couldn't have been more than ten or eleven and I'd been ill with rheumatic fever, running a temperature high enough to make me delirious. I'd almost died, and when the fever finally broke, I fell asleep and had this incredibly vivid dream. The memory of it was so alive that I began to share it with David without first asking myself whether or not that was wise.

"I was riding a Pegasus through the sky," I said, taking a sip of mineral water. "The fields and forests were rushing past below me and the wind was blowing in my hair. My big sister Nan, whom I adored, was riding bareback in front of me, leaning forward and grasping this utterly wild creature by its mane, while I sat behind her, holding her around the waist, and, uh ..." I paused awkwardly because I'd almost confessed a shameful secret.

"And *what?*" David asked.

"No ... that's all I remember," I said.

"Bullshit! I know dreams like that. You're holding something back."

He'd rightly guessed I'd left out the most difficult part, and I decided I might as well tell it. "Okay," I said. "The thing is that Nan and I were both naked, and my penis was rubbing against her behind. Christ, if felt so wonderful I had an orgasm. My first ever ... it was like I just melted into her."

David sighed. "And you, raised a devout Catholic."

"I was sure that even dreaming of incest was a mortal sin, and I was too ashamed to tell it at confession. What made it even worse is that Nan died of leukemia two years later at seventeen."

"Ouch!" David said. "And you thought her dying was God punishing you for that dream. If I was a priest, I'd tell you to skip the 'Hail Marys' and have a shot of this bourbon."

"No, it had nothing to do with God," I said. "See, Nan was ... well, kind of homely. But she was such a good soul and I'd have done anything to make her happy. She was sure that no one would ever marry her because she was so plain, and for years after she died, I wished I'd told her about the dream ... just so she'd known that someone had imagined her sexually, even if it was only her creepy little brother. But how could I tell my own sister a dream like that?"

David reached over and put a hand on my shoulder. "You're nothing close to being a creep, Baba. What you are is a *mensch*."

I didn't know the Jewish word, and he thought a moment when I asked for a translation. "Let's see ... A *mensch* is someone who cares about people and tries to do what's right by them. Not to get God's approval, but just because it's the right thing to do. It loses something in translation, but a *mensch* is what you are, Baba."

It was one of the kindest compliments I'd ever gotten, and it touched me, yet the irony was bitter. I wanted to think of myself as a *mensch*—a decent man, or at least something close. But David was my friend, and I had pledged to betray him.

We sat silently for a minute, just contemplating the stars, until I asked: "Are Jews as afraid of death as Catholics are?"

"Death?" David said. "Nah, we're not afraid of death. It's *life* that scares the shit out of us."

It took a few moments to process that, before I began to laugh.

When you're a Changeling and your Shepherdess asks a favor, it's almost impossible to refuse. After the *Edartina*, you're sexually and spiritually bound to her, and there's a strong compulsion to do whatever she asks. Still, her requests are usually benevolent and meant to help you and other Changelings sail effortlessly through transformation.

So what Aneel asked me to do a few weeks ago seemed innocent enough. "I need you to go back to the Lower Village and help a new Guest named David," she said, as she, Janaynie, and I were having dinner at *Les Verges* in the Upper Village. "He needs a friend to steer him in the right direction."

It happened that way sometimes; a recent arrival became more difficult than most, before the minute doses of *Calda* the Meliai spiked our food with had time to take hold. In cases like this, a Pandic Changeling like me might be sent back to the Lower Village to befriend and help them adjust.

That was fine and I gladly agreed, but it was Aneel's second request that made me uneasy: "I also need you to make sure that David doesn't learn that Janaynie is the one who brought him to Ausonia ... and not her Full Sister, I mean." I gave her a quizzical look and Aneel smiled. "Just so he has a chance to get used to Janaynie's energy before she takes him to the Temple for the Edartina."

When I told her I still didn't understand, she said: "Look, securing the right human is even harder for Full Sisters than the rest of us, because the twin who goes to *T'Erenya* has the added responsibility of finding a human who can bond not just with her, but with her sister too."

Every set of Meliai Full Sisters drew their immortality from a single Drys tree, meaning they needed just one Changeling between them. But for reasons I wasn't clear on, just the First Born twin was allowed to go to Earth to find a human to replace their dying tree. Only if the First failed or died was the Second Born allowed to go. And that was what had happened in Janaynie's case.

"Jill is the one who found David," Aneel continued. "And she was meant to bring him here for transformation by both her and Janaynie. But she died before she could do that. And since David was already in love with Jill, Janaynie will be impersonating her ... just to keep things simple."

"My tree will die soon, and I don't have enough time to start over with David," said Janaynie, who'd been uncharacteristically silent through most of dinner.

"So the simplest thing now is for David to go on believing she's Jill," Aneel added. "Once he's had his first portion of *Fleen*, it won't matter, and he'll be just as devoted to Janaynie as he was to Jill."

I'd met Janaynie, who was Aneel's lover, soon after Aneel brought me to the Upper Village, and she was hard to like. She was vain and manipulative, with a sense of entitlement that surrounded her like a glass shell. I didn't even know David yet, but for me to help Janaynie masquerade as her Full Sister to fool this fellow just sounded wrong. Transformation was supposed to be voluntary, wasn't it?

"It will be," Janaynie said when I pointed that out. "He'll give his full consent before the Tribunal ... just as you did for Aneel."

Aneel put a hand on my knee. "Really, William," she said. "Everything will be done within the bounds of *Sufadel*." That was the Meliai Code of Law, and their Tribunal wouldn't allow a transformation to proceed if they believed a Meliai had violated any part of *Sufadel*.

"Well, doesn't tricking a human into accepting transformation violate your law?" I asked.

"My Full Sister was First Born," Janaynie said, neither answering my question nor trying to hide the bitterness in her voice. "And now she's gone, so by right David should be mine."

"But why can't you just tell him who you really are?" I asked. "I mean, if your sister is dead, wouldn't it be best to court him as yourself? If he'd be willing to accept transformation for Jill, why wouldn't he do it for you?"

I saw how naïve my question was by the exasperated look Janaynie gave Aneel. "He's your Changeling," she said. "*You* explain it to him."

Aneel ignored her rudeness and took a sip of white wine. "It's like this," she said, taking my hand. "Jill wasted so much time with David on *T'Erenya* that the tree she shared with Janaynie has two years left at most, and that's barely enough time for a transformation to complete. It took Jill months to get him to the point where he seemed ready. If Janaynie tells David she's not really Jill, who knows how he'd react?"

"It's not like I didn't keep pleading with her to bring him while there was still time," Janaynie grumbled, plucking a live getchi from the bowl in front of her, dipping it into the sweet sauce, and then popping it into her mouth. "But, no ... she had to keep him for herself, *and* keep him human."

"What she means," Aneel said, "is that Jill was inexcusably selfishly thinking only of her own desires, and that's put Janaynie's life at risk ... not to mention jeopardizing the entire Meliai Clan. You wouldn't want that to happen, would you?"

"If I don't start his transformation soon," Janaynie said sullenly, "I'm as good as dead, and there'll be one less Meliai in Ausonia."

Aneel leaned over to kiss Janaynie's cheek. "Don't worry, *Pleesha*; we're not going to let that happen, are we, William?" She turned her seductive gaze on me. "There's just not enough time for Janaynie to court David as herself and then find another human if he turns her down. So making him believe she's Jill is really the best way."

"But won't he see the difference right away?" I said. "I mean, Full Sisters' left and right eye colors are reversed and ... oh!" I caught myself because, of course, both Janaynie's eyes were gray, which meant both of Jill's had been gray too. For a Dryad to have two eyes of the same color was virtually unheard of, and it would make such "freakish" Full Sisters virtually impossible for a human to tell apart. Still, there was actually a *tiny* difference in the eyes. Janaynie showed me the little golden flecks in her left eye, which were so subtle I'd never have spotted them, and she said that Jill had had those same spots, but in her right eye.

"Humans are so unobservant he'll never notice," Aneel said confidently. "Oh, William, stop frowning like that. Your lovely face will get all wrinkled."

"Okay ... so what do I have to do?" I asked.

"Almost nothing," Aneel said. "Just become his friend, and make sure he doesn't learn the truth. Do or say whatever you have to, and always remember your oath."

Ah, right—the solemn oath each human took before the Tribunal, sworn to and sealed when they drank the *Fleen*: To do whatever was necessary to ensure the survival of the entire Meliai Clan.

I'd never liked my fellow humans much. We were a stupid, cantankerous lot, and I preferred my solitude when I could get it. What I hadn't counted on was developing such a bond with David. He made me laugh and I truly liked the man. Now I was between a rock and a hard place—bound to keep my word to Aneel and unable to warn David about Janaynie and what she had in store for him.

As we sat on the porch, David pointed at the mountains that marked the eastern border of Meliai territory. "What's beyond there?" he asked. "I mean, Ausonia is a whole planet, isn't it? But what's on the other side of that mountain range?"

"The Meliai call it 'Seeta Callan'—the Unknown Country," I said, shrugging. "It's wild and full of dangerous creatures, and they seldom go there. That's all I know."

David rocked forward in his chair and pointed in the direction of the faint blue glow coming from the Upper Village. "Well, what about that? You think that's really Nob Hill back home? People say Ausonia is an 'alternate universe' Earth and that all the landforms are the same."

"I think so," I said. "Earth and Ausonia have a common geography, and I'm pretty sure that would be Nob Hill in San Francisco, with California and Powell meeting right about there, just where the glow is brightest."

"What makes those trees shine like that?" he asked.

"Something phosphorescent in their chemistry," I said. "Quite a few of the local flora and fauna have it, like the Shari. But these trees really go wild at night. Weird, isn't it? I mean, Nob Hill was once the swankiest part of San Francisco, all gutted by the 1906 fire, and here in Ausonia it's a Drys orchard with fruit trees that glow at night, almost like they're on fire. Without those trees, the Meliai would all die."

David took another sip of bourbon. "Is that for real?" he asked. "I keep hearing people say that, but I mean, have you actually seen a Meliai die because her tree died?"

Unfortunately, I had, and it wasn't pretty. "As long as her tree stays healthy," I said, "a Dryad can stay young for thousands of years. But kill her Drys tree and she crumbles to dust in weeks." I told him that I'd seen a Meliai whose tree had succumbed to blight die in agony, with her weeping sisters in attendance inside the Temple.

He shivered. "Fuck! I hope I never have to see one of these girls die like that."

"The death of a Dryad's tree is the greatest tragedy they face," I said, "and a lot of them are dying of slow blight right now."

"Does that blight thing have something to do with why the Meliai are bringing us here?" he asked. "How are we supposed to help fix their trees?"

Despite two months in the Lower Village, David's mind was still sharp, but it was a question I was not allowed to answer. Humans didn't learn why the Meliai were bringing us to Ausonia until they went to the Upper Village, and most stopped asking meaningful questions well before that, which was what the Meliai counted on.

This was how they worked their spell: First they offered a human transcendent sex on Earth until he or she was thoroughly addicted. Then they brought them to Ausonia and left them in the Lower Village for a time, putting them on an erotic starvation diet, while a life of total ease and subtly drugged food made them pliant.

Only when these humans were deemed ready did their Meliai lovers come back and take them to the Upper Village, where they learned the full truth of this place, and more transcendent sex became the irresistible bait to lure them into accepting transformation. The process was as insidious as it was delicious.

"C'mon, Baba," David said when he grew tired of my tense silence. "Answer the fucking question. What do these girls want with us?"

I sighed and reached into my pack for the journal with the worn leather cover I'd found hidden under a floorboard in my cabin when I first came here. I was sure that none of the Meliai knew of its existence or they'd have burned it long ago. "Here," I said, handing it to him. "Read this and don't tell anyone about it … and I mean no one."

I'd been carrying it around for a couple of days now, wondering if the pledge of silence I'd made to the Tribunal would actually make it impossible to give the book to David. It didn't. Apparently promising not to 'tell' him what really went on in Ausonia didn't prevent me from giving David an old handwritten journal the Meliai didn't know about.

David flipped it open and read the title page aloud: "'Being the journal of Noah Burns—1862.' What the hell is this?"

"Call it an unauthorized guide to Ausonia," I said. "It was written over 150 years ago, but things haven't changed much since then."

He flipped the page and began to scan the handwritten text inside.

"No, not now," I said. "Read it when you're alone."

He set the book down. "Did Jill give you this to give to me?"

The question caught me off guard. "Why would you ask that?"

His response sounded angry. "The note she left me said she'd be back in six weeks and it's been over two months. You've been to the Upper Village. Did you meet her, and did she give you this book?"

"No!" I said, truthfully, though it came out sounding defensive.

He poured the last of the bourbon into his glass and downed it in a single gulp. "Tell her I need to see her now!"

"I've never met her, and you shouldn't drink," I said. "It makes you stupid." His mind could be so keen, yet when it came to Jill, he was thick as a brick. I wanted to shake some sense into him and give him a fighting chance against her twin. But the words were literally locked inside me by the promise I'd made to Aneel to help Janaynie deceive him. Still, I hadn't sworn not to tell him my own history, had I?

"You know," I said, "I was married in my early twenties."

"What? I thought you were a monk."

"That came later. I was married for two years and totally, blindly in love ... with a girl named Lylee."

He quickly got the wrong idea. "And she cheated on you, which is what drove you into the Ashram, right?"

His drunken assumption annoyed me. "No, she drowned in the bathtub while I was out buying cigarettes. She was the love of my life ... and she drowned while I was out buying goddamn cigarettes."

He seemed genuinely horrified. "What? How does a young woman drown in a bathtub?" Then his eyes widened. "Suicide?"

"The medical examiners said she'd probably had a seizure, but she didn't have any history of epilepsy."

I'd never believed that absurd story they came up with, but it wasn't until after Aneel got ahold of me years later that I saw the truth about Lylee, and why she'd taken her own life. It shouldn't have come as a shock that she'd been a Meliai too, but it did.

Falling romantically in love with her human is a disaster for a Meliai because her choices are so limited. She can alter her lover beyond recognition, or else release them and sacrifice her own life in the process. Beyond that, because their numbers are falling so drastically, every Meliai's death delivers yet another blow to the survival of her entire clan. The pressure to succeed on each girl who goes to Earth to find a Changeling comes from all sides, and it's tremendous. Failure is simply not an option. Lylee was as in love with me as I was with her, and the choice she faced would have been unbearable; it must have been the same for Jill with David.

"Damn! I'm sorry about your wife, Baba," David said, sadly. "That sucks."

Remembering Lylee was like poking an infected tooth with your tongue to see if you could still make it throb. After a while you became addicted to the pain and actually sought it. I took another gulp of mineral water because my mouth was so dry. "There's one more thing you should know about Lylee." I paused a moment. "She had a cousin whose name was Aneel, and Aneel was a Meliai."

He got it immediately. "Your wife was a Dryad?"

"I'd been at the Ashram nearly two decades when Aneel showed up," I said. "She told my Guru this bullshit story about wanting to be a nun, but she'd really come to get *me*. I was terrified when she first spoke to me because it was like my wife had come back from the dead. I mean, Aneel didn't look like Lylee, but she had that same accent and was so much like her in other ways that I thought I was losing my mind. The Meliai will do that sometimes; one of them releases you and a relative of hers eventually comes to claim you." I was skirting the edge of what I was allowed to say, but I got the words out.

David put the rest together for himself now. "You're telling me that Jill's Full Sister is the one who brought me here, aren't you? Fuck, she told me she had a twin who worked as a hooker in Germany."

I had to laugh. "A tiny lie, but I'll bet it gave you a thrill, didn't it?"

David was silent, trying to assimilate this, taking it far better than I thought he would. He looked up at the night sky, seeing the same constellations he'd be seeing if we were back on Earth this time of year. The only difference was those two moons. "What are the Meliai doing to us, Baba? Tell me!"

I shook my head. "I can't, David. I swear. But read the journal. It's all in there. Listen, you've told me about the disease that killed your father and how it might get you too. You can go back home to whatever awaits you, or you can stay here and give the Meliai what they want. Just don't forget you have a choice."

We both spotted them at the same moment: Two Dryads, tall and regal, had suddenly appeared out of the forest. Despite the chill, they were naked, skin shining like bronze in the moonlight, strolling regally like a couple of amazons along the tree line, seemingly oblivious to us.

My breath caught. This was what the Shari had warned me about on the path. "Shit, David … they're Oreads!" I knew there'd been increasing tension between the two Dryad clans lately, and the Oreads were supposedly prohibited from coming to the Lower Village. What were they up to?

"Hey, ladies!" David shouted, waving in their direction. "Over here!"

"Don't be an idiot," I whispered harshly. "Those girls are dangerous!"

"Nothing that gorgeous can be dangerous," David insisted.

But, as if to prove my point, a large rocat emerged from the trees to stand between us and the Oreads, growling softly, its eyes shining with reflected moonlight.

"Oops," David said.

"Yeah," I said. "Oops is right. It's their pet."

The animal began moving deliberately toward us, but it stopped in its tracks at a curt command from one of the Oreads. *"Shatak!"*

The Oreads stared at us, then turned to each other and conferred briefly. And now they both pointed—clearly at David and not at me. Obviously they could sense I was already another Dryad's Changeling, so of no use to them, but David was still fair game.

"Look, Baba. They like me … Holy shit!"

The two Oreads began beckoning to David like a couple of Sirens, and I could smell their sex scent on the breeze, even from fifty feet away. "I don't like where this is going," I said. "Let's get inside right now."

"What are you, crazy?" he said, getting up out of his chair. "I haven't had sex in six months. I'm going out there."

"David. It's not what you think. They'll eat you alive."

"I should be so lucky," he said, taking a step toward them.

He was drunk, and I grabbed his arm to keep him from walking to his doom.

David tried to free himself, but I was bigger, stronger and sober, and my grip made him flinch. "Shit, Baba, let go … that hurts!" I gave him a yank and he fell back into his chair, staring at the Oreads, who now seemed to realize he wasn't going with them.

"*Vashkalla!*" the Oread on the left shouted, pointing at David again. Then they both turned and walked back into the forest, trailed by their rocat, who gave us a last hungry glance.

"*Vashkalla,*" she'd called David. My Pandoric was quite good and I knew that word. It had multiple uses, but loosely translated it meant 'prey,' an animal to be killed and eaten by a predator.

Chapter 30

⚮

DAVID

*B*aba stayed until after midnight, and by the time he left I was too tired to make sense of the journal he'd given me. I did flip through a few pages at random, but Noah Burns' handwriting was tiny, and his style was so long-winded I wanted to scream.

Now that Yemanya had set, it was darker, and the winking of the starflies in the field was hypnotic: red, green, blue and white. The only sounds were the rustling leaves, the crickets, and the murmur of the stream behind my cabin, a stream which ran back into the forest and down the mountain, where it emptied into that river; what was it called … the *Ninaya?* Baba said there was an Alanoie settlement at a fork in the *Ninaya*, and I really wanted to meet one of those Naiad girls. But how could I get down there alone through a dense forest without getting lost or gobbled up by a rocat?

My eyes ached and I set the journal on the table, figuring I'd read it in the morning when I was fresh. I stood and stretched, picking up the nearly empty snack plate. If I left it out overnight, it would be covered with purple ants in the morning. They were tiny as pinheads and would get into anything edible, swarming by the thousands.

Walking into the cabin, I yawned and turned off the porch light. The room was stuffy, so I damped the pellet stove, brushed my teeth, and got into bed. I was exhausted but couldn't stop my mind from racing. Was it actually Jill's twin sister who'd brought me here? Baba had implied she might soon be coming to take me to the Upper Village. I was sex-starved enough to chew nails, and if Janaynie offered herself to me, should I even care that she was an imposter? I was stuck in Ausonia for now, and if I could get some consolation from Janaynie, maybe I should just play along and pretend to believe she was Jill—at least for a while. But what did she even want with me? It was crazy to think she'd taken me from that party and brought me here just for sex, when she could have that from practically anyone without going to all that trouble.

The clock on the bedside table said 12:55. My stomach felt queasy, and I knew I'd be hung over in the morning. Groaning, I got up, turned on the light, and took a swig of mineral water from the half bottle Baba had left. I went to the bathroom to take a leak and then walked into the kitchen. A little food might settle my stomach, so I had a bowl of goat yogurt mixed with a bit of granola and a few cuddleberries, which helped a bit.

I crawled back into bed and tried to sleep again, but I was just too wired. The clock said 2:32 and I should have been asleep hours ago; but no matter which way I turned, I couldn't find a comfortable position. I moaned and curled myself around a pillow, trying to think of something pleasant, but I couldn't even work up a decent erotic fantasy.

That was when a voice whispered my name: *"Dayyvid ..."* It was more like a croak than a whisper really, and at first, I thought I'd imagined it. But then I heard it again, and this time a hand grabbed my ankle through the blanket. "David, look at me."

I screamed and turned on the light. And there, perched on her haunches at the foot of my bed, was an old woman—a crone, really. Her stringy hair was gunmetal gray, her skin ashen and wrinkled, eyes pale and rheumy above a nose like a mottled beak. It was a scrawny vulture of a woman, staring at me like Death itself, and I could smell decay in her sweat.

"Who the fuck are you?" I demanded, my heart pounding.

"A girl who needs your help," she said.

Girl? She looked like a goblin, and she was in terrible pain. I could feel her agony and it was choking me.

"Help me, David," she hissed. "Give yourself to me, and I'll make a heaven for you."

"Ugh!" I'd sooner have given myself to a corpse, and I kicked at her with both feet, hitting solid flesh and bone.

"Oww!" she said. *"Ipchak alkat!"* And, without another word, she disappeared with a hiss, like the air going out of a balloon.

The clock said 2:33, so the whole episode had lasted only a minute. There was no way I'd sleep now, so I threw back the covers and got out of bed. Maybe a little cool night air would ground me—convince me that it was just a by-product of the bourbon and staying up too late. I put on my socks and sandals, then my looba, turned on the porch light, and went outside to sit for a while.

Salome had almost set, throwing just a glimmer of light on the field in front of my cabin. The starflies were gone and the forest was in darkness. I sat in one of the rockers, thinking I might try reading from the journal, but before I could reach for it, I heard a whirring sound above my head, something like a hummingbird.

I'd never seen one before, but I knew it was a Shari the moment she settled onto the table and looked up at me. She was glowing with a violet light and was so adorable my first reaction was to laugh. It must have startled her, because she mewled and jumped back a step. After a moment, though, she relaxed and smiled at me, and I saw she had one green eye and one blue.

I held out a hand to see if I could make her perch, wishing I had some food to offer, a slice of apple, a bit of cheese, or maybe a cuddleberry. But she still accepted my invitation, leaping into my palm, her wide-set eyes never leaving mine. The Shari's wings kept buzzing and she was tilting her head this way and that, trying to get a better look at me. Then, with a tiny voice, she said two words very clearly in English: "Immortal bee."

I stared at her. What the hell was an immortal bee? Baba said the Shari could be trained to talk, a little like parrots; but their own language was mostly hand signals and facial expressions, and sometimes their attempts at using words came out as nonsense.

The pixie began to squirm and gesture, doing a weird little dance, whirling a few times and crossing her arms over her chest. She wiped her feet on my hand like it was a doormat then cupped her ears, pointed at her eyebrows, and touched each side of her nose with an index finger.

"Immortal bee," she said again, then held her palms up like she was blessing me and buzzed off into the night.

I sat for a minute, thinking about the strange encounter, then picked up Noah Burns' journal and opened it. I started at the beginning and read straight through.

From the Journal of Noah Burns (1863)

Though the accounts herein given may seem farfetched, yet I am obliged to set to paper all that I have learned since coming to Ausonia, as this world is known by its perilously seductive inhabitants. These facts I report truthfully and to the best of my ability, regardless of how they may affect civilized sensibilities. If what I write seems indecent to some, I must say, 'so be it,' for decency in the betrayal of knowledge is mere intellectual cowardice.

How I arrived here is a tale I shall make brief. Unlike most humans, I came entirely of my own volition, chiefly to study and learn, rather than through surrender of my will to one of these alluring, immortal females. Suffice to say that, while on holiday, I was met by a fey girl named Érichea, who laughed and sang to me in a strange tongue, as I was on a solitary walking tour through the woods on a fragrant May morning in County Kerry. This was in the year 1862, Anno Domini, when I was but two weeks shy of my twenty-ninth birthday. When Érichea persuaded me of her true nature and invited me to visit her world, there was for me, as a scientist, no way to refuse, but whether I shall survive long enough to see my family and home in Coventry again, I cannot say.

How a man or woman can be remade into a tree is the greatest of all mysteries in Ausonia. I can cite the steps the Dryads take and the rituals they employ to bring about this transfiguration, but I cannot explain what is actually at work within the bodies of the Changelings. To all appearances, this bizarre process is indistinguishable from what the alchemists might have termed magick, replete with potions, incantations, and erotic frenzies.

A human who agrees to become a Drys tree to save the life of his beloved Meliai does so at a Pagan ritual called an Edartina. Here he is given to drink a potion made of the sap from this Meliai's dying Drys tree, mixed with a small amount of her bodily fluids (typically saliva, though urine may also be used). This ensures that the healthy tree this human shall become only gives life to the Meliai who is transforming him (for it is true that a Dryad will perish without a living tree of her own). Perhaps it is some microscopic creature living within the sap that brings about the eventual transformation of human to tree, but I have not the tools to test this theory in any way.

The potion, of which a large dose is initially given (followed by smaller doses taken weekly until the transformation is complete), is called Fleen, and is first administered at the Edartina ceremony. There is nothing in modern human experience with which to compare the Edartina. It appears to be part religious service and part bacchanal, and it would not surprise me to learn that the Meliai adopted at least some of this ritual from rites they witnessed when they had colonies in ancient Greece and Rome.

After the Changeling has consumed the initial bowl of Fleen, there follows a virtual orgy of intense and deviant sexual activity engaged in by the Changeling, his Shepherdess (the common term for the Meliai whose tree this Changeling will become), and any other Meliai who care to participate.

Copious sexual activity between Changeling and Meliai continues on a daily basis until the transformation is complete. This frequent congress appears necessary to see the process through to a successful conclusion.

Once begun, the transformation cannot be halted or reversed, and failure to ingest sufficient amounts of Fleen or a cessation of sexual activity for any length of time will result in the death of the Changeling. Thus, partaking in the Edartina sets a human upon a path which he or she must keep walking until the inevitable destination is reached.

March 9th, 1863 (approximate)

There are three requirements a prospective Changeling must fulfill prior to formally accepting transformation at the Edartina.

First, he must witness an Edartina without yet partaking in it. Does the sexual ravishment he will experience attract or repel him? If repelled, it means he lacks the correct emotional makeup to become a Changeling and he will be returned to Earth with all memory of Ausonia hypnotically erased. If, instead, he longs to be used in this way, he has passed the first crucial test.

Should he still desire transformation after witnessing an Edartina, he moves on to the next "lesson," which is to observe an actual Edarta, the moment of final transformation. An Edarta is even more shocking than the Edartina, and to witness a woman or man turning fully into a tree before your eyes is utterly riveting and sometimes horrifying. Most humans who ask to be returned to Earth do so now, when the full significance of what will happen to them becomes apparent. If, at this point, they still hunger for transformation, there is but one final test.

The prospective Changeling must now witness the gruesome death of a Meliai whose tree has perished without a ready replacement. Humans do this in groups, as they must wait for the moment when such a tragedy naturally occurs. It is a horrific sight, but few humans decline transformation after witnessing it. In fact, this final lesson usually has the effect of galvanizing a human's determination to proceed; for one who is deeply in love with his Meliai and has remained steadfast through the first trials cannot bear the thought of his beloved dying in such an agonizing manner.

The Stages of Transformation

The full conversion of human to Drys tree typically takes 18 to 24 months, though intervals as short as four months or as long as 30 are not unheard of. Curiously, humans with severe emotional disorders appear to complete the transformation more rapidly.

The changes in a human are mostly internal at first, and do not become outwardly evident until the final weeks of the process, so that a Changeling who is a year or more advanced in the transformation might yet appear fully human to a casual observer. But a Meliai is easily able to tell how advanced any Changeling is, simply by touching him.

There are five main stages in the transformation process:

1) Pre-Natal: "Guests," as they are usually called, are humans who have not yet begun transformation. They initially reside in the Lower Village, where they are subtly brought to the state of emotional surrender required of a Changeling. When they are deemed ready, Guests are brought to the Upper Village for further preparation.

2) Pandic: Humans who have taken the Edartina and are newly minted Changelings.

3) Doric: Changelings who are roughly halfway through the biological and psychological changes which begin at the Edartina ceremony and end with Edarta itself.

4) Pre-Edartic: Changelings who are approximately ninety percent of the way through transformation and beginning to exhibit certain emotional states, which may include a deep sense of well-being and a ravenous sexual hunger.

5) Edartic: the final stage, which generally begins anywhere from one to three weeks prior to Edarta. Sexual desire on the part of the Changeling quickly peaks and becomes virtually insatiable. Shortly before the final consummation, Changelings are planted in the Nursery to become gradually acclimated to the life of a tree.

In order to help other Changelings recognize the status of their fellows, the Meliai clothe them in filmy green gowns whose particular shades identify a Changeling's progress. Guests wear gowns of a very pale green, while the Pre-Edartic's gowns are of a deep forest green. The Pandic and Doric Changelings wear greens in shades that are in between the lightest and darkest green. Edartic Changelings are kept naked, or "sky clad."

When Guests are brought to the Upper Village, they finally learn what is wanted of them. The truth is, of course, shocking, and they are allowed an emotional adjustment period of several weeks before viewing an Edartina. In an ironic sense, Guests in the Upper Village are like novice nuns preparing to take their final vows. Even if they wish to accept transformation, they may still be turned away, much as a novice may be turned away by the head of her religious order if she seems to lack a true vocation.

While they reside in the Upper Village, awaiting their destiny, Changelings are thoroughly pampered by the Meliai; many entertainments and other 'diversions' are available. The lodgings the Meliai provide here are far more sumptuous than the simple bungalows in the Lower Village, and the Dryads become extremely free with their sexual favors.

Food in the Upper Village is especially fattening, as high caloric intake is vital if the Changeling is to make a successful transition from human to Drys tree. The transformation requires great reserves of physical stamina, which perhaps accounts for why humans older than middle age are seldom taken from Earth.

Chapter 31

JANAYNIE

Month of Reed/Month of December

In all Dryad history, I doubt there was ever a set of Full Sisters with eyes like mine and Jilaynie's. Lorelle, our mother, said the midwife's hair stood on end when she got her first look at these twin Nymphs, each having two gray eyes. The little gold flecks, Jilaynie's in her right eye and mine in the left, were the only visible difference between us, and you had to look closely to see them.

If we'd been born Oreads, with all their superstitions, they'd have called us demons and the two of us would have been left to die of exposure in the forest. But the Meliai medics understood our strange eyes were due to a genetic anomaly that had come from our human father. It didn't make us demons, though we were still teased by the other Nymphs, who called us *"sa cheena patella"*—the freak sisters. Still, the teasing fell away when our beauty emerged, and once we'd bonded with our tree and became adult Dryads, we were courted as lovers by almost everyone.

Part of it was our sensuous mouths, full breasts, flawless skin, and long elegant legs. But it was mainly this one unique feature that drew girls to us like starflies to goat's milk. Imagine a Dryad whose eyes are both gray. Then visualize two identical girls each with two gray eyes, both courting you! We touted our mystique constantly, saying our eyes were Kayla's 'mystical' mark to inform every Dryad of our divinely ordained skill as lovers. That was how the exotic Ashe sisters became legendary throughout the Twelve Mountains.

Dryads don't need to look at eye color to tell Full Sisters apart, but humans, who lack the *kash* sense, do. On the surface, Jilaynie and I were so identical that Aneel was sure David would never see the difference, and I could only hope she was right.

He hadn't noticed which eye my spots were in when I'd snatched him from Selene's party that night since he had only moments to take me in before I drugged him. But spending any length of time with me would be another matter, and the more I thought about it, the less convinced I was that I could bring this deception off.

What if Aneel's Changeling actually had the better idea? What if I just approached David as myself and seduced him with the kind of dominant sex he craved, just as Jilaynie had done? Maybe that would be enough. If I could bind his spirit to mine that way, there'd be no need to deceive him.

But that was even riskier. If I just appeared and told him I wasn't his precious Jill, he might be furious at how I'd stolen him and demand to be sent home immediately. On the other hand, if I could fool him into thinking I was her, even for just a few hours, I'd at least have a chance to seduce him properly. Then, with the sexual bliss I could grant him, we would see if he had the willpower to give me up. And once he took the Edartina and I became his Shepherdess, he'd adore me—or at least understand it was too late to turn back, and so accept his destiny.

Jilaynie had told me about a lovemaking technique she'd developed for David. She called it 'Devouring Bliss,' but I had no clear idea what that even meant, let alone how to use it. My entreaties for an explanation of Devouring Bliss just led to vague answers that confused me even more: "Think of a rocat consuming a deer," Jilaynie once said. "Now imagine that cat putting so much tenderness and compassion into eating that deer that the *vashkalla* is oblivious to the pain; instead he actually feels it as ecstasy and falls in love with the predator as she devours him. Now substitute my soul for the rocat's teeth, and that's how I make love to David. I eat his soul with mine, and he becomes part of me." It sounded like nonsense, but I knew my Full Sister must be onto something because David was so mad for her.

I asked Aneel what she thought Jilaynie meant by Devouring Bliss, and she said it sounded like David and William were similar in their erotic tastes, and that she'd developed several tricks of her own to arouse a submissive human male like William. She then offered to teach me, having me practice with several of the male Changelings in the Upper Village. I accidentally put one of them in the infirmary before I got the knack of it, but fortunately our healers are experts at treating kidney injuries.

With Aneel's own version of Devouring Bliss added to my already potent sexual arsenal, I might actually get David to the Edartina quickly enough, without giving myself away as an imposter.

Now, the moment had arrived. It was time for me to become Jill and offer him the erotic heaven of the Upper Village that all Guests longed for, and either he would believe I was her or he wouldn't.

Sky clad, I headed for cabin #28, knowing David would be there because William said he always came home to read for a couple of hours after breakfast. He was there all right. I could feel him with my *kash* and sense the months of sexual frustration in him even from fifty feet away. These cabin doors had no locks, so I would just enter and overwhelm him, and he would lose himself in 'Jill's' luminous flesh before he had a chance to look too closely at my eyes.

From the Journal of Noah Burns, June 17th, 1863 (approximate)

To fully understand the pestilence called slow blight and its ravages upon the Drys trees is to better comprehend the complexity of the Meliai's dealings with the humans they desperately need in order to survive. Stark parallels from nature come readily to mind For example, the seductions of that ravenous lady, the Venus flytrap, who draws insects to her honeyed bosom, then crushes them in her grip to devour them whole.

But this analogy, while compelling, does not do justice to the Meliai-human relationship, for there is clearly more at work here than "Nature red in tooth and claw." One has only to attend an Edartina at the Temple of Kayla to understand that this is so. For it is not merely the savage sexual rite where Changelings are made; ironically, it is also a tender and deeply romantic sacrament. That these opposing faces of Love could coexist seems unimaginable, until one actually witnesses an Edartina and feels its profound allure. Then, for all its savagery, this otherwise profane ritual appears almost sacred, though not in any way a Christian might credit.

Some of what I write here is taken from what I have been told by the Dryads themselves. Much else is simply conjecture based upon an understanding of my mentor, Professor Darwin's, ideas on the evolution of species. As to what I report of the Meliai way of life and their hypnotic power over humans, this is taken from my own observations.

Having spent much time in conversation with the Meliai Clan Mother, I have learned a few things directly from her. Tristelle Mayweather claims to be well over two thousand years old, having dwelt in Rome during the time of the Caesars, as well as Medieval Europe and China, the Indian subcontinent, and a variety of other lands in many epochs. Indeed, Tristelle's own birth mother Antalla claims to have lived in Ancient Babylon, where she was a lover of Sargon the Great.

Tristelle is fluent in at least a dozen languages I can recognize, including several varieties of Gaelic, which she learned during the time she and her clan dwelt in lands that are now Ireland, Scotland, England and Wales. Indeed, the Meliai sing many enchanting folk melodies in archaic forms of Gaelic, Middle English, and Welsh.

Exactly how the Dryads and their aquatic cousins, the Alanoie, came to be is open to debate, but the fact that all are able to mate and produce offspring in conjunction with human males offers incontrovertible proof of their Earthly origins. This is fortunate for both Dryads and Naiads, as there are no males left among their own kind; in fact, there apparently have been no males among them since shortly after their human progenitors first entered Ausonia, some thirty-five thousand years ago.

It would appear that a primitive tribe of human men and women came upon the Portal in what is today Southern Europe, while fleeing a rival tribe bent on slaughtering them. Just what this passageway between worlds is I cannot say, though I have seen it and, like all humans in Ausonia, have passed through it, with no small discomfort.

The tribe made good its escape, discovering here a virginal paradise, filled with abundant vegetation and game, but wholly devoid of sentient beings able to compete with them for dominance.

The human tribe soon discovered that two species of local trees (the Drys and Oros) had the power to impart virtual immortality by allowing humans to 'bond' with them in an extremely bizarre manner. The girls of the tribe found that, after taking the sap of one of these trees into their bodies in a way I must decline to describe, they grew to young adulthood and then stopped ageing. In each case, a particular bond was formed between a girl (or else a pair of remarkable sisters) and a single tree, and this was a lifetime bond that could be broken only by the girl's death through some mishap, or by the death of the tree itself. The human females who bonded with the Drys trees were to become the Meliai Dryads, while those who bonded with the Oros trees became the Dryad clan known as Oreads.

How the females of that original tribe discovered this 'bonding' process I cannot say, but the Meliai believe the secret was imparted to their ancestral mothers by the trees themselves through some sort of telepathy. Of course, as a man of science, I put no store in telepathy. Rather, I believe there must be a logical explanation for the phenomenon, which I hope someday to uncover.

Because of the manner in which the tree sap was absorbed by the young girls, this bonding process afforded immortality only to females. Furthermore, when these now immortal girls grew to adulthood, they could bear only female children. As a result, within just a few decades, there were no males remaining in the tribe. To perpetuate their race, the females found it necessary to return through the Portal to Earth, in order to abduct human males for mating. It was necessary to bring these men to Ausonia because each girl could only be impregnated when mating beneath her own tree. (Similarly, an Alanoie must be immersed in her native waters.) Thus did the

Dryad and then the Alanoie species (for the Naiads are surely a sub-species of Dryad) evolve from humans.

Each Dryad can give birth just once during her long life, either to a single daughter or else to a set of mirror twins called Full Sisters. This is enough to maintain their populations at more or less a constant rate. About 2,500 years ago, the Meliai began bringing both male and female humans to Ausonia as part of a grander design.

Though the Meliai are uncertain of exactly when slow blight first struck their Drys trees, it was in roughly in the year 4,100 BCE by my estimate. Still the Drys managed to survive this pestilence until about three thousand years ago, when the blight became more virulent and began to imperil the lives of the trees and of the Meliai themselves; for it is true, even as legend has it, that no Dryad can long survive the death of her tree. The same does not, of course, apply to the Alanoie, whose bond is to the ocean, rivers, and lakes in and around which they live. The Alanoie are also extremely long-lived, though through what agency I know not. Perhaps it has something to do with the nature of the waters themselves, though the selfsame waters do not seem to affect humans in any unusual way.

Chapter 32

A CLEVER GIRL FROM BROOKLYN

Month of Reed/Month of December

Sarahleah Kahane buzzed about her neat kitchen like a girl possessed, on a mission that would brook no interference from anyone, least of all Willie Ludlow. Sarahleah thrived on clearly defined goals, and she was never as content as when occupied with household tasks that required her full concentration and creativity. This was how she expressed her love, and all the women in her large family had thus been raised, generation upon generation. Sarahleah knew she would never herself have children—that was a given considering what would soon become of her. But though leaving no children behind saddened her, she would not let it affect her ability to be a devoted helpmate to the girl who needed her now.

In the few weeks since Willie had come into her life, Sarahleah's main objective had been to care for her—to keep their little home tidy and comfortable, and to keep her lover from brooding too much over what couldn't be helped. Not that Sarahleah herself didn't miss Nellyn, who had become too busy with Meliai politics to have much time for her. But Willie's moping over having been abandoned by Selene wouldn't become despair if Sarahleah had anything to say about it.

Despair was the price one paid for obsessive thinking, and the best antidote for too much thinking was to keep busy. This was a lesson she'd learned from her mother, Zipporah, though applying the lesson to her own life was not always easy. The thought of her mother frequently sent a pang of sorrow through Sarahleah—and, of course, a stab of guilt. Zipporah's face was always before her, her voice ever in her ears. Would Sarahleah meet her again in the next world? Did it even make sense to think of a "next world" now?

No! She had no time to dwell on such things. Right now, Sarahleah was in *this* world, and her proper focus today was to fix Willie a traditional Sabbath meal—minus the meat, of course, since there was no kosher meat available in Ausonia. A nice brisket would have been lovely, its succulent aroma filling the bungalow, making their mouths water. But Sarahleah could live without meat if there was fresh fish to be had; and there was plenty of that, thanks to the Alanoie. So, tonight, there'd be stuffed carp—or at least something carp-like—plus roasted potatoes, green beans, and a cucumber and red onion salad, marinated in red vinaigrette.

Of course, in such rainy weather there had to be soup, so she'd been simmering a hearty bean and barley concoction all day. To top it off, she'd prepared a sumptuous dessert made of broad noodles, stewed cherries, and sweetened cottage cheese. Goat cottage cheese was a little odd, but with enough sugar, it would even have passed muster for her finicky father—a man who would shake his head and gravely push his plate away without a word if something tasted even the slightest bit off. Had his occasional silent criticism of her mother's cooking ever insulted Zipporah? If it did, she had borne it stoically.

Willie had never met anyone like Sarahleah. She was a mass of contradictions: on the one hand, a vivacious free spirit; on the other, obsessively traditional and domestic—a sensuous little mother hen who could laugh at her own fastidious foibles. Yet there was also a hint of melancholy about her that Willie couldn't quite pin down. It didn't show itself often, but when it did, it could send a chill through Willie, like an abrupt change in the weather for which she was inadequately dressed.

Bemused, Willie had watched her new girlfriend tie on an apron and take command of the kitchen shortly after breakfast. She'd been at it ever since—cutting, grinding, chopping and boiling, mixing, kneading and baking; sampling this and that with a finger, muttering to herself, then rushing over to the spice cabinet to find whatever it was this dish still lacked. She did it all without a word of complaint, totally in her element and appearing to love every minute of it. Sarahleah's cooking was mostly yummy but insanely fattening, and if this relationship continued much longer, Willie feared she'd become a blimp.

As her new lover scurried about, Willie felt utterly useless because Sarahleah stubbornly refused to let her lift a finger: "No, Willie. You relax. This is my dinner. If you want, you can try cooking Sunday—though from your pooh-pooh salads, we would both soon starve. And by the way ...your PMS jokes aren't funny ... *period!*"

Willie stared blankly for a moment, then got it and laughed despite herself. "Shit, girlfriend ... that's gotta be your worst one yet." Sarahleah had a limitless supply of puns, all of them dreadful. But the earnestness of her delivery and her timing were brilliant, and they usually caught Willie off guard. If nothing else, Sarahleah made Willie laugh, maybe more than she'd ever laughed with any other lover.

The girl was young, twenty-two, and even smaller than Willie, which made her about five-foot-nothing. She was certainly easy to look at, though, with those big brown eyes, porcelain skin, full red lips, and thick black hair that was always worn up—except when they went to bed and Sarahleah would take the pins out, letting it tumble down her back like an ebony waterfall. Willie loved to bury her face in that sensuous mass of hair.

Someday Sarahleah would probably go to fat, but for now, her body was beautifully proportioned, with generous curves in all the proper places. Still, it was her brilliant smile that stood out most. The girl didn't smile just with her mouth; she smiled with her entire being. And it had been with that smile, so like an embrace, that Sarahleah had crept into Willie's heart.

They'd met in front of the General Store just after sunrise one morning, during one of Willie's infrequent forays from her cabin, when she'd been forced out of seclusion by the annoying fact that she'd run out of coffee (an odd thing, since she could have sworn she'd left nearly half a pound sitting on the kitchen counter).

As far as possible, Willie had been avoiding all personal contact, keeping mostly to her own cabin, often sitting on her porch at night reading one of the books the library had to offer. She'd never delved into James Joyce, much less Robert Heinlein. But with all this time on her hands, losing herself in someone else's thoughts helped keep her from obsessing about her loneliness.

The "six weeks" Selene had promised until her return had become ten, without even a word. Willie had asked several of the Meliai Guides when she was due back, but though Selene had great status here, none of them seemed to know.

Willie had been preparing all her own meals, having ventured up to the Dining Commons only once, because she preferred her privacy. The reclusiveness she'd acquired almost from day one was entirely out of character for Willie, the gregarious friend and businesswoman, the ever-eager joiner of this club or that worthy cause. But she'd changed radically since landing in Ausonia. She was furious at having been abducted, at having control over her own destiny snatched from her hands, much as Harry had stolen it all those years ago. And the fact that her freedom had been appropriated by the woman she'd loved—well, that made it all the worse. So, since Selene's note had encouraged Willie to explore and make new friends, she would live like a hermit just out of spite.

That morning, when Willie had ventured out for coffee, rounded the last bend in the trail that led to the General Store and seen Sarahleah standing there, her impulse had been to duck out of sight. She'd come early, certain there'd be no one here but Nyleen, and that all she'd have to do was get her coffee and leave. But the girl waiting outside for the store to open spotted her immediately, shouted a friendly greeting and waved in her direction. So Willie sighed and prepared to endure a few inane pleasantries with a stranger.

The weather was lovely for this time of day, without a trace of the usual morning fog drifting in off the ocean. The pale sunlight was filtering down through the forest canopy from the east, and there was only the lightest breeze and a lone mockingbird twittering in a nearby tree.

"So which of us is the early bird and which is the worm?" Sarahleah had said when Willie walked up. It seemed an odd comment, trivial on the surface, but one that could have hidden layers of innuendo if you wanted to look for them. *The early bird catches the worm?* Willie gave her an appraising look, but there seemed no guile there, just a good-natured flirtatiousness, and she was quickly drawn into easy conversation with the quirky little creature.

Sarahleah was wearing shorts and a t-shirt beneath her translucent gown—like Willie, declining to surrender her modesty to the semi-nudity almost everyone practiced here. A grinning acknowledgment of their mutual propriety helped kick-start the bond between them, and they soon discovered they had much in common. Both were lesbians who came from families where orthodox religion was tightly woven into daily life. Sarahleah was the oldest of eight children from a Hassidic Jewish family in Brooklyn, and her parents had expelled her after she'd announced her sexual preferences at age seventeen, three weeks before she was to enter into an arranged marriage with the son of a prominent rabbi.

Her mother had been the first she'd told, and Zipporah, though shocked and heartsick, had advised that she go ahead and marry Bennie anyway, continuing her relationships with girls in secret if she must. Sarahleah had actually considered that option for a while. After all, though homosexuality was a grave sin for men in Judaism, the rules for women were somewhat vaguer.

"In olden times," Sarahleah had explained to Willie, "women were not considered full persons, so nothing they did sexually that didn't involve men counted as much. I'd never had sex with a man, so by Jewish law, I was a virgin, and pure enough for marriage to the son of a rabbi. But, in the end, I just couldn't go through with it. There would have been children, and if I couldn't stand the marriage and

263

had to leave, I'd have lost them. It was a trap that would have killed me." This was before Willie had told Sarahleah her own story, but her heart completely opened to the girl.

The attraction between them was mostly friendship at first, a recognition that here was someone who resonated with you like the neighboring string on a harp. The sexual part had followed naturally enough, though lovemaking was more something they did for comfort than any great need. For Willie, there was none of the insane urgency she'd known with Selene. Instead, it just felt natural and sweet. As for Sarahleah—well, a little sweetness was all she wanted, since she'd never before experienced the kind of intense passion she had with Nellyn, and didn't expect to with anyone else. Only one of the Shining Ones could ever make her cry out and beg for total annihilation that way.

Willie had encountered virtually no Jews until coming to the Bay Area, where she'd met a lot of them. Most particularly, she'd met David and then Glenda, her future business partner who'd been in her women's group. But though both David and Glenda were Jewish, they were thoroughly assimilated, and neither was especially religious. So to Willie, they were more like curiosities than the menacing "Christ killers" she'd been warned about as a child. They were simply David and Glenda, both of whom she came to love, and that was that. Sarahleah, though, was another matter. She was Orthodox through and through, and she wore her religion like a badge of honor.

Sarahleah had had no dealings at all with Christians during her childhood. Her little community was even more insular than Willie's had been, and the warnings she'd received about the *goyim*—the gentiles who were out to hurt her—had been every bit as gruesome as Willie's were about the Jews.

Culturally, Borough Park was not much different from the *shtetl* (the quaint little Jewish town in Poland) Sarahleah's great grandparents had lived in—just a lot more urban and without the constant anti-Semitic pogroms by outsiders. Her first real exposure to the wider world had come when her family had cast her out, at which point she'd been thrust into a totally alien environment. She might as well have been fired off the earth in a rocket ship, without even a guidebook to help her learn the curious customs of the Martians on whose planet she'd landed.

But Sarahleah, who'd always been a rebel at heart, was a quick study, and the girl from Borough Park soon adjusted to the polyglot culture of Manhattan, and then San Francisco, where she'd gotten a job as a translator for a law firm. In fact, not only had she adjusted, but she'd done so with fierce determination, loving her newfound freedom, blossoming and making friends among the natives.

It wasn't until the boundaries of Sarahleah's circumscribed life had fallen away that she realized how narrow they'd been. For one thing, romance and passion with other women was now possible, without the need for secrecy. Lesbians were everywhere in San Francisco and lived right out in the open. For a time, it was heaven on Earth.

Then, about six months into her new life, she'd received the crushing news that her mother had succumbed to a stroke. Her heart had broken and Sarahleah fell into a deep depression, blaming herself, convinced her mother had died of the grief she'd inflicted upon her—not so much for being a lesbian, but for shaming the family by announcing it publicly.

Why had she gone to such extremes when she could have canceled her wedding in private on some plausible pretext? The answer was she'd felt she had no choice. The Gay Pride event Sasha Rosen had taken her to had filled Sarahleah with a new kind of passion—all those people standing up in public to tell their own courageous stories.

She'd never tried to hide the fact that she was a Jew, because that was what she was. So why secret away this other important part of herself? Sarahleah was tired of living in darkness. She wanted to live in the light, but how could you live in the light if you were afraid to turn it on for fear of being seen? Sarahleah was a lesbian—an orthodox Jewish lesbian, and she would not continue to hide that fact from her family, her community, or the world. Well, she'd broken free all right, but at a terrible cost. She hadn't even been permitted to attend her own mother's funeral. "No," her father had said when turning her away. "The fruit has fallen too far from its tree. It cannot return to the branch."

Sarahleah's remorse was not over being a lesbian, but because something she couldn't help—this innate part of herself—had caused her family such anguish. What sort of world was this, in which a woman could not live as she'd been made without destroying her loved ones in the process?

She had learned to believe in herself, in what her body and spirit decreed. Now, though, doubt began to haunt her. Was this how God judged you for your sins—by destroying not you, but someone you loved, like the slaying of the first born in Exodus? That was absurd. She didn't want to believe in a vengeful God—a vengeful male God, as the Torah had it. It was Man himself who destroyed the innocent, not the Blessed One. And yet the results were no less devastating, the grief no easier to bear if human beings could condemn you unto death, even if *HaShem* held you pure and blameless.

This was why she could offer herself so freely to the Meliai. They neither judged nor punished anyone—they bestowed their blessings equally upon all: woman and man, Jew and Gentile, rich and poor, embracing even the most wretched. And how could they do anything else, when they were angels? It was Nellyn, and later the other Meliai, who had brought Sarahleah back to life, given her hope and helped her heal. She owed them everything and would repay them with the same love and generosity they had shown her.

"I don't care what you say. I'm setting the table," Willie said, when dinner was almost ready. The luscious, though unfamiliar, aromas filling the kitchen were making her mouth water and her stomach rumble.

"No, I told you to relax," Sarahleah, replied, wagging a finger in Willie's face. "You can open the wine if you want something to do."

Willie laughed and opened the half-liter bottle; not much of a chore, since it was a screw top. *It's almost like Sarahleah thinks of me as her husband,* she thought, finding the idea both amusing and unsettling. For all her relationships with women, she'd never been in one with so many echoes of stereotyped male-female gender roles. It made her feel like some caricatured lesbian out of the 1940s, an old-fashioned dyke, as out-of-date as the Betty Crocker kitchens all these Guest cabins had.

Unlike Willie, whose cabin had remained just as she'd found it during the weeks she'd lived there alone, Sarahleah had put a definitive stamp on her place, with potted plants, curtains and wall hangings, and even a little religious icon called a *mezuzah*, which she'd obtained from the General Store and nailed to the front door frame. It was astonishing how eager and able the Meliai were to provide their Guests with all these special items, though Willie had determinedly refused to ask for anything with which to "brighten up" her own cabin.

She wanted no comforts that might defuse her anger, but when Sarahleah had invited her to share her home, the offer was impossible to resist. Sarahleah's cabin felt so much cozier than her own, and the asceticism Willie had determinedly cultivated evaporated without a trace. She knew the Meliai discouraged humans from "coupling up." But they had sought no permission and received no reprimands from any of the Guides, who just turned a blind eye to their arrangement. It seemed strange to Willie, though Sarahleah just shrugged it off: "Oh, the Meliai are too busy dealing with the Oreads to worry about two human girls sharing a bungalow."

As housemates, they mostly got along well. The chief exception was that Sarahleah liked the cabin quite warm, so the pellet stove was going constantly, and the place always felt stuffy to Willie. To keep Sarahleah happy, she was constantly lugging eight-kilo sacks of stove pellets home from the General Store—the man's role again. But, after all, she *was* physically stronger, and it did help her work off the endless stream of homemade cakes and cookies Sarahleah was constantly urging on her.

Here at home, neither Willie nor Sarahleah had any qualms about being naked, and they often walked around that way, sometimes reaching out to touch each other affectionately as they passed. Even dinner was often eaten in the nude. "The Lord meant for lovers to adore each other with their eyes," Sarahleah said the day Willie moved in. "Modesty is proper among strangers, but here, with just ourselves, why should we hide behind clothes if we don't need them for warmth?" In this respect, she admitted, she was a most unconventional Orthodox Jew, but if Adam and Eve could be naked in the Garden, why not two Eves in their own little paradise?

Sarahleah had been promising Willie this Sabbath feast for a couple of weeks now, and she'd gone all out to deliver the genuine article. Tonight, they'd decided to wear their Meliai gowns to dinner with nothing underneath. They were the closest thing to finery the women had, and the filmy things seemed oddly appropriate for what felt like a spiritual occasion.

They'd brought the table and chairs out from the breakfast nook into the cabin's main room, and Willie watched as Sarahleah dimmed the lights, lit the candles, and uttered an incomprehensible blessing in Hebrew, moving her cupped hands over the twin flames in little circles, then pressing her palms to her eyes, as if she were gathering the candles' light into herself so that she could radiate it back into the world.

"This is a woman's ritual," Sarahleah explained. "It evokes the sacred feminine, which is at the heart of Judaism. Of course, our *Rebbe* might disagree, but he's not here, so tonight my interpretation goes." She tapped her own chest with an index finger, giving her girlfriend a wolfish smile. Then she seated herself opposite Willie, the candles slightly off center on the table so the women could see each other's faces in the flickering light. Their skin shimmered and glowed beneath their filmy gowns.

After Sarahleah had said two more blessings, first over the wine, and then the bread, she extended the fresh-baked *challah* to Willie. The braided bread was not meant to be cut with a knife; rather, custom called for each person to use her hand to pull a chunk from the loaf, which came apart easily where its braided sections crisscrossed. It was a sweet tradition, Willie thought, like some kind of communion.

She broke off a piece and took a bite, after which Sarahleah did the same. The loaf was still warm, its crust a golden brown and slightly crunchy, the pale yellow inside fluffy, steaming, and fragrant. "Yum," Willie said. It reminded her a bit of the fresh-baked brioche she loved back home.

Sarahleah raised her wine glass for a toast. "I drink to my Eve," she said.

"To *my* Eve," Willie replied. The deep, red wine was too sweet for her taste, but it went straight to her head. "Yikes, this stuff packs a kick!"

"Kosher wine from New York," Sarahleah replied. "The Meliai get it for me."

"Wine has to be kosher?" Willie asked. "I thought it was only meat."

Sarahleah made a dismissive gesture. "Don't even ask. I get this wine because I like it … Here, have some soup."

She ladled the thick concoction into Willie's bowl, and Willie dug in with enthusiasm. "Wow, Sarahleah … this is great … real comfort food."

"By us, it's all comfort food, Willie. We don't just eat to live. We live to eat."

"Well, you're a wonderful cook," Willie said, "and gorgeous as Queen Esther."

Sarahleah rolled her eyes. "Where the heck did you come up with Esther?"

Willie shrugged and took another bite of *challah*. "Hey, your little *shiksa* did study The Old Religion in Sunday school," she said, chewing. "Esther was the most beautiful woman in all of Persia, and the most courageous. She became queen and saved the Hebrews from being slaughtered."

Willie's take on the *Book of Esther* made Sarahleah giggle. Of course, the daughter of an evangelical minister would refer to Biblical Jews as "the Hebrews." "Yes, well, it's sweet of you to compare me to Esther, dear, but please don't talk with your mouth full. Food is not meant to be seen once a person starts chewing it."

The admonition stunned Willie for a moment, then she laughed so hard she nearly choked. *Her girlfriend, her husband … now it's like I'm her daughter.* "You really do take care of me, don't you, Sarahleah?" she said, when she'd caught her breath. "I know I don't always show it, but thank you for all the kindness and love you're giving me."

Sarahleah looked down demurely, then smiled. "Well, someone had to see to you, Wilhelmina. When we met, you were so alone you never went out of your cabin." No one in her memory had ever called Willie "Wilhelmina" without drawing her ire, but coming from Sarahleah, it felt like an endearment.

Willie smiled weakly, taking another sip of the rich wine. "It doesn't really matter if I leave the cabin or not, Sarahleah. Wherever I go, whatever I do, I'm in jail here. I don't even know if Selene is ever coming …" She stopped herself because, suddenly, mentioning Selene when Sarahleah had gone to so much trouble to prepare this meal for her seemed rude and ungrateful. "Oh, I'm sorry, honey. I didn't mean to …"

But Sarahleah shook her head. "No. We should be honest. We agreed from the start that this was only temporary, didn't we? I'm waiting for Nellyn. You're waiting for Selene. So what? We're both floating in the same boat. For now, we make nice company."

"Yes, but don't you ever want to get out of this place?" Willie demanded. "I mean, that boat we're floating in, it's a fucking prison barge!"

270

Sarahleah's lips tightened. "We are not prisoners, Willie. We're the Meliai's honored Guests. We should be grateful to be so wanted and loved."

"Wanted and loved? Girl, sometimes you have this total slave mentality! It's like you're back in Egypt serving the Pharaoh and perfectly happy right where you are."

"Willie! Stop it! I don't like such talk. I know you're unhappy here, but I am allowed to think for myself, thank you very much."

Willie sighed. They'd been down this path before, and all it ever did was upset Sarahleah. Like most humans here, she'd come to identify with her captors. It was a classic case of Stockholm syndrome, or else some kind of mass hypnosis the Meliai practiced. *So why the fuck do I seem immune,* she wondered.

Willie knew she'd gone too far with the slave mentality remark, but a half-hearted apology was all she felt like offering, given how dense Sarahleah was about the Meliai and whatever their mysterious intentions toward humans might be. "Yikes. Of course you're allowed to think for yourself. Look, let's just change the subject, okay?"

Sarahleah nodded brusquely, avoiding Willie's eyes, then busied herself serving.

Shit, all I've done is ruin a romantic evening, Willie thought. *Me and my big mouth.*

"Here, have some *gefilte fish,*" Sarahleah said. "No bones, so you shouldn't choke, and if you do, I can Heimlich." She looked up, stony-faced for a moment, then broke into a broad grin and gave Willie a mischievous wink. They both laughed and Willie breathed a sigh of relief.

She took a bite of the odd, pale thing Sarahleah dropped onto her plate and remembered the dish now, having eaten something similar years ago, when she'd joined David and Lester for a traditional Passover meal at some aunt's house. It was like a cold meatball, only made of ground fish instead of meat.

The jellied fish sauce that went with it looked repulsive but wasn't that bad when you sopped it up with the *challah* and ate it

271

that way. The horseradish helped a bit too if you ate just a little at a time, but this dish was clearly an acquired taste, and Willie tactfully declined seconds, saying she wanted to 'save room for the rest of this wonderful meal.'

The green beans with almond slivers were good, if a trifle overcooked, but the pan roasted potatoes were delicious, as was the cucumber salad. The gut-stuffing dessert, which Sarahleah called *kugel*, was scrumptious, and went especially well with the sweet red wine, which was beginning to grow on Willie enough so that she was probably drinking too much of it.

Sarahleah, her good cheer restored by the wine, spoke animatedly about her past—not of her life as a member of a Hassidic community in Brooklyn because Willie had already heard about that. Instead, she spoke of leaving that behind her. She talked about finding an apartment in San Francisco and about attending community college. She talked about becoming a legal translator and then meeting Nellyn, the attorney who'd become the love of her life.

"I'm curious about how you became a translator," Willie asked. "What languages do you speak?"

"Besides English, Yiddish and Hebrew, I speak Polish, Russian and German. The Russian and German were what got me work because I'm very fluent."

"You learned all those languages in school?"

Sarahleah shook her head. "My family is from Eastern Europe, so some of them we spoke at home, the rest I just picked up. I've always been good at languages. That was why Nellyn's firm hired me."

Willie poured them each another glass of wine. "I've been meaning to ask you this," she said, "and I'm not even sure how to put it, but did you ever think that Nellyn had … I don't know, some kind of 'unearthly' power over you? I mean, that's what I felt from Selene. It was like supernatural seduction or something." The startled look on Sarahleah's face stopped her. "Oh, is talking about this uncomfortable for you?"

"No, not at all" Sarahleah said. "It's just the way you put it. See, I knew exactly what Nellyn was the moment I set eyes on her. She was just so ... so luminous. I said to myself, 'Here is one of the Shining Ones, one of the *Hashmallim*.'"

Willie gave her a puzzled look. "The what?"

"*Hashmallim*. The Shining Ones: the fourth loftiest among the ten ranks of angels. To be taken as a lover by one of them is among the greatest gifts a human can receive."

Willie was stunned. "You can't actually believe the Meliai are angels!"

"But of course they are. What else can they possibly be?"

Willie had no idea how to respond to such an outrageous notion. There was so much she hadn't revealed about her own history with Selene. Would Sarahleah even know what a dominatrix was? How could she ever explain these things to such an innocent? Suddenly, Willie remembered that painting in Wynter's gallery with Jill sprouting angel's wings as she calmly dug the heel of her shoe into the stomach of a submissive. The wine was really getting to her now, and she tried unsuccessfully to stifle a grin.

"What's that smile about?" Sarahleah wanted to know.

Willie shook her head. "I was just remembering something ... 'angelic' about a girl I once knew."

"Come on, Willie, tell me," Sarahleah pleaded, like a preteen wanting to be let in on a grown-up secret.

Willie put a hand over her mouth to stifle a giggle. "It's hard to explain, honey. Ask me again another time."

Sarahleah shrugged and changed the subject. "Listen, since it's finally stopped raining, how about we take a hike to the Upper Village tomorrow?"

"What? There's no way up there except through the forest, and that's dangerous without a Meliai Guide."

Sarahleah made a dismissive gesture. "Oh, baloney to all that. I'm not afraid. I'll get us there safe and sound."

"Oh, right," Willie said. "And just how would you keep us from getting lost?"

"Easy. I know the way because I've been there ... three times, in fact."

From the Journal of Noah Burns (1863)

Miscellany:

1) While Pandoric is the native language of both the Meliai and Oread clans, the Alanoie speak an entirely different tongue, which more resembles birdsong than any human speech. The Dryads can speak this odd language, but, to my knowledge, no human or Changeling has ever mastered it.

2) The savage Oreads are bonded not to the fruit-bearing Drys trees, but to the Oros trees of the deep forest, which are massive and not susceptible to blight. Because of this, the Oreads themselves almost never die and therefore have virtually no need of human males to replenish their numbers. Yet they will mate and reproduce occasionally with males bartered to them by the Meliai. This usually happens only after some freak event, like the fire that decimated the Oros trees of Fifth Valley three centuries ago, taking hundreds of trees and the lives of as many Oreads with them. The Meliai exacted a steep price in raw marble and clay for the human males they lent the Oreads, and since the Oreads had no access to the Portal, they were obliged to pay it. The Oreads resent how the Meliai treated them to this day.

3) The mysterious Portal (called the Balacampa in Pandoric) connects Earth to this strange world. It has one end whose location remains always fixed at a single point in Ausonia, that being in the center of a grove of walnut-like trees whose exact site the Meliai keep secret. On Earth, however, the Balacampa's opposite end continually shifts from one place to another, flicking here and there like the tail of a whip, before remaining stationary for some arbitrary period of time.

For centuries, the Balacampa's Earthly end point was on one of the smaller Greek isles, before later moving to the Indian subcontinent and then to Northern Europe. It has existed in forests and caves and, from what I have been told, even in human dwellings, and particularly inside houses of worship. Tristelle claims that the Earthly end of the Balacampa spent some four decades in a hidden chamber inside the Vatican archives, and that a number of high Church officials were seduced and brought to Ausonia for transformation.

Chapter 33

SARAHLEAH

I was leading Willie up the mountain—climbing, panting, climbing. It was murky, damp, and overgrown in this forest, with not so much as a narrow path to follow. When I'd come this way with Nellyn, I always felt safe. But now, the calls of strange birds and animals were making me anxious and my heart was pounding. Even worse, my guilty secret was that we were not going to the Upper Village, as I'd promised. Instead, we had a secret appointment with the crazy Oreads—the *Lilot*, as I thought of them.

In Jewish mythology, the *Lilot* are female demons, succubae that suck the souls from men. According to legend, Lilith, Adam's original wife, was the first *Lilot*. The Lord had fashioned her from clay, just like Adam, thus making man and woman full equals at the birth of creation. But something went "wrong" with Lilith and she declined the role God assigned her. Did she actually try to devour Adam's soul, as he claimed, or was he just telling tales to God because he knew he wasn't man enough to satisfy her?

Sasha Rubin, my first lover, told that version of the myth. She said that Lilith longed to be loved by another woman, and the Lord, seeing that His commandment to "be fruitful and multiply" was not one she was likely to follow, simply shrugged and started over again, growing Eve from one of Adam's ribs. After all, of what possible use was a lesbian Lilith to Adam? It wasn't like he needed a tennis partner with big breasts in Eden.

Of course, Lilith was just a fable invented by men to scare rebellious wives into obeying their husbands for fear they'd be replaced by more accommodating women. The Oreads, though, were all too real. And if they were a threat to the Meliai, wasn't it my duty to help foil them? Of course it was, and it should be Willie's duty too, though I could hardly explain to her something she was not yet ready to understand.

I had no idea how she would react to the Oreads when they came for us because she was not one who took well to being ordered about. But while Willie's resolve comforted me most of the time, it worried me now because patience was just as important as strength. I could be patient as meat in a freezer, though resolve in the face of danger often failed me. In that way, we were like two halves of one whole person, Willie and me. Together we were complete, but individually, not so much. Willie could stand up for herself as well as any woman I knew, but if she tried to resist the Oreads, there would be trouble.

Still, Willie's reaction to the Oreads was not my main concern right now. My big problem was that we were lost; or, at least, *I* was lost. It was late afternoon and the greenish light was turning to emerald blue—usually a lovely time of day, but it was frightening here in this forest.

The Upper Village was over to the west, and I was trying to steer us just north of that using Salome, which was in the sky during the day right now, as a guide. Nellyn had shown me how, but the clouds had rolled over in the past hour and I'd lost track of where the big moon was. Were we still going the right way? I thought so, but I was no kind of jungle explorer, just a clever girl from Brooklyn who'd learned to read street signs when she was four but knew nothing of getting around in the wild.

In the city, everything was clearly marked. Every street had a name, each house a number. You read the numbers and street signs and knew exactly where you were. But here all directions looked the same. If it were up to me, each tree would have a big, white number painted on its trunk, numbers that glowed in the dark. And there'd be signs that read Trees #1100-1250, or #1375-1500, with arrows pointing the way. I wished with all my heart I was really taking Willie to the Upper Village where I knew my way around, but in this forest, I was lost. And if I couldn't get us to that clearing soon, would the Oreads even find us?

"I think we turn left here," I said, pointing to a thick pine tree whose bark was torn with a ragged gash. I had no idea if a Meliai had made this slash, or if some beast had just used the bark to sharpen its claws. Maybe it was a mark left for me by Nellyn, but what direction was I to glean from a gash in the bark of a tree?

"You think we turn left?" Willie said, sarcastically. She'd been *schlepping* that backpack all the way up the mountain, and she stopped for a moment to adjust its weight on her shoulders. "You fucking *think*? Shit, Sarahleah. We're totally lost, aren't we?"

At one time, Willie's constant swearing would have shocked me. But I'd lived for years in Manhattan and San Francisco among all kinds of people and had learned not to be bothered by vulgar language, nor by many other things that might once have horrified me. Even Willie's tattoo didn't trouble me—though for observant Jews, marking the body in such a way is considered a sacrilege. Of course, I no longer believed that.

Sasha Rubin was the girl who'd "brought me out" and she'd been both an observant Jew and a militant feminist—"a punk kike dyke," was what she'd proudly called herself. At age seventeen, she'd had a series of scenes from *Exodus* tattooed round and round her body, inside the outline of a thick, coiling serpent. She was a big girl, and when she was naked, you could circle her three times and read it all, going from bottom to top, like an illuminated scroll, with the arrival at the Promised Land portrayed inside the snake's huge head, which arched across Sasha's breasts. It should have been blasphemy, but to me it was sublime. She published a little magazine for radical Jewish lesbians called *Dafka*, which meant "In Defiance," and Willie reminded me of her because she was always telling me I didn't know my own power.

I looked at Willie and tried to joke my way through the fact that I had no idea where we were: "We're not really lost," I said, "just a little *farblonget*." She gave me that exasperated look she got when I used a Yiddish word she didn't know, and I explained that "a little *farblonget*" just meant "a teeny bit misplaced" or "gone slightly off course."

"In other words ... totally fucking lost!" she insisted, glaring at me, hands on hips.

"Well, yes ... lost," I replied. "But not as lost as *totally* lost would be. I mean, we know we're in a forest, right?" Instead of laughing, as I'd hoped she would, she just rolled her eyes.

She had a point though. *Farblonget* was not a good thing to be with night closing in and that clearing nowhere in sight. I should have gotten us there hours ago, and now I was growing desperate. I thought about what Nellyn had said when I'd last seen her: "No harm will come to you or Willie, I promise. And your courage will be well rewarded." She didn't have to explain what that meant. I was still merely human, so "well rewarded" meant everything to me. I didn't want Nellyn to replace me with another girl like Lilith had been. If my Shining One turned me away unaltered, if I was sent back to Earth as mere mortal clay—I couldn't bear it.

I looked around uneasily, trying to get my bearings. Everywhere I turned, there was gloom and chaos, the trees so dense they seemed to squeeze the very breath from me. The fat, clumsy roots were always under foot, and the thin, whippy branches clawed and snapped at us as we fought our way through them. It reminded me of that evil forest in *The Wizard of Oz*, which Sasha had taken me to see on our second date. I was not allowed to go to movies by my parents because they were considered sinful, along with so many other secular things like nonreligious books. I had to lie about where I was going, and that was my first true act of rebellion, though far from the last.

We trudged on, Willie still grumbling as the forest grew denser and darker. To the right, a pool of stagnant water reeked of death. And suddenly, a six-legged frog as big as a rabbit jumped from behind a rock, making me shriek. It splashed into the pool, croaked, and sank beneath the water, leaving a trail of bubbles. My scream made Willie laugh, and I laughed too, though it felt hollow.

We'd gotten a late start this morning, after eating the delicious breakfast I'd made for us: oatmeal with milk, honey, and raisins; then omelets filled with sweet red peppers, onions and tomatoes. And there was buttered toast, cuddleberries and cream, and a pot of the extra-strong coffee Willie loved. After all, it was going to be our only meal before the hot supper I'd promised would be waiting when we reached the Full Sisters Inn.

That was the exquisite guesthouse with its fancy restaurant, and those adorable suites whose windows overlooked the English gardens, and the sapphire lake where the Alanoie camped when they came to trade fish, shells, and colored stones for the finished goods the Meliai made. That was the story I'd told to tempt Willie into making this trek. But it wasn't like these wonderful things didn't exist—they did. It was just that our arrival at the inn would be delayed awhile.

I'd wanted to make a 9:00 a.m. start from our bungalow, but by the time we were ready to go, it was 10:30. That should still have been early enough to get us to the clearing by 3:00, but by now it was after 4:00, and the evening fog was already curling through the trees. Such a simple thing this journey should have been to lead, but I'd failed miserably. I stopped walking and turned to face Willie. "I'm sorry," I said, fighting back tears. "You're right. I have no idea where we are."

She put an arm around my shoulder, not admonishing me again, though she had every right to. We sat down on a couple of tree stumps to rest, and now I began to weep in earnest. "I'm such a fool," I moaned.

"C'mon, honey, we're big girls," she said. "We can survive one night in the woods. Think of it as an adventure. I'll make a fire, and we'll both be nice and warm."

"Sleep in the woods?" The idea terrified me. "But there are *things* out here."

"Lions and tigers and bears, oh, my!" she gasped, feigning terror she clearly didn't feel. I stared at her, astonished. It was like she'd read my thoughts when I was remembering *The Wizard of Oz* only moments ago. This world had a way of doing that to you. Minds could merge in the strangest ways, and it just felt so natural—as if we were all a single thought in the mind of God.

I confessed to Willie that I'd never slept in the woods before.

"Really?" she said, astonished. "You never went camping when you were a kid?"

I shook my head. "In my family, we didn't do such things."

Willie smiled. "Don't worry, sweetie. You're with the original Girl Scout. I brought some matches, so I can build us a nice fire." She began to rummage through the backpack she'd set at her feet. "Let's see ... we've still got lots of water, a bag of roasted mullnuts, and a couple of chocolate bars. Plus, look ..." With a wink, she produced a full bottle of brandy. "Between this stuff, a fire, and our loobas, we'll be warm and toasty."

I gave her a little nod, huddling close for comfort. My uncle Mordecai, not yet forty, had been killed by a mugger right outside his home in Park Slope, so I knew how quickly and horribly death could overtake a person. Willie did not suspect the wonderful thing the Meliai had in store for us, but if we perished here tonight, before they could transform us, whose fault would it be but mine?

I did what I hadn't done since leaving my parents' home: I petitioned the God of my Fathers: *Dear Lord, if you send Death for only one of us tonight, please let it be me and let Willie live.* It should have been a generous prayer, asking that Willie be spared and I be taken in her stead, but I quickly saw its selfishness, which was nothing more than a plea to depart this life quickly myself, leaving Willie to suffer alone whatever terrors the coming night might hold.

I still loved the old rituals, like blessing the Sabbath candles and the food we ate, but this was why I'd abandoned asking for things in prayer: because no matter how selfless you tried to make your petition sound, your own needs were always at the heart of it. A pious woman prayed her husband would survive this heart attack, her innocent child this cancer—but was her prayer really to spare *their* lives, or because she couldn't bear being left alone? How we humans deceived ourselves, believing in our own virtue. Would there be a purer, more sacred life in that remade self I longed for? I fervently hoped there would—no, I *knew* there would! I had seen and felt it when I'd attended my first Edarta. But now it would never happen because my blundering had ruined everything.

I began to cry again, and of course Willie misunderstood why. It wasn't because I'd gotten us lost in this forest. I was weeping for my mother and uncle, who were gone forever, at having been cast out by my own family simply because of who I was. Most of all, I was weeping for the sad fragility of life, and the terrible insult of death that took away all that we loved, with such callous indifference to human suffering.

And then another memory came to me: I couldn't have been more than seven, and one Sabbath, after the service, our *Rebbe* gave a talk to the congregation. The women, of course, were seated behind the *mehitzah*, the curtain that separates the men's section from the women's, so that the sight of females should not turn men's minds to impious thoughts in the synagogue (as if women were to blame for male lust). The subject of the *Rebbe's* talk was, "Why is there human suffering?" And instead of falling asleep on my mother's shoulder, as many children would, I followed the talk attentively.

The *Rebbe* gave many reasons for human suffering, mostly having to do with sin, all of which I'd heard before. But then he posed the question of why the Lord allowed even the most innocent, like sinless newborns, to suffer. After giving us a moment to consider this, he said, "We must remember that *HaShem* does not think as we do, nor does He feel as we feel. *HaShem* is transcendent. He is not flesh and blood, so He does not have a human heart like ours."

This was a staggering new idea for me. Did the lack of a human heart make the Lord greater or lesser than we were? Was all the misery of the world there because He was incapable of feeling human pain and so remained unmoved by it? It was like no concept of *HaShem* I'd ever heard before. This seemed an alien God, cold and remote as the moon. But it might explain the many things that were so obviously wrong with the world: murder, rape, war, famine, disease, genocide, and all the other horrors.

And then I had an amazing thought—one so astonishing that, against all propriety, I spoke up loudly from behind the *mehitzah*, saying, "Well, if *HaShem* doesn't have a human heart, maybe it's our job to help Him get one."

Immediately, I realized what I'd done and clamped my own hand over my mouth. It was as if someone other than me had spoken these words, as if Sarahleah Kahane had been possessed by a *dybbuk*. There was an audible gasp from the congregation, and then stunned silence. Not only had a girl child spoken out of place, rudely and inexcusably interrupting the *Rebbe*, but she had dared to suggest that mere humans could help the Lord get something He actually needed, something mere mortals had but that He Himself lacked. My mother, sitting beside me, gave me a painful pinch on the arm and told me to hush. I knew I would be in terrible trouble with my father tonight.

The silence in the synagogue seemed to last forever. But now an odd thing happened, a thing which, at the time, I did not fully understand: The *Rebbe* began to laugh, not just a chuckle either, but a full-throated, gut-wrenching laugh. The congregation began to laugh with him, though tentatively, since they had no real idea what they were laughing about. When the laughter finally stopped, the *Rebbe* spoke a single sentence: "Oh, from the mouths of babes." That was all he said, and then he sent us home.

I was no longer crying when Willie touched my cheek. Something inside me had suddenly shifted. "Look," Willie said. "We're in this together, okay? The thing to do is find a place to build a fire and get some sleep. Then, in the morning, we'll head back down to the Lower Village the way we came."

But my mind was clear now and my will unshakable, as I remembered the task Nellyn had given me. How could I even dream of surrendering to despair with so much at stake? "Go back to the Lower Village?" I said. "No, Willie, we will not!"

She looked at me as if I was mad. "Fuck this, Sarahleah!" she said. "We can't keep wandering around this godforsaken forest forever, with no idea where we're going."

"I know exactly where we're going," I insisted. "We're going to the Full Sisters Inn, and I will find it."

"Bullshit, girlfriend," Willie said, pointing a finger at me. "You said it yourself. You're totally lost up here! Now listen to me. Once it's light enough to see, we will turn around and head downhill. We're sure to come out in the Lower Village somewhere."

"Oh, and you know this how?" I demanded, challenging her with a ferocity that surprised me. "We might come out on the far side of this mountain and be even more lost than we are now."

"I don't care!" she said. "As soon as it's light, I am getting down off this mountain, and you can wander around the fucking forest all by yourself if you want. The only thing I'm interested in finding now is that damned Portal so I can go home!"

Well, wasn't this something? Now she was the hysterical one. And suddenly, I was perfectly calm, calm enough to realize that, though I hated the thought of spending the night up here, it wasn't wise to keep fighting her. So I pretended to relent. All right—we would find a place to camp and go back to the Lower Village in the morning. I would play the meek role she expected of me, but I had no intention of going back down. Morning was a long way off, and who knew what might happen between now and then?

<u>From the Journal of Noah Burns, October 1863 (approximate)</u>

I theorize that slow blight first came here from Earth, inadvertently brought through the Portal by the Meliai's own ancestors, perhaps as spores from somewhere on the European continent, where it may have existed in a far milder form. The disease then became more virulent here, where the Drys trees possessed no natural immunity to its ravages.

Blight attacks first the tree's bark, coating it with a gummy white plaque. From there, it gradually works its way into the Drys tree's heart and roots, depriving the tree of its ability to draw moisture from the soil. In essence, it gradually dies of thirst. The Meliai's subsequent death resembles this in form, in the drying up of her bodily fluids and flesh, though she herself may not begin to exhibit outward signs for decades after her tree first becomes infected. However, during the latter stages of the blight, she suffers from increasing thirst, consuming huge quantities of water.

It matters not how far removed physically a Meliai is from her tree. Even if she is living on Earth, another world entirely, should her Drys die in Ausonia, the Meliai's own demise is certain. It is as if each Dryad were part of a single being made of two invisibly linked bodies—one appearing quite human, the other a tree—with each dependent upon its counterpart for its survival.

How these trees managed before the Dryads' ancestors came here, I do not know. Perhaps the Drys previously bonded with some now extinct native fauna but found human females more congenial as symbiotic partners.

The Drys themselves are not sentient as we understand the term, and yet they are much more than mindless plants. They possess a keen awareness that can often be sensed by humans through physical contact. I myself have felt it, though the experience is difficult to describe. Imagine, if you will, a kind of dynamic presence with no sense of time, but fully alive in the moment. It bears witness to all around it yet is without thought. Many humans who have sensed it find this state one of transcendent bliss, while for others, it is a terrifying loss of selfhood. Those who find the experience alarming are of no use to the Meliai and are sent back to Earth. For me, the sensation has been a combination of both extremes, but, for now, I remain here, continuing to learn what I can.

That slow blight takes decades to completely destroy a Drys tree accounts for its name, but though it is 'slow,' its effects are always lethal in the end. Yet it is fortunate that the protracted nature of the blight's progress allows a Meliai the opportunity to take the measures that alone can save her.

If the source of slow blight is indeed Earthly, it may account for the Changelings' natural resistance to the disease, since Changelings themselves are of human and thus Earthly origin. Can a human carry some natural immunity to a disease that affects a single species of alien tree? It seems an absurd notion, but far more plausible conjectures have failed me. Maria the Jewess (the ancient Mother of Alchemy) might have been more at home in Ausonia than I, a scientist of the modern world. To an alchemist, the witch's brew the Meliai feed their Changelings might fit the natural order of things quite well.

Chapter 34

WILLIE

$\mathcal{I}$'m done with this bullshit," I said. "You obviously have no idea where we are, and as soon as it's morning, I'm heading back to the Lower Village. And you, girlfriend, can either come with me or keep wandering around the fucking forest alone until you fall into a rat hole." It was like I was threatening to trade her to the Gypsies for a stewing chicken, which, the way I was feeling, I might have actually done if there'd been any Gypsies around with a bird ready for the pot.

My ultimatum worked because she suddenly went meek as a kitten. "All right, Willie," she said. "We'll go back down in the morning if you think that's best."

I dropped to my knees to adjust the straps on the backpack on the ground, furious at her for getting us lost; but the weird thing was I wasn't even sure I liked winning this argument. For a moment there, she'd actually been standing up to me, sounding more like a strong independent woman than a helpless wife. I've always liked a little heat from my lovers—a touch of emotional struggle that works like a pressure valve to release the simmering boredom that can build up in relationships. Sarahleah standing firm about not going back to the Lower Village showed me a new side of her. But then she'd slipped right back into her usual passive role.

Maybe she was being submissive because I was just the third relationship she'd had and she was afraid of losing me if she held her ground. And maybe that's why she did all the cooking and cleaning at home, spoiling me rotten to keep me from leaving. It had annoyed me from day one—even while my lazy part loved the pampering—because a dynamic like that is unhealthy for adult relationships. How could I explain to a girl as naïve as Sarahleah that sometimes you got more points by getting in your lover's face and growling at her than you did by giving in? To a tame puppy like her it would make no sense, but to an old she-hound like me it was as basic as knowing how to bury and guard a bone.

Physically and emotionally, Sarahleah was wired for women. That much was obvious. But she'd grown up with lots of male energy at home—a stern father and six brothers—and it was like some part of her still needed to sniff a little testosterone to give her direction, to make her feel protected and feminine. Sometimes I wondered if what she really craved was a man in a woman's body, though Sarahleah, who'd never been in therapy, would have laughed at that idea.

She once told me that she'd never even imagined having sex with a man, much less done it—as if being a dyke was some kind of noble cause and she expected me to be proud of her. I didn't call her on it, though of course it was bullshit. You're turned on by who you're turned on by, and that's the end of it. The freedom to love whoever you want—now *that's* worth fighting for, but who you're attracted to isn't a cause, it's just how you're made. I sighed as I thought of David. If only I'd remembered how he was made when he first told me he was in love with a dominatrix. I wished he was here now, so I could tell him how stupid and self-righteous I'd been trying to 'save' him from being who he was.

The backpack's straps had been pinching my shoulders since we'd set out, and I grunted, trying to loosen them, but they were damp and stuck tight in the buckles. I dug around inside the pack till I found the Swiss army knife I'd picked up at the General Store, but none of its clever tools gave me enough leverage on the buckle.

"Can I help?" Sarahleah asked.

"Yeah," I said. "Get down here and work the strap while I use both hands to pry this thing open."

Sarahleah's insistence that she was some kind of 'pure lesbian' was a case study in denial. I'd been into girls since middle school and had nothing to justify. I loved female energy and women's bodies. I loved their humor, their spirits, and their nimble minds, and I never once thought I needed a male to take care of me. I loved having sex with women, but sometimes I liked getting it on with men too. So what? Women might be my center of gravity, but that didn't make them my Eleventh Commandment. Anyway, how could you know you were really a dyke without at least trying a man, without knowing how a flesh-and-blood cock felt moving inside you?

Sarahleah was tugging too hard and getting the strap stuck tighter. "No," I said. "Work with me, here. Push in to loosen this side, then pull here to make it longer."

The Meliai had no men of their own, but they never called themselves lesbians, pure or otherwise. In fact, Pandoric didn't even have a word for lesbian. I knew there were a few gay men and heterosexual women in the Lower Village—people whose main attraction was to men—and the fact that the Meliai could seduce them so easily had to mean their power over humans crossed sexual preference lines, reaching down to something more basic than gender.

Whether you were male or female didn't seem to matter to the Meliai. Of course, they were aware of gender, but for them it was more about polarity—the flow of energy from one being to another. As long as there was a 'transmitter' and a 'receiver,' there was attraction, energy flow and pleasure. On the other hand, putting two transmitters or two receivers together was like trying to mate the two positive or negative poles on a couple of bar magnets. As hard as you pushed, they kept repelling each other.

The first strap came loose, and we got it adjusted. Sarahleah beamed, pleased with herself. "Okay," I said. "Good girl. Now let's do the other one just the same way."

Back home, I had friends who were into Wicca, a kind of nature religion that involved 'white witchcraft.' Glenda was totally involved with it and was forever trying to get me to join her coven. There was this thing called 'Sex Magic' that Wiccans practiced. It used spells and sexual arousal to focus energy on attaining some benevolent goal. Glenda said that Sex Magic was great for making yourself irresistible to anyone you wanted as a lover—not necessarily a benevolent goal in my view, unless you thought you were doing these people a huge service by fucking them. Of course, Glenda always seemed sexually deprived, so it was probably bullshit.

But was it really? Maybe the Meliai were using something like Sex Magic, and that's what made the dommes at Nyala so good at their jobs. If it was real, it couldn't be just the Meliai at Nyala who used it, though. All the Meliai must be doing it to keep their humans in line. And Jill would have used it on David too.

Jill! That was another revelation I'd had, because it was obvious she'd been a Meliai too. I'd worked that one out pretty quick after Selene dumped me here, while I was holed up in my cabin with all that time to brood. Jill's work at the club, her connection to Selene, and then the way she'd pounced on David; it all fit.

Why else would a wild girl like that want someone as tame as he was? If Jill was Meliai, it made sense that David was the perfect match for her. The polarity between them was obvious any time they walked into a room together. She owned him sexually and he loved it, and sometimes that annoyed the shit out of me.

But Jill, though she seemed to relish her power over David, never used it to humiliate him, at least as far as I could tell. She'd accepted his worship as her due, but never abused it. In fact, she repaid it with tenderness. I was convinced that she'd really loved him, but I also knew that if she hadn't died in that accident, David would be a prisoner here too.

The second strap came loose, and we got it adjusted. "That does it," I told Sarahleah as I stood and looked down at the backpack, feeling exhausted. Why the hell had I brought those books? It was like some part of me thought that once we got to the Upper Village, I would have nothing but time to read.

"You must be tired, sweetheart," Sarahleah said. "Why don't you let me take the pack for a while?"

I shook my head. The thing must have weighed as much as a couple of bowling balls. "No," I sighed. "It's too heavy for you. I'm fine."

"Don't treat me like a child, Willie," she insisted. "I'm stronger than you think."

I doubted it, but what the hell. "Okay," I said. "Since you're the one who got us *far-blongered*, or whatever you call it, let's see how you do. Stand up with your back to me."

She stood erect, presenting her back and squaring her shoulders like a soldier. I hefted the pack off the ground and harnessed her up. "Okay," I said, temporarily supporting the pack's weight. "Lean forwards a little, like you're walking uphill. No, not that much. Yeah ... like that."

But the moment I let go, she staggered, let out a cry, and toppled backward onto the ground, where she began to flail like an inverted turtle. The sight was just too hilarious and there was no way to keep from laughing, which I did until my sides ached. Even Sarahleah had to laugh at her predicament. "Let me try again," she said. "It just caught me by surprise."

I took her around the waist and hoisted her up. "No, honey," I said. "I'm used to hiking with a pack. You'll slow us down and we need to find a place to camp before dark."

It was near sunset, and we'd stopped to catch our breath and rub the cramps from our legs. The underbrush up here was so thick there wasn't even room to sit, much less spread our ponchos for sleep. I figured we had at most an hour until pitch dark, so I marched us off again double-time.

After a while, we came to a little gully where the brush was thinner, but the ground was way too muddy to make camp. "Everything is so wet," Sarahleah said as we squeezed our way between moss-covered trees. "Are you sure you can start a fire in this?" I assured her I could and kept my doubt to myself.

She was actually the one who spotted it. Veteran camper though I was, we would have missed it if not for her sharp eye: "Look, Willie! Up there!" In the growing gloom, through a break in the trees, I saw a circular clearing, a real campsite on a little rise in the terrain. It was maybe thirty feet wide and looked perfect.

We made a dash for it, shouting and laughing with relief. "Check this out," I said, dropping the backpack. "It's got a fire pit." It looked like the campsite hadn't been used in a while, but who cared? The elevation created some natural drainage, and the ground wasn't too damp. There were a few tree stumps to sit on, and someone had even thrown a tarp over a big woodpile to keep it dry. I let us rest a couple of minutes before prodding Sarahleah into action again. We needed to get a fire going right away, and I gave her instructions on what to look for.

The wood under the tarp was split, but the pieces were pretty big, so we began scrounging up anything that might work as kindling. The stuff we gathered was still a little damp, but I would make do. I really had been a Girl Scout; that was one of the few useful things Harry had given me. He'd made me join, saying, "Scouting will help you get your head on straight."

Get my head on straight with the Girl Scouts. I didn't laugh when he'd said that, though I could have because it was so moronic. But whatever he was, Harry wasn't a moron. He was a master manipulator. *How old would my daughter be now*, I thought. *Seventeen? Just a few years younger than Sarahleah. Christ! I'd give anything to have watched her grow up.*

I forced the self-pity out of mind and focused on the task at hand. Using just four matches, I worked the twigs and dead leaves with total concentration until a tiny flame took hold. There was a lot of smoke at first and it stung my eyes, but with Sarahleah cheering me on, I built the fire, carefully adding larger and larger sticks till it could handle some of the smaller logs from under the tarp. By the time it was totally dark, I had a fierce little blaze going. It hissed and crackled in the clearing, warming our hands and making our faces glow.

We piled leaves and pine needles about eight feet from the fire, spreading the ponchos over them as makeshift bedding. Then we relaxed and huddled close, wrapped in our loobas, passing the brandy back and forth, taking tiny sips to make it last. We ate the chocolate and the nuts, and there was comfort in just a little casual touch. Sarahleah was telling me some of those silly puns that always cracked me up: "Do you know how Moses made his tea? Hebrewed it," and "As a teenager, I had this job at a bakery ... but only because I kneaded the dough." Why did I keep laughing at this cornball shit?

The fire was all we had to see by, and it was eerie how quiet these woods were tonight. The fog had lifted and the sky was crawling with fat, fuzzy stars, like in that Van Gogh painting. It was a gorgeous night, and I felt totally content—content with my fire, content with the brandy, but mostly content to be here with this strange girl who had come to share my life. An hour ago, I'd wanted to strangle her. Now I just wanted to have her in my arms and tell her how beautiful she was.

I leaned over and kissed her, gently forcing her to the ground. The chocolate and brandy we'd had made her taste like one of those liqueur-filled European truffles as I ran my tongue around her lips, feeling her moan into my mouth. Her lovemaking was so passive—so different from the violent urgency I'd had with Selene.

Sarahleah gave herself to me like a lamb surrendering to the slaughterer. This was how she liked to be loved, in complete submission, so much like what Harry had forced on me, to the point where I'd begun to crave it. Sometimes, when I was making love to her, I'd actually imagine I was Harry, overpowering myself as a child. It was disturbing that I could find so much pleasure in that. Of course, Sarahleah wasn't twelve; she was an adult. At least that's what I kept telling myself.

Suddenly, just as my hand was creeping up under the hem of her looba, Sarahleah squirmed away and sat up, her expression anxious. For one awful moment, I felt as if she'd read my mind, seeing herself through my eyes as a helpless child, seeing me as someone using her for pleasure or simply to have power over her.

"What's the matter? Did I do something wrong?" I asked.

Sarahleah smiled. "No, honey, it's just been a long day and I'm totally exhausted. I don't think I can keep my eyes open a moment longer."

"Ah ha, so my lovemaking is starting to bore you," I said, trying to disarm this first- ever rejection with a joke.

"No!" she said insistently. "It's nothing like that. It's ..." Then something at the edge of the forest caught her eye, and she gasped. "Oh, Willie, look! Look at all the Shari!"

Beyond the clearing, the woods were dancing with blue and purple lights. It was like a forest full of Christmas trees.

Sarahleah laughed and clapped her hands. "Oh, Willie, they're lovely! And there are lots more over here ... and there too."

The little pixies were flitting all around us, and they were forming these incredible shapes in the darkness—arranging themselves into patterns, like giant snowflakes, rosettes and hieroglyphs. It was a dazzling show, and they were performing just for us.

Sarahleah clapped her hands again. "They're welcoming us, Willie. This is wonderful news. If there are so many Shari around, it means we're already near the Upper Village ..." Her voice trailed off and her expression darkened again.

But I didn't have time to wonder about it, because a flock of Shari began circling us like a diamond bracelet. I could hear their wings buzzing, their tiny voices singing something that sounded like "immortal bee." The words were silly, but the melody was pure and magical, and my eyes filled with tears.

All my misgivings were gone, and I felt a flood of exquisite energy and love for Sarahleah that had nothing to do with sex—

well, almost nothing. "Listen," I said, putting my arms around her. "Forget about going back down the mountain. If it's like you say, the Upper Village isn't far. Does that inn serve breakfast?" I was feeling giddy, and the idea of getting to the Upper Village suddenly seemed more important than anything.

But Sarahleah still had that dark expression on her face. She seemed to be listening for something, and it was making me uneasy. "What's wrong?" I said. "We're going to the Upper Village. Isn't that what you want?" She didn't answer, just stared at me with those big, limpid eyes. And that was when I felt the foreboding.

In a heartbeat, the Shari vanished with a *whoosh*—not just the ones circling us, but even ones that were playing in the trees. Startled, we both jumped to our feet. Sarahleah was staring over my shoulder, focused intently on the woods behind me, and I turned to see what she was looking at. All I saw was a few bobbing lights in the trees, and my first thought was that some of the Shari had stayed around or come back. Then I realized the lights were torches, and I made out the shadowy figures holding them aloft. Ten or more of them were melting out of the woods, floating into the clearing like apparitions. Finally, they came into the firelight, and that was when I screamed.

What the fuck were these creatures? They were tall and slender, but the hooded loobas they wore hid every other feature. Five held burning torches aloft, and I felt an intense, jagged energy—like static electricity before a lightning strike.

Then I saw they were female and knew they could only be Dryads, but they were unlike any Meliai I'd ever seen. Their apparent leader was a giantess, and the way she was eyeing me made me feel like a snail about to be dipped in garlic butter and swallowed whole. I wanted to scream again but held myself in check.

Sarahleah was still standing behind me, but I hadn't heard a peep out of her. And when I turned to look, it was all there in her face. Oh, my God! She was relieved, like she'd actually been expecting them.

"What the fuck is going on?" I demanded, grabbing her arm and squeezing it. "Who the hell are they?"

"I'm sorry, Willie," she said, avoiding my eyes. "They're Oreads, and they've come for us. We'll be safe. I promise."

Oreads! I should have known. "Is this why you brought me up here?" I said, furiously. "To be taken by these … these trolls? You little bitch! Why?"

"Willie," Sarahleah said, her voice barely audible. "I had to. You'll …"

"*Kashtok!*" The command came from the Oreads' leader, who walked over and stood glowering down at us. Whatever Sarahleah was going to say, she buttoned her lip.

The leader was slim as a willow, at least a foot taller than we were, and she was wearing some kind of red and black face paint—a bunch of squiggles and circles on her cheeks and forehead. Her lips were blackened too, teeth stained bright red with the same gunk. If the 'war paint' was meant to scare us, it was working on me just a little, but the flickering firelight made her look almost as ridiculous as she was menacing—like a cartoon savage in an old Donald Duck comic I'd once seen, wearing the badly applied makeup he'd gotten from the white traders who'd come down the Amazon river in a smoke-belching steamboat.

I tried my best to meet her gaze without flinching, and she picked up a branch and walked to the fire pit, where she started poking at the flames. "*Seklah, el-bekomlit!*" she said to the others.

Four of them ran over and began kicking dirt on my precious fire. They were very efficient, and in a couple of minutes, only a few orange embers were left. Then they crouched over the pit, lifted their loobas, and peed on the embers. The steam smelled like cedar and green apples.

The story continues in Book 2, Edarta

ACKNOWLEDGMENTS

Many thanks to my amazing editor and coach, Jean-Noel Bassior, without whose support this book could not have been written.

Thanks also to my cover artist, George Patsouras, for his wonderful work, and to the many people whose proofreading, copy editing, and suggestions were invaluable: Betty Chase, Dennis de Marco, Eldri Jauch, Steve Lackow, Deborah Schiller, Mary Sheridan, Pia Tsuruda, Raven Wolfe, and many others.

Special gratitude to Carla Green for her cover design, formatting expertise, and seemingly endless patience with suggested changes.

And many thanks to Steve Lackow for his hard work on the website development.

Made in the USA
Middletown, DE
24 October 2020